Mark Stanton

AN AFRICAN WARRIOR:
CITY OF STONE

© Copyright 2013
Mark Stanton

The right of Mark Stanton to be identified as author of this works has been asserted to him in accordance with the Copyright, Designs and Patents Act 1988.

All Rights Reserved

No reproduction or transmission of this publication may be made without written permission.
No paragraph of this publication may be reproduced, copied or transmitted save with the written permission of Mark Stanton, or in accordance with the provisions of the Copyright Act 1956 (as amended).

Any person who commits any unauthorized act in relation to this publication may be liable to criminal prosecution and civil claims for damages.

A CIP catalogue record for this title is available.

2nd Edition

**ISBN-13:
978-1481989565**

**ISBN-10:
1481989561**

Disclaimer

I know that any historical work of fiction is open to interpretation and I am sure there are more qualified historians out there who may find fault in what has been written.

I realise that the Zulu nation was not a combined nation until later on in history, around 1709 and that the term Bantu refers to many tribes throughout Africa who began moving southwards from Western African 2000 years ago, but for the sake of writing a story which allows for fluid transitions, I have taken the liberties with the historical timelines.

Unfortunately, as there is no known written narrative covering this period, in the region, hard and true facts are difficult to come by, so again I acknowledge that there may be some conflicts with what has been included in this book.

It is a book with no allegiances or political bias; it is just a story about a time when Africa was master of itself, proven by the fact that there were civilisations well advanced in technologies. Their full impact seems to have been lost in the annals of time although their imprint is still clear to see on the Zimbabwean landscape, by way of numerous stone monuments, the crown jewel being the beautiful city of stone at Great Zimbabwe, Masvingo, standing proud centuries after the people who built them had passed and of course let us not forget the legendary image of the Zimbabwe Bird.

By these admissions, I absolve myself of any claims but do apologise if I have caused any discontentment.

Acknowledgement

I acknowledge the input of so many people but in particular I wish to thank my father, Henry Stanton, for the very first read of the manuscript, Nigel Jones, Wendy and Christine Rapson, Nina Stubbs and Helen Gohil for their valued editing comments.

My wife and daughters for putting up with me, "trying to get it right."

Let me also not forget the young men from The Kings School, Witney, who helped with the chapter, "A Foolish Thing", written together after a hard outdoors activity away day and in reward for agreeing to go to sleep on time at "lights out"

To those friends who encouraged me along the way and in loving memory of my mother.

Preface

Great Zimbabwe, an ancient enigma, a city of stone situated in the south-eastern portion of current day Zimbabwe, Southern Africa. It was built between the 11th and 14th century by the descendants of the Bantu race who still live in the region. It is a stone monument, spread over an area of five square kilometers, which rivals even the mystical Geza pyramids in Egypt, with many hundreds of lesser ruins cast throughout the southern African region, each within a day's walk from the next; a virtual network of settlements offering excellent communication and trade routes.

The old metropolis consisted of two major sections. The first and oldest was a hill fortress with mammoth stone walls and defensive structure; the second, a circular enclosure with almost modern day prison quality walls interspersed with large stone towers. The city may have hosted tens of thousands of people at its peak and was undoubtedly a central hub to an advanced civilization which dominated the region.

How and why this great civilization disbanded and disappeared into the annals of time remains a mystery. How did such a technically advanced people not leave a recording of their passing? I am sure its explanation is still waiting to be revealed however, just maybe, this is the story.

Regional Map

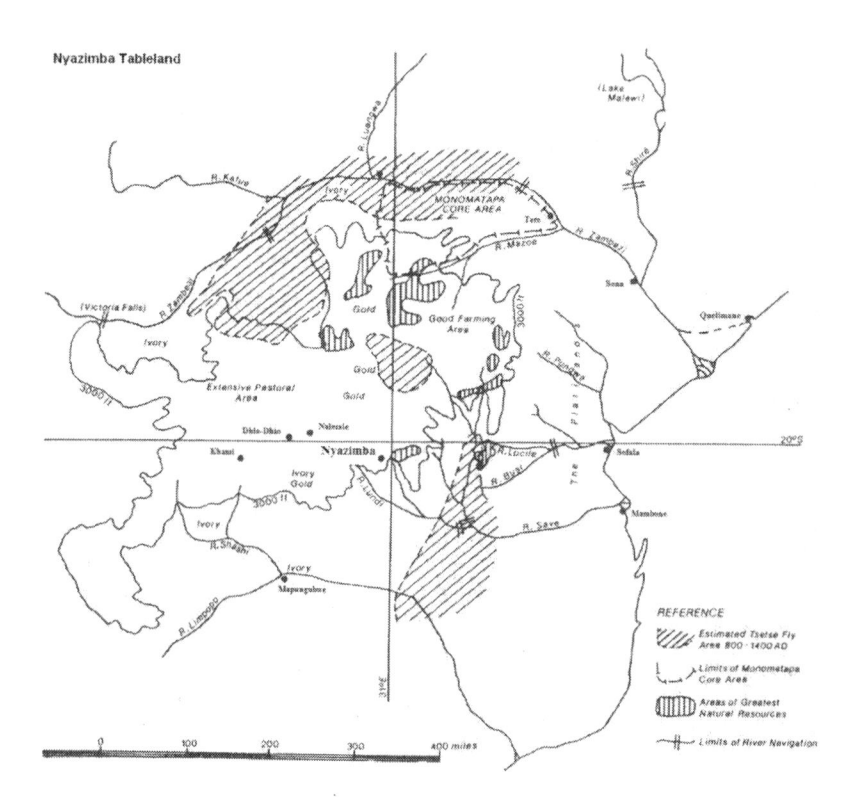

Chapter One
In the beginning

The sky was bright blue and clear with not a cloud in sight from one expansive horizon to the other. The sun was halfway across the firmament and the mix of warm sun and gentle breeze had a soothing effect on the skin. Sounds of bleating goats carried on the wind, drifting over from amongst the hills, which gently moulded into one another like perfect domes stretching away into the distance, each module a tint of gray or green interspersed with scrubs, boulders and trees.

The domestic animals sounds were added to by the numerous birdcalls of the wild, the constant echoing coo of the wood pigeon; the larking chirp of the warblers and weavers. Insects completed the orchestra with an underlying buzz of excitement. The insistent chorus paused when the sound of a flute being played stretched its melody across the landscape. The first domesticated animal ambled into the glade and paused to tug at the new grass, tearing the roots from the ground in the destructive manner of the goat. The rest of the herd appeared and whenever a particularly savory patch was discovered by one of the animals, the other members of the group rushed over to nestle themselves into the spoils, nudging and pushing to get at the succulent fodder. The resonances of nature were overlaid with a tuneful musical melody fading with the chasing eddies of the wind from a blown flute. The tune stopped and in its place a voice pitched with youthfulness called to the senior lead goat.

"Come on Zeni, move on. Keep on moving. We've still got a long way to go."

A youth came into view. He was tall with a muscular torso and strong limbed. His skin stretched tightly over his strapping frame, with well defined muscles moving freely as the young man moved. His head was shaven closely although the re-growth of tight peppercorn-like hair had already begun to amass.

Over his shoulder, he carried an animal skin bundle containing a calabash of water, a small package of fresh food wrapped in the dark broad green leaf of the banana tree and a knobkerrie*, which was sticking out of the top. In his hands was the formerly played musical instrument, which he put back to his lips, to play another tune.

As the boy strolled along, the herd of goats moved with him, safe in their numbers and under the perceived protection of the herds' boy. A little distance ahead of the procession, a small bush stirred, caused not by the movement of the wind but by a number of little bodies at its base, four boys were huddled in a conspiratorial pack.

"Ha, there's Zusa. Look he doesn't even know that we are here," whispered one of the boys, his eyes alight with excitement. "I cannot believe he hasn't seen us yet!"

"Shush," hissed the leader of the group. He was not the leader by vote but just by the fact that he was the biggest out of the set, a full head taller than the rest of the gang and proportionally as wide."Be quiet, we don't want the enemy to know we are here," he urged.

The group looked at each other questioningly at the mentioning of the word enemy; they exchanged puzzled glances, and looked back at the speaker who just ignored them, and they wisely decided to let the strange comment go. It would simply not be worth the effort taking into consideration the agitated state of the larger boy.

Earlier on during the day, the group of boys had been playing on the nearby riverbank but after a while the boredom of splashing through the shallows had struck home and they had decided on a new, more exciting game. They had hoarded clumps of river clay, twice the size of their closed fists, which were piled at their feet. As a means of distraction, these lumps could be compressed onto the

*The knobkerrie is a basic form of fighting stick cut from the root of one of the hardwood trees, where the arm-length straight handle is crafted with a bulbous end.

ends of their knobkerrie's shaft and all it took was a simple flick of the wrist, and the semi-hardened clay would be propelled in the direction of the cast. It was an exciting game to play by any measure, and the anticipation was heightened by the understanding that a direct hit by one of these missiles on an unprotected part of the body could result in considerable discomfort and pain.

Just as they were about to start their boisterous game, the sound of Zusa's flute floated past the place where they had assembled and instead of the group deciding to take each other on in battle they had changed their plans. Their attention shifted at the direct insistence of the older boy.

"It will be fun I promise" he said in support of his argument. The unsuspecting target continued to approach the huddled group in hiding, totally unaware of the menace ahead, followed calmly by the goat herd.

The lead goat ambled on, tugging at grass roots as he passed, delightfully ignorant of the silent gathering ahead. It was only after a few more steps that his natural instincts eventually sensed that something was amiss and he froze in alarm. His legs stiff, he held his head still with only his ears twitching and twirling in an attempt to determine the seriousness and direction of the threat.

Zusa turned at this time to call the animal again and noticed that the whole herd had followed the fearful stance of the herd leader and that they had all paused apprehensively.

Zusa dropped the flute to his feet, the wooden musical instrument clattering against a stone and in a puff of dust, the fine power sticking to the wet mouth piece as a darkened patch. He slowly reached across his shoulder for his fighting stick, not wanting to spook the unknown threat into an early action before he could ready himself.

His heart raced at the sudden tension and sweat burst across his forehead. Controlling his breath, he allowed his eyes to move from side to side, trusting his peripheral vision to sense any motion and attempting to locate the source of the danger.

Suddenly there was a whirl and buzz in the air, like a

swarm of bees, as the ambush party flicked their clay projectiles at their quarry.

"Attack!" the group of boys screamed at the top of their lungs as they rose as one and rushed towards their target, their battle cries increasing in intensity. Their missiles were a blur in the dazzling sky with three of the shots going wide of their intended target. Zusa reacted in terror at the attack, his eyes not believing what was happening before him. He jumped back in alarm, his mind reeling and confused at the shock of what was going on. One of the clay balls caught the unfortunate herd boy on the side of his head, felling him with the impact and he dropped to the ground, his body lying flat in the dust.

"Charge, we have got him!" the attacking group's leader shouted as the gang ran forward. Their surprise advance scattered the docile herd in all directions, with their once gentle bleats changing into squeals of panic and fear. "Yaaaaa!" the raiders cried as they ran up to where the prone form of Zusa lay on the ground. Three of the boys pulled up short as they saw Zusa begin to stir and watched as the injured boy made a vain attempt to get to his feet. The group's leader, Pimi, continued to run in from his position rear of his attacking force and just as Zusa managed to sit up, he kicked the dazed boy in the chest causing Zusa to fall to the ground again, clutching his side in protection, a scream of pain escaping from his mouth.

"Pimi!" shouted one of the other boys. "What are doing? You are really going to hurt him!"

"Shut up," Pimi snarled in response, spittle flying from his mouth with the naked aggression. "He is the enemy! We stalked him, attacked and we have beaten him. What's wrong with you? You can't just give up!"

There was a wild, angered look on his face, his eyes open wide and his saliva drying as white flecks on his lips, but the unadulterated look of triumph was still clear for those around his to see.

His three colleagues took an involuntary step backwards at the cruel passion of the shouted statement, their eyes darting between the large bulk of Pimi and the prone form of Zusa stretched out on the dry ground.

"We, we, we did not want to hurt him, Pimi, we were just playing a game," one of the others pleaded in a stutter. "Look, he is bleeding."

A bright welt of blood had stained the side of Zusa's face, vivid scarlet at the wound, turning to a dark purple as it ran onto his dust-covered face.

"What is wrong with you all? Why are you standing back?" Pimi shouted. "We got him!" He walked toward his audience, ignoring his victim on the ground, his arms outstretched in question.

Given respite, while Pimi argued with his men-in-arms, the prone lad managed to regain a resemblance of his senses and gradually an understanding of the situation he found himself in. His mouth was dry from fright and the sudden increase in adrenaline pumping through his body. The fine dust which filled the air around him irritated his nostrils and caught in the back of his throat. He sneezed and his head ached with the effort.

Looking around he realised that the sound he had made had been ignored by his attackers. Shaking his head, he tried to get to his feet; pulling himself semi-erect, he felt dizzy and stumbled once again to his knees. Pausing for a few more moments, he made another attempt and this time he was able to stand and remain upright, although wobbly, he looked around. He was confused and the pain of his open head wound compounded the effect, his mind spun as he grappled to understand the situation. His belongings had been scattered in the short melee, the gourd of water was smashed into the ground, its liquid drained into the parched soil, and his food had been crushed under foot.

Crucially, he noticed that his fighting stick had been knocked over to one side of the clearing they were in but it was just beyond his immediate grasp.

Whilst the exchange of words between the gang members went on, Zusa's senses gradually restored. On face value, he realised that Pimi, a local bully from their younger days, had banded together with a small group of boys from the surrounding kraals and that they had laid a trap for him. He truly accepted the danger he was in and he drew a number of long, deep breaths in an attempt to gain control of the fear that gripped his heart. Obviously, from the reaction of the rest of the group, what had started out as a few hours of fun had taken a drastic turn as Pimi had used the opportunity to gain a little revenge on Zusa.

The retribution was based on a distant feud between their families. The grudge going back as far as their fathers younger days, who had competed for the attention of a woman. Zusa's father had eventually won her over and married her. *A strange thing for a young boy to be angry about, especially as it is my mother, as the fathers' had put the youthful argument aside many years ago.* Zusa thought to himself.

With the verbal exchange heating up, Pimi knew that he had lost the element of surprise and that his "army" was wavering in its support for him. Even as he looked at them, he could see their courage evaporating. He knew he did not have long to maintain the initiative over Zusa and putting the thought of his rebellious men aside, he looked around. His mind was set for the settling of old scores, although its root cause had been handed down from father to son, based on something which had occurred before he was born. The feeling of revenge was sweet and the power and control he had over the situation filled his mind to distraction.

From the corner of his eye, he sensed a movement and his heart skipped a beat; turning on his heels he saw Zusa launch himself at his discarded knobkerrie which was about ten paces away and behind the position where he had been knocked to the ground.

With a few quick strides, Zusa threw himself forward into a roll, which resulted in him finding his fighting stick at his feet, without having to stoop for it, he managed to pick up the weapon in an easy flowing motion and rolled away again, just as Pimi threw his own stick at the spot where Zusa would have been if he had decided to stop before his second acrobatic manoeuvre.

Getting to his feet Zusa turned to faced Pimi who had used the few seconds available to him to counter the move by striding forward in an attempt to retrieve his thrown stick. His large frame, lacking any grace or athletic prowess, wobbled as he moved.

Realising what Pimi was going to do, Zusa moved as quickly as he could in an attempt to cut his attacker off from the discarded weapon but his adversary arrived two paces ahead of him and Pimi managed to pick it up and, with a renewed look of accomplishment on his face, he waved the fighting stick in the air in triumph. As they faced each other there was a lull in their movements and both boys used the time to take stock of the situation. The physical difference between the two rivals was clearly apparent.

Zusa was tall and lean with a well-defined muscle structure, whereas Pimi although almost as tall, was slightly larger in build. His shoulder slumped inwards and a layer of fat made him appear more heavy set and much bigger.

The waiting game over, the opponents crouched slightly and began to circle each other in a clockwise direction. The dust was stirred into the air to knee height; their arms outstretched with their knobkerries held vertically, the rounded heads just over the level of their shoulders.

Pimi attacked first and lunged forward aiming his stick at Zusa's head. Having to duck out of the way, Zusa inadvertently stepped into the radius of danger and Pimi swung his knobkerrie in a reverse direction and managed to catch Zusa on the right side his rib cage with a wet smacking sound, bruising the bone structure and causing an immediate darkening to the skin. The injured boy fell away and back out of the circle of danger and a sharp shout of pain escaped from his mouth. Zusa pressed his injured side briefly with his free hand but realising that he was far from being safe he fell back into a defensive stance, regaining eye contact with his foe. Harsh breaths were expelled from their mouths as the tension and fear mounted at the jousting.

A sly smile reached Pimi's lips and his eyes glinted as he noticed Zusa favouring his right side. His bravado was strengthened by the apparent discomfort of his enemy.

Pausing for a moment, Pimi straightened fully up, looked left and right then changed the direction of the rotation. Zusa immediately realised with the change in motion he was going to be attacked on the weaker side, where he had been injured in the opening gambit. His concern for the outcome was growing by the second.

The next attack came just as he had expected. However, for Pimi to get to Zusa's injured side he had to use a slower swing followed by a straight feint for the head, which led to a reversed downward strike re-aimed at Zusa's bruised ribs.

Sensing this, Zusa managed to block the strike, sliding his fighting stick the length of Pimi's weapon and catching his assailant's knuckles with a crack making Pimi drop it, and pull his hand to his chest in pure agony accompanied with a loud cry of pain. In a quick follow-up, Zusa kicked the fallen instrument further away, leaving the bully unarmed and defenceless.

Pimi stared in disbelief at how quickly the situation had changed. His initial thought of a quick win faded and his bravery evaporated just as the water spilt from Zusa's broken water bottle was disappearing in the heat of the day. What had started out as an easy target and where he had had the upper hand, had now swung completely around and his opponent was now in full control of the situation. His colleagues, who had gathered at a distance to observe the fight, looked on in disbelief at the sudden turn in events, scared for their own safety.

"Zusa, Shamwari, *my friend,*" Pimi said. "You know we were only playing around with you." His voice a high pitched whine and his sentence ended in a croak as his mouth dried in fear. "It was a game that's all!"

Zusa didn't reply straight way, he just looked at his foe. His mind filled with turmoil and disbelief.

"What?" Zusa said, in an even toned voice, full of incredulity at the easy statement and the obvious attempt by Pimi to try and talk his way out of the situation. Zusa spoke again "Oh, now I understand." He paused as if in thought. "Do you mean like last summer when you left me tied to a tree for the whole day to let the fire ants pinch at my skin until I bled, hey? Or was it like the time you pushed me into the Takwane River and I was swept downstream and only managed to save myself by grabbing on to an overhanging tree trunk?" He looked straight back at his foe holding the gaze until Pimi looked away and said, "It looks like this is not the way you expected game your game to turn out isn't it?" he paused. "I am tired of being your source of entertainment Pimi and it has to end here and now!"

Pimi nervously shuffled his feet, his eyes darting from left to right, looking for an avenue of escape. The tension between the two had reached a peak; both boys knew that now was the time to settle this for the last time.

The silence hung between the two for a few heartbeats, when in interruption, the plaintiff cry of a goat rose above the ambient noise. The sad bleat repeated, but this time it carried a sense of desperation as it increased in pitch and length. Its lonely sound was followed by a blood-curdling howl- a wild hollow scream tapering off into a rasping gasp. It was a sound of the wild - a sound which brought the hairs on one's body to stand erect in fright.

"Mbada!" shouted one of the three bystanders, his voice full of terror at the sudden and very real danger.

"Mbada!" the other two and Pimi screamed in chorus and in unified panic. As one they broke into a sprint and scattered in all directions in search of safety.

The goat cried again, this time more feebly as if sensing its own demise. A clatter of hooves announced that the rest of the herd had also scattered at the harsh sound, disturbing stones and pebbles, which marked their desperate escape.

Leopard. Zusa immediately knew and the panic that had gripped the other young men seized his own heart. His first instinct was also to run, however, his next was, *my father's goats. I am responsible for their safety, I can't run away.* Sweat burst across his forehead, diluting the blood oozing from the head wound and he reached up to wipe it away, the act stretching his stomach muscles which flared, reminding him of his other injury. *It's no good me waiting here,* he thought to himself, *they are my charge and I have to do something to protect them.* He steeled himself for what he knew he had to do.

Without any more uncertainty, Zusa took a firm hold of his knobkerrie, turned away from the direction in which Pimi and his fellow gang members had fled and moved towards two large boulders about twenty paces away from where the chilling sounds were emanating. The natural gully toward the rocks formed a grasscovered pathway. This belt of fresh fodder must have been the temptation which had caused the troubled goat to move away from the safety of the herd and while Zusa had been distracted with his fight with Pimi.

Moving towards the gap, Zusa again wiped the dripping blood from his head wound away from his eyes, leaving his hand stained red. His mouth was dry from the rush of adrenaline caused by the need to defend himself a short while ago and the more urgent need to defend his charge, the goats herd, against a far more dangerous, aggressive and unpredictable enemy.

The wild scream sounded again, trailing off into the familiar hollow growl of the leopard, the most dangerous to man of all the wild cats.

The leopard's natural prey was the numerous baboon found amongst the rocky outcrops of the area. Therefore they were most skilled at attacking the human form.
After stalking their quarry, leopards would spring, digging their front claws and wide fang-lined jaws into the animal's head whilst their back clawed feet tore at the stomach of the prey eviscerating the abdominal cavity, tearing the entrails from the body in bloody and irreparable strands. Normally the cranium would be cracked open by the powerful jaws whilst the scalp was torn from the skull, a painful but quick death.

The opening between the rocks opened into a cul-de-sac: the two boulders at the entrance stretched above Zusa's head while a number of huge stones, which had fallen at angles across each other, blocked the far end of the enclosure. At the base of this natural structure, a small refuge had been formed and it was where the young goat had been able to scramble once it realised its life was in peril. At the entrance to the safe haven the leopard was stretched out on its belly, down on one shoulder, its forearm stretched into the mouth of the cave trying to snare the trapped kid goat with its sharp claws.

Zusa bent over on the move, picked up a large rounded stone and, without any hesitation, threw it with all his might at the prone feline.

Although his target was intent on its prey the leopard sensed the movement behind itself or it may have heard the grunt that escaped Zusa's lips with the effort of the throw, and it was already retracting itself from the hollow as the stone landed with a thud on its right back paw. With a scream of anger and pain the animal spun on its axis to face the new danger.

It went down on its haunches, front legs outstretched, its hind legs coiled like springs. The leopard stared back with a hiss, its mouth wide open, rich red in colour, and lined with sharp fangs, its pale yellow eyes unblinking and penetrating. The animal unleashed itself at Zusa, who in turn skidded to a defensive halt.

Instead of jumping directly at the boy, the leopard sprang to one side and sprinted up and against the enclosing wall of the rocky area.

This brought the cat to the height of Zusa's shoulder as it curved around his position and, at the last moment, leapt at his form in the age-old natural rhythm of the kill. Zusa moved to the opposite side from where the animal was attacking, wildly swinging his fighting stick.

Halfway through the jump the leopard reached out and dragged its left paw across Zusa's shoulder tearing at the skin, its claws digging deeper, causing ruts in the flesh and muscles which instantly filled with blood. As if in a co-ordinated dance move, the knobkerrie continued in its arc and connected solidly with the flying animal's shoulder with a crunch of splintering bone. The leopard screamed and instead of landing with the normal grace of a cat it landed in a tumbling heap, its front leg giving away causing it to somersault, throwing up dust, which irritated its eyes and filled its mouth with the fine powder.

In a bout of pain Zusa fell to one knee. His weapon dropped to the ground at his feet as he gripped his severely injured shoulder with his right hand, blood springing from between his fingers, his lungs gasping at the pain and exertion.

He realised that he was in a far more serious situation than he had been a short time ago with Pimi. As soon as the leopard had turned back on him he knew he was in a fight for his life. The thought of a painful death deadened his senses and he knew that he might not live past the encounter. Thoughts of his parents, that he might never see them again, briefly brought to his eyes tears of frustration and sorrow. Annoyed with himself at the sense of self-pity, he steeled himself for what might be the last round with the wild cat.

Panting heavily the leopard managed to recover from its tumble and withdrew a few paces back whilst facing the young man and finally it crouched in a defensive stance.

After a few moments the animal slowly rose to its feet favouring its injured front shoulder and rear paw. Taking an unsteady step forward, its head unmoving, slunk below the height of its hunched shoulders, its eyes unblinking, staring, assessing its target.

The throbbing of his wound had caused Zusa to lose his concentration and hence his contact with the beast and with a start, he realised that he was also unarmed. He looked around and found his weapon just within arm's reach from where he was kneeling. Beyond that was the crouched form of the leopard. He forced his hand away from his wound and gripped the staff of the fallen knobkerrie. He found his bloodstained fingers too slippery to maintain a firm grip on the weapons shaft. He released the weapon again, rubbed his hand in the talcum powder-like dust to absorb the fluid and then re-gripped the
fighting stick more firmly. All the while he maintained eye-to-eye contact with the leopard knowing that to lose this connection at this stage would make the animal attack,
feeling that it had overawed its enemy. *Don't just wait here to die, attack.* He thought to himself. Gritting his teeth Zusa leapt forward with a loud shout.

The wild cat, taken by surprise, turned slightly as if to flee but changed its mind as it realised that there was no escape; the surrounding boulders hemming it in. It moved back into its poised position. Rising up on its haunches it reached out flaying with its one good paw. Zusa broke through this blocking defence and with another swing brought the rounded head of the fighting stick against the animal's skull.

The leopard fell into a heap at Zusa's feet, its golden furred head crushed to the bone.

Swaying, Zusa looked around dazed. Slowly he let the fighting stick fall from his hand. Moving his head made him dizzy and his vision blurred. *It's getting dark,* he thought. *But it can't be. It is still midday!* With his head spinning, he collapsed to his knees, wobbling for a few seconds before he fell onto his face next to the kill. The scent of the wild animal's fur, the fresh blood and the dry dust filled his nostrils because his sense of smell became heightened as his other natural senses of sight and sound faded with the lost of blood.

The background noises of the wild bush were echoing in his ears and in the distance he could just hear loud voices raised in alarm. *Who were they? Were they coming to his rescue?*

His eyesight began to grey over and his last clear vision was that of the stricken goat emerging from its safe haven. After a tentative look around it began tugging at the bright grass, which had been the temptation that got it into trouble in the first place. There was a last urgent sound of bare feet padding on the ground behind him and a pair of strong hands lifted him, leaving the imprint of his body in the sandy soil; its impression stained with his blood.

Chapter Two
Red sky in the morning

The orange rim of the sun had just appeared over the horizon staining the sky with a purple-tinted hue. Gradually it arched its way into the new day and steadily its strength grew until it reached a certain point where the firmament began to glow with a red flush expanding with time as it stretched across the heavens from east to west. From a bird's eye view, numerous hills and valleys broke the ground below but where vegetation should have been there was nothing but expansive desert except for the sparse growth which gave way to lesser trees all stripped of their foliage. Forlorn, their dried trunks stretched with lifeless limbs to the heavens. Dry watercourses were etched into the sun-baked ground like finger nail scratches onto parched skin; the few remaining drinking holes were stinking patches of mud patterned by the multitudes of spoor from ever-hopeful wild animals in search of the precious liquid of life. Dried carcasses lent testimony to where they had failed to find enough water to survive, finally resulting in their agonising demise. The ever-present carrion birds, even this early in the day, gave the land a constant overture of death.

The deep valleys were still shrouded in shadow but as the sun reached over the towering peaks of the surrounding mountains more details on the ground became clearer. At the centre of the basin was a wide clearing encircled by curiously beehive-shaped dwellings, many with fenced-off areas interlinking a number of similar buildings. The open, sand-covered arena appeared from above to have been engraved with dark lines that wavered as if being stirred by the breeze.

Closer inspection revealed the moving lines to be

warriors clothed in simple leopard-skin thongs; headbands complete with large feathered plumes; matching armbands and leg covering of some long-haired animal skin.

Regiments of these men stood in silent expectation, each with a single short spear, an assegai, clasped in one hand and in the other a long oval shaped, rawhide shield, tapering at each end to a point, almost as tall as the warrior. Various coloured and patterned shields indicated the identity of the individual regiments.

To the front of the assembly, a collection of grander huts with guarded doorways stood proud with talismans fluttering in the wind. One of the door coverings stirred and through it oozed a number of diminutive, hunched-over beings, whose sudden appearance caused an uneasy murmuring amongst the gathering. They were dressed with animal furs and hides adorned with the tools of their trade; skulls and severed paws, bloated bladders on sticks and kudu horns of muti, *medicine.*

Without out any pre-announcement, the figures moved with purpose up and down the ranks of warriors. Two large guards armed with wicked-looking war axes, whose iron heads glinted in the first light, flanked each of the six spiritual healers. Spitting and gargling, cursing and laughing, speaking in mystical voices, they moved in and out of the gathering. One of the healers had moved down the second line sniffing at the air when she suddenly jumped into the air and spun around to face a particular warrior who, once he realised he was the source of the interest, recoiled with horror, and took a slight step backwards. "You betray yourself," screamed the witch, pointing out the individual with her charm-encrusted stave.

Immediately, her accompanying guards seized the young man and dragged him wailing to the front of the arena. They threw him on the ground, raised their giant battleaxes above their shoulders and beheaded him with a clean blow. The severed head bouncing on the hard surface with a wet smack, the body jerked in the spasm of death as the arterial blood from the heinous wound spurted its life force onto their legs and feet.

All along the line, other men were being singled out and despatched in a similar, violent manner. Their cries of anguish prior to death, echoed across the arena, each of the warriors relieved to have been passed by. The cleansing ceremony continued until the sun had cleared away the last of the predawn shadows. In its full brilliance it highlighted the execution site, stained scarlet with the blood of two score warriors whose bodies had been deposited in an untidy pile in front of the sorcerers' hut, left for them to pick over later to further their practice. The ground where they had been dragged was a quagmire of stinking mud, which squelched as it was walked upon, sticking to the lower limbs of the executioners.

By this stage no one made any unnecessary movements, so as not to draw attention to themselves, and the lines stood perfectly still. A bass drum began to sound deep from within the kraal to the front of the assembly and after a few minutes an elephant of a man stepped into their view. It was the Zulu King, Zeneni. He was equal in height to his door guards but twice their width. A majestic headdress of ostrich plumes set on his bold pate gave him the appearance of being taller than those in the gathering. His neck was an extension of his head moulded onto his gigantic shoulders over which draped a cloak made of lion skin. The teeth from the same beast were strung around his neck and they jingled as he moved. His stomach, true to the traditions of African wealth, was huge and overhung his leather skirt, and the calves of his legs were adorned with numerous objects, which rattled with each movement. Strutting forward he did not deign a glance at the macabre result of the concluded witch-hunt.

"Bayete," he shouted the royal salute, raising his decorated assegai above his head.

"Bayete Nkomo, bayete, bayete," responded the gathering.

The King allowed the ensuing silence to hang in the air for a while, creating further an air of anxiety and expectation. "You can see that we have singled out from amongst you those who have been the cause of the great drought which has befallen our land this last season." He stared as hard as he could deep into the front ranks inviting any sign of defiance. "You see that we have been able to ascertain who was responsible for the misdeeds within the nation, and you can see that we have delivered the punishment it truly deserved." He finished by lifting his assegai into the air as if in proclamation.

"Bayete, bayete, bayete," was the fervent response. The King waited for the echoing of the repeated shouts to die away. "But there is more."

The crowd held its breath as the sorcerers minced their way back amongst those standing on the parade ground. The King stepped onto a raised stage in front of his hut. "I have had a dream." A hum rose from the massed throng. "And Mwari, *God,* has spoken to me, his appointed messenger." At this the witch doctors voiced their approval, shouting in agreement with what he had said.

Wary eyes from the gathering looked nervously around trying to decipher what was going to happen next.

"I have had a dream and Mwari spoke to me of other reasons for our misfortune." Feet shuffled nervously at the statement. "Mwari has told me that the nation of the Nyazimba have hoarded their cattle and grain while trading the yellow metal with others. They have gathered their wealth while we, their closest of brothers," this brought a number of curious stares amongst the gathered warriors, "continue to go without food and our families," he paused for effect, "and our children go hungry."

Zeneni strutted across the raised stage, with one hand on his hip and the other clasping his assegai, his head nodding at what he had just said and at the obvious truth of it. "It is true. Our children starve, our women weep and our livestock die. It is their fault; they have employed their ancestral spirits to withhold Mwari's provision from us. It is time we took back what is rightly ours."

"Zee," was the affirmative, hummed response from the captive audience who all along were being scrutinised by the score of witch doctors for any hint of doubt shown by a lacklustre response.

"Go," the King, shouted. "Go my warriors," and he pointed his spear to the north. "Go and bring back our heritage to appease your King, your people and our ancestors." He stabbed the air with his weapon. "Go and bring back our heritage to appease your King, your people and our ancestors," he repeated, "Go I say."

The muted drums that had continued in the background began a more urgent and louder beat, which was steadily added to by numerous other instruments spread around the village compound. The deep, repetitive sound dragged one's soul into itself, numbing the mind; the stricken feeling of fear was replaced by one of outward anger at the injustice and relief of having been spared. Steadily, the mass of warriors began to move their feet in rhythm to the beat of the war drum, as its sound fuelled their mind now cold from the reprieve of not being singled out earlier for retribution.

"Zee," they hummed, as the regimental chief moved forward to lend support to the great King's instructions. A high-pitched voice called, "What are we?"

"We are the night," the horde responded, dragging the words out.

"Who are we?"

"We are the Jackal!" In a clear voice, a singer began singing, "Wazei, wazei," and the massed throng of warriors replied in bass and baritone voices, "Amalia, amalia." The repetitiveness of the song was hypnotic in its form and the lines of men slowly swayed in an all-enveloping resonance. A new deep bass drum matching one's heartbeat swelled the effect and rumbled through the lines. It was not possible to understand how long this went on but suddenly the drums fell silent and a clear but
dragged-out call of "Nzulu" was met with a triple clash of assegai against hide shield. *Shoo, shoo, shoo,* the sharp clattering reports echoed around the valley. The call was repeated a second, third and fourth time with the same response.

A tall warrior stepped forward and in a clear tone he shouted, "We are ready, Oh great King: Lead us, we ask. Show us, your children, where it is you wish us to go."

Jumping into the air the speaker lifted his right leg high above his head, in time with the increasing drumbeat, and stamped it to the ground, stirring dust into the air. Repeating the action, the mass of warriors swelled outwards as the regiments gave each other room to perform the same high footed action. The sound of the stamp in unison caused the ground to shudder at each blow. Assegais were rattled against shields and the sound resonated about the valley until the direction of the source became indiscernible. *Shoo, shoo, shoo* like the downpour of a heavy rain fall.

The imposing King stood upright with his own assegai held high as one by one the individual impi leaders turned and saluted their monarch. A sweeping motion indicated for their own warriors to follow them out of the arena at a trot towards the distant goal. Impi after impi, regiment after regiment, five thousand men in total passed by their ruler receiving his royal blessing. The Moles, the Hyenas, the Civet Cats, the Buffalos and the Kudu regiments all moved toward the northward passage out of the valley, towards the great river, and towards the promised riches of Nyazimba. Once the last of the warriors had left the arena, the regimental chiefs, who stayed near the King, were directed to gather at the Royal kraal for a final time of detailed planning and instructions.

There were twelve elders and fifteen chieftains as well as the King and his three advisers. No council of war would be complete without the obligatory priests and priestesses who continued to hover around the perimeter of the tribunal so as not to be too far away from the decisions that would be made affecting their society.
The meeting began with the normal greeting and gestures of respect especially as the King was close enough to monitor any hints of disrespect which could easily be the prelude to signs of dissent within his kingdom. The group stood about a central fire, its smoke being expelled through a hole at the pinnacle of the dome, within the palace's largest hut. This was where the King normally dispensed counsel or judgement to his people. The King's intricately carved wooden throne was set in the centre of the back wall.

A number of lower wooden stools had been set about

for the distinguished company and woven grass mats were laid for the remainder of the delegates.

The King turned to Modena, the most senior chieftain and the selected leader for the forthcoming expedition. He had been instrumental in preparing the base camp to which the regiments were now heading, an easy half-day's journey to the north, following an earlier indication of the King's desires two moons ago. "Modena, what is the state of our preparations?" the King enquired.

"My Lord, the base camp is complete and ready to receive all five impi. By this evening we will have five thousand warriors on the Bantu border and only a short walk from the great river."

"What about the depth and speed of the waters? Are we able to cross at the ford yet?"

"Yes, my sire, the waters have receded enough and the key rocks have emerged above the level of the water and, provided we take care, we will be able to cross safely. I have had a scouting party on the other side of the river since last month ensuring that our planned crossing place was not stumbled across by anyone." Modena glanced around the assembly. "We will begin the crossing the day after tomorrow and I will have the Hyena regiment form a picket line further inland from the crossing point. Once two more of the impis are over we will send the couriers across with the provisions for the campaign."

One of the other chieftains spoke up, "In my day the Zulu ran on what we could carry and were not hindered by a baggage train. Why are we doing it this way? Everyone knows how scarce food is right now."

Sensing some dissent, Modena responded in a measured tone, "We are intent on attacking the nation belonging to the Great City of Nyazimba this time, looking for cattle and slaves at the King's wise suggestion."
He looked at Zeneni who nodded in acknowledgement.

"It would take up too much time during the inward drive to have to forage for basic food so this is the reason why we will carry our own for the opening stages. We are also attacking at the end of the rainy season and our journey will take us very close to the belt of the sleeping sickness so we want to spend as little time as possible in this dangerous region!"

The King interjected, "What is the planned route, Modena?"

The chieftain took a breath and replied, "After we have traversed the first section of the country it is my intention to move on to the position of the trading settlement at Shashe on the morning of the eighteenth day. I know we will take it by surprise as the villagers will be expecting the floodwaters to be protecting their southern border. Once we have secured this village we will move north to take the towns Masole and Zezani on days nineteen and twenty. I will use alternate impis for the overlapping attacks to allow for some rest and recovery. Each attack will begin at dawn and the distance in between the target villages performed at double time so that enemy lookouts are not able to raise the alarm."

A titter was heard from the assembly at the apparent concern for his warriors' well-being and at the statement to allow for rest but the King swung his head in the direction of the sound and no more was said.

"What will you do with the captured territory once you move on from these villages?" another asked.

"I plan to leave fifty garrison troops in each of the towns we have seized to control the prisoners and to gather any cattle and spoils. The men will be instructed to await the return of the porters who will be released gradually from service as we consume their loads. As these porters pass homewards they will gather anything collected by the garrisons and carry them back to the King's kraal. Any slaves taken will also be escorted back to a single location so that once we have completed the campaign the whole army can accompany them back to our kingdom under a strong guard. If our expectations are
realised then the number of captured Bantu will require a large escort so as to prevent stragglers and escapees."

"Will this not deplete your strength as you progress, leaving men behind like this?"

"No," Modena responded, "it will leave clear lines of communications home so that messengers can keep you aware of our progress; it also leaves our route home open."

"Go on, Modena," the King instructed.

"Our path north will be via the village of Makado, then across the open plains towards Masase where we will take the first of the Nyazimba remote stone fortresses at Chimnungwa. At this site, the Bantu normally have a token guard of around five hundred warriors. I do not expect them to put up much of a fight and the town will fall to us in no time." He paused to make the point. "We will then use the fort as a base to raid the surrounding country, including the villages of Mwenzi, Chidembeko and finally Belingwe. I trust this part of the operation will take less than five days," and he looked at his monarch as if seeking approval the King's face did not give any indications as to his thoughts and his dark eyes just continued to watch Modena as he hesitated in his narrative.

"Yes five days," someone added in a loud voice. "Five days in which to have the Bantu King of Nyazimba alerted to our presence."

Modena interjected, "We will blanket the area with patrols and set up picket guard posts between the area and the city of Nyazimba to stop any messengers getting through, but if we are to reap the fruits of these raids then we need to ensure we gather plunder as we progress."

The King beamed at the prospect of the riches involved and, in his mind, he was already counting his soon to be acquired wealth.

Modena carried on narrating his plan. "At this stage I expect to have stationed about four hundred garrison troops behind us at the sacked and captured villages and I intend to leave at least this number again as well as any walking wounded at Chimnungwa, safe within its walls. It will be the pivotal point from which we will launch the balance of our attacks. We do not expect to have suffered too many casualties up until this stage so I predict that our army will still be four thousand men strong." He looked around the gathering for any signs of doubt. "Within these five days we would have managed to strip the surrounding countryside and move across the Mtanda Mountain range ready to swoop onto Pambuka. At this stage, we can expect the Bantu to be aware of our presence or at least alert to the fact that something was stirring. The main Nyazimbian army would likely react and move towards our position. Once their scouts have located our main force, I intend to engage them on a battleground of our choosing, somewhere on or near the Munaka hill range. This encounter should go well as we have trained and planned for it. Following the mass destruction of the Nyazimba army, I plan to move slightly north in anticipation of meeting the Bantu King's brother's regiment, which could arrive in support of the army at around that time. We need to ensure that we do not have to fight this combined force." He paused a little in thought then went on. "That is if he decides to come to his King's aid at all." A few heads turned to look at him. "I believe he aspires to be the nation's leader and what better way for him to take over than if his path to the throne is vacated by the death of the Bantu King in battle!"

An uneasy silence hung over the room at his comments and realising that he had spoken aloud, Modena looked at his own King, who stared back with eyes black and depthless.

"Sire, an abomination to think about but it is a task that may well suit your Majesty's own desires, goals, and objectives."

Zeneni nodded at Modena's statement, knowing it was not something which could occur in his own kingdom as he had simply had anyone - brothers, sisters, and close relatives with a claim to his throne killed as soon as he had been appointed to it. With an indication from the King, Modena continued. He picked up a stick from the fire place and used it to scratch into the bare ground a number of lines indicating their planned route into the Bantu country where the main battle with the Bantu could take place. "Depending upon the time taken, I may allow a number of my regiments to raid a few more of the Bantu settlements before their populace get a chance to escape. Finally, we will begin our move on the capital city. It is only one and half days away to the east from the position we should be at that stage in the campaign."

"How do you expect to penetrate these impregnable walls we have heard so much about?" The question was again from Kwaka, possibly Modena's biggest critic amongst the gathering; however, the tone of the enquiry was well guarded in its delivery to instil enough esteem whilst throwing some doubt on to the master plan. Modena smiled at the attempted snipe but countered, "The Bantu King would have had to strip his garrison in order to mobilise enough soldiers to meet us in battle on a point of almost even numbers. We have firm intelligence that the north facing defences, although still impressive and protected by a steep mountainside, have not been completed to a high enough standard to prevent a determined and select group of warriors entering under the cover of darkness. Once our men are within the perimeter, they will overcome the gate and wall sentries and they will open the portals for the rest of the force to enter through." Sitting back, Modena spread his arm wide indicating his receptiveness to any comments. The room remained silent with all eyes upon the still figure of their King seated on his throne.

King Zeneni held his chin in his left hand, his elbow resting on his knee in reflection. After a few moments' pause, he spoke. "It is a good plan, Modena. I am pleased with your forethought and detailed planning. Defeat these people and I will reward you well and you will be able to grow old on the riches you gain from my favour." It was left unsaid what the payment for failure was. The remainder of the group smiled at the King's acceptance and any misgivings were forced from their minds.

"How long do you and the army expect to be away?"

"I expect to be at the city walls within thirty-two days and home in victory, within three moons!"

The King rose from his seat and grasped Modena's arm, shaking his hand in a two-handed manner. "I am very pleased with *your* arrangements and I now know it was the right course of action to put the nation's future and trust in your hands!"

Modena stepped back, surprised at the amount of

praise being offered and in front of so many of his peers. This declaration by the King strengthened his position within the political standing of the army. Others also noted the King's words and wisely chose to join in with the congratulations and offerings of support in the venture.

At a sign by the King the meeting adjourned and each of the members took his turn in bidding farewell to those who were going with the army. The King watched the individuals leave one by one; with Modena being the last to leave. The King's eyes bored into the back of his commander as he exited the meeting hut.

Chapter Three
The great crossing

Modena stood on the bank of the fast-moving river, which for the duration of the perennial rains became an uncrossable barrier while at other times of the year was as dry and barren as the desert or the surrounding plains. The Zulu chieftain had carefully chosen this position for his army to cross because of its extreme width and hence shallower and slower waters. This came with its own problem and that was to get five thousand men, weapons, and provisions across without being attacked by the resident hippopotami and crocodiles or risk being swept away by the rapid-flowing waters. On both sides, the river embankments were high with well defined paths to the river edges, pointing like an arrow to a line of boulders that was just appearing in midstream. These stepping-stones had become more pronounced over the last couple of days as the level of the water fell.

The river water was purple-brown in colour and so its depth was unfathomable. Occasionally whole trees could be seen being dragged downstream by the strong currents, slowly rotating in midstream but totally at the mercy of the flow. More sobering were the carcasses of dead animals that had fallen to this same current; a grim reminder of the hidden force within its waters, their bodies bloated and with stiff legs.

Ropes made from the twisted fibres of the sisal plant stretched in six lanes across the full width of the natural fording place, almost five hundred paces long and secured to large tree trunks on both sides. At intervals along these ropes, Modena's scouts had pushed narrow wooden stakes into the riverbed to give some stability and support to the ropes and to prevent them from touching the water.

The men who had completed this initial task could be seen on the far side watching the proceedings unfold before them. For over two weeks, Modena had had a hundred of this advance guard on the far side watching for any sign of discovery or organised resistance. He had given them strict instructions to remain out of sight. Their main assignment had been to observe but not to get too close to the communities which they would soon be attacking. The only time they were allowed to venture inland was for the task of scouting for the first planned raids on the villages of Shashe and Masole and to assess the fighting men they could expect to encounter. Both villages were almost equal in size with about two hundred inhabitants of which there were only forty-seven and fifty-three men of warrior status, respectively. These same scouts had also spent a lot of their time preparing the ropes and poles for the mass crossing.

With a wave of an assegai the scout leader on the far riverbank indicated that all of the preparations were now complete, that the final arrangements were in place, and that the crossing could begin. Modena turned to his lieutenant and said, "We can begin the crossing now. Send the two senior impi, then the porter column, followed by the remainder of the warriors. I want to be fully across by mid afternoon."

"Yebo, baba, *Yes, father.*"

The man turned away and hailed his own lieutenants who indicated to others beyond the line of sight from where Modena stood. Within no time, the first strings of men in single file could be seen snaking over the southern riverbank from the forest beyond and marching towards the river. With some trepidation, the leading men of the six columns stepped into the water, one hand on the rope the other holding shield and weapons high and clear of the river. Their first few steps were shaky as the men tried to get the feel of the riverbed, which was strewn with large boulders and loose shingle piled up by the ebbing floodwaters and extremely unsteady to the step.

However, the ever-constant pressure of those behind moved them steadily onwards and within a few steps the water was up to the first of the men's knees. As they made progress, the depth varied but only reached as high as mid-thigh where the pulling and tugging of the fast flowing water kept the men constantly off balance. It took longer than the chieftain had expected but eventually the first of the river crossers stepped onto the far bank, dripping water and clearly exhausted by the effort and concentration required for such a feat.

For half the morning warriors continued to cross without any major mishap, except for the occasional misplaced step which resulted in a number of men falling and becoming totally immersed. The majority of these still managed to keep a grip on the rope but two warriors completely lost their grasp. Fortunately, as their rope lines were upstream of the others, they were quickly pulled from the torrent to the callous laughter of those who were equally nervous of their predicament and used the situation to vent their own pent-up anxiety. Shouted laughter and conversation lent an air of gaiety to the event.

It was not until the porters had begun to cross the river that disaster struck. The day until then had gone by reasonably uneventfully and the men had allowed themselves to become less vigilant. Suddenly in the middle of the crossing on the last rope downstream there was a loud sound of splashing and shouting as if someone else had slipped into the water. The sounds did not end with the culprit regaining his feet sheepishly but continued. The initial shouts of fright turned to screams of panic. Other porters close to the disturbance began running in all directions throwing their precious bundles into the water whilst seeking an avenue of escape.

As the impi induna, *chief* ran across to see what was happening, the water midstream erupted and an enormous crocodile, almost twice the length of a man, surged up, holding in its jaws the unfortunate porter who was being thrown from side to side as if he was weightless.

With the increased activity on the hemp rope, it soon parted under the extra strain and scores of other porters were then swept downstream adding their fearful and panicking shouts to the confusion. Two other fountains of water exploded as more of the reptiles sort out this easy prey, latching on to their targets and spinning their bodies in the water to disorientate their catch before dragging the unfortunate men underwater to drown. The foaming waters became tinged with red to mark the places of these tragedies.

Those not caught by the reptiles were left to float downstream. A few who had taken the time to learn the rudimentary basics of swimming as children struck out towards the river banks but at least twenty others were not as fortunate and drowned before the eyes of their comrades, their bodies disappearing downstream to feed the ever-present scavengers. Nothing in nature is wasted.

Modena and his chiefs hurried about trying to reassemble some order but the sudden and ferocious attack had filled those who had witnessed it with dread at the thought of committing to cross the natural obstacle.

Without a second thought, Modena waded into the fast flowing water and personally directed the rejoining of the parted ropes. This took a lot longer than he thought it would but eventually the lines were spliced together and the staves put back in place. During this time, he also set dedicated guards to watch out for more of the crocodiles and, to set an example, he stayed midstream with the sentries whilst the remainder of the army once again began to move across the water barrier under the cajoling and shouted orders of his senior induna to keep the men moving.

Eventually the last of the regiments completed the crossing but the day was almost at its end. It had taken almost twice as long as Modena has envisaged and the men wearily sat down on the northern riverbank. With the last man across, Modena eventually waded ashore and immediately called a council meeting, his limbs tired by the constant fighting against the flow of the water and his hands and feet wrinkled due to the time they had been submerged. As soon as the gathering sat down in a circle, one of the travelling witch doctors spoke aloud, "The signs from our ancestors are not good, bad spirits have attacked our men during the crossing."

"They were crocodiles not spirits," someone threw in angrily, a passionate statement from someone who was tired of the medicine men's apparent ability to read the gods' or ancestors' mood swings after an event had occurred.

"Then why didn't we see them coming?" the priest countered.

A few other voices lent discourse to the conversation. "Why didn't you think to warn us of this so called spirit before we attempted the crossing?" Modena asked the man. He stood up and all conversation stilled. He stretched out his arms, "All that has happened is that we have suffered a very small setback and our losses were minimal. In fact they were far less than I thought we would have lost crossing a flooded river. I knew it was always going to be a risk crossing the Limpopo so early in the season but we needed to do this to catch the Bantu off-guard. They have become used to having the river protect them during this time of the year. We will rest here for a while so that the men can re-form, but this evening we will move off, as planned, towards Shashe so that we are in a position to attack early tomorrow morning." *I trust our scouts are familiar with the way,* he silently thought to himself.

"What about the men, my Lord, they are shaken and weary?" one induna asked, his voiced pitched with concern but the sentence was respectfully spoken.

Modena turned on him quickly, his eyes wide at the remark, "If you need me to tell you what to say to your men to get them motivated then I would have no need of you!" he shouted. "You decide what you need to say to motivate your own men."With a wave of his hand, Modena dismissed the group.

Once he was alone he stared back across the river that had caused so many problems so early on their venture. *Was it a sign?* He thought to himself. Taking a deep breath he looked around, the camp was alive although there were many groups sitting in circles on the ground. He knew it would be no good giving up so early in the campaign and having to face his King with the failure –

a failure which would be his personal problem if he did. *No. He thought to himself. Turning back was not an option.*

After time to rest and under the command of the senior men, the regiments were persuaded into regaining their composure. By this time the sun was well down on the horizon and the dark of night was not far away. The large impis broke into smaller groups under the local command of lieutenants and the men stood by, awaiting the final decree to move out.

Scouting parties had been despatched earlier on in the day accompanied by those who had camped on this side of the river mapping the land and routes over the previous couple of weeks. The main task of this force was to ensure that the way was still clear and that no one was around to see the large raiding party's movements.

The terrain near this major river was barren and although most rainy seasons saw a barrage of water flow along its length, other than the riverbanks that teamed with wildlife, trees and bushes, the surrounding area remained practically a desert. Its soil consisted of grit, the remains of larger rocks scoured by weathering, and it was well on its way to eventually becoming fine grain sand. Sparse bushes and thorn trees were haphazardly dotted across the plain, which undulated as far as the eye could see, torn in some parts by deep dongas, some of which were big enough to swallow whole regiments of men.

These natural ravines were caused by the heavy rains, common in this part of the country, whose swift run-off tore through the sandy soil, which did not have the benefit of plant roots to hold it together.

It was going to be a difficult part of the journey, which was why the decision had been taken to cross it in the cool of the night air. The difficulty was compounded by the approach of nightfall.

Modena had spent the rest of the afternoon going over final arrangements, after getting over his earlier fit of anger. He took the time to speak to a number of his warriors, gauging their morale, which he found had remained reasonably high as expected of true warriors. Food and water were allotted to ensure the men would have no need to stop during the night march. As the sun began to set, with the sky dimming while the horizon burned with an angry orange, the regimental chiefs gathered their troops for a final briefing, and once the surrounding shadows extended across the African plain, the groups of men struck out in the direction indicated by the scouts.

Chapter Four
Recovery

A strong smell of dry grass hung in the air, intermingled with the scent of wood smoke and dry ash and an underlying sense of the dampness of water used to control the dust in the kraals and surrounding courtyards. To begin with, Zusa was confused as to where he was but he soon recognised the tell-tale smells of home and the familiar feel of his own bed fitted with cured skins upon which he lay, safe in his father's house.

Sounds became clearer and more familiar, a little bit at a time. Soft voices of people chatting outside the hut were apparent along with the pleasant chuckle of hens, which were occasionally raised in pitch whenever someone moved too close to them or as they scrambled over pickings on the ground, and on top of that the calling of the wild birds that surrounded Zusa's father's kraal.

Zusa tried to open his eyes, they were still heavy with fatigue but, safe in his environment, he decided to take the opportunity to rest a little more and, comfortable within the sounds of the family homestead, he fell back into a more restful unconsciousness.

A while later he again awoke but this time there was not so much confusion; he knew he was home. He slowly opened his eyes and through the slight gap he saw the glare of the outside sun streaming through the hole in the top of the grass-roofed hut where the smoke from the fire exited. The brightness made him squint but in the shaft of light he could see dust hanging, suspended in the air, moving as if with a will of its own, a feature one is never completely without in the dry climate, even throughout the rainy season.

He moved slightly and his bed coverings rustled. The face of his mother came into view and her initial look of concern changed rapidly to one of delight as she saw that his eyes were open.

"Zusa, umfana, *my son,* you've returned to us." Her face had a radiant glow, which overflowed into Zusa's heart and his own expression returned the love he had for her.

"Amai, *mother,*" he tried to say, but it escaped as a croak instead.

"Baba," his mother shouted to his father waiting outside the hut while reaching for a ladle of water, which she held to Zusa's mouth for him to sip at. "Baba, your son has returned."

There was the sound of bare feet at the entrance to the hut and the animal hide covering the doorway was pulled aside; the bright sunlight beyond momentarily blinding Zusa. Its glare was quickly blotted out by what could only have been the bulk of his father, the familiar shape of his head and torso apparent. The door covering dropped back into place as he stepped toward Zusa.

"My son, you are awake," he said in a joyful voice. "You have returned!"

Zusa pulled away from the offered drink and tried to raise one of his arms in greeting but a burning sensation tore through his body causing his head to spin and his eyes to lose their focus.

"Be still," his father said gently. "You are home and safe, my brave son." He put his strong hand to Zusa's chest to prevent him from trying to rise again. Zusa had so many questions to ask. *What had actually happened? How did he get home? Is the herd safe?* When he tried to speak again he could only let out another croak and he realised how dehydrated he was. His mother leant over and gently squeezed a mash of a plant root to his lips and he was able to let the liquid dribble down his parched throat easing his thirst. He could feel each drop at it carved its way down his dried-out gullet, as if it was scoring its way down to his stomach. The water was tinted with sweetness. It was pulped sugar cane in water; its re-hydration properties were phenomenal, and as each drop glided down his throat, Zusa could feel his energy beginning to return.

He closed his eyes for a moment and the memory of the fight with the leopard came flooding back to him. The reason for the burning sensation in his left shoulder also flashed back to him. Opening his eyes again, he slowly moved his head to see if he could observe the extent of the wound but even this slight effort caused his vision to swim.

"Son, you need to keep still," his mother said gently, but Zusa knew he had to know the degree to which he had been hurt. His eyes opened wide as he managed to twist his head enough to look at his shoulder. All he could see was a covering of damp moss but of more concern was the smell of corruption emanating from beneath the layer of natural herbs. A look of horror sliced across his face with the sudden realisation and understanding. He turned his eyes to his father.

"The wound was deep, Zusa," his father said. "The leopard's claws left dirt, which has caused the injury to become septic." He rested his hand on his son's forehead. "Your temperature is almost normal now. Gemba has been here since he heard what had happened and he has been treating you with his own muti."

At the sound of Gemba's name Zusa relaxed slightly, knowing of the old man's reputation for knowledge and his remarkable healing powers. There were those who said he should have been a Nanga, *a witch doctor,* but the old man had always scoffed at the idea saying his services were always to be free and then he knew he was trying to help from his heart and not for the sake of a reward. The fact that Gemba was here, a close relative, an uncle from his mother's side of the family, was a comfort. *He must have travelled quickly to have got to his father's kraal from his own home almost a day's walk away to the north,* Zusa thought to himself. A little confused at the time over which this appeared to have happened, Zusa asked, "How long have I been asleep?"

His mother stepped over and took his hand. "You were brought home more dead than alive eight days ago now. You had lost so much blood that we could hardly feel your heart beat." She sobbed and lifted her hands to her face in memory. "We thought you were not going to make it through the first night and so we sent for Gemba. He arrived the following day and he has been here ever since attending to you."

At that point, the doorway cover was again pulled to one side and the aforementioned Gemba stooped through the opening, looking up as he stepped through, and his eyes fastened on Zusa stretched out on his bed. He straightened up and maintaining eye contact, he walked across the room and over to the bedside. The hut was now becoming crowded and Zusa's mother excused herself saying that she had evening food to prepare, and with a last gesture of relief, she touched her son and stepped out of the hut, another flash of daylight marking her exit.

"Sekuru, *Uncle,*" Zusa said, lifting his hand slightly in greeting.

"Zusa, my son, I see you," Gemba said in a strong and clear voice belying his aged appearance. He stood tall and slim in the traditional dress of a time-honoured warrior, with his headband adorned with battle awards of feathers and talismans. Underneath this his hair was a mass of grey and white that bespoke well of his seniority and hence the respectful standing he was afforded within the community.

"I am glad to see that you have decided to wake up at last," he added, but the attempted joke did not go far enough to hide the kind look of relief washing across his face. "I was wondering how the young men of today decided when they have been in bed long enough!" Zusa's father, Jabulani, reached out and shook Gemba's outstretched hand, firstly by gripping the palm of the hand then shifting to a mutual hold of each other's thumb base and back to the palm grip, in the style of the African handshake.

Gemba slapped his other arm in greeting. "I told you he was a strong young man," he said, then bent down to examine his patient.

As the moss dressing was turned back the unsavoury smell became more pronounced. Zusa looked at the wound and saw a small number of white maggots moving around within the wound; his eyes opened in disgust. Sensing the change in the demeanour of the boy, Gemba spoke without looking up. "Don't worry!" he said concentrating. "I put them in there to clean up any of the dead and dying flesh. Anyway it's time for them to come out; they have done their job well." He opened a small container made from a large seedpod and using a split stick, he carefully picked each of the worm-like insects from the open wound and placed them in the box before securing the lid again with them safely inside.

Holding the old dressing away from Zusa he put his nose closer to the lesions and sniffed in an attempt to sense any new infection. Looking up he smiled, his eyes lit up with joy. "Ha, all is well, my son." He opened another small container and applied a small part of its contents, a mix of herbs in animal fat, to the obviously raw parts of the injury. "I am going to leave the moss covering off for while for the wound to dry out. This ointment will keep the weeping parts from becoming infected again and it will also fight off any of the poison left from where the leopard's claws scratched you."

At the mention of the cause of the injury, Zusa father looked into his son's eyes. "What actually happened on that day Zusa? We still don't fully understand," he enquired. "The other boys have given mixed accounts."
Zusa related the events as he could best recall them, glossing over the run in with Pimi and his "gang". He explained how once he had heard the leopard roar he knew that his father's herd of goats was at risk of being attacked by the cat once it had finished off the cornered kid. He said he knew he had to do something about it. He went on to say that he had intended only to frighten it away and had not expected it to turn back and attack him.

His father said, "Well it looks as if it followed the young goat into the area so when you came up behind it, it felt trapped and so it tried to fight its way out, a natural reaction!"

"But how was it that I was found so quickly? I remember someone getting to me just as I blacked out," Zusa said.

"One of three boys who were with Pimi came running past shouting about a leopard attacking someone and I knew where you normally led the herd so we came running as quickly as we could. You must have held the animal off for quite a while because I heard the sound of the blow with which you managed to kill the wild cat. And yes, I did manage to get to you as you collapsed in the sand."

His mouth spread in a wide grin. "You killed it with your knobkerrie, son. You did not even have a spear or knife, and you showed bravery well beyond your years."

"Do you mean bravery or stupidity, Father?" His head hung low with the uncertainty, his eyes downcast as he awaited his father's reply.

"There is a very fine line between the two, my son!" Jabulani looked to Gemba for confirmation. His voice tenderly toned.

Gemba chuckled as well. "Yes and the good news is that you are well on the mend and I have just received a message from Nyazimba. The King has heard of Zusa's exploits and he has been invited to attend the festival marking the end of the rains. This is due to take place at Nyazimba next month so you have a lot of mending to do in the meantime if you are going to be fit enough to make the trip!"

With all this to take in, Zusa's head began to spin and Gemba said that he needed to rest for a while. "Get some more sleep; we will come for you before it's time to eat, okay!" making the statement more of a demand than a request.

Zusa gratefully put his head back on the pillow and, closing his eyes, he easily went back to sleep.

It did not seem as if he had been asleep for long but when he awoke, he felt a lot stronger and suddenly realised how hungry he was. The resonance of the village surrounded him. The playful sounds of the children contrasted with the more measured speech of the gathering men and the quicker and higher-pitched conversation of the women working, all interspersed with an easy, relaxed laughter.

Zusa lifted himself, his left shoulder aching with the

effort and with the movement. He felt some of the dried scabs break under the stress but it was the beginning of the healing process and he knew he had to get to his feet. He was able to take a rest on the other arm, which took his weight before swinging his feet off the bed and placing them on the cool floor of the sleeping hut. He felt dizzy again but not as badly as he had earlier on in the day. Taking a deep breath, he eased himself to his feet and slowly padded towards the doorway. He pulled aside the door covering and blinked in the bright daylight. There was a squeal and a call of surprise as his young sister Rudo ran over to him grabbing at his hand while calling out his name in delight, "Zusa, Zusa, Zusa."

All the children she was playing with also chanted in unison. Zusa's younger brother, Mende, walked towards him, not wanting to be associated with the infantile larking of the young children but still eager to be able to greet his older brother. Zusa noticed him hovering on the edge of the circle of children and he reached out his hand. "Canjan, *How are you,* Mende," at which the sibling ran and hugged his torso in a tight embrace. "My brother. I am so glad to see you!" Mende beamed at the attention.

His mother looked up from the fire where she had been supervising the making of the evening meal. Her eyes were slightly red from the rising wood smoke but her smile lit her face at the joy of seeing her son on his feet. Leaving the preparations to the other women she walked over to where Zusa was surrounded by six or seven children, the tallest of whom only just reached up to his waist. Each of them called out in excitement, asking for details of what had happened to him.

"Amai," he said returning her smile, as she shushed the children away so that he could walk uninterrupted to the sitting place where the older men had congregated. These visitors had gathered at the news of Zusa's recovery. His father, Jabulani, rose and pulled another carved wooden stool closer to his own. Taking over from the mother, Jabulani took Zusa's arm and helped him settle into the chair. One by one the other men rose slightly and reached over to take Zusa's right hand in a simple grasp of greeting, each with his own word of welcome. The second to last to extend his hand was Gemba who spoke loudly for all to hear.

"And here he is at last." He stood and turned to the gathering. "Here is Zusa, son of Jabulani, who left home eight days ago a young boy, as a goat herder, but he has been returned to us now as a young warrior!"

A chorus of agreement arose. Those whose eyes Zusa glanced at showed their pride and admiration. Strangely he did not feel as if anything of consequence had occurred and was rather embarrassed at the attention he was receiving. It was not as if he had cleanly slain the leopard, his injuries were the true testimony of that. It was as if he was receiving the credit for something which he had only half participated in. Lastly, Zusa's eldest brother stretched out his hand in greeting. "I see you, Zusa!" Chenzira said. He had the strongest understanding of what Zusa had been through having only just handed over the responsibility of his father's herds last season.

At the bidding of one of his father's older brothers, Zusa was asked to recite the happening for a second time that day. Taking his time to collect his thoughts, he began to speak in a quiet but clear voice. The tale unravelled, occasionally being interrupted as someone asked for additional details, whilst the rest of the gathering relished the relived story. As Zusa explained how he had found the kid goat trapped the whole area quietened as the women and children gathered closer to the men's circle, drawn in by the steady and even-toned recital.

Reaching the final part where he awoke in his father's house, he looked down at his feet and his voice finally broke with emotion as he spoke further of his thoughts and fear of the unknown. He said that he felt that all he had done was what was expected of him as a goat herder. Zusa stopped talking and the silence followed for a few heartbeats. He realised that he might have offended those who had gathered in honour of his father; he looked up and found that everyone was quietly looking at him. When he turned his head he saw the tears of pride glistening in the corners of his father's eyes, his forehead wrinkled in an attempt to control his sentiments. Slowly, Zusa looked from person to another; each of the men was sitting in contemplation of the detailed account. One of his older uncles, his head a mass of respected silvered hair, a man whose battle honours were still woven into his headdress, had tears unashamedly etched down his face, his mind thinking of past conquests during the recitation.

Gemba stepped over to where Zusa sat, and placed his hand gently on the young man's shoulder. "That is why we have welcomed back Zusa the warrior. Only a grown man would come to the self-realisation and the true reality of the situation. A man who has left the boy he once was behind in the bloodstained soil of the kamusha, *the wild,* and returned to his homestead an adult."

For a while, Zusa sat in contemplation. He looked up, smiled at his father and the rest of the group, and taking a deep breath he said, "What's for dinner? I'm starved!"

The assembly burst into laughter and a few mild comments were thrown at his father about Zusa being his father's son, always thinking of his stomach.

Zusa was surprised, as a clay pot of mild draft beer was thrust into his hands. He looked at his father seeking confirmation and Jabulani nodded his head in encouragement for him to drink. He lifted the purple brew to his lips, and took a mouthful of the fermented liquid.

Slightly gagging at the first full taste, he held the rest of the gulp in his mouth then slowly allowed it to slide down his throat. Once he had taken a few mouthfuls he laid the pot to one side and wiped the beer froth from his upper lip with the back of his hand, a natural "Ahhhh" escaping from his mouth in the time-honoured satisfaction of drinking beer.

The women had gone back to the preparation of the evening meal. His mother called from her place near the fires, "We have cooked your favourite meal this evening in your honour, Zusa, Sadza ne Nyama yembudzi, *roasted goat's meat, and millet corn meal."* At the mention of the meal of cooked goat, Zusa looked around in guilt. Laughing, his mother said, "No it is not your father's goat that got you into trouble, we haven't taken revenge on the kid. It is from Pimi's father by way of a peace offering for his son's behaviour and in celebration of you recovering so quickly."

On the fireplace was an earthen pot in which water was boiling. Next to the fireplace, a U -ended hollowed out tree trunk, set base first in the ground, was being pummelled with a couple of large wooden mallets by two of the younger women. They were rhythmically lifting the long mallet vertically between themselves and pounding it down into the mortar bowl grinding the bulrush millet into fine white flour called *sadza rezviyo.*

The cooking and eating of the meal involved a degree of social politics. Firstly, the meal was prepared in a very meticulous manner. The milled grain was put into another large clay pot and a measure of cold water was added to be absorbed by the powder. The mixture was stirred with a *mugoti,* a large flattened wooden spoon, until it became a very thick white mixture. While one cook stirred, another continued to add the boiling water, a little at a time, to stop the sadza from settling and hardening on the bottom of the pot, a result called *Sadza rine Mapundu,* literally meaning sadza with pimples.

As the mixture heats up, the texture changes from rough to smooth. More of the boiling water is carefully added, to loosen the mixture and to allow it to boil with enough movement. An upward spattering occurs at this phase called *kukwata.*

At this stage, the sadza is in a porridge state. If the mixture is just right, the sadza will boil without spilling over. It is left to boil for a few minutes on a hot fire and more ground maize is added a little at a time. By now the sadza requires relatively heavy stirring as it thickens and the mugoti is passed from one cook to another once they tire, remaining vigilant and careful so as not to allow the mix to become too hard, known as *chidhina,* literally brick like, or to the other degree overcooking known as being *rakaneta.*

After the sadza reaches the desired texture it is removed from the heat, covered and left to sit for a couple of minutes before serving.

Whilst this process was going on, the slaughtered and butchered goat was receiving attention on the other cooking fire. After its skin had been removed, the stomach cavity had been slit open and the entrails removed. The liver and heart were chopped and kept in a separate pot. The delicacy of the stomach lining was cut into strips and wound into sausage shapes, using the water-cleaned intestines. This was then cooked on a hot flat stone at the edge of the fireplace.

The carcass was also sliced into strips that were hung on green sticks above the fire where the heat gently roasted the meat. These spits were rotated every so often, the smell of the fat making empty stomachs rumble in anticipation of the meal.

Eating was a social event in the community, and the food was served from one or two bowls from which everyone helped themselves. The cooked sadza and roasted meat was placed in the centre of the seating area and the whole family and friends gathered around.

Once these preparations were finished, a number of women brought bowls of water to the gathered party where the important ritual of the washing of hands was completed. One hand cupped the water to cascade over the other, and then both were gently dried on a leather cloth.

Zusa reached into the communal bowl and took a small chunk of the white sadza, moulded it in his right hand into a small ball and then dipped it into the vegetables and gravy mix to season. He took a small bite. Chewing slowly, he looked around at the rest of the gathering as they all helped themselves in a similar manner.

The evening moved on and dusk turned into twilight and with the suddenness of the wild, the night was soon upon the village and the only light was from the flickering of the main fire, which cast shadows across the walls of the huts in the kraal. The boundary of the hamlet was a solid wall of darkness; what lay beyond was impenetrable and foreboding.

As the conversation dwindled, one of the men began to sing a song, low pitched and mournful in tone. The group picked it up and together they continued to sing, long Into the night, a melody offering comfort in its surrounding effect. Clay pots of mild beer were passed from one to another as stories were recited of other heroes from the past.

In the background chirped the milliards of Cicada beetles, their high-pitched noise rising and falling in synchrony, while beyond the safety of the gathering the wild resonated to the call and cries of numerous animals as the circle of life continued.

.

Chapter Five
Still they come

For the last eighteen days, the Zulu army had continued moving northwards. Day after day they ran at the trot which they were accustomed to, driven on by the desire to carry out their task and by the fear of knowing what the ramifications would be if they were to fail in the quest set out by their King.

Each day, two hours before darkness was due, the commanders called a halt to the day's advance and each of the regiments settled into a their trained routine of camping by setting overlapping fields of defence. Campfires were lit, but kept shielded. As soon as the food was cooked and before it got pitch dark, the fires were extinguished so that their existence in their enemies' territory could not be noted. No matter the vastness of the African bush, it was still difficult to hide the passing or presence of so many men, and their numerous campfires at night would act like beacons announcing their position. The sleeping men would have to rely on the camp sentries to keep the wild animals at bay.

Game and wild fowl had been hunted towards the end of each afternoon, a few zebra or similar beasts were stalked, and with finality, the hunters would rush in and stab their prey with their assegais. During one of these actions, a hunter had got too close to his prey and had received a hoof to the head for his efforts. Having been knocked unconscious, his head continued to swell and after the first hour he had not awoken. One of the senior men had looked at him again a bit later on in the evening and the swelling had still not gone down and the outlook was grim; the injured hunter's breathing became shallower with each gasp.

The induna in charge of the foraging party knelt down beside the prone man and his comrades, one of whom looked up from the injured man shaking his head. With a hint of regret in his eyes, the chieftain realised that their march northward was going to be too fast to have stragglers attached to the column.

The leader gave a final look around the circle of men, whose eyes silently acknowledged acceptance of what had to be done. Without any further hesitation, he drew his razor-sharp assegai blade quickly across the throat of the prone form, pulling the spear away quickly to prevent the spurting blood from drenching his arm. A well-practised stroke. The injured man gave a hollow, blowing sound, almost a rattle, as his last breath left his body. Standing erect, the induna then made two fast incisions in the abdomen to free his spirit before instructing the attendants to perform the appropriate burial.

Back at the main camp picket guards were set one hundred paces from the perimeter of the resting main body of the army, so as to be in a position to raise the alert if they were attacked or to dissuade any curious animals attracted by the smell of cooking food.

On this the eighteenth night since crossing the river, the four regimental chieftains and their senior company commanders gathered around a fireplace in council. Instead of sitting directly on the ground they squatted on their haunches, knees up under the armpits with hands held loosely in front of them, their shields and spears close at hand on the ground next to them.

Modena opened the meeting. "We have travelled well so far and our scouts have managed to guide us according to the plan around any settlements which we did not want to disturb."

The group nodded in agreement and a few murmurs responded to the statement.

The chief went on. "But we cannot expect this to last for long; someone will eventually see our regiments from afar and out of the range of the pickets and the word will be out.

We need to move fast over this last section and

strike before any warning is given." He used his arms to emphasise what he was saying and the tired men around him nodded in agreement, their whole attitude one of professionalism although weary from the hard march. He looked around the group to ensure that he had their attention. "Tonight we move forward over this hill in front of us and leave the first impi in place to be able to attack Shashe, which is just on the other side of it, at daybreak tomorrow."

Shashe was one of the southern-most villages belonging to the Bantu nation. It was perched on the border of the barren land and the more fertile Low Countries but high enough so as not to suffer from the effect of the sleeping sickness and insects found in the lower valleys.

"We expect just over one hundred Bantu warriors to be in the town but with surprise on our side they will be quickly dealt with. While this attack is being set up, the second impi will curve around, well out of sight, moving towards Masole, and I will take the third beyond that to Zezani so that these two towns are simultaneously attacked the morning after tomorrow."

"What resistance will we find at these other towns?" someone questioned.

"Even less than the first town," was the response from Modena, "Over the following three days we will do the same to the towns of Makado and Masase. Once we have occupied each of these towns we will leave a garrison to keep control of the area and to hold captive any Bantu women and children."

One of the induna's added his affirmation and support to the success of the past few days and the other men in the group nodding their heads in agreement.

"We will wait at Masase for the impis from Makado to catch up with us and consolidate our forces before the first of our major attacks on the Bantu fortress at Chimnungwa. We expect their warrior force to exceed five hundred and they might be able to despatch a messenger to their King, warning of the attack."

A few more murmurs of agreement greeted this

statement. The leader went on. "For this very reason I want to be able to throw a cordon around the village and fort well before the dawn attack. It will be their task to be in positions to intercept anybody that manages to get out of the town with a warning."

The sense of this was obvious to the gathering, as they still required their presence in this strange country to be kept as quiet as possible at this delicate stage of the campaign. It was their intention to refortify the fort at Chimnungwa and use it to launch further raids on the other major trading cities of Naletale, Dhio Dhio and Khami where the plunder was expected to be considerable. These cities were known to be open cities with central refuges for the population to retreat to during time of strife. If the Zulu wanted to increase their bounty of slaves, it was important that any attack would have to be swift enough to catch them before they got to safety.

The spoils of war would be substantial, as any fleeing populace would leave possessions and food behind in their haste to escape the attackers. The porters would follow the army to help carry back the plunder, which would be taken to Chimnungwa for storage before it was transported back to their own land.

That thought was for the future though, for before them was the first real test for his men and the main objective of the campaign. The group discussed details including the final formation of the attacking regiments and the subsequent handling of the plunder and prisoners.

Modena stated, "Anything captured needs to be accounted for! I do not want to have to explain to the King where the missing bounty is. Let your men understand the penalty for not bringing everything in!" He looked at those seated around him to accentuate the point. "Prisoners!" he said next. "All women and children are to be kraaled together and kept healthy and well provided for with
shelter, food, and water. We want them to be in a good enough condition to make the long walk back to our homeland."

"And what about the men folk?" someone asked.
Modena's eyes glinted like steel in the dying firelight. "Kill

them!" he simply said, his voice iron hard to match his look. "We cannot leave any trained or even resentful men to our rear and in direct line of our communications home. Anyone old enough to hold a spear must be put to death."

A few more arrangements were discussed but eventually it was agreed that all that could be considered had been covered and the final order was given to move the regiments in preparation for the morning raid.

With a few sounds of disturbed grass swishing from the passing of many bodies, the first impis moved out on instruction. No more commands needed to be relayed as all involved knew what was expected of them and in no time the remainder of those in the camp found themselves in silence, other than from the noises of the countryside around them.

Chapter Six
Learning and training

Zusa eased his injured arm in a slow circle, feeling the damaged flesh; muscles and sinew stretch as he increased the movement. He took in a few deep breaths to ease the pain. He looked around what had become familiar terrain surrounding his uncle Gemba's kraal. Unlike his father's homestead, Gemba had semi-retired to a picturesque area set on the side of a large hill, in the more mountainous area of the country, north of where Zusa had grown up.

These highlands were coated with vast forests, which offered a break from the gust of winds that were funnelled through the region by the steep walls of the mountains' sides. Some areas had been left open by nature, completely void of vegetation, due the shallow depth of the soil covering the mammoth granite domes beneath it. In these parts a hardy grass still managed to cling on to life and offer fodder to the few goats and wildlife which lived in the area.

In between these hills were large open areas of flat ground with patches of new shoots of green grass bursting through the topsoil, a direct result of the recently ended rainy season, which had blessed the area over the last four moons. The larger rivers, although still full, had ceased to flow with the power of the heavy rainfall and the water holes teemed with the promise of new life for the whole countryside. Trees and boulders had been washed clean of the previous year's accumulation of dust so that everything almost shone with newness in the bright morning sun.

Just then, Gemba walked up behind Zusa and said, "Are you working that arm, young man?" Zusa turned and replied with a smile, "Yes, Uncle." He swung it again to prove what he was saying. "It hurts at the beginning of each morning but the pain gets easier as the day moves on."

The older man stepped up to examine the damaged shoulder. He pushed and pulled and not totally satisfied, he decided to prod one of the larger scars, to which he felt Zusa shy away and take in a hissing breath in pain. "I do not want you to rush the healing process, Zusa!"

The young man disengaged his arm from the healer's firm grip. "I know, Uncle. You have told me many times that unless I let nature take its course; I may never regain the full use of my arm."

"And it is true. Time is the greatest healer."

Zusa smiled at the quick affirmation and statement. "I am feeling a little better each day and it only gets stiff at night, so I like to get it moving as soon as I can each morning." He swung the arm again in reinforcement; careful to hide any expression of discomfort from the older man, but Gemba was not fooled, as the beads of perspiration that broke across the boy's head told their own story.

Keeping this observation to himself Gemba simply said, "All right then, let's get on with your warming up and then I will watch you run the course we have set out for you. You have been off your feet for too long and we need to get you fit again."

With this instruction, Zusa moved off at a settled pace, his face set with determination as the jarring of his run sent needles of pain through the damaged shoulder. Gemba was able to see this in the manner in which the young man swung his arms during the run. His wounded left arm only swung up half the distance of the right, which in turn caused the runner to become off balanced at times. Gemba's eyes did not leave the figure of his charge during the circuit, watching and scrutinising his every move.

Zusa ran on a path that cut diagonally down the hillside, using the convenient stones and boulders stairway to assist his way, whilst taking care not to step on a loose stone in his haste. The rush of his descent whipped away the sweat that had initially formed on his body and, as the path bottomed out, he picked up the pace.

His next major obstacle was a cold mountain stream, which had stepping-stones across its narrowest point, but he elected to make his way through the refreshing water at a place where the bottom of the watercourse was made up of firm sand. As he left the water he lost his footing and slipped on the far riverbank. As he reached out to save himself immense pain tore through his body and for a moment he thought he had opened the wound again. Using his right arm he pulled himself upright and continued on the course feeling the gaze of Gemba upon him. His path looped around another hill and, during this time when he knew he was lost from Gemba's sight, he looked down at his smarting shoulder. It was with relief that he saw that it had not torn open and, with renewed energy, he headed towards the last part of the circuit, an uphill run back to the start point.

At this point his mind wandered back to the day after the celebratory evening meal. His father had sat down with him so that they could discuss his immediate future. It had been agreed that his brother, Chenzira, would take over the full responsibilities of the herds, as it was time that Zusa concentrated on his hunting and fighting skills. To this end his uncle and healer, Gemba, had agreed to take Zusa back to his own homestead for a couple of weeks, where they would explore the martial skills. The old uncle was still well renowned for his expertise in the art and skill of war. As a young man, he had led a number of regiments and patrols during times when the countryside was still untamed and uncivilised. During this period, the Bantu nation's advancement and increase in wealth through trade and industry had not gone unnoticed by the surrounding tribes and nations.

As land became tightly contested, countless battles had been waged in an attempt to usurp territory or to capture goods, livestock, women and children.

Gemba had fought on all of his nations borders. His first exposure to battle had been in the west against the San people. It had not been so much an open war, more like a number of elaborate tactics for gaining land. The San was a nation of diminutive people. However their reluctance to give up their lands was shown in the fierce skirmishes experienced, hit and run battles, which were their chosen strategy to fight instead of an outright battle. Their art of hunting with the bow and poisoned arrow meant that they were able to attack from within the concealment of rock outcrops or dense bush. This manner of death caused more than one Bantu warrior to become hesitant in chasing the San down into these dense warrens. Eventually the desert people had made the mistake of meeting the Bantu in an open battle where the mass tactics of the Bantu wiped out the fighting heart of the San nation. In his old age, Gemba had reflected on these occurrences with the San. He had thought deeply that there might have been a better way of handling these unique people instead of reducing their numbers in such a way. The few survivors simply migrated further west into the vast expanses of the desert where they knew no one would want to take the land from them because of its severe climate.

    Wars with other tribes had been easier to justify, normally following the invasion and killing of his Bantu kin. These attacks from the north and south were pitted against similar civilisations equally armed, and areas exchanged hands a number of times before the unified might of the Bantu nation forced these protracted wars into nuisance skirmishes.

    Lost in thought for a time, Gemba's mind snapped back to the present as Zusa arrived back at the starting point, his breath rasping in his throat, his chest heaving at the tough climb back to this place on the mountainside.
Looking at the young man Gemba said with a smile, "What took you so long?" Before waiting for a reply, he turned and walked towards the group of huts.

    Zusa just stared at his retreating back not able to force a reply but the glint in Gemba's eyes said to him that his mentor was pleased with his progress and after a few more moments to recover his breath he followed the old man.

    It had been three weeks since his arrival at his uncle's kraal and in that time his mother and father had visited them twice to check on his progress. Zusa had been allotted his own sleeping hut within the main kraal, the first time he had been afforded this privilege. However, the pleasure soon wore off as he missed the comforting sounds of his brothers and sister snoring in the same room as him during the night.

His time at Gemba's home had begun with him just sitting around with his uncle who spoke at length of wars and hunts gone by but, within the first week, the lack of activity caused the young man to become restless. Sensing this, Gemba took the lessons and discussions into the surrounding mountains, giving the young man a chance to stretch his legs and mind and for the opportunity to explore. Eventually, even this caused Zusa to wonder when he could expect to get on to the exciting reason for his time with his famous uncle. Discipline and respect prevented him asking outright but every day he wondered when was he going to get the chance to practise with a spear and shield and to learn the way of a hunter-warrior?

Trying to catch up with Gemba, he was pleased to notice that his recent exercise regime had really helped him in regaining and improving his fitness. He had lost sight of Gemba but a rattling sound caused him to look up and, there before him, his uncle stood with a spear and shield. Zusa rushed to him and silently took the offered weapons from his teacher. Gemba turned away to collect another set of weapons.

The remainder of the day was spent in instruction of how to care for the weaponry, including running field repairs and maintenance.

The following day, after his usual run, he was coached on how the spear and shield should be held, along with the basic' moves, both offensive and defensive manoeuvres. Pitted against each other, Zusa learnt the vital importance of footwork during the different phases of a one-on-one duel with an opponent and he received more than one painful strike to his body, arms and legs if he lost concentration even for a moment.

When Zusa slept at night, his body ached in many forms. There was the ever-present deep pain of the leopard wound, which caught him at different times with a sudden sharp ache. There were the numb bruises from his teacher's well-aimed strikes and on top of all these there was the throbbing of exercised limbs from all the running and fighting he had completed. Another week passed during which he was taught the finer art of stabbing with the spear using the point whilst defending his body with the shield.

Once the teacher was satisfied that Zusa had understood the basics of fighting with their main weapon he decided to introduce something new. The bow and arrow had been used for hunting throughout many generations as its superior accuracy over a considerable range, compared to that of the thrown spear, made it a better tool to use for hunting smaller game. Unfortunately, its lack of power against larger game such as elephant, rhinoceros and wild cats meant that the long spear was still considered the weapon of warriors. "I am sure you have seen and even played with a bow while you were growing up, Zusa," Gemba said, "but I am not sure if you have ever seen one like this!" He handed the large bow to the young man for his inspection. It was longer than the bow his father had kept for hunting and appeared to have been made from two different coloured pieces of wood. It was a dark brown, almost red on the inside curve whilst the away face was light in colour with the grain of the wood clearly visible. Taking the offered bow Zusa looked more carefully. He discovered that it was not two different pieces of wood but in fact it had been carved from a single, solid piece.

Looking up he said, "Uncle, this is magnificent. You are right. I have never seen such a beautiful weapon!"

"Its design and construction is not just for the sake of being handsome to look at, young man." Gemba looked at his nephew with a raised eyebrow. "It has been carved from the heart wood of an iron tree."

Zusa looked at his mentor. He knew that the Mukwa tree was one of the hardest trees to fell and he was surprised that Gemba had said that he had carved the bow from it. "It must have taken a long time, Uncle?"

"Yes. You are right. I blunted more than one axe on the wood."

Pulling back on the bowstring, Zusa felt the power in the design. Gemba went on. "The dark part is the very centre of the iron tree and is extremely strong, giving the bow its power. The lighter wood is the softer part of the tree and it allows the bow to be bent in the right direction and for the spring action."

Zusa was only able to pull the sinew string back as far as his elbow, all his effort being concentrated on the pull.

"No, young man. You are pulling on the string. That is not how you draw a bow! Let me show you." Taking the weapon back, Gemba selected an arrow and fitted it to the instrument. Looking down range at the straw targets they had used to practise their spear throwing, he lifted the bow so that it was pointing at an upward angle. Taking a deep breath, the old man simultaneously brought the weapon downwards whilst drawing on the string and, with a ping, the arrow soared across the distance to the targets and disappeared through the straw bundles. Zusa looked surprised at the old man's ability to draw the bow fully and at the accuracy of the strike.

Gemba perceived his unasked questions. "Don't look so surprised young man." His eyes glinting mischievously. "It is a matter of training and practice. I want you to begin using this to give your injured shoulder a chance to rebuild up its strength." Handing the bow back he went on, "Use a deep breath to increase the stretch across your chest and you will find the draw easier."

Looking up at the sun, he nodded his head. "Good. You still have enough time in the day to get some practice in," and he walked away without another word.

Zusa watched his mentor disappear from sight before turning back to the straw targets. He took an arrow from the bundle close by, notched it and pulled back on the string. He was sure he had managed to get the string back further than the last time and he let loose. The arrow petered out of the weapon and landed with a slap about thirty paces in front of him and to one side of the target.

He looked around him to see if Gemba had witnessed his opening attempt but the old man was no longer in view. With a sigh, he turned back to the bunch of arrows with a little bit of disappointment. *I am going to get through these in no time.* Then under his breath he uttered, "It is going to be a long afternoon."

Three times during the remainder of the day, he used and then retrieved the fired projectiles and after a while, he found his left shoulder feeling as if it was on fire with each arrow shot. It was a deep burning which overwhelmed his being and the continued effort caused him to sweat profusely, the salt laden moisture stinging his eyes with its downward passage. The inside of his right arm was bleeding from where the returning bow string had caught his flesh a couple of times, reminding him to curl his wrist a bit to keep it away from his skin. That night he lay in bed with his body aching from the effort of using new muscle sets in addition to the pains of past and recent injuries.

For the following week, he rose early each morning to get some unobserved practice in before his mentor awoke. The rest of his training day was spent in a mixture of increased exercise regimes and weapons training. The nights were spent discussing all manner of subjects with Gemba until it was time to retire for another well-earned rest.

It was towards the end of the twentieth day that he had been at Gemba's kraal, when the old man announced they were going to hunt for the evening meal.

"Tatenda baba", *Thank you father,* Zusa said, his heart racing at the thought. He had hunted many times before but it had been limited to the young boy's game, rabbits and wild birds but now he was hunting for the pot.

Lost in thought he was jogged back to reality when Gemba prodded his arm, "Come along lad, we don't have all day you know!"

The two men headed towards one of the mountain forests overlooking Gemba's homestead, armed only with their bows and a clutch of arrows. The initial climb was accomplished at a gentle pace but as they entered the tree line they separated a little bit, leaving a gap of about ten paces between them. Moving parallel to each other, they took slow measured steps through the foliage, their eyes casting well ahead for the first signs of prey. Zusa had also played the hunting game many times with his father but this would be the first time when the success of the stalk and kill would be his sole responsibility. Moving deeper into the woodland, the hunters took care where they trod, as any sound would be enough to scare the game away. The multiple shades of green caused their staring eyes to swim. From the corner of his eye, Zusa practically sensed, as opposed to actually seeing, a slight movement in his peripheral vision. Raising his arm into the air, Gemba halted. Zusa turned his head slowly in search of what had alerted him.

For a few tense moments he did not know what he had seen, and it was not until there was another shift in the backdrop of the wooded area that he could make out what was causing the movement. There it was again,
a black and white flicker, which was out of place in this sea of green. Zusa shifted his gaze to see what it was he was looking at. "Where did it go?" he asked himself. Then another larger movement, deep in the natural vegetation backdrop, made him realise that he was looking at the tail of a deer, which the animal had used as a whisk to swat away settling flies.

Now that his eyes were focused, its fawn-coloured body became clearer to see, with its white under-belly hide reflecting the natural light. Curved antlers rose upwards,
almost camouflaged by a tangle of branches from a large bush against which it stood.

Gemba saw the animal at the same time and they both sank to their haunches in the long grass. The old man picked up a small piece of grass and let it go on the breeze. It blew back towards him so the hunters knew that they were safe from their prey picking up their scent on the wind.

Using hand signals the two co-ordinated their movements forward a few paces at a time. Taking care, pausing to observe the deer, which continued eating the succulent leaves from the bush, unaware of their presence, the gap decreased until Zusa could hear the animal actually feeding. From the ripping and tearing of the fodder to the grinding of the cud in its mouth and the gentle gurgle of its stomach.

Zusa eased himself to a full standing position, his bow held at arm's length, the arrow secured by his right hand on the bowstring. In a practised motion, he took a deep breath and brought the weapon downwards to sight upon his target.

In the same moment the deer sensed the presence of the man and brought its head around to locate the danger. Reacting naturally, it tensed its legs for immediate flight.

With a buzz, Zusa let loose the arrow and it crossed the short distance in an instant, embedding itself deep into the chest of the deer, destroying its heart, killing the animal in mid-spring.

Zusa ran forward, his excited yelps echoing through the forest as he closed onto the position where the beast had fallen. His youthful jubilance made Gemba smile as the surrounding wild bush was filled with the rushing of many other animals, each scurrying away from the danger. Gemba walked up to where Zusa was and looked on in admiration of the clean kill and at the skill this young man had picked up over the last three weeks. Well at least they would eat well over the next couple of days before it was time for them to travel back to Mafuri, to Zusa's father's kraal.

Zusa was still chatting to his uncle, explaining again and again how he had seen the animal and how he had delivered the killing shot. Smiling to himself, Gemba just listened, letting the young man tell the story of his first true hunt, a story which would be retold around many campfires for many years. Thinking to himself the older man reflected on his own first hunt story. *If only time allowed for us the stay in the moments of our youth but while we dwell upon them, life moves on around us.* A sense of foreboding chilled Gemba's heart for a moment, unsure at what caused him to think that way. The older man looked around as if sensing a physical presence watching them.

Zusa caught him looking around and asked, "Is everything okay uncle?"

"Yes, yes young man" He paused again, "Nothing to worry about, let's get our dinner home shall we?"

Nodding in agreement, Zusa effortlessly slung the dead deer across his shoulders and they made their way back towards the homestead.

Chapter Seven
Travelling

Now back at his father's homestead, Zusa's wounds had healed to such an extent that he was now able to exercise freely without causing the scabs to break open again and it would only be a few more days before these eventually fell off of their own accord. The wounds would still be a raw pink against Zusa's dark brown skin, but at least he would have been fortunate enough to have regained full use of his limb. The time with his family had been some of the happiest he could remember. It had always been a good life with his parents and family around but recent events had made him realise that he could not remain a boy forever. He knew that new challenges and responsibilities were opening up and he understood these could well be the last days of his youth at home.

The day arranged for them to begin their trip to the nation's capital, Nyazimba, began bright and soon after a satisfying breakfast both Zusa and Gemba set out on the journey. Although advanced in age, Gemba set a pace which stretched and warmed their muscles within the first hour's walk. The first section of the journey was on narrow footpaths leading out of the district of Zusa's family's influence and beyond the normal pastureland for the village's goat herds. The gentle hills became more densely covered in vegetation and the trees grew in thicker patches almost into full forests. A number of neighbouring kraals were passed. These were built in cleared areas, which allowed the people to cultivate the fields around their homesteads and which provided a line of site defences so that the inhabitants could not be surprised by wild animals or man.

On two occasions they skirted more intricately

prepared defensive structures whose wooden walls guarded the village within, only greeting those who were in earshot.

Once they had been away from signs of population for almost an hour a movement within Zusa's peripheral vision revealed a group of warthogs in the clearing of a forest glade.

The animals' hind legs and tails stuck upright and stiff whilst down on their front knees digging away at the ground with their tusks searching for roots or nuts. The wild pigs lived in ground burrows in which they spent most the day, foraging during the night and until the early morning. This was a species not known for its kind temperament and which one wisely left alone; more than one brave soul had been chased by a disgruntled boar or sow if it was startled in the wild. On the good side, the meat of the warthog was almost white when cooked and the outer layer of fat crisped to a satisfying golden covering when roasted. It was remarkable that with this rich layer of lard the deeply grained meat remained fat free and strong tasting.

Ignoring the antics of the beasts, Gemba kept up a steady conversation, explaining the relationship between certain villages or reminiscing over something he remembered from the past. Some parts of the road also held special memory for him and he launched into stories normally beginning with, "When I was younger ... " Zusa took in any new information but sometimes closed his ears to stories which he had heard so many times before, letting the old man continue his speech but not forgetting to interject with the correct respectful tones such as, "oh yes" and, "aha baba".

Other times during the day were spent in silence as the men worked at consuming the distance they needed to traverse, knowing they had to reach the traveller's lodge before dark or run the risk of spending the night in the open. The frolics of the abundant wildlife kept them entertained, from the tall baboons, manlike in appearance when they stood on their hind legs, to the cavorting of the silver grey, furred vervet monkeys, *Makudo.* The young monkeys jumped from one member of the troop to another culminating with a sudden rush to cling to their mothers' backs if startled by something like the passing of the travellers. The monkeys' faces and well-formed humanoid hands were a very dark black against their contrasting light-coloured pelts.

    The district in which Zusa lived was on a hill covered plateau but their journey took them on a route where the ground flattened gradually into open grass plains and was particularly expansive on their right hand side. A range of high hills was seen on the far horizon to their left. Its distant colours mingled into shades of green and grey over which there was an occasional interruption by the flash of the bright colours of birds on the wing. These birds were startling in their vivid plumage, with all of the colours of a rainbow present from the light grey of the wood pigeons, the bright yellow of the weaver, the orange of the bishop bird through to the iridescent glossy starlings. Their calls blended to create a chorus of sound unlike anything which could be reproduced by man with a full orchestra of musical instruments.

    The grass of the plain reached to their knees but it would not be long before it grew above the height of an adult's head. The grassland was still damp in patches from the recent rains and the pools of water were well trampled by the hooves of countless beasts. These would gradually dry out over the next two months and soon after that not a drop of water would be found above the surrounding ground for a great distance and then these valuable sources would become the centre of existence for many of the animals.

    The smell of the veldt was still mostly, aromatic. There was the herbal fragrance of the wild scrub and bushes while the soil had the mixed scent of the underlying moisture. The top layer of the earth had begun to dry but not to the point where it could be disturbed into dust by the gentle breeze. Bright yellow knee-high plants gave an oily bouquet in contrast to the sweet smelling, long black prickly and sticky seeds, which stuck to the hairs of man or beast as they passed and these in turn, spread the flora's domain further.

Mixed herds of zebra and buffalo in their hundreds were seen in the distance and what was visible on the herds' perimeters were the ever-present hyenas and lions, waiting for an animal to die or to become a straggler.

Newborn beasts were an easy source of food to the felines as they could be effortlessly cut out of the herd for the kill. The passing of the gigantic herds was marked by the strong ammoniac smell of urine and lighter odours of their droppings that were interwoven with strands of undigested grass.

At midday Zusa and Gemba stopped to eat some of their pre-packed provisions and to drink from their precious clean water in the shade of a large baobab tree. A tree with a strange appearance, it was key within the great circle of life in the African surroundings as, when bare of leaves, the spreading branches of the baobab look like tree roots sticking into the air, rather as if it had been planted upside-down.

The Bushmen had a legend that told of the god Thora who took a dislike to the baobab growing in his garden. Pulling it from the ground, he threw it over the wall of Paradise to fall to the Earth below and, although the tree landed upside-down, it continued to grow with its roots pointing skywards. This would adequately explain the shape of the branches. Some of the tree trunks are so thick that twenty men holding arms outstretched could not encompass its girth. Many trees have stood as long as the oldest members of the community could remember and others became hollowed out by disease or rot to offer an enclosure and form of shelter. The tree was so very different from any other on the plains. Its massive trunk was smooth and shiny, not at all like the rough bark of other trees, and pinkish grey or sometimes copper coloured.

The baobab tree has large whitish flowers, which open at night with a unique sweet scent. The tree has many purposes; the fruit of the tree, which grows as long as a man's forearm, can be soaked in water to make a tasty drink; the bark can be pounded to make rope, mats, baskets, and thin cloth; and even the leaves can be boiled and eaten. Finally, a glue-like substance can also be made from the pollen of the flower, a truly convenient combination of usable commodities from a single source.

During a lull in conversation, Zusa touched one of the newly budded flowers of the tree that had sprung from a knoll at head height.

"Careful, umfana! You do not want to be eaten by a lion do you?" Gemba said, his eyes looking on in amusement at Zusa. Common folklore stated that if you picked a flower from a baobab tree you would be eaten by a lion, but on the other hand if you drink water in which a baobab's seeds have been soaked you will be safe from crocodile attack if you are trying to cross or swim in a river.

Zusa snatched his hand away from the blossom in case he inadvertently knocked it from its stem. "Is what they say true, Gemba?" he enquired.

"I couldn't really tell you, my boy, but I would rather not take a chance as I wish to stay well away from both those beasts!" Gemba replied with a hint of mischief in his voice.

By this time the sun had passed overhead and with both men well rested they continued with their eastward journey to Mushindi where they planned to spend the night. The path they were on had begun to slope downhill and the green plains of the low veldt were visible, stretching out before them. The vegetation had once again changed and they saw it was becoming denser as they looked further down into the valley below. Step by step they moved towards the dense tree line.

The forest consisted of what was more commonly known as the umbrella tree. These forests were crowded at the leaf canopy height, affording good shelter from the sun, but left the area below clear of clutter other than some lower bushes. Their tree trunks were a light grey in colour and rose above the ground in a single stem before forking in to two or three branches to spread the foliage above.

In the near distance the higher peaks of the Mtanda range continued to stretch above them and the pass
through which they intended to walk was clearly visible as a break in the stone barrier

The well trodden path through the forest opened into a open grass plain and, with the closing of the day fast approaching, there were many wild hares nibbling at the short grass whilst their smaller offspring bounded about in playful abandonment. Gemba put his arm out to stop Zusa from going any further and lowered himself to the ground, pulling Zusa with him.

"How about shuro meat for dinner this evening?" he asked.

Zusa smiled back, thinking Gemba spoke in jest, as he knew they did not have time to set a snare and wait for their quarry to return to be caught in the trap. He also knew from his youth it was pointless to attempt to chase the animals down; their fleetness of foot was well beyond that of man.

Sensing the hesitance in Zusa's eyes, Gemba reached into his shoulder bag and took out a looped bundle of twisted leather and cattle sinew. When unravelled and stretched out the string proved to have a loop at both ends. Gemba took the first end and fitted it over the tapered end of his walking staff. Once in place he wound the sinew thong around the tip two or three times before turning the rod around and putting the first end to the ground. Leaning on the stick, he bent its form into a bow, securing the other end of the bowstring in another tapered and grooved slot. Once this was done, he eased back from leaning on the shaft letting the bow take its natural curved shape.

After resting for a few seconds he again bent the bow and performed the double looping of the string to help secure the string in place and to increase the tension on the instrument.

Once its form was evident, Zusa looked carefully at what, only a minute ago, had been a walking aid and which was now a weapon. Seeing its appearance the reason for the centrally carved handgrip became apparent. Copper wire had been wound around the middle part of the bow and this clamped a piece of darker wood to the rear of the device to lend strength for when it was pulled back in tension.

In complete silence Gemba finished readying the bow and after making a final inspection he handed it to Zusa. "Don't let the string touch the soil and get damp, otherwise it will break when it is pulled," he said quietly.
From his pack he removed three arrows, their heads pointed, black and fire-hardened. At the rear of the arrow Gemba affixed a large feather, sliding it into a pre-cut slot and then binding it into position with a thin piece of leather, leaving a short portion of the shaft at the end clear. Once all three arrows had been prepared, Gemba tested each for weight and balance then holding them each up in turn to the sky and twisting them between his fingers he checked for the trueness of the shafts.

Smiling, Gemba reached out to Zusa for the weapon and indicated for him to wait where he was. Fitting one of the arrows loosely to the bow, slotting the string into the groove at the back of the projectile he rose slowly to his feet looking around for his prey. He caught the flash of white under tail almost fifty paces towards the edge of the clearing.

In a crouch he slowly moved forward knowing that if the alarm was raised the entire field of hares would empty in a blink of an eye as they fled for safety in the nearby tree line or into the numerous rock cavities.

Placing one foot carefully in front of the other so as not to step on a stick or disturb the loose leaves under foot; Gemba remained in a hunched-over position until he had cut the distance between his target in half. Not wanting to risk disturbing his prey attempting to get too close, Gemba halted and stuck the spare arrows into the ground at his feet, point first for easy retrieval. He checked for a final time the placing of the arrow he had already fitted to the bow.

From his stooped over position he straightened his left arm, gripping the bow in his strong hand. The arrow was held in position with the fingers of his right hand and, after a final check on his position in relation to the gathering of hares, he singled out a particularly large animal. Taking a deep breath he straightened his stance in a fluid motion whilst pulling back the bowstring to a position at eye level, sighting down the length of the arrow. Using the string as an aiming point, he aligned his sight and simultaneously let loose the arrow.

From his position behind Gemba, Zusa caught a blurred glimpse of the arrow in flight although he was unable to see the target. This was rectified when he saw one of the animals rise high above the grass, being catapulted backwards to land lifelessly on the ground. With the sudden appearance of a stranger in their midst, and the sound of the twang of the released bowstring, the thirty or forty other hares scattered in all directions. Some seemed not to understand why there was a panic and found themselves actually closing in on the source of the disturbance only to twist away once they saw Gemba standing upright. The field had exploded with small furry animals, their lighter underbellies and fur coats flashing in the daylight disturbing birds and insects into flight, creating miniature clouds, and within seconds they had all disappeared as if they had not been there in the first place.

Gemba looked at Zusa and beckoned him forward. At a run, the young man headed for the position where he had seen the animal hit and the two arrived at the spot at the same time. The arrow had taken the animal cleanly through the chest, killing it in an instant. It was indeed a large animal and it would feed the hungry travellers well.
Zusa bent over and retrieved the arrow, which had to have its stabiliser feathers removed and the shaft pushed further though the carcass as the design of the arrowhead was barbed to prevent it being withdrawn easily.

Zusa tied a leather thong around the feet of the rabbit and slung it over his shoulders with the bow and as one, they headed toward the place they intended to spend the night. By this time the sun was low on the horizon and the companions increased their pace to ensure they reached the safety of the travellers' refuge at Mushindi before dark.

The end of the day seem to drag on and just as Zusa was wondering when they would arrive the familiar shape of a rock and brick enclosure appeared on the next rise, silhouetted against the vivid dusk.

The path was clear all the way up to the entrance and to one side of the refuge a stream ran freely, adding the laughter of flowing water to the sounds of the insects and rustling leaves of the trees.

The sanctuary had been built with thousands of even-sized granite bricks and was circular in construction, about twenty paces across. The walls reached Zusa's shoulders in height and once they stepped into the refuge he could see that the floor was bare ground although covered in parts by windswept leaves and foliage. The door was as narrow as a man and had a gate made from interwoven branches which could be slotted into vertical recesses, effectively securing the occupants once inside.

"Let us gather firewood before it gets too dark," Gemba said.

Fires were lit first once camps were set as they served two main purposes other than the need for heat and cooking. The smoke and noise from the crackling flames scared away any unwanted animals, insects, and reptiles and secondly it served as a beacon in case those foraging for the camp became disorientated in the unfamiliar territory.

The men laid their possessions just within the entrance of the miniature fort and moved around picking up fallen twigs, branches and dried grass. Within a short time they had managed to gather enough material to ensure the fire could be kept burning all night. With a stone flint and a bar of iron, Gemba started a campfire in the centre of the enclosure, a white fluffy weed ensured the sparks caught quickly, which when gently blown on, producing a flame. He then speared the recently skinned hare on a spit made from a newly cut green tree branch hanging above the flames and rested the carcass on another wooden fork set into the ground so that it could cook.

Once these initial meal preparations were completed both of the men went out of the stone encirclement and across to the stream to wash the dust of the road from their bodies and to take their fill in a deep and satisfying drink of cool water. As they returned to the campfire the sun finally dipped below the horizon and with the suddenness of an African sunset the night was upon them. At the instant the bright disc disappeared from sight, the gentle chirp of insects paused and the slight breeze reversed as if it took a sharp, short breath inwards. From a discernible level of low light the countryside was plunged into an almost total darkness and as if a switch had been thrown the daytime sounds was replaced by those of the night.

Zusa and Gemba secured the wooden gate in its place and settled down near the fire, tending the gentle flames whilst turning the carcass in order to give it an even roasting. The men took out their bundles of pre-prepared sadza and divided it into two meals, a portion for that night and the remainder for the morning breakfast. They used the large stones surrounding the fire to heat the cakes of maize meal.

Both men had taken the time to enjoy the silence of the sunset but gradually as the evening worn on they began conversing as strips of meat were sliced from the carcass and added to the warmed sadza, each morsel of food was popped into their mouths and chewed with delight.

Once the fare had been consumed, Zusa looked at the bow that Gemba had used to kill the hare a while ago. He reached across and picked it up.

"I have not seen a bow of this construction and dual use before," he said. It was yet another design away from the unique dual-coloured wood bow he had learnt to hunt with while he was at his uncle's kraal.

Gemba smiled. "It is something I picked up from the San people who live many weeks travel west of your village. Normally the shaft is a strong but flexible walking stick and, when you attach the sinew string to create the bow, you are able to shoot these lightweight arrows over quite a distance. Fired correctly they can bring down even the largest of animals." He thought further and continued.
"In fact the San use reed arrows with detachable heads which they poison with the pulped bodies of a grub. The poison does not actually kill the animal. It makes it drowsy

and it eventually falls asleep. The San are expert trackers and they will follow their target for many hours and once the animal has fallen to the ground they take the time to apologise and explain that their families are hungry and that they need to eat ... and then they cut its throat." His voice trailed off.

Both men stared into the fire, their minds working over the tale. The mature man's eyes misted with understanding at the closeness with which the San interacted with nature, killing only when they had to so that they preserved their limited and scarce resources. The younger man's mind ticked over with the excitement of learning something new before he spoke aloud and broke into Gemba's thoughts. "I understand why they only use a small amount of poison. If the hunter used a larger dose to kill the animal it would corrupt the meat and they would unable to eat it!"

"Yes, that is true, Zusa," Gemba said, saddened by the fact that the young man was not astute enough to understand the fine line between life and death or feast and famine which governed the African wild. The silence continued and Zusa realised that there was more to the story than just the technicalities. They continued to sit near the fire, each of them deep in his thoughts.

After a while Gemba asked if Zusa wanted to try the bow. Nodding acceptance Zusa cautiously experimented pulling on the weapon's bowstring. Giving instructions, Gemba told the young man how to assemble the instrument from being a simple walking aid to a weapon of death.

When he had constructed the weapon Zusa sighted with one eye closed, the other looking along the bowstring and body of the arrow shaft. It was of a lighter construction than the model he had trained with. After a few failed attempts, which made both men laugh, Zusa managed to loose an arrow successfully.

"Don't forget what I taught you. Use the effect of taking a very deep breath to stretch your chest; this will help you to pull the string back as far as possible!" Gemba advised. "With practise this will make sure you can fire faster and further."

Gemba was pleased to see that his charge had an almost natural rhythm which allowed him to pick up the art of shooting various bow designs with ease. A couple of times thoughout the evening, Zusa ran forward to retrieve the spent arrows so that they could be fired again and he was enjoying himself so much that the evening drew inwards and eventually the weary travellers had to put aside the bow and lay out their sleeping mats.

On opposite sides of the fire they stretched out on the ground with their monkey-skin blankets pulled up to their shoulders to keep the slight chill off their bodies for the night.

Lying on his back staring into the clear night sky, its black canopy filling his view from horizon to horizon, Zusa contemplated why Gemba has gone strangely quiet at the recounting of the bushman hunter's story earlier in the evening. Suddenly Zusa had an insight into the discussion and the older man's reactions and looked over towards his mentor. "Sekuru," he said gently, "the San, they hold nature with great respect for their apportioned provisions don't they? That is why the hunter takes the time to explain to the animal why he has had to kill it!"

Gemba opened his eyes and looked back at Zusa, his eyes glinting in the firelight. "You are becoming a man more and more each day, my son," he said. He gave a sigh of delight, before turning away to go to sleep.

As the gentle snores of Gemba rose above the sounds of the night, Zusa laid awake, listening to nature all around him and staring at the panoramic bright sky filled with an uncountable number of stars.

Chapter Eight
Fort Chimnungwa

It was early morning; five days after the first Bantu town of Shashe had fallen to the invaders. The Zulu forces now surrounded the unsuspecting village and military fort of Chimnungwa. The sun was due to rise within the hour and their chieftain, Modena, had taken a position on the hill overlooking the inhabited area. His plan was simple, as soon as it was light enough to make out his signals, the co-ordinated attack would begin. The fort, their main goal, was on a small rise with the associated trading town spread below it on a plain leading down to a river. As a fort, it was only an enlarged stone brick circle with no definitive defensive structures to it. It was more a refuge than a military building and was manned by a small detachment of warriors.

As this regiment was far away from the influences of their city leaders in the nation's capital, poor discipline had crept into the garrison at this remote outpost, where it was common knowledge that "nothing ever happened." This break in regulations had meant that the majority of the garrison troops had moved out of their allotted army barracks into the more comfortable surroundings of the village after finding wives from within the local community or having their families move to the town once they had been permanently stationed there. In the past it had been normal practice for the Bantu army commander in Nyazimba to move his garrison troops from one military site to another on a regular basis.

However, since the army had been handed over to a new commander called Kadenge, he had not enforced the standing regulations. He had felt that a few changes had to be introduced to coincide with his new appointment so that his stamp of authority was recognised.

He did not want to feel under the constraint of the rules of the previous commander, Zabesi, who had been a conscientious army commander and who had been rewarded by being promoted to the chieftain's post of the King's Palace personal guard.

Unwittingly, this lapse in command by Kadenge had favoured and abetted the Zulus' plans and the town and fort slept silently, the populace totally unaware or the pending assault.

Modena had taken personal command of this attack following his successes over the proceeding weeks with seven villages and over three hundred slaves in his hands. Cattle and goats numbering many hundreds had also been seized and in his mind he was already calculating his share of the spoils.

His own casualties had been light and the combined force below was just waiting for his signal to begin the attack. He looked again towards the east but it was still not light enough for the attack. With a mass assault by so many of his men against a defending force of around five hundred Bantu warriors, they needed the benefit of the daylight so that they did not risk killing each other in the expected confusion. He could picture in his mind what was about to happen. A repeat of his proven tactics, a sudden, silent rush, the first hysterical screams and cries of panic followed by the howling of fear as many were put to the spear.

Modena had set a ring of skirmishers utilising a complete impi of over one thousand five hundred men around the target area to stop anyone escaping and these men had strict instructions to remain in place, no matter how strong their desire to join in the battle, to ensure that news of the attack was kept a secret for as long as possible.

He again took the time to survey the layout of the village below. The fort had been one of the first defensive-type settlements to be established in the Bantu homeland many generations ago. The Bantu had had numerous smaller settlements spread for many weeks' walk in all directions but this site was considered the true beginning of the nation as it was known today.

The site for this town had been chosen primarily as a central point due to the presence of iron and the ore-producing mines spread throughout the area. From this, a community had arisen in the wilderness and the true art of extracting iron from the ground was developed. The population learned how to tease the precious commodity from the surrounding mines mainly through trial and error. What had initially attracted the ironworkers to the region was the large number of iron-ore nuggets just lying about on the ground, although they were highly oxidised from their exposure to the elements for countless seasons.

These easily accessible samples permitted the experimentation of furnaces and eventually a combined system of using the natural draw of a chimney with the added pressure from leather skin bellows allowed the fire to reach a high enough temperature for the ore to smelt. The art of producing this raw material became an almost religious ceremony and the few selected masters kept its secrets, jealously guarded the knowledge, only handing on their own tricks of the trade to carefully selected apprentices who would in turn one day take over the forge, or who could be dispersed to other areas to extend the ever-growing need for iron tools and utensils.

Its malleable quality when under extreme heat was also refined in this time and the uses for the finished, hardened products were soon discovered to be limitless. During this period, man became the true clear masters of the world as their advantage of being able to manufacture tools and weapons beyond those gifted by nature, such as tusks, claws or teeth, meant that they could kill any other beast on the earth.

This industry attracted the best and the worst of society. There were the skilled and learned men who improved on the new science of ore extraction and metalworking; the artisans who supported them and the traders and hunters to supply food for the concentration of population. Unfortunately, shanty towns sprang up on the edge of the new society where malingerers and drunkards who had been cast aside by the progressive commercial trade or simply due to their own laziness, eked out a harsh living.

Once the village had become a town with its own market place and self-sufficient industries it required protection from marauding gangs who were tribeless and a law unto themselves. The newly-forming nation united under one leader whose seat of power at that time was further west at a place called Naletale. The first Bantu King imposed his will and projected a sense of peace by decreeing laws and maintaining a standing army to enforce them.

During this lawless era and time of transition, the quality of the iron tools was really put to the test. The first tools were brittle and many broke if used under harsh conditions and nothing tested men more than when hunting a wild buffalo, elephant or man to have your main advantage, your iron weapon, break at a critical moment.

A higher-grade quality of ore was found only a short distance below the surface of the soil and could still be gathered with just a little more effort by digging strip trenches. Unfortunately these resources were also depleted within a couple of generations and other sites, rich in abundance with the ore, were found north-eastwards in an area called Belingwe.

With this shift in location of such a strategic resource much of the metropolis moved with it along with the technical expertise and knowledge. Almost fifty smaller sites were established, each with its own smaller stone-built stockades for protection. It was no longer possible to maintain warriors in the field at all these locations on a level large enough to have an effect on raiders so a degree of self-defence was vital. This was in conjunction with a marked improvement in the state of security across the nation as smaller tribes were assimilated into the Bantu' race and those not willing to accept their ways were swept aside to extinction.

At this time, the seat of power of this iron-fashioning nation was moved to the city of Nyazimba as Naletale's influence on this mineral-rich area waned with the increase in distance between the sites and, shortly after these occurrences, Nyazimba was declared the nation's capital.

Through this occurrence the City of Stone was founded. Its economic foundation was largely dependent on the trading of the iron and its products from the surrounding region. Trade between other nations became widely spread as they also had an insatiable desire for the wondrous material. Some of these nations were soon able to perform their own iron mining, smelting and manufacturing but nowhere near the commercial capacity or quality of the Nyazimbian produce and so it remained a valuable trading commodity.

Unfortunately, over time, these new iron ore sites began to dwindle and the nation thought that they were going to have to uproot their society again and be forced to replant themselves where the next iron ore fields were found. This semi-nomadic lifestyle would not work as easily as it had in the past. Other nations had managed to establish themselves and their boundaries were jealously guarded, and any major move would have involved an all-out war and displacement of many thousands of people.

A chance discovery by one of the open-cast mine diggers revealed a solid seam of iron ore angling downwards below the normal level of the trenches. A few days' work proved this a find of almost pure iron.

Unfortunately its presence was no longer in easily smelted nuggets and it was found to be embedded within the rock. More mines were opened in search of larger deposits of the ore and there was a marked increase in productivity, which meant its costs reduced considerably and even more uses were discovered for the material.

The practice of breaking the rock with fire had been in place for many generations, which was used in the open granite quarries to build the stockades, forts and residences of the society.

Although well proven, this technique was something very different when used underground where space was limited as the shafts were sometimes only the width of the miner's body and the dangers of suffocation from the smoke of the burning fires were extremely high.

Casualties, injured and dead, began to increase in number, but that was only human life, cheap when compared to the rewards the products of iron returned. Other metals were found during this process, one the colour of the setting sun, reddish orange, which remained soft and pliable and was used in the production of jewellery and for winding around spear shafts to add weight and strength. Another metal found was the true colour of the sun, golden. It was thought to be of particular beauty but not enough of it could be refined to be of real value. It fact it was too soft to be of a practical use and so ended up being added to the jewellery production.

The fort over which Modena looked was far from its days of glory and this was reflected in the run-down condition of the dwellings around the stone-ringed barricade. The fort was manned by Bantu warriors and its existence was purely due to the fact that it was the furthest point from the city and it could be used to intercept raiders from the south, namely Zulus like himself or one of the other eight tribes who lived south of the Limpopo river.

The small amount of iron still produced there was just enough to support the village which had lost its status to be called a town many years before. However, it was still of significant importance in maintaining control of the surrounding area and Modena knew he had to take ownership of the defensible position before he could attempt to raid the district further afield. Once the disciplined Bantu military force were alerted to the presence of an attacking enemy in its territory, it would expect to use this position as a safe refuge with its guard posts fully staffed and prepared. From its walls they would be able to sortie out from its relative safety and it would remain a safe haven for other villagers and a warehouse for supplies to keep the Bantu warriors in the field long enough to see off the menace.

The reality was it needed to be taken and held against all cost. Its present stocks were a further incentive for the attack as it was still used to store the season's production of metal, weapons, food and general supplies.

As an added bonus, the town's wooden cattle stockade would make an excellent prison for the captured Bantus.

By now, the sky had a flicker of light on the eastern horizon and Modena knew it would not be long before he signalled his men to attack the sleeping township. He sneered to himself; the lazy Bantu had not posted sentinels and they deserved to die in the beds where they lay.

A slight shuffle close to him announced his attending lieutenants anticipating his command but he decided not to address their impatience and ignored their attempt to get his attention. He did not want his men to blunder into a fixed or well-planned defence so he was waiting until he was able make out the land below.

The minutes dragged on but as Mware, had made the moon to measure the seasons, he used the sun to mark the hours of the day. As it rose, its first fingers of light touched the valley in which the fort was situated.

Modena finally rose from his concealed position on the hill and raised his assegai above his head to attract the attention of the impi leaders below.

He was distracted for a moment as something in his peripheral vision made him look at the hill slightly beyond his own position. He thought he had seen something move on the hillside overlooking the village. Modena paused and stared at the place where he had sensed movement but it did not recur. *It must have been an animal or possibly the wind moving a bush* he thought to himself. *If it had been someone witnessing what was unfolding below, then his net of warriors who formed the outer picket line would surely catch them.*

Even in the few seconds he took to ponder these questions the light had strengthened further and he was able to make out the uplifted faces of his men looking at him as he stood with his arm above his head.

He jabbed his assegai upwards and waited for a response from the three regimental chiefs below. Once they had all acknowledged his gesture he looked around to ensure all was in place. Without any additional delay and with a swooping motion he over-emphasised the action of his arm and pointed his assegai three times at the rural community below. His command was repeated by his aides to relay the attack command to the regiments who had the responsibility of securing the extreme perimeter and for them to prepare to stop those who would take flight at the first sign of danger.

To begin with, Modena thought there had been no reaction to his command, but then he was able to make out the thin lines of his warriors as they silently converged on their objectives. A simultaneous and coordinated attack was vital to their success so that there was no warning to anybody in the dwellings or the fort. Even as he looked, the first regiment was closing on the southern portion of the village and as it reached its perimeter the men spread out in an extended line to form a scooping net which swung around the buildings encompassing them in one stroke.

Bursting through thin wood and hide-covered doors with loud battle calls the Zulu warriors showed no mercy to any man found within the buildings. Although against direct orders some women and children were killed in the confusion and gloom of the interior, their cries for clemency and their begging arms raised in desperate entreaty were ignored, as their bodies were pierced by the broad-bladed assegais.

Whilst this occurred, the other two full Zulu regiments had closed on the area near the fort and the associated barracks. In a similar manner they broke into the soldiers' billets near the fort and killed all of those within. Many of these were despatched in their sleep or in the act of getting up to defend themselves.

In the strengthening morning light, Modena could see that the attack was progressing well. However, some shift in the movement of the lines below made it clear to him that some military discipline was still in force in the besieged town as a half-sized regiment of almost two hundred Bantu warriors spilled from the fort and attempted to form into a defensive line. Their chieftain could be seen shouting his orders, his voice audible at that range, even over the harsh din of battle. Worst of all for Modena, the Bantu chieftain's commands were also being enacted, even as the Zulu commander looked on, and its success was evident from the way the Bantu force was responding.

Modena remained surprised that this group of garrison troops had managed to arm and equip themselves properly in the little time given and it was now moving into a defensive formation at a position just outside their fort's main gate. *It might have been more sensible for them to have held the fortress wall,* Modena's military mind thought. The Bantus' reaction must have been based on those inside believing that they were being attacked by a small group of bandits and not by a full fighting force of Zulus!

In the melee below, outside the fort, the Bantu commander, Kete, soon realised the extreme danger he and his men were in. The attackers had now been correctly identified as Zulu invaders. Based on the time he had had to gather what was left of his force, he knew that he was greatly outnumbered. As if reading the thought of Modena observing from above, he said to himself, "I should have kept my forces inside the protection of the stone walls."

One of his lieutenants standing close by thought he was being spoken to and replied questioningly, "Sir?"

"No, I was not speaking to you, soldier. I was thinking aloud to myself." He stopped speaking as another forward rush by the attackers pushed his right flank away from the fort's gateway closing the option he may have had in regaining the safety of its high stone walls. More of his men fell as he watched and it was their deaths right before his eyes that galvanised him into action.

He grabbed the lieutenant, who had just addressed him by the shoulder and shouted above the din of battle,
"Get all the men to form against the wall, curving outwards slightly with any walking wounded inside the boundary to act as reinforcements." The man nodded his head in understanding and moved away to issue the command.

Set before the Bantu chief was a wall of struggling humanity but their regalia allowed him to distinguish between the two sides. Screams of anger and pain filled the air as arms rose and fell delivering death-dealing blow after blow. The crash of shields against each other assaulted the ears while the smell of blood and punctured bowels invaded the senses. A large Zulu warrior broke through the melee and ran towards Kete, whose insignia announced his seniority. The attacker's large shield blocked Kete's view but his eyes were drawn to the savage weapon in the warrior's hand. The blade reflected the rising sunlight and he found himself mesmerised by the contrast of the points of brightness and the dulling caused by the scarlet droplets of blood from an earlier kill. As if in slow motion, he watched the blade swing down towards his exposed throat.

    The look of glee on the Zulu's face at what appeared to be an easy kill, changed to one of confusion as Kete, a seasoned warrior for fifteen years, sharply deflected the assegai's path with his shield. This counter-manoeuvre forced the attacking Zulu off balance and as Kete sidestepped his assailant, he dug his spear into the now exposed torso of the warrior, deep and under the ribcage to tear the heart muscle and lungs asunder. The cry of surprise from the Zulu at the change in circumstance and pain turned into a gargle as a bright spurt of blood leaped from the Zulu's mouth and he fell at Kete's feet, tearing the spear from his grasp.

    The noise of battle filled his mind and he looked around to see that the last of his men had begun to react to his last command to re-form. Realising that he was without an offensive weapon, Kete bent down to retrieve a spear which had been dropped by one of his fallen men.

    His action of bending over saved his life in that instant, but the assegai, which had been pushed at him by another attacker still raked across his back and split the skin which opened like a ripe plum, before the gash flooded with blood.

    Kete fell forward; two of his men reached out and snatched him into the safety of the newly-formed defensive back line before killing the Zulu who had wounded their chief, both spears finding their mark and making short work of the assailant.

    The injured chieftain lay on the ground for a few moments, biting down at the intense pain which racked his body, each deep breath and beat of his heart adding to the excruciating throbbing in his back. He searched for the wound with one hand and shuddered as his fingers located the opening across his left shoulder. Pulling back his hand, he saw that it was coated with his blood. Angered at the assault, his face set fiercely and with a loud shout he rose to his feet. Looking about, he realised that he had less than one hundred and fifty men left to command, a large portion of his force dead or severely wounded were strewn across the battlefield.

At the top of his voice he shouted, "Pull back, pull back! Get up against the fortress wall." Those who heard it took up the command repeating it to those around them and in response the formation retreated to secure the safety rear guard of unmoveable stone and rock.

The Zulu force kept up a constant attack and another twelve Bantu warriors were killed during the re-formation manoeuvre. A long spear was thrust into Kete's empty hand by one of his warriors, whilst the weight of his shield and the wound to his shoulder meant that he did not have full control of his personal defence. Realising that he would be more of a hindrance in the front line he continued to command from within the semi-circle of men, directing the final defence and co-ordinating his dwindling reinforcements into place, if a front line warrior fell, plugging a gap in the perimeter.

Once the shield wall had formed, the longer spears of the Bantu showed their advantage over the shorter assegai as it kept the attackers beyond arms' reach.

"Don't let them close with you!" Kete kept on shouting. "Do not let the Zulu engage you shield to shield, use the reach of your spears."

The Bantu reserves in the inner semicircle pushed their own spears through the gaps towards the enemy to present a formation bristling with deadly quills and kept the Zulu at bay. The clatter of spears and assegais against shields assaulted the ears while the battle cry of success and death shattered the mind. The long drawn out calls of pain grated the nerves sending shuddering sensations down the spine and causing the scalp to itch at the sound.

For a moment the noise eased and Kete looked

around to see that the Zulus' frontal assault was pulling back and a clear gap appeared between the two battling forces.

Seizing on this small gain he shouted further words of encouragement to his men to re-form lines and pull back to shorten their front line. He knew that although he now had fewer men on his perimeter, it also meant that the Zulus could only send a limited number of men into the attack. He thought to himself. *Have we managed to fight off the attack?* He looked around to see if he could make out what was happening and his mind froze in terror. His face stayed a mask of discipline even as he saw that the Zulu had only pulled back to restructure their line and as he watched, the reinforced formation swept forwards, their battle cries renewed just as was their strength in manpower.

Kete suddenly realised that it was now just a matter of time. The sheer mass of surviving Zulus far outnumbered his total command at the beginning of the battle and his greatly depleted force was nowhere near the size needed to act even in a holding formation.

The renewed clash of shield against shield drew his attention to the fact that the Zulus had closed once again with his men. The Bantu spears were dragged down with the impaled bodies of the Zulu warriors and had become useless and, with the efficient use of the Zulus' close support weapons, the last of the Bantu defence collapsed.

At the same time other Zulu warriors dropped at their rear from the top of the walls, after gaining access to the fortress via the open gates. The enemy was amongst them and it was over.

Rallying his men in a last defiant act, Kete led the final rush towards the attackers. Being shield-less he took three assegais to his body but he remained on his feet, battering anyone who came within reach of his spear. His men fell; one by one, overwhelmed by superior numbers and eventually another thrust of an assegai between his shoulders caused the Bantu chief to fall and his blood-soaked body draped across those of his men, arms outstretched as if in a final act of protection: The garrison had fallen to the Zulus.

The sounds of battle gradually faded but the screaming and shouting of the captured women and children was carried on the wind and Modena decided to make his way down to lay claim to the final prize for himself.

Rape was not an acceptable act of war in the region and was instantly punishable by death, so the disciplined Zulus, after containing their captives, ransacked the homesteads of anything of personal value like small knives, jewellery and trinkets. The strategic commodities such as food, clothing, livestock, women and children belonged to the King and no one dared take from the King that which was now recognised as being rightfully his. The captives were herded together, their terror apparent by the way they stumbled and tripped through the debris of battle broken fences, shattered clay pots, smashed wood, furniture and torn cloth towards where they were to be impounded.

By the time Modena had made his way down the hill and inside the fort, his senior men had managed to regain a semblance of order. The prisoners had been commanded into silence, although a number of younger women and children quietly wept at the suddenness of the attack and the even quicker change in their status, from proud Bantu to captive slave in a blink of an eye.

During the forced entry into a number of the huts, some fires had been kicked and their hot embers set the grass and wood on fire. The flames had spread to nearby structures and now smoke from a number of burning huts swept across the town, the acrid smoke catching in his throat and stinging his eyes.

"Get those fires put out," Modena shouted. "Do you want to signal our presence to the rest of the country?"
Groups of men ran towards the burning buildings to tear down the structures so that the flames could be beaten out with tree branches or snuffed with water and sand.

Other commands were issued and men were being directed to numerous tasks. The bodies of the slain were piled to one side for quick disposal, as the ravages of disease associated with the closeness of dead bodies in Africa were well known. The Zulus did not want the stench of the rotting corpses to affect the habitability of what was going to become one of their main base camps for the campaign.

Once the streets and buildings had been cleared a party of Zulu had the surviving young boys dig a large trench so that the dead could be buried. The Zulu army had only lost thirty-seven dead and forty-one wounded but the overall Bantu garrison had lost over five hundred men in a short, cruel morning.

Modena summoned his senior men who soon brought him up to date on the overall tactical situation. From the report he knew that additional guards had been stationed around the town with one of the regiments being tasked with remaining in a state of readiness in case there was any counter-reaction to the forceful taking of the town. Halfway through the briefing there was a disturbance from the eastern perimeter of the township and a large body of his troops broke through the outer tree line pushing before them a group of individuals. They were the Bantu who had managed to escape during the initial attack and who were captured by his cordon of warriors. Amongst the dejected captives were seven men and four women, each with their own young child. As the group arrived to where Modena was holding his meeting the prisoners were forced to their knees in front of the Zulu commander. The Zulu patrol leader reported to Modena stating, "We caught them all trying to get away towards Nyazimba! What do you want me to do with them?"

Modena looked back at the man and replied with a sense of incredulity that such a question needed to be asked. "You have received your orders lieutenant; I thought my instructions earlier were clear. You know what to do!"

Realising his mistake the warrior indicated to his men and without any further hesitation four of the warriors pulled the women and children to their feet and dragged them away to be incarcerated with the rest of the village folk.

The men were not so fortunate and realising this, one man threw himself to the ground sobbing for leniency. His whimper echoed in the open village square but Modena was unmoved as he knew that their fate had already been sealed.

The first cry for mercy was taken up by the other men on their knees, each with a Zulu soldier standing over them. At a nod from the induna, the prisoner furthest away from Modena had his head pushed forward. The point of the guard's assegai was forced through from the back of the neck to sever the spinal column before its tip emerged from his throat, killing him instantly. He did not even have time to let out any sound - he just died. The hand span of assegai blade sticking out of his flesh was stained scarlet red with his blood and on retrieval, with a sucking sound, the blade practically decapitated the corpse and the head flopped sideways before the body crashed to the ground in a puff of dust.

Taking this violent act as encouragement, the other Zulu guards decided to see who could find the most creative way of despatching their particular prisoner. Some of them had their heads drawn back so that the exposed neck could be sliced open, while others were stabbed from behind so that the head of the assegai emerged from the chest after passing through the heart.

Some died quietly; others not so and their screams of pain and panic caused the wailing of the women and child prisoners to halt their weeping as the horrors of what was happening to another of their kin became a stark reminder of what could happen to them if they continued to try the patience of the Zulus.

With a dismissal flick of Modena's wrist the bodies were dragged away to the newly dug burial site leaving the earth where they had fallen stained with their blood. Without another thought of what had just occurred, Modena walked away to assess his newly-gained bounty. He was pleased with the way the attack had gone and, although he mourned the men who had died from his regiments, he considered it a small and acceptable price to pay for such a rich trophy. He knew his King would also be pleased and if the King was pleased then his personal reward would be even greater.

Growing old in my own village surrounded by my wives and children, he thought, *Now that is the way I want this to end.* Smiling to himself he dismissed the men around him and walked into the captured village to assess its value.

Chapter Nine
To Nyazimba

It was still early in the morning and the pair of travellers were awakened by the harmonic chorus present at the break of dawn. The barking of the baboons in the surrounding hills and the cries of the roosting birds in the forest were evident. The sun had just begun to announce its existence upon the horizon to the east and the soft ruby glow spoke of the promise of a hot day ahead. The sky was clear but with a tinted spectrum extended from the west. The deepest blue of the night had changed to a pale shade of grey in the direction of the new day. With a burst of energy the skyline became spotted with the early gatherings of birds taking flight in search of the first food, sweeping and swooping, before forming into larger flocks.
There was light dew on the grass upon which Zusa had slept and the smell of the moist soil was sharp in his nostrils. It was a scent not unlike the taste one gets from placing the tongue on a piece of bare metal. Tangy, wholesome and belonging to the earth. It was the taste of *simbi:* iron.

Stretching his arms and legs Zusa arose from his sleeping mat. The surrounding circular stone-bricked wall had managed to retain some of the heat from the watch fire whilst outside the fort the ground was shrouded in a fine mist caused by the lower night temperature. Gemba had also risen and opened the wooden gateway by lifting it from the grooves in the door frame. Leaving it resting against the inner wall they walked out to work off the stiffness in their muscles after a night sleeping on the ground. "Mangwanani baba*"*, Zusa said.

"Morning Zusa", his mentor replied, "I trust you slept well?"

"Yes, I did, the long day really made me tired but I am looking forward to getting to look around the city later on today! I have heard so much about it."

"It's going to be a good day young man and the city is going to be everything you expect it to be." Grinning he pushed Zusa's shoulder; "We should eat and get back on the road."

A breakfast of cold sadza was hastily eaten, washed down with the last of the weak beer brew. The small stream allowed the companions to wash their faces and to rinse the fine talcum powder dust from their bodies after their night on the ground. The banana-tree leaf wrappings, which had contained the last of their food, were buried and the night fire dampened but its stone circle left intact for the next traveller to use. Their calabashes of water, *called mundende,* were refilled from the gentle stream and they carefully ensured that the stoppers were fitted tightly. Finally the sleeping mats were rolled up and tied with bark string and slung over their shoulders.

In the reverse order from the evening before there was an anticipatory stillness in the air, a moment of calm, as if Mother Nature was drawing a breath and gathering herself before the fresh start of the new day in the never-ending cycle of life. Even the multitude of insects paused in their incessant clamour. For just a few heartbeats there was silence. Then the breeze returned and with it the fulsome and live sounds of the surrounding country.

Without another word the two men looked at each other and moved towards the now glorious sunrise leaving their night-time refuge behind. It was the start of a beautiful day, full of the promise of new and exciting ventures and for one of the pair sights that had stirred the imagination since the first stories had been told around the fireplace at the kraal back home.

Their first hurdle for the day was getting through the northern pass of the Mtanda mountain range. Their place of rest from the previous night had been built in the shadow of the twin high peaks that indicated from afar the gash in the natural stone barrier and the way through the mountain range. This was the most commonly used route to Nyazimba for those arriving from inland although another route through this barrier existed further south from this position. It was a narrower gap to pass through and Gemba was familiar with the mountain range and its common and lesser-known secrets as he had grown up in the area.

Zusa and Gemba continued to walk at a steady pace, their strides falling into that of long-distance walkers through the ages, where mile after mile is consumed by the urge to move forward. The path, worn from age and use, led like a pointer to the City of Stone, occasionally meandering amongst the large rocks but always heading eastwards. This section of the road was of a particularly fine sand, slightly off white in colour, and where the recent rains had fallen and the waters had run freely across the ground, areas of the trail had become flattened and smoothed in wide patches. As a foot was placed, the ground gave way with a gentle squeak with each step, leaving clearly defined tracks of the person passing. Zusa decided to have fun with the phenomenon and laughed as he managed to make the ground emit the unique noise for about ten paces.

Gemba looked back and with a stern expression although there was a hint of a smile in his eyes and said to Zusa, "If you were being tracked and hunted by an enemy, even a chipembere, *a rhinoceros,* could find you with a trail like that." He nodded at the tracks left behind them.

Zusa returned the smile, his mind and heart in youthful buoyancy with excitement.

"Ehe baba," he replied, "but who would call us his enemy here, this is our land."

For a moment, the madala's eyes shifted with the memories of times gone by and where peace had not always been taken for granted. *Ah, but for the true innocence of youth,* he thought to himself.

Flat-topped trees stretched as far away as the travellers could see, their gnarled trunks, a mix of greys and browns with deep rutted bark, which broke away easily to the touch. The leaves were of all shades of green from the light pale colour of the new shoot to the dark green of the sun-deepened outer foliage that curiously flattened at the top of the tree as if sawn off by a mighty blade. This left the ground beneath clear of foliage, giving an almost unrestricted view and openness under the forest canopy, whilst offering protection from the unrelenting sun. The shade, a welcomed relief, was interspersed by bright flashes of museve wezuva, *arrows of sunlight,* as the soft breeze shifted the natural umbrella-like covering, making the ground flash with speckles of light before the eyes.

The surrounding hills became more pronounced and rugged as the morning's travel drew on, stretching to the horizon, dark green in the distance, with bright splashes of white and grey where the granite beneath had broken through the topsoil. Reflecting lines on the hillsides wept trails of water, like that of the persistent tears on an elephant's cheek, caused by natural springs leaking the earth's lifeblood into the deserving soil. These blessings were gratefully received by nature for, at the base of the hill where the water collected, life blossomed to its full. The area was abundant with overgrown vegetation, with older trees stretching their limbs high above while below their sentinel stature, numerous bushes and plants teamed with wildlife, choking the ground.

The combination of water, shade, rocks, grass and bushes offered almost every animal its own ideal habitat and, if a predator appeared, then natural refuges were available, high in the trees or deep under rocks and soil.

What was difficult to comprehend was the fact that the wildlife seemed to accept the few oases as a place of neutrality and although some kills were made within the environment, most beasts seemed to respect the almost spiritual quality of the place.

Certain times of the day were reserved for particular visitors: birds and small rodents used the water holes early in the morning with large antelope, giraffe and zebras happy to drink from morning until past mid- day. By late afternoon monkeys, baboons and smaller deer used the resource before the large cats arrived in the evening.

Zusa and Gemba saw a number of these natural sanctuaries as they travelled and by mid-morning their path began to climb towards the hills; the natural forest had begun to thin out and axe-cut tree stumps were visible, a sure sign of the proximity of man. The breeze carried to them the whiff of smoke and gradually foreign sounds could be heard over the background of the wild.

These new noises became more pronounced and at one point there was a series of louder exclamations and shouts followed by the chatter of human voices accompanied by a sudden roar and a long and drawn out rumble.

Zusa looked questioningly at his mentor. "What is that, sekuru, what are those noises?" he inquired.

The old man smiled. "You will see soon enough, young man," he replied as he stepped onto a new path that had intercepted the road they were on. Zusa had stopped walking when he saw the old man change direction and he had to jog to catch up, his sleeping mat and water gourds bouncing on his hip with each stride. The strange sounds became louder as they walked on the narrower pathway and the scents carried on the air grew stronger. Around another bend in the path, a light plume of smoke could be seen winding its way skyward, occasionally shifting with the breeze.

The path passed through a stone gateway with a large stone lintel over the top of the entrance. On top of the entryway Zusa could see that a flat walkway had been constructed and from it an armed guard could easily defend the entrance, but as there was no one in sight, they entered without a challenge.

Once through, the way in front of Zusa and Gemba opened into a cavernous valley the shape of a buffalo's hoof with the curved granite walls, sloping at an angle where a human could walk on with little effort. The boundary of the stone quarry was marred with the weathered colours of older stone slashed into with the bright scars of what were newer workings.

Up on the incline the source of the smoke could be seen. Hot, burning embers were glowing in narrow troughs of clay laid out in measured lines across the granite mother-lode. From the discarded waste the fires were obviously made from a mixture of dry grass, leaves and light wood, which once alight, ignited the "Iron Wood" placed on the top, burning a hotter, steadier and more intense heat. Gangs of men on the far slopes were laying out two more of these structures. On one of the slopes the fire troughs had quite evidently been burning for a while as the embers were ferociously glowing with heat and the stone beneath it was of a darkened hue, almost a dull red, which bespoke its containment of latent heat on a narrow band. As Zusa watched, a group of men hauled cured cowhides full of water to the summit of the slope above the dying inferno. The drag marks leaving a snail like trail on the rock surface.

A shout from behind them made them both spin around. "Sekuru Gemba, is that really you?" A man was walking towards the travellers with an out stretch arm.

Gemba laughed and reached out to shake the offered hand, "Sibanda, how are you? It's been such a long time since we last met."

"Yes my friend it has been a long time, too long as far as I am concerned."

"Well I realised that, which is why I decided to stop to see you on our way to Nyazimba"

With the mention of the word "we", the man looked at Zusa who had remained quiet during the exchange.

"And who might you be young man?"

"My name is Zusa," the boy answered and a light of recognition appeared in Sibandas eyes.

"Zusa. Yes I know who you are." He turned to Gemba, "You are travelling to the King's ceremony."

Gemba nodded his head, "That's right. Its Zusa's first time to the capital."

"Well Zusa's exploits have travelled before you. Come you must be thirsty, take some time to rest and have a drink." He looked around and waved to a woman who had been watching them speaking.

The woman approached the pair balancing a gourd of water on her head. Walking beside her was a child, a girl about eight years old, who carried a carved wooden stool for the visitor, which she placed under the shade of a tree.

Sitting down, the madala, *old man,* spoke in greeting. "Mangwanani, Amai, *Good morning, Mother."*

"Mangwanani baba," she replied and cast her eyes downwards in respect. On completion of the greeting ritual, she stretched out her offering of refreshment.

"Tatenda, *thank you,"* he said. Taking the hollowed-out pumpkin gourd by its conveniently curved handle he drew it to his lips and drank deeply. With half its content consumed and with an appreciative, mouth-smacking sound he turned to hand it on to Zusa, he smiled at the young man who took the water and drank whilst looking at the activity that had continued around them.

Sibanda spoke again, "You need to tell me what this young man has been up to, are the stories true?"

They continued to speak but Zusa closed his ears to their conversation and stood transfixed taking in the immensity of the industry around him, his mind reeling at the sights and sounds. Even as he watched, there was a warning shout, "Chenjura moto, *beware of the fire"* and with a gusty roar the men above hurled the waterfilled skins onto the dying fire where their landing place was marked by a large cloud of hot ash. A leather rope anchored the full hides so that they would not slide down the granite slope after the throw. The skins were accurately placed in what had been the centre of the blaze. As if in an anti-climax the skins seemed to just sit there for a while, steaming.

Zusa noticed the workers running as fast as their legs could carry them away from the fire troughs and water sacks and was wondering at their haste when suddenly the skins burst as the super-heated rock face burnt through the hide. It started with a light snap, followed immediately by a whoosh of steam and an ear-rending crack, which made Zusa flinch at the sound.

The water had cascaded over the rock face, cooling the top rock to a uniform depth and causing a straightline fracture in the granite and this whole section, now loose from its foundational hold, slid gracefully away with a deep rumble to end in convenient and manageable pieces at the bottom of the slope. Man had just proven his ability to speed up nature's action of grinding down rock into sand, and man completed that which took nature millennia in just half a day's effort.

Looking around in wonder Zusa realised that this had to be the birthplace of Nyazimba, the breaking of the stones, which just like seeds once planted on new foundation would rise again.

The new rock fall remained shrouded in dust where it had fallen. Another group of workers was operating on what was an earlier rock fall. They were scouring and chiselling straight lines on the mined rock with iron tools, each a measure equal to the depth of the slice of granite.

Once this had been done, the slabs were levered up and spacers placed beneath them. With a sharp report of heavy hammers, a slice of the granite the length of two men and almost perfectly square to that of a man's hand width fell to the ground. It was pulled away by six men who moved it to another site at the other end of the quarry. This column of granite was once again scoured with the metal chisels at measured distances about the length of a man's foot. After being struck the result was a uniformed sized brick of bright white stone. These were piled at the end of the quarry, row upon row, many thousands of evenly sized bricks, now finished and awaiting the next part of their journey.

Taking another mouthful of the offered refreshment Zusa cleared his throat and the two older men laughed. "We had almost forgotten you there."

After a pause Zusa asked, "Why have we come here, Uncle?"

"Well I am sure you have already gathered that this is the source of the building blocks for Nyazimba," the old man replied.

Sibanda cut in," For generations, just before each rainy season, stonemasons have worked these hills. During the dry months, wood is gathered from afar and cattle hides are prepared. Once everything is in place the quarrying begins. Firstly, hot fires are left to burn for half a day before the rock surface is suddenly cooled with water. The result is as you see before you."

Looking around Zusa nodded his head in understanding. He noticed that the housing for the stonemasons had been constructed from the spoils and rejected bricks from the rock-breaking industry. Uneven rocks, some with major flaws, made up the walls of the ten or twelve buildings, each topped with newly-cut grass thatch. The old man continued with his narrative. "Any man visiting Nyazimba is expected to pass by the quarry and carry two stones to the gateway of the city and deposit them with the city guard's structures. Once you have deposited your stones you are welcomed into the city." He indicated the pile in front of them where a stack of bricks was carefully tied in pairs with a piece of tambo, *bark string,* so that the burden could be slung over the carriers shoulder.

Gemba and Sibanda continued to talk for a while and Zusa used the time to lay under the shade of a tree and fall asleep. He was awoken a while later with someone nudging his leg. When he opened his eyes, blinking in the bright sunlight both of the older men were looking down at him.

"I guess you didn't sleep much last night then young man," Sibanda said "Well at least you will be well rested to carry the stone bricks onto the city then?"

Gemba laughed and added, "Get up Zusa, we need to get back on the road."

Zusa got up and thanked Sibanda for his hospitality and with promises to see each other again the travellers moved across to the quarry stockpile. They each took a pair of stones, which they strung across their necks. The path out of the quarry looped back on itself and joined up once again with the main road and as they moved away the sounds and scents of the quarry faded and were soon left behind.

The undulating hills became more widely spread and between them loitered large herds of cattle which were grazing on the prime pastures. The different groups of cattle were being watched over by young herd boys just how Zusa had guarded his father's livestock only a few weeks before. Many of the boys had taken positions of height in trees or upon anthills to be able to watch over their roaming herds. Each was armed with a narrow iron-tipped spear or a leather sling. Some of the children had small bows slung across their backs next to an elongated pouch holding a few reed arrows.

One of the young boys suddenly went very still. Then with care, he slowly unwound his leather sling and fitted a choice stone taken from a riverbed. Sighting carefully, his arm outstretched in balance, he twirled the weapon three times around his head before letting it fly. The stone flew true and his target, a fat pigeon, tumbled from a tree in a puff of feathers. Running forward with a shriek of delight the hunter raced ahead of his friends to arrive at the prey first. Snatching the bird from the ground he twisted the head to ensure the animal was dead before walking back to his original position. He knew that any contribution to the family pot would be gratefully received at home.

Only a short while later Zusa watched one of the older boys use his bow to fire a reed arrow at another bird. He too was rewarded with a wet impacting sound and another puff of feathers as the bird fell to the ground.

"Good shot," Zusa shouted and the boy waved back in acknowledgement.

Typically of any male, Gemba had not been distracted by the activities of the herds boys but he was pleased to see his nation's wealth on display all around him and he openly admired the health of the cattle. Their colours varied from completely black to a tan and varying mixes in between. There were a number of almost pure white examples whose presence on the open plain made a complete contrast to the natural environment. The tips of the cattles' horns were as wide as a grown man's outstretched arms and their body size dwarfed the majority of the herd boys. Egrets, *tickbirds,* stark in their white plumage, with orange legs and yellow beaks, rested patiently on the backs of the animals, their eyes alerting them to catch a flying insect or to peck at the grass ticks that attached themselves onto the cattle as they walked through the long grass.

Further down the road, the open grazing lands made way to larger open fields where selections of crops were under cultivation. The end of the seasonal rains had left the ground well prepared and the first of the millet crop seedlings had already broken ground in their burst for life.

The unforgiving sun would have made short work of their new shoots if it were not for the irrigation canals which had been cut in straight lines through the fields, being fed from large water reservoirs. These canals had been built slightly higher than the surrounding fields so that small gates could be open for the liquid of life to flood onto the fields and meadows. The green shoots appeared bright in the dark brown, moist soil.

The smell of mass habitation assailed their senses long before they laid their eyes on the city; a low drone of the many voices of humanity could be almost sensed; the murmurs pierced by the shrill sounds of children playing as well as the shouted conversations and the call of traders selling their wares. All the sounds mixed into one another, reflecting in echoes by the surrounding kopjes and granite outcrops, each forming a part of a natural auditorium. It caused a slight sense of confusion and the young man moved his head around trying to track the direction of the sounds. As they walked around a final bend in the track the weary travellers were rewarded by the site of a stone-walled gateway set before them guarded by six armed warriors. The walls either side of the city gate curved away to the left and right, ending at the river's edge which ran across the plain. This was not only the source of water to the irrigated fields but also provided water to the city. In addition it was also a natural barrier against attack from the north-east pathway. Beyond this was an incredible view of the city stretching above them and across the hilltop. An immense monument of stone designed especially to impress the first-time visitor and Zusa was suitably awed. The large walls of the city were covered with a plaster made from a mix of mud and ox blood. They had been highly decorated with earth-coloured murals, their patterns and designs
announcing the degree of civilisation beyond. They had arrived at the city of stone, their capital, Nyazimba.

Chapter Ten
On to Belingwe

The Zulu army had rested at Fort Chimnungwa for a few days. The regiment which had not taken part in the assault on the town as they had been acting as a perimeter guard was despatched during this time to raid the Bantu town of Masase. These men were content with their assignment as they had borne the brunt of light hearted jokes such as playing the role of the hunters' beaters, normally a task reserved for young boys who were used to scare game onto the hunter's positions for an easy kill. They were more than happy to have been given a chance to earn the right to wear battle honours. Masase was a large market town of approximately four hundred inhabitants and with no organised military presence. The only arms were those owned by the men folk who resided there. Some of these men were retired warriors but it did them no good against the co-ordinated surprise attack by the Zulus.

Again, the attackers used the night to conceal their approach and raided at sunrise. The results were the same with the men of arms bearing age being immediately put to death and the women and children captured along with large herds of livestock and stores from the warehouses and granaries of the town. As a market town the pickings were exceptionally rich with many trade goods from all over the Bantu Kingdom being found.

By midmorning, once full control had been taken of town, the impi chief sent out a few smaller raiding parties to mop up the few settlements around the area and to bring in any other captives and animals.

It had been agreed that the regiment would stay at this position for the night whilst the area was brought under control but they were due to continue with the lightning attacks northwards the next day after leaving a small group of garrison troops behind.

Early the next morning, the chief, Digane, left the small guard of fifty warriors to maintain their control over the area and to look after the captured bounty while he led his regiment to the north, towards their main goals for the next day - Naletale and Dhio-Dhio. He knew that one of the other Zulu regiments was scheduled to travel north-west the next day towards the last ancient city of Khami. These three strategic sites had to be taken swiftly to catch as many of the Bantu as they could before they managed to retreat into their city safe-keeps designed for their defence.

The advance was carried out on the trot with the accompanying chief occasionally indicating that smaller groups should peel off into sections of men to perform the individual tasks of assaulting the small kraals and homesteads along their route. Although they ran the risk of being detected from a distance the Zulu command felt that their rapid approach would still be the best way to catch the trading cities unaware. Many of the side raids were designed to cause mayhem and confusion amongst the Bantu populace with the rewards, slaves and materials being herded back to form larger groups which would then be escorted back to the holding areas.

It was one of these side raids, on a particularly large homestead at the base of a rock-covered kopje, which the half- sized impi induna had decided to lead himself. Indicating to his personal guard of ten men to follow him, he moved off on the run leaving the main body to keep on moving northwards.

As they made their final approach, they discovered another smaller kraal in their path nestled in a hollow of the high ground. Without breaking their pace they charged into the group of huts scattering the few chickens which had been peacefully pecking at the earth, only to find an old man and his similarly aged wife sitting in the open on wooden carved stools.

Both of these people were too old to be useful as slaves and so they were killed where they sat, their bodies falling across each other in death, whilst a flaming torch from the fire on which they had been cooking was picked up and thrust into the thatch of their run down home. The dry thatch burst alight and a dark towering plume of smoke and flames reached skywards within seconds.

Without wasting any more time at this barren target the group of warriors moved on in single file towards the better appointed dwellings a few hundred paces further away. This group of huts was more richly decorated and the site had been semi-fortified with a wooden stockade and even as he looked the Zulu chief observed two men hurrying to close the gateway to the premises.

At a shouted command his men broke into a sprint to catch these men before they were able to mount a more effective resistance. The assailants spread out into an attacking line to maximise their impact on the defences but, as they reached the wooden framed fence, a spear was thrust through a gap between two wooden poles to take one of the Zulus in the centre of his chest. His scream of agony sounded loud even above the breaking of the wooden spars as the remainder of the dead Zulu force broke through the wooden spar barrier.

The two men who had been seen closing the gate, one a large man with another who could have been his son, could be seen on the other side of the forced entry point. The attackers shouted their defiance as they pushed forward. The defenders managed to kill another warrior, stabbing the first assailant through the broken stockade with their longer spears.

Whilst the defenders were distracted, the second part of the Zulu group, with the chief, made their way through a second break in the fence and took the family group from behind not giving them a chance to face their attackers. They simply plunged their broad bladed assegais into the exposed backs and in a matter of minutes it was all over.

The Zulu group was down to eight men and, once they ensured that there would be no more danger; they turned their attention to the huts from which they dragged a middle-aged woman and two children, a boy and a girl.

The captives were thrown in anger onto the open dusty ground in the centre of the ring of buildings.

One of the Zulus shouted, "We should kill them to avenge the deaths of our brothers," indicating the two lifeless forms of their fellow-warriors lying beyond the stockade, and he lifted his assegai looking for permission from his chief.

Although tempted the leader knew better than to allow personal emotions to dictate over the clear and precise orders from his army commander. Modena would not be happy to discover that three prime slaves had been killed due to the emotion of warriors seeking to avenge the stupidity of some of his men who had been inept enough to get themselves killed by an old man and his son.

"No! We will not kill them," he commanded. The warrior who stood over the captives lowered his weapon. Although his blood lust was high he also knew the results of disobeying a direct instruction. "Tie them up and search the huts for plunder then set fire to the buildings."

The attackers went swiftly to the task and it was quickly achieved. Soon the homestead was well alight. He looked at the bodies of the man and his son lying on the ground. With his assegai he indicated, "Throw those two Bantu baboons onto the fire and make sure our fallen men are dealt with properly." In response, the father and son's corpses were dragged across the bare ground, their heels lifelessly leaving twin trails of their passing in the sandy soil, and they were unceremoniously tossed into the burning building. The roof of the hut collapsed, followed shortly by the mud caked walls weakened by the conflagration. The flames were so intense that the Zulu warriors had to retreat quickly as soon as their task was complete.

Anything useful from within the houses had been stacked to one side to be collected by the porters who were following the regiment.

The prisoners were pulled to their feet and with a few well-aimed blows from the warriors' assegai handles the captives were forced to move, heading southwards under the guard of two warriors.

With a final look around to ensure all had been dealt with the chief gathered the remainder of his group and led them off towards the assembly point set on a large hill on the horizon.

****

Modena had allowed the main body of his army a full day of rest although half an impi, led by his senior induna, Digane, had been despatched that day with orders to assault the towns of Khami and Dhio-Dhio. The remainder of this impi was expected to leave the next day once their current position had been consolidated and brought under the full control of the invaders. Initial reports from the regiments in the field indicated that the attack on Masase had gone as planned, much like the rest of the campaign, Modena thought to himself, and already the porters were busy gathering the spoils of war. Instead of having the baggage carriers travel the longer distance between the town and the fort he had directed these bearers to bring the goods to the area of the next town due to be attacked, Belingwe, confident in the ability of his men to meet the task set before them.

Now on the road again he knew that he had to keep his men moving forward as far and as fast as possible. They were still not quite sure of what the Bantu army's reaction was going to be, although the eventual outcome had already been decided in his own mind.

This next assault would be slightly different from those which had occurred before, with the attack going in at mid-morning. Due to the large number of minor settlements close to the iron-manufacturing town there was no safe haven where his men could encamp for the night and still expect to remain undiscovered.

With this in mind, the two impi with him would travel this evening and storm the surrounding area at first light, rounding up prisoners as they penetrated the layers of iron mines and miners' homesteads around the key target mining town.

Not only were the pickings expected to be

exceptionally bountiful but the location of the site would be ideal to support the continuing raids throughout the Bantu Kingdom. Its position, just west of the mountain range, would hamper the main Bantu army sallying from their city and having the luxury of counter attacking at any point of their choosing along his line of communication. Instead, the two passes governing the approach through the natural barrier would allow him to blockade the forces against him from this side of the range and it would funnel any military response by the Bantu King into surveyed kill zones.

The assault on the iron-mining district went well and numerous mines and kraals were gathered in the far-flung net of Zulu warriors. By mid-morning, his main army had managed to converge on the outskirts of Belingwe and, so as not to allow any alarm to be raised, the Zulu army simply broke onto the streets of the industrial town killing and maiming as they spread out across the metropolis. A special section of warriors had been tasked with dealing with the small garrison in the stone stockade and the gate guard was effectively silenced without the chance to put up too much resistance before any armed men were over powered by shear numbers.

During the foray into the town, a fire had been started in one of the homesteads and this spread to a number of dwellings, and the smoke added to the mayhem. Modena again found himself directing a group of men to extinguish the flames before they could spread to the remaining structures, which he knew he needed in order to meet the accommodation requirements of his troops.

Again, in what had now become a well-rehearsed manoeuvre, the women and children were gathered and enclosed in one of the empty cattle pens while their houses and properties were searched.

After setting guards at a number of points overlooking the surrounding terrain Modena installed himself in the town chieftain's house.

By late afternoon, the porters from the other conquered sites began to arrive with their contribution of captured goods and slaves. The valuable commodities were secured in the large warehouses already in this trading town whilst the captives were forced into more of the cattle pens. Modena had allowed the enslaved women and children to erect sun shades as protection against the arid elements and a select few were directed to collect sleeping mats and covers from the town houses so that they could be used by the prisoners over the next few days until the time when they would be moved towards the captured fort at Chimnungwa.

Food and water was distributed to the surprise of the multitudes. It was not an act of kindness by Modena, more the actions of a wise man who knew how to look after his property that is, until they were sold.

Chapter Eleven
The City of Stone, Nyazimba

With the city on the hill as the centrepiece to the backdrop of the landscape, the road Zusa and Gemba were on led straight towards the main entrance. The guards' stance reflected their rigorous training regime, tight skins stretched over well-defined muscular bodies. Their attentiveness indicated an overall state of awareness and their eyes followed the approaching pair.

The entrance to the city had been constructed from the now familiar granite bricks, the left hand side curving to the edge of the river which in itself formed a natural barrier to the city, the other disappearing to the right in a wall of stone. Although not a strong deterrent, both the river and wall, by design, would at least slow down any sudden attack by an approaching enemy giving the populace and the army time to react to any aggressive manoeuvre.

The gateway was only as wide as the shoulders of a grown man. With the edges of the doorway curving inwards three sculpted steps gave way to rise to the passageway through. Zusa realised that the defensive wall must have been quite thick because, as they approached, two warriors appeared on top of the wall giving them the advantage of height especially in defence. Another soldier stepped toward the travellers, raised his hand in greeting and asked for their identity.

Gemba responded and went on to indicate that the King had summoned them both to the city and that Zusa was to attend the planned ceremony in the afternoon. At the mention of his name, the guard perked up and turned to the young man.

"Ah, so you're the boy, who killed a leopard with his fighting stick, aren't you?" he said.

Zusa, uncomfortable with the direct statement, looked at Gemba for support. "And modest with it too, young warrior," the man said when he noticed Zusa's uneasiness.

"Yes, I am Zusa," the young man replied and quickly added, "we have brought these bricks from the quarry, where do you want us to put them?"

The guard smiled and indicated a neat pile of stone bricks off to one side of the path. "Put them there," he said, "Nyazimba welcomes you, Zusa, and sekuru, Gemba."

Both visitors went to move on but Gemba glanced back to speak to the guard who had a wide grin across his face. Squinting he said, "Is that you Tichawona?"

The man beamed back, "Yes uncle, it is me!"

"I have not seen you or your parents for many years, I see you have grown well and hold a position in the royal guard!" The guard's cheeks shone in embarrassment at the comment and he responded, "Yes, I have been with the King's regiment for two seasons now."

Nodding his head in understanding Gemba mentioned that he hoped to speak to him again soon but it was time for them to make their way into the city.

Zusa faced his mentor and said "Isn't there anyone you don't know sekuru?"

Gemba laughed, "When you get to my age you to would have crossed the paths of many people, you never know when you may need a friend."

Zusa followed Gemba, single file, through the city entrance. A few paces in, Zusa noticed that the passage narrowed with a grooved slot on either side at a single point. Above this position was an opening where he thought a gate could be lowered to block access more than likely at night. A few more steps took the men back into the open with a stone causeway stretching across the river over which they continued to proceed.

To their right a reservoir of water had been created by the manmade land bridge which further protected that flank whilst supplying water to both the city and to the irrigation scheme outside the walls. A number of women were on its banks gathering water in earthen pots. Others who had already completed that task were walking back towards the inner city, gracefully poised with the full containers perfectly balanced on their heads. Their bodies moved as they walked whilst their heads remained fixed not spilling a drop.

Once Zusa and Gemba were over the narrow causeway, the path rose steadily towards another gate, larger and even more impressive than the first. Its walls stretched for the height of two men and they were thicker in depth. The extended walls curved away from them forming a formidable defensive structure. They too were, like the acropolis above, plastered with a mixture of mud and ox-blood plaster, richly decorated with symbols and patterns in the earthen colours of brown, red, orange and yellow. The design consisted of repeated squares or triangles one inside the other, each a different colour.

However the most remarkable symbol was that of a hawk-like bird sitting upright with an enhanced, sharp beak. It was the easily recognisable icon of the city and indicated the presence of the King. These stark murals had been outlined with narrow black lines making them appear to be standing proud from the surface on which they were painted.

The large stone wall was further defined by a unique finish along its top edge, with a chevron or fish-bone pattern being used to lend added splendour to the palace of Kings. The thick walls were topped by a number of smaller stone towers, only knee height upon which a fire-darkened clay structure was placed.

Quizzically Zusa looked at Gemba and said, "What are those for?"

"They are for the night watch fires to provide light for the guards and to keep away wild animals." He stopped and turned around, "This area is known as the water gate entrance and it protects the north-west road to the interior of the fortress," he said.

Nodding his head in understanding Zusa walked towards the main entrance. Once through this more impressive city wall the hill climbed across an open area of the hill. Rocks had been haphazardly set by nature and ankle-length grass carpeted the ground. Within fifty paces the hill began to steeply climb whilst the path they were on entered a stone bricked corridor, open to the skies with the sides of the wall almost two men in height meandering from left to right for twenty paces opening into a section of the hill which was filled with dagga, and thatched dwellings, with a large number of people going about their daily chores, cleaning, mending, or cooking. Smoke from the wood fires mixed with whatever was being cooked on the open fires in three-legged *potingere* iron pots. Chicken and goats on spits dripped hot fat onto the coals of the fire before its flavour was spent in a sharp hiss to join the rising plumes of smoke. The mouth-watering smells reminded Zusa that he had not eaten since the morning and his stomach rumbled, and when the wholesome smell of sadza being prepared also assailed his nostrils he turned to Gemba and asked when they were going to eat.

"Soon Zusa, we only have a short distance to go."

By this time Zusa was high enough up on the hill to be able to look back down and across the defences and irrigated fields and he was also able to make out in the distance the smoke caused by the stone-quarrying activities half a day's walk away.

The pathway entered another stone-lined, high-walled passageway open to the sky. Within eighty paces it widened considerably at the intersection of three doorways, two on the left and one on the right, all leading to what appeared to be separate village areas. These dwellings higher up on the hill were finer in status. This was clear by their richer decorations and some of the buildings were larger than the standard hut and had been built with stone brick walls.

The constant flow of human traffic along this pathway had necessitated its paving with flagstones or by chiselling numerous stairs into the living rock to keep the climbing effort to a minimum.

By now the passageway had become congested, with water-bearers moving in both directions: empty jars downhill, full containers uphill and all manner of foodstuff,

The "Eastern Enclosure" or Audience Chamber

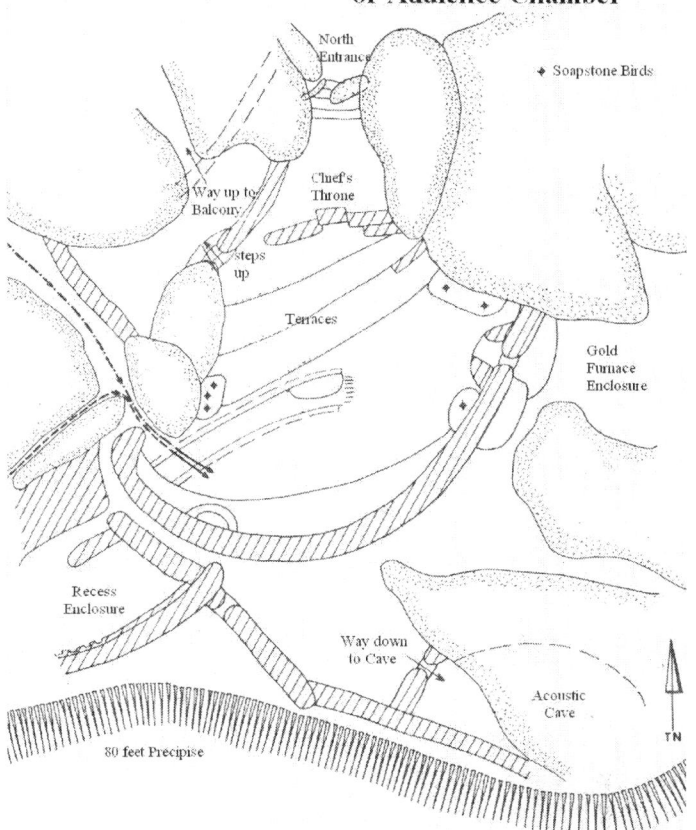

such as grain and meat as well as firewood, was being ported into the city as if feeding a gigantic animal. Zusa realised with a start that that was what a city really was, a living being that needed continuously feeding and guarding.

Yet another large gate loomed before the travellers, even grander than the previous entrances, this one reaching higher than three men standing upright.

Once through to the immediate right of the doorway was an opening in the wall that on further inspection led to a number of what appeared to be soldiers' barracks. It had a bare patch of earth, which was being used as a parade ground and fifty warriors were jousting in mock battle armed with spear and shield, all under the shouted orders of two instructors. The noise of clashing shield and the snap of sticks kept Zusa watching for a few minutes.

Moving onward, the travellers continued up the stairway and across an area of bare rock. The pathway turned to the left and ran along the main fortress wall before disappearing into a tunnel, which was yet another excellent defensive measure. Within the tunnel the temperature of the air dropped noticeably and after twenty paces the passageway opened into an enclosure which could have accommodated a gathering of over five hundred people. This area set aside for the visitors had five sides to it and unusually, the stone wall ran up and across three large boulders, which nature had placed on the near summit of the hill, to keep the enclosure wall at a uniform height.

On top of these thick fortifications were more of the miniature stone turrets used to offer firelight during the night. The walls were decorated with more of the mud-based murals and the parts consisting of natural rock had depictions of armed men in acts of war or the hunt. This was, overall, an impressive display of wealth, especially to visitors to the city for the first time.

As they stepped into the area a city official greeted Zusa and Gemba and once they had again identified themselves they were directed to a seating area where other newly arrived travellers were already waiting. They sat down on the carved wooden stools provided to rest and a number of servants offered refreshments. True to form, Gemba again recognised several of the other guests and spent a while exchanging pleasantries and catching up on past news and events.

Zusa, in the meantime, had noticed that there were a few younger men amongst the group all, like him, sitting in silence either out of respect for the combined company or else in awe at the splendour of the seat of power in their nation. Looking about he saw that the walls were thick enough to enable guards to walk along the top. He also observed a small natural cave structure in the immense rock. Inside the deep recesses of the cavern he could just make out a group of people performing undefined tasks.

A meal was soon served, during which additional guests continued to arrive. The cheerful fellowship and conversation went on whilst the sun marked the passing of time across the sky.

From a position above the enclosure a trumpeted alert called the crowd to order and to gain their attention. Once the assembly had quietened down they looked expectantly at the platform above where a number of guards dressed in ceremonial splendour stepped into view to join the trumpeter. A messenger announced in a clear voice, that the King was now ready to receive his subjects and asked the gathering to accompany him to the royal audience chamber. He indicated an armed guard who had appeared from an entrance below his position, who in turn raised an arm in the air, and turning with a whirl of his monkey-tail skirt, he lead the way between the cleft rocks.

The gathered visitors, almost sixty in total, rose to their feet and shuffled forward towards the natural gap in the rock. It was paved with worn slabs of stone set into the ground. The tunnel led into another corridor open to the sky that had a number of guarded entrances leading off it and, after a hundred paces, the group joined another crowd of individuals entering the same main passageway via a second corridor coming from the south of the hill complex. The noise level increased carrying an air of expectation and excitement, the voices mixed in a number of local dialects. It was truly a gathering of the clans indicated by the manner of dress, headdress plumages and armband designs on display.

A short time later, the combined group passed through a final narrow entrance and the large group continued over a hollow-sounding wooden floor before bearing right into the open-air hall. They had arrived at what was clearly the grand audience chamber, which was the same size as the visitor reception area, but better appointed in design.

Nothing could have prepared Zusa for the magnificence or the splendour of this structure. The retaining wall on his left curved inwards and towards a barred entrance, terminating at a large rock outcrop. The walls had been brightly decorated with more vivid coloured designs, but Zusa's eyes were drawn to a number of bright green statues, stark in their appearance against the duller walls and which had been set in recessed alcoves.

They had been expertly carved from a soft stone, quarried from an area North East of Nyazimba. The stone, when sanded smoothed, oiled and polished had a soapy texture to its surface, the grain of the rock offering a mixture of high and low lights making the image appear alive.

The carvings depicted the symbol of Nyazimba, the Hawk. Crawling up each of the long columns were sculptured animals, one a crocodile, elephants and another was a lion. The bases of these were set on heavy stone mantles. Their place of setting was designed to receive the sun's rays which caused the mix of soft and sharp angles to reflect. The figurines shimmered as if alive and, in particular, the eyes of the birds had been coated with a reflective substance which insinuated a sense of life from within.

These statues represented the King's powers, authority and were the national identity. It had been foretold throughout the ages that as long as they stood in this place the nation would prosper in unity.

Three of the statues were set to the left of the area, two more on the right side of the arena and another was set at the back but in direct line of sight to the throne.
This statue was the largest of them all, by almost four times. Zusa was too far away from it to study it in detail but for some reason he felt drawn to this particular effigy.

Glancing around, Zusa saw that within the enclosure there were three terraces leading to a large stage area upon which was an intricately carved wooden throne set into a stone-backed wall. To the left of this was another guarded entrance and overlooking the whole area was a balcony set as high as four men, upon which more than twenty well-armed warriors stood silently looking at the gathering below.

The backdrop to the arena was the largest boulder

on the hilltop; it was well placed as its bulk offered shaded relief from the heat of the sun in the southward-placed amphitheatre. As he continued to study the design of the complex, Zusa realised that the building of the hilltop fortress was by no means a matter of luck. It had been designed with careful judgement and design, balancing the need for physical security or against the unstoppable forces of nature.

The gathering now numbered in excess of two hundred men excluding the royal guard. A drumbeat began to sound from within the deep recesses of the royal enclosure and was perceptible beyond the wall where the wooden throne was set. Other drums, including the great, bass-note war drums joined the initial instrument and the nature of the granite walls caused the sound to swell and fill the auditorium until the senses reeled under the deep methodical bass interspersed with the higher toned tom-tom drum.

The crowd stood in silent expectation, unmoving; their eyes looking towards the royal podium. The line of guards stirred and came to attention as a trumpeted call from a curved kudu horn sounded and the drums stopped. With authority Yasini, the King of Nyazimba, stepped into view and walked along the wall at the top of the stage.

Pausing as he reached the majestically carved throne, he looked upon his subjects, taking the time to catch the eye of those he recognised in the audience. For a moment, Zusa thought the King had looked directly at Gemba. Was it his imagination? It must have been as he also thought the King had looked at him, just for a split second!

King Yasini was the twentieth regent of the Nyazimbian nation, spanning back almost four hundred years from the time when the first of their Bantu descendant had used the natural form of the hilltop as a refuge in a wild and untamed land. Once the capital had been moved to this site, each successive ruler had increased his legacy to the community by adding to the building of the city on the hill as memorial to his ruling,

The "Eastern Enclosure" or Audience Chamber

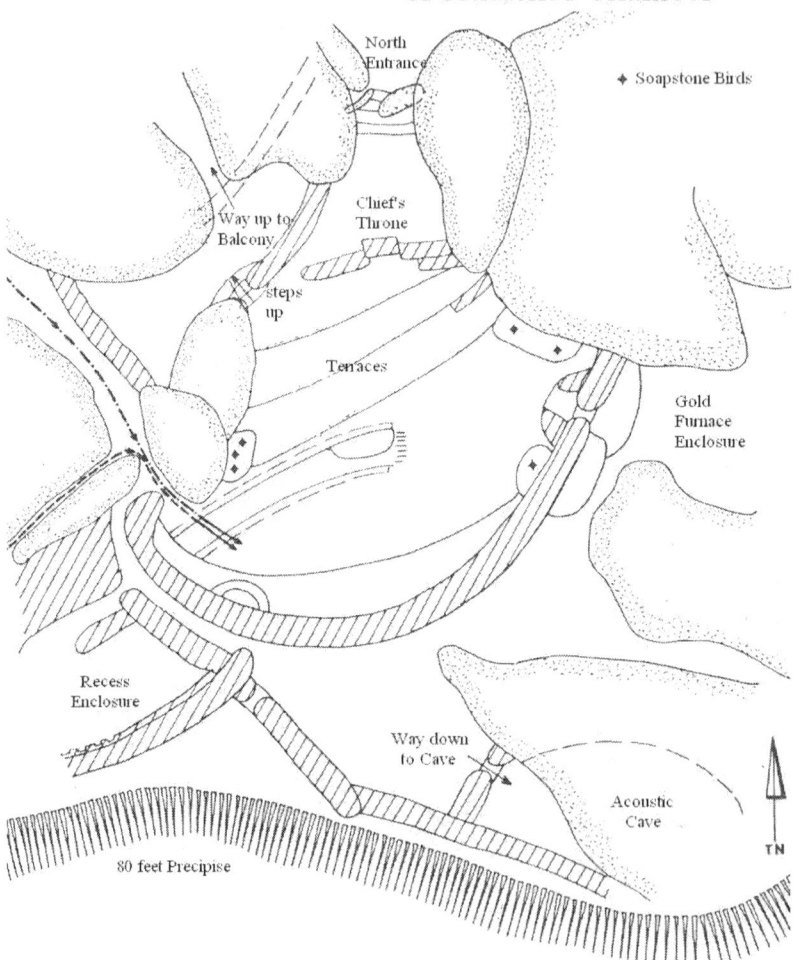

even after death. The King was advanced in years. He was a large man but not overweight as his frame expressed his dignity well. In spite of his age, his head was still covered in dark tight curls of hair whilst his evenly-cut and sculptured beard was startlingly silver, indicating his cultural wisdom. Such an uncommon feature in a community where an abundance of facial hair was rare had earned him the respected title within his immediate circle of family and advisors of "Mandevu, *the bearded one*".

The King's headdress was a simple hide band with a number of majestic ostrich feathers sticking out of it, which twitched with every move he made emphasising the action of his head. The hide bands were replicated on his upper arms stressing the shape of his well-defined muscles.

Across his broad shoulders was a cured leopard skin, the sight of which, made Zusa shiver at his more recent memory. The King's loincloth reached to his knees. In his right hand was a ceremonial spear that glinted in the bright light but it had an effect of glowing along its full length with the colour of the sun. It had been fashioned generations ago when ndarama, *gold*, was first teased from the mines to the north and smelted within the city's furnaces. In his other hand was a shield, larger than those carried by the warriors. It had been constructed with a pure white ox hide and was stretched across a wooden frame for shape. Out of the top of the shield were more ostrich feathers and two polished knobkerries were attached diagonally across the back of the shield.

Without any further ceremony the King sat down and two of his warriors took up guard positions either side of him. The advisor who had extended the invitation earlier to Gemba's group stepped across the stage to stand at the left hand side of the King while another finely robed man, a royal priest, indicated by the adornments of his clothing, stood on the right.

A wide smile broke across the King's face and he spoke in a deep, clear voice, "Welcome to you all to the City of Stone." His arms out stretched to emphasis the greeting.

The crowd responded "Ehe baba, *yes father*".

The king went on, "We welcome you all in the name of the Rukodzi, *the hawk*." He paused for effect, his voice echoing around the enclosure. "You have been summoned on this day so that you may be presented to your ruler. It is an opportunity for our remote communities to meet and a time of celebration. Many of you here, in the past year, have either achieved great things for your nation, or you have contributed wisdom or wealth in order for our land to thrive." The King paused as sounds of approval were made by the crowd. He continued, "This year, our ancestors are pleased and accordingly we were blessed with good rains. The soil is well prepared to receive the first of the seed and already the women are busy in the fields with the new planting." He indicated the activity outside the city with a sweep of his arms. He signified to his advisor to take to the stage centre and he sat back into his throne with a thoughtful expression on his face.

The King's servant stepped forward and began listing from memory the up-to-date status of the economy. "Mining continued through the winter whilst the fields were empty and large quantities of iron, *simbi* have been mined from the west. It was smelted into bars and delivered to our ironsmiths where the metal has been fashioned into tools, cooking utensils and weapons. At the same time Ndarama has also been wrestled from the hills to the north and sent to the royal refinery," he pointed at the guarded doorway at the back of the auditorium, "and this too has been turned into bars of trade ingots. Our fearless hunters have brought in the teeth of the Ndzu, *Elephant* from the far north." This time he indicated the wooden floorboards, the audience had crossed when entering the meeting area.
"We are in a good position to receive the traders from across the endless river this year and Mware, *God* has truly blessed us." Having finished with his report he stepped back.

The Royal Priest took his place and raised his arms into the air, and gave praise to the ancestors and Mware. The drums began once again, but with a more melodious tone and to the front of the stage a line of women moved slowly into sight, bare-breasted, their grass skirts swishing with each step. Each woman in line held the elbow of the woman in front so that the linked arms rose and fell in a wave-like motion as they danced in time to the beat of the drum. Their bare feet shuffled on the ground and the dance became a story depicting the flow of the seasons and the impact a good year had on the nation. The line moved backwards and forwards across the stage in celebration of the prospect of the new harvest and provisions collected, with each event marked by a separate action or movement, keeping their audience spellbound until eventually they moved off through the same door by which they had entered.

During this orchestrated distraction other women had wandered amongst the gathering offering calabashes of water for refreshment. The music eventually stopped and King Yasini rose to his feet. "It is now time for us to recognise those who have been summoned before us today."

It began with an old man being called forward because of his role in improving the way iron ore was mined and another for his skills in working the iron into useful implements; a third was a weapon smith. Household staff were called to be promoted in their stations within the royal camp and a number of warriors were awarded praise for the state of readiness of their regiments, others for acts and deeds across the nation.

Finally the King turned and looked into the crowd, his eyes searching for someone. His eyes rested on Gemba and this time they shared an open smile. The King spoke, "We have recognised so many people today for so many different things, but we also have with us a young man from Mafuri beyond the town of Mashaba." Zusa's heart leapt at the mention of his village area. The King continued, "I know many of you have already heard the tale of how a young man defended his father's goat herd single-handedly against a leopard. Killing the animal, not with a spear or bow but with his knobkerrie and he received severe injuries as a reward." He looked directly at Zusa and beckoned him forward. "Come here, young man!"

Zusa stood still for a while, transfixed, then after a gentle nudge from Gemba; he stepped forward to where the King was beckoning him. The crowd parted as if an invisible hand had divided the gathering, multiple eyes following him as he walked to the front of the auditorium and up the steps leading to the platform. Sounds of approval and encouragement were voiced; a few cheered and called out his name in salutation.

With his heart pounding as if it was trying to burst out of his chest, Zusa continued to where his King was seated. In an unprecedented show and outside recognised etiquette, King Yasini rose to his feet and stepped from his commanding position to emerge from beyond the guarded entrance. Initially reaching to take the young man's hand he seemed to change his mind and he grasped the boy's shoulders instead, pulling him into a great hug. A sound of astonishment arose from the crowd at the outward show of emotion from the King.

"Zusa," the King said in a loud voice, "you are truly a son of our nation, your bravery knows no bounds and it will be upon you that the future of Nyazimba will one day fall."

The crowd cheered and applauded his words whilst Zusa squirmed at the attention and praise directed towards him. Raising his hand to quieten the crowd, the King went on. "And in recognition of your deed and the fact that you killed a leopard single-handedly I hereby offer you the privilege of wearing the skin of the animal you have slain."

At this point, a court official stepped forward with a bundle in his outstretched arms. The King took it and turning back to Zusa, let the parcel unfurl itself into a full-length cloak. Its design and cut was of such a quality that the King's personal tailor must have prepared the skin for the result was truly magnificent. The leopard fur shone in the sun with the vivid black spots highlighted against the golden glow of the white and yellow fur. The cut of the hide was such that it fitted Zusa's shoulders perfectly and a leather thong with a bright gold clasp was attached near the throat to hold the cloak in place.

Stepping back, Zusa realised the significance of the King's gesture towards him and he was truly awed by such an event. The crowd continued with its shouts of delight and the King turned back to the audience and said, "The future of our society is in the hands of such men. Come let us greet Zusa, a man of the nation!" Those present clapped wildly and cheered at the King's words and Zusa was directed from the stage in a slight daze as the next recipient of an award was led on.

Chapter Twelve
Just another day

Waking the next morning Zusa's head felt sore, which he correctly assumed was due to the amount of celebratory beer he had had forced upon him the previous night at the dinner hosted by the King. He saw that his newly-presented leopard skin cloak had been spread over his body and he smiled at the thought that Gemba had still found the time to tend to him after the festivities. His back was also tender from the countless congratulatory slaps he had received during the event and he had lost count of the number of times he had had to recite his tale. The evening had stretched far into the night and he had some distant recollection of being assisted back to the sleeping hut which he shared with Gemba where he had fallen into a deep and dreamless sleep. Looking across the room he realised that Gemba's sleeping mat was empty and, although he was tempted to go back to sleep, he knew he did not have a lot of time left to explore the wonders of the city before he and his mentor were due to return home. With a groan he pulled himself to his feet.

Stepping out of the abode he realised that it was past midmorning; the sun was bright in another cloudless sky but he still seemed to be one of the first to appear in the enclosure where all the visitors for the event had been accommodated. He expected to see his mentor close by but, now that he was outside the hut, Gemba was nowhere to be seen.

Some cooking fires were being attended to by a group of women, who had simmering pots containing some form of breakfast meal, but his delicate stomach rebelled at the thought of food and he decided to go for a walk in an attempt to clear his head and possibly work up an appetite.

He splashed some water onto his face from one of the large bowls set aside for this purpose near the door of the huts entrance. He then took a couple of gulps of fresh water from the separate drinking bowl before heading towards the encampment's gateway.

The visitors' area had been recently refurbished and repaired apparent from the newly-laid thatch of the accommodation huts. The majority of the mud and dagga walls had been decorated with fresh paint, in honour of this year's event. Like the rest of the fortress, the area had been specifically designed for its function. There were thirty circular huts set in five rings of six buildings, with all the groups built around a central open area while another quarter reserved for food preparation and cooking was set to one side. Ablutions were on the far side of the in an area partitioned off by a grass fence.

The southern sector was formed on one side by the inland approach corridor through which Zusa and Gemba had entered the city the previous day. There was a lower wall where there were more of the stone cones used for the night watch fires. Only a sharp eye realised that the placing of these and the obligatory watch towers and gate were in fact the best way to keep any visitors to the city under observation. The only gateway led back into the city via the main corridor entrance almost at the top of the hill. It was "guarded" by a number of the royal troops. Large wooden gates presently closed off the two other entrances in the walled area.

Recognising Zusa from the previous day's events the guards greeted him by name as he approached the exit. "Ha, mangwanani Mbada, *Good morning leopard*" one of the men said in greeting.

"Mangwanani sekuru, marara sai?" *Good morning Uncle, how are you?* Zusa responded.

"You are a strong one Zusa; you are one of the first to arise after last night's festivities!"

"Yes but maybe that was my mistake, getting up so early," Zusa replied. "My head feels like the inside of a war drum and someone is beating it hard!"

Laughing, the guards let him through without

another word. Once into the main entrance passageway Zusa turned right and walked downhill at a leisurely pace, passing a few men and women and exchanging polite greetings as he went. Lower down the incline he passed through the open water gate, before he arrived at the city's water hole beside the causeway which the capital's citizens and visitors from the interior used to cross into the metropolis.

A group of women were at the water hole filling clay pots with fresh water. A few children had accompanied them and some of the mothers had babies strapped to their bodies, their infant's legs splayed with the sides of their faces against their mothers' backs. Again he exchanged greetings and some of the younger unmarried women gave embarrassed smiles in return while shyly averting their eyes, their cheeks shining as they recognised Zusa from the descriptive stories going around the community.

One young woman caught Zusa's attention although she had not looked at him directly. She was in a group of maidens who were obviously keeping her informed of Zusa's movements. As if in a passing gesture she dipped a hollow gourd into the water before pouring its contents into her water jar and Zusa watched her until it was full. Getting to her feet she stretched her arms and turned around as if to simply look about. Her round face shone in the soft morning light as she turned and her friends giggled at her actions as she whispered something to them and they burst into fits of merriment. The tone of her voice carried to where Zusa was although he could not make out what it was she said it was music to his soul.

Zusa just stared at the young woman. His breath caught short in his chest and his ears pounded as his heart raced. She was tall for a Bantu maiden but her womanly curves were not completely hidden by her garment whilst her legs and arms were shapely from healthy living and exercise. She was clothed in a leather skirt with an additional strip covering her breasts; an uncommon apparel, however it indicated she was from a family of status.

This thought was further supported by the glass

bead bangles around her delicate wrists along with those interwoven into her jet-black hair which had been carefully plaited into a unique design.

However it was her petite face which drew Zusa's gaze. Her head was small but gracefully poised on her long neck. Her light brown skin was flawless in its texture, and her fine- boned features almost outlined her face. Her nose was delicately shaped, but it was her eyes that transfixed Zusa. They were large and dark brown, the colour of the pure liquid honey that dripped from wild beehives. Her mouth was wide and inviting and when she smiled her teeth were perfectly set in her rose-tinted lips, bright in the natural light.

Zusa couldn't stop looking at her and when she eventually glanced at him from the corner of her eye, his heart leaped with the direct contact and he inhaled her complete beauty. She quickly looked away as if nothing has happened and the huddle of girls around her burst into another fit of giggles, their hands covering their mouths.

One of the more comely women filling jars at the waterhole noticed the exchanges and she rose quickly to her feet at a speed unexpected for her size and rushed over to intervene. With a loud voice she scolded the young women, shouting that they all had better things to do than to look at boys. At her forceful instruction they began to pick up their water jars. When the loads were carefully balanced on their heads and resting on a ring of twisted hemp rope, they were ushered away. The gracefulness of the woman with whom he had exchanged glances, walking with a heavy load on her head, filled Zusa's stomach as if it were full of locusts.

Zusa continued to gaze after her and just as she entered the stone-lined corridor, she turned to look straight back at Zusa and she gave him a wide smile.

Then she was gone from sight.

By now others had witnessed the episode around the water hole and a few voices were raised in conversation. Realising this, Zusa knew he had no defence, but to leave unceremoniously would further impact on what was
being said so he calmly bent down to take a mouthful of

the clear cool liquid before splashing a couple of handfuls across his face. Then, with as much dignity as possible, he beat a hasty retreat.

The climb back up the path was less taxing, now that he had managed to quench his thirst. He felt refreshed but this was more than likely due to the glimpse of the beautiful young woman he had seen a short while ago. *Who was she, what was her name?* Hoping he might catch up with the group he increased his pace, but as he climbed further up the hill he realised that they had disappeared and so he decided to head towards the fortress's summit. Gradually he lengthened his stride to work his legs whilst taking deeper and deeper breaths to help clear his head. Building up his pace he walked by the entrance of the main village area for the fortress and passed the gateway opposite to the area where his sleeping hut was situated. He had thought to enquire as to Gemba's state or whereabouts but he was enjoying his lone exploration and decided to continue on his own. He reached the reception area of the previous day and just as he was about to walk through the entrance he noticed a small open and unguarded side gate to his right with Nyazimba's unique curved steps leading upwards. Hesitating for a few seconds Zusa looked around but saw no one paying him any attention and he decided to step through the portal to see where it led.

Taking the steps two or three at a time Zusa noticed that that the stairwell spiralled up and backwards on itself. Open to the sky Zusa realised that the steps were going to take him to the top of the wall above the reception area, from where the guards had been able to look down on the assembly.

As his head became level with the top of the buttressing he hesitated and carefully looked around. Again seeing no one he slowly climbed until he was on top of the partition. It was wide enough to allow two men to pass side by side and it had been paved with smooth stone slabs to aid anyone walking around its perimeter. From this position of height Zusa was able to see the full layout of the city below him and all of its intricate defensive arrangements, its design stretching away In front of him like lines etched into the ground. Most of the fortress' thick walls joined each other to allow for the fast movement of troops from one defensive post to another whilst some breaks in the design were obviously part of the concept to confuse and restrict some access in case the walls were ever captured and used by an attacking force.

Sloping away downhill other features became obvious in their function and the young man marvelled at the structure of the city.

Behind and to the left of where he stood was the garrison troops' kraal. It was complete with larger thatched huts which accommodated the young warriors in training whilst more permanent stone-walled buildings held the armouries and food supplies. Others were where the senior officers were housed. These buildings were situated around an open parade square but again not many people were in sight and none of those who were paid any attention to the lone figure on the wall above them.

In front of the wall on which he was standing was the city's village area, a congested mix of buildings, groups of which had their own wooden stake barriers to give each head of the home some privacy. There were a large number of people milling about performing numerous daily tasks.

The visitor's area where he had slept was slightly to his right but the placement of some of the buildings made it so he was not able to see the hut he had shared with Gemba. A few more people were walking about. At least the camp was waking up at last, he thought to himself. Further to the right, he could see the mountain range which formed the valley in which the city was located. It extended northward to the horizon in what appeared to be an impregnable barrier. Its hills and slopes were slashed with sheer vertical granite sides, bright in the morning light, studded with hardy bushes and some trees whose roots had found a firm grip amongst the narrow cracks and crevasses, desperate to hold on to life and to thrive.

Turning to his left, he walked along the top of the wall which widened considerably until it was almost ten paces across. Zusa passed by two of the turreted lighting pedestals which smelt of dead embers and there was a more pungent smell which assailed his nostrils, something that kept the fires burning through strong wind and rain he thought. He continued to walk another forty paces over the portal of a tunnel gate between the main village and the garrison troops' settlement, which had been constructed across two natural rocks. The wooden gate was in the raised position allowing common and free access below. Five more stone light pedestals sat upon the wall which curved to what appeared to be the southern boundary of the hill fortress.

Taking smaller and smaller steps Zusa eased himself towards the edge of the wall where the view before him astounded him. The hill on which the fortress stood gave way to an open flat-bottomed valley further surrounded by a number of lower undulating and gentle hills which became more mountainous in the far distance.

The height he was at above the surrounding terrain sucked away at his belly and for a moment he felt dizzy and disorientated. He realised he was standing on the hill fortress' extreme southern wall which had a near vertical precipice of a hundred paces reaching down to the valley floor.

He could just make out a stair-lined path snaking from the top of the hill, past his position and folding back on itself before making its way to the bottom. It was as narrow as any corridor Zusa had seen so far. So this is where the other group of visitors came from yesterday, he thought to himself.

From his high position he could see that many lines of granite partitions intersected the valley basin in various stages of construction. An outer wall reaching from the water gate, slowly swept around interlocking a number of large boulders and rocky outcrops and completed the perimeter defence before disappearing from his view which was blocked by the bulk of the hilltop fortress rising above him.

Within the valley, he could see people moving about but his eye was drawn to a hive of activity on what appeared to be a building site. Over three hundred men were working on a near circular enclosure within the boundary of the valley complex's encompassing walls. Most of these workers were laying or carrying bricks while a few others were chipping and cutting the stones to size before putting them in place. The sharp report and tinkling sounds of iron hammers and chisels upon rock could be clearly heard. As he watched one of the workers Zusa became curious at the sight of the stonemason striking his chisel only to have the sound reach Zusa's ears after he had lifted the hammer into the air again, as if the noise was coming from the uplifting of the tool instead of the impact on the rock!

The walls that were being constructed were as high as the tallest giraffe and were four or five paces thick at their base. It must have taken a number of years to get it to this advanced stage of completion. The major construction site was almost central to the valley basin and dominated the environment with its presence.

The enclosure consisted of two more inner concentric walls within the larger main outer wall which was the highest and widest in form. Two conical towers, one as tall as the height of six grown men, the other a third of the size, were nearing completion in and to the western side of the complex, separated by about fifteen paces, their use much less apparent than the stone wall. Grass thatched buildings were scattered in a haphazard way.

Zusa could sense that time had been taken in the preparation of the structure, for intricate patterns had been inserted in the walls around the top of the stonework. Instead of the granite rock bricks being set in the normal parallel manner, the stonemasons had aligned the stones in two lines of alternative diagonals offering more of the fish-bone effect and chevron designs he had seen when he had entered the city yesterday giving the great structure an air of majestic splendour.

The dark green grass carpet of the vale floor was interlaced with lighter-coloured narrow paths between the different areas of the valley complex and what seemed to be isolated settlements.

Two more frequently used paths were shown by the increase in width on the bare ground from the regular passing of many feet. One led from the centre of the valley towards a small water hole that seemed to supply the valley complex. The other path extended from the bottom of the hill fortress out of what appeared to be another main gate whose road disappeared towards the south-east. Zusa correctly assumed that this was the other trade road to the far eastern coast.

"You shouldn't be up here, Zusa," a loud voice said from behind him and he started in surprise. Turning around he saw Makonde, the King's trusted friend and adviser, standing behind him. A stern look on his face.

"I am sorry," he stammered to begin with "I was just looking around, trying to clear my head after last night's celebrations," Zusa said in response, the second sentence spoken with more conviction than the first.

Makonde continued to look at him and then smiled, "So you also have a headache, hey?"

Zusa realised that he was not going to get into trouble for trespassing and turned back to the scene below. "It's amazing, our city is getting so large, I can't believe what's being constructed down there," he indicated with an outstretched finger.

The chieftain walked closer to look. "It's not really an extension to the city, Zusa." He stopped speaking as if contemplating what to say next. "It's almost a second town as its construction has been brought about more by necessity than by desire." He took a deep breath as if to continue but decided to hold something back. Makonde placed a hand on Zusa's shoulder and said, "Let's take a seat over here." He indicated a section of wall which had been made from one of the large natural boulders, its sharp edge dropping away into the valley below.

They sat with their legs overhanging the precipice and after a short delay the senior man went on with a softer tone in his voice. "You see, there is a problem that is building up even as we speak and it is getting bigger every day. Every year our city is attracting more and more visitors from across the land and even from beyond our borders. These people are attracted to our way of life and many of them do not want to leave once they have visited. I am sure you are aware that as the larger tribes and nations stretch their influences across the land, the weaker tribal groups seem to gather closer to us for protection. Don't get me wrong, this arrangement has worked well for us as these groups have provided labour for our iron and gold mines plus the building of the walls below."

Zusa knew of this arrangement as mining was an extremely difficult and dangerous occupation. There were two types of mines, open cast and tunnelling, the latter being the more hazardous. This type of mine normally consisted of narrow tunnels between thirty and one hundred pace's long, angling deep into the earth. Some had vertical mine shafts and the workers were lowered in using rope ladders.

The ore, both iron and gold, was extracted by using fire setting, a similar technique to that used by the granite quarrying he had seen the day before, but he imagined that in an enclosed area, the working conditions must be appalling. Once the ore had been ripped from the mother lode it was carried out piece by piece, in woven baskets before it was smelted by groups of workers on the mining site. Finally, the metal was delivered to Nyazimba's skilled smiths for working into useful implements.

Makonde has paused in his narrative as he watched Zusa who was obviously taking in what he had been saying. Zusa realised the chieftain had stopped talking and said, "Yes, I understand what it is you are saying."

Makonde went on, "The settlements which sprang up from this migration have begun to encroach on the fortress' boundaries which in turn compromised the safety of the King and the city. Based on this we eventually gave our blessing for the construction of the town you see below you. It is clear that the different tribes and groups have set themselves aside from the next in their own communities but with each passing season the number of people living below the safety of our walls has grown and the society is becoming a single entity."

Zusa nodded his head at the statement and asked, "I

can imagine there are more than just these concerns." Raising an eyebrow Makonde indicated for the young man to go on, interested in where his thought had taken him. "I am sure nature would also have some difficulty in looking after so many people in one place. It's never really been done before. Our tribe has for countless generations lived in smaller sized communities so that the surrounding land does not fail us."

Makonde smiled. "You are correct in your thinking. Our city fathers were concerned about the increased risk of disease and the strain this amount of people would have on the rest of the land. As you have already said, firewood needs to be provided and food both cultivated and hunted in order to support them all."

Zusa realised the impact such a large number of people had on the delicate environment which is why the initial descendants of the Bantu civilisation had survived by spreading its people across the land in smaller, grouped kraals which lessened the impact of land degradation and the consumption of natural resources. "So when do we know when enough people are here?" Zusa enquired.

Makonde looked at him for a while. "That is the big question. For generations we have lived off the land, moving on once resources began to dwindle. Since we settled in the cities, we have had to learn to cultivate grain and other plants to eat. We have had to breed and herd cattle, while limiting the hunting of wild game. We have learnt to use other fuels for fires but we have had to maintain forests for the ever-constant requirement for wood. It has taken us as a civilisation a long time to learn these things and even more time to master them."

Zusa marvelled at the thought. "Each of these commodities seems finely balanced, each relying on the next. I guess it would not take much to upset the fine balance of things." He stopped to think a while. "So as we learn more, such as new uses for iron, then we have to increase iron production, which needs more wood and more labour which needs more food and accommodation." He paused at the magnitude of the situation. "It's an almost never ending cycle isn't it?"

"Yes, I see you have understanding beyond your years, young man, it is a pity others do not understand the seriousness of it all. One day our city may simply collapse with the pressure of the humanity surrounding it," Makonde said, "The King was wise, in recognising you in such a way and as a man of our future!"

The two stood in silence for a while, each in his own thoughts. "It doesn't simply end there though, Zusa." The youth turned to look at him.

His voice taking on a more serious note Makonde said, "We could have managed the changes brought on by our own making, where each of our commodities, wood, food, iron and water have been supplied by nature and with our ancestors' blessings. But the whole issue is being distorted by the recent arrival of the foreign traders from over the vast waters."

"Are these the traders who have brought fine knives, glass beads and white cloth?" Zusa asked, his mind flashed to the glass beads worn on the wrists and in the hair of the young women he saw near the water hole that morning.

"That is the problem," Makonde responded. "We know how much effort it takes to harvest our natural commodities and therefore they have an agreed trade value, but as soon as there are new goods, such as you have mentioned, on offer, then everything is distorted." His eyes narrowed at the thought. "The foreign traders' demand for gold is unquenchable and the worst development is that just before they left last year, they asked for us to consider trading people - men, women or children - so that they can be taken back as bought workers to their own country."

Zusa expressed his shock at such a request and although serfdom had been practised for many years in the region, with some Nyazimbian households and other tribes paying tribute to the King by sending their people to work for Nyazimba, forced labour, slavery, had never been accepted. "And what did the King say to that?"

Modena smiled, "The King would have nothing to do with it although the idea did receive the approval of his brother and a number of other city officials. From a trading point of view, it would reap great rewards. However, the King is really worried that the foreigners' inhumane request is going to receive more and more support from within the council as some of its members like his brother feel we should be supplying the foreigners needs which in return will enable our nation to trade even more goods." He stopped in his narrative for a while as in thought and Zusa let the silence carry on. The older man went on, "That is why we are building that large enclosure in the valley. It will be offered to the travellers as a safe refuge and to protect their goods whilst they are with us."

"And it will keep them in a place where we can keep a watchful eye upon them," Zusa finished.

"Yes, young man," Makonde said, laying a hand on his shoulder, "but the winds of change are upon us and I feel it is moving at a pace where we will begin to struggle with it, but like the rising of the sun each day it is something that cannot be reversed."

"Well as a nation we have changed so much over the last few generations, it must be difficult for us to hold on to our core values at times." Zusa said.

"Values fine," Modena replied, "but not our culture for, it defines us as a body of people and it must never be forgotten for if we do not remember our errors and faults from the past it means we are doomed to making them all over again in the future."

By this time, the sun had passed its zenith. Makonde turned his back on the valley and said to Zusa, "Why don't you and Gemba have dinner with my family and I this evening. I am having a number of other guests and we will be delighted to have you to share our meal with us."

"Thank you," Zusa said. "On behalf of the both of us I would like to accept your invitation and we look forward to joining you."

"Good. Ask anyone for directions to my kraal, near the army barracks and I will see you soon after dark." With that, Makonde turned and walked away while Zusa was left alone to continue to look over the wide view of the city and valley complex below.

Chapter Thirteen
A dinner invitation

Following his conversation with Makonde on the wall high above the city, Zusa decided to make his way back to his appointed accommodation in search of Gemba to inform him of their invitation for that evening. He found the return route quite easily; nodding greetings to those he passed along the way. Once off the city wall he proceeded along the high-walled passageway to turn into the accommodation encampment. Most of the visitors and revellers of the previous night were out of bed with only those who had seriously over-indulged still lying prone on their sleeping mats in the huts. Gemba was sitting on a carved wooden stool amongst a circle of men who were in an animated conversation; a few of the voices were very loud in discussion.

Zusa approached the gathering where he caught Gemba's eye, who nodded his head and smiled in greeting. He indicated with his head for Zusa to take a seat next to him before turning back to the discussion. As Zusa sat, he heard a man voicing his opinion on some matter.

"I am telling you the truth; although the Limpopo River has been flooded since the beginning of the rains, there have been some strange goings on, a number of goats and cattle had gone missing over the last couple of weeks, a trader arrived yesterday and was also talking about it in the market place. I was in the area about ten days ago and it was the talk of the villages"

"Could it just be that they are losing them to the wandering lions and hyenas?" another responded.

"Yes, I suppose so, it could be the case," the first speaker said, "but there have been other things as well, strange tracks and spoor."

Gemba's ears pricked up at the mention of this and he cut in. "What tracks are these?" he asked in a serious voice.

"Well not tracks actually," the man said hesitating a little. The rest of the group laughed at his discomfort. Thinking a little more before responding, the speaker swallowed and went on. "It's not what tracks we saw," his trailed off, "but more like what tracks we didn't see!"

"So you are worried about something you didn't really see then?" another man in the group said. "Ha, based on that, my whole life would be a worry!" The group burst into merriment. They had gathered to share a midday meal after their night of celebrations and a number of topics had been raised and discussed before the man had voiced his concerns. These topical discussions were always light-hearted in nature and were used to spread folklore, community news and gossip.

Allowing the laughter to fade away, Gemba addressed the man again. "So what were these tracks which weren't really there?" The group fell silent at Gemba's insistent query.

"Well, when we were looking for the missing animals we managed to track them to a point where their tracks just ended."

"Ended?" Gemba questioned.

"Yes, ended. They were there to see and then they just stopped."

The gathering remained quiet, listening to the discussion. "But what was strange was that there were no tracks around, of any animal, domestic or wild. As if, as if?"

"As if someone had wiped the spoor," Gemba completed in a soft voice full of thought. "And only someone with something to hide covers their tracks in such a way!"

"Rustlers!" another voice stated.

"Animal rustlers would be the least of our concerns I think," Gemba added.

The conversation moved on to discussing recent betrothals and deaths, the health of the national herds, crops and mining, but Gemba sat in contemplation for a while, only half listening to the exchange and banter going on around him. Sensing Gemba's withdrawal, Zusa sat in silence awaiting his mentor's acknowledgement again knowing that he should leave the old man to his thoughts

One by one the group gradually broke up as each member wandered off to attend to his own needs. The sun had passed its peak and by the time Gemba had finished his own thoughts it was well into the afternoon. With a final grunt Gemba blinked as he realised that that Zusa had been sitting quietly to his left. "Ah, Zusa! I am sorry; I was lost in thought for a while. I must admit I am concerned about this talk of rustlers in the southern low lands."

"Why, sekuru? What is it that are you worrying about?"

"Well I remember a time, eight seasons ago, when there was a similar occurrence but this time on the eastern border which we share with the saManica (a tribe north-east of Nyazimba). Domestic animals went missing for a few weeks at the end of the rains. A week later our nation was attacked by a large army of the Bemba people. They had used the heavy rains to hide their movements after travelling down from their own land to the north before cutting eastward through the Manican mountain range."

"But why did goats and cattle disappear before the Bemba army arrived?"

Gemba looked into Zusa's eyes, paused, and then said, "Well, their forward scouts had to have something to eat whilst they were performing their reconnaissance, didn't they?"

One of the women hosts interrupted their discussion, offering them a calabash of cool water to quench their thirst. With relief they drank their fill and thanked the woman, who curtsied her response before moving on to the next person.

"So, my young warrior;' Gemba said, changing the subject, "where were you this morning? You were gone by the time I got back to the hut after my early walk. Did you actually go to bed last night I wonder?"

Zusa smiled a response, his cheeks glowing at the insinuation. "Of course I did, Uncle, but I woke up with a thousand drums sounding in my head so I also went for a walk to clear it!"

He went on to recount his morning's escapades, the downhill walk through the city, skimming over his chance meeting with the beautiful girl near the water hole. He spoke at length of his amazement at the new complex being built in the valley and lastly his conversation with Makonde, including the invitation to dine with him that evening. There was a pause in their conversation.

"So was she beautiful?" Gemba asked. Zusa immediately realised to whom he was referring and blushed at the directness of the question, stumbling in response.

"I don't know what you mean, Uncle!"

"The girl of course, the girl you met near the water hole. You mentioned her and moved on so quickly I knew you must have noticed her a little more then you acknowledged! Who was she?"

"I am not sure, her aunties called her away so quickly and I did not have a chance to find out."

"Heh heh, my young warrior. Slayer of leopards, guardian of your father herds yet tongue tied at the first sign of a beautiful woman." He nudged Zusa's arm, "Don't worry, you are not the first and you will most definitely not be the last man to be confused around the opposite sex."

Changing the subject as quickly as he could Zusa reiterated Makonde's invitation to share this evening's meal.

"Do you know much about this man?" Gemba asked.

"No, not a lot really," Zusa replied, "Just the stories we hear when we were growing up. I know he has been with the King since they were children. They grew up together. Later on in their adult life, he was appointed by the King to command the army. He remained in that trusted position for many years. After that he was given the responsibility for the King's personal guard and now he oversees the training of the new recruits. Another senior chief called Zabesi replaced him as commander of the palace guard, I think."

"Yes, you are right in what you say. Makonde has shown himself to be a loyal supporter of the King and has gained many battle honours over the years but more importantly, he has gained the King's trust. His kraal is in fact part of the palace guard barracks area. The barracks have been strategically built between both of the entrances and the city's largest suburb of dwellings, almost as a buffer zone."

"Nothing seems to have been left to chance during the building of the city, has it?" Zusa asked, reflecting on the layout he had seen from the high point over the city.

"Well, it has been developed over many generations, where lessons have been learned the hard way. Determined attackers in the past have found ways into the fortress, which have thereafter been sealed in defence against further incursions. I must admit the hill fortress can be considered to be fairly complete - it's not often they make changes now. Most of the new construction is in the valley complex and the work is moving along a lot faster than that done in the past because of the experience gained." During their conversation, they had been strolling about the encampment. Gemba pointed to the ground at the foot of the stone wall. "Look at that for an example, the builders had to ensure that drains were inserted at the correct place into the bulwark so that rain water can flow away so as not to cause a flood. They worked this out by pouring large vats of water onto the ground and observing where the water ran and more importantly where it collected which is where they would leave a drain hole through the wall."

The drains under discussion were stone-lined chambers leading under the mammoth structures, each large enough to allow a grown man's arm to be able to retrieve any debris that caused blockages. Gemba continued, "Also if you look closely at the construction you will notice that the walls are thicker at the base and they taper off the higher they go. This is another way strength is maintained in the structure."

"Yes, I see what you are saying, Uncle," Zusa agreed. "I have noticed the narrow entrances and approach corridors which limit access and flow of people and I guess more importantly, an attacking enemy!"

"Yes. The city has been built over many generations and has become our refuge and the mainstay of our society. Its presence on this hill governs the immediate area and projects the power of the King into the surrounding area and it is ideal in holding off raiding parties. However in battle it is sometimes best to meet the enemy before they get to the walls."

"But why? The walls are high and strong. Our army is well protected inside them."

"Yes, but don't forget it is the surrounding country which sustains the city and if the water and food was cut off in a drawn-out siege then the population inside would suffer considerably. We have large water vats hidden in caves in case we lose control of the water gate but they are only big enough to keep the garrison alive for a few weeks. Grain and other food have been stored against such emergencies but our army is trained to meet the enemy in the open field rather than to stand behind the walls."

They discussed the structure of the city for a while until Gemba suggested it was time to prepare for their evening appointment with Makonde. Both men took a slow walk down to the point downstream from the water hole where the city's populace bathed.

The water at this spot ran quickly, swirling about in a number of pools where different groups had congregated for their bath. Fingers of the riverbank afforded some privacy stretched into mid-stream. However, in Nyazimbian society, modesty was not a high priority and most people present simply stripped and waded into the water. Only matrons kept their skirts on as they stepped into the bathing area.

Stepping into the cool water, Gemba and Zusa washed the dust off their bodies and after a while they waded out of the stream and sat on a large sloping rock to dry off. The place they had chosen to dry off was overhung by the common, flat-topped trees familiar to the area; their shade a respite from the relentless sun. Whilst lying back on the rocks, Zusa noted multi-coloured lizards all over the hillside. They were almost as long as a person's forearm and had dark-blue coloured heads. This hue faded to a medium green at their neck and upper bodies before gradually changing through a spectrum of colours to a burnt orange near their hind legs and finally to a yellow at the end of the tail. Some of the more courageous reptiles crept closer to the prone men, stopping, observant in a heads-up pose, front legs stiff, back legs poised, ready to flee at any sign of danger. Their heads had a leathery serrated crown that was the same colour as their body. Their eyes were as still as their bodies whilst their tongues flickered in and out, sampling the air.

It was not long before the soft rustle of the wind through the trees, interspersed with the sounds of cheerful people about them and the reflected warmth of the bare rock lulled the men into a peaceful sleep.

The long shadows thrown by the sinking sun awoke Zusa, the shade caused by the high peaks to the west crossed his face and he stirred at the changing light. Sitting upright he touched Gemba on the shoulder so that he gradually awoke.

"I needed that sleep but I see that it's almost time for us to join Makonde," he said. "We had better make our way back into the city!" Standing up they stretched their relaxed muscles and limbs and began the climb back along what had now become a familiar route and behind them the sun continued to descend towards the horizon.

At a steady pace they walked past their place of accommodation and for the first time, turned right through the gateway to enter the army training grounds. The area around Makonde's kraal was almost full with almost twenty visitors and as they approached they were welcomed at
the door by a chieftain who showed them to where the gathered group sat. Makonde rose to his feet on their entry.

"Welcome, Zusa, welcome, sekuru Gemba. You are most welcome in my home." He indicated two wooden stools to his left set facing the entrance, "Garapasi, *please be seated*." Nodding their acceptance and extending their greeting to the guests the two took their seats.

Makonde's kraal had been built at the top of the area reserved for the army's training. It consisted of four mud and dagga, grass-roofed huts each about eight paces in diameter and built in a semi-circle about the main dwelling. The construction of this stone house spoke of the high regard for his senior position within the city as it had been built with the granite bricks and was, unusually, rectangular. The doorway was high enough that one did not have to bend over to enter like the standard housing, and it had a solid wooden door set in its frame. The roof was still thatched grass; however, it sloped up and against one of the fort's main walls against which it had been built. A chimney was at one end through which smoke could be seen rising in the cool evening air. A low grass and wooden stake fence finished the enclosure marking its extent.

A large fire had been set in the central fireplace surrounded by a ring of irregular stones. It had burnt ferociously earlier and was now a heap of dull red glowing embers emitting enough heat to ward off the night chill as the setting sun continued to descend below the horizon.

With the suddenness of the African sunset the sky lit in bright splendour with the burnt orange disc of the sun staining the skyline in the same colour, whilst higher above, the few clouds glowed golden, as if in final farewell, all set against a backdrop of a darkening blue sky. With a final, observable motion, the sun disappeared below the rim of the earth and correspondingly twilight moved quickly into dusk.

Their seating area had been placed in an optimum position giving a westward view of the city below.

Behind the gathering, with a whooshing sound, three wall lanterns were ignited, giving luminance to the area, followed in turn by other fire lamps spreading across the city. There were a number of indiscernible hails from afar as the city gates were closed and the night watchmen took their posts.

The conversation around the fireplace was low-voiced in respect for their patron and two or three groups were discussing a number of issues. Gemba had taken up dialogue with another man seated to his right, while Zusa sat deep in his own thoughts.

The smell of cooked food was carried upon the

evening breeze. Zusa recognised the aroma of roasted goat meat, and boiled sadza mixed with the herbal scent of thickened, meat-based gravy. As he looked around, a number of women walked demurely into the centre of the gathering. Eyes cast downwards they knelt in front of each guest offering a bowl of water so that they could wash their hands. Out of habit Zusa reached into the bowl offered to him and cupped water from one hand to the other, when his attention was drawn to the woman serving him. He had sensed her eyes and looking towards her face. His heart took a leap as he recognised the serving woman to be the young girl from the water hole that morning. Instead of keeping her eyes downcast she had been watching his face for a reaction and at his start she looked directly into his eyes for a brief second, her mouth holding back a smile as he finished cleaning his hands. Without another glance she rose from the position and retreated with the hand basin while Zusa's gaze followed her until she disappeared behind one of the huts in the kraal.

Turning his attention back to the conversation, he was in time to hear, "Isn't that true, Zusa?"

"Ah, what was that, sekuru?" he said.

"Baba Matte was asking after your injuries and I have told him you have recovered well, isn't that true?"

"Ah yes. I am feeling a lot better now and my wounds have healed properly" He tried to get his mind back into the conversation but his thoughts kept wandering at the thought of the girl who had once again disappeared before he had had a chance to find out her name or anything about her.

Women began filing back into the gathering, this time carrying large, flat, fire-baked clay platters of roasted meat and round pots of the maize meal and flavoured sauce. Wooden platters were also carried in, loaded with fresh fruit and nuts and others containing a mixture of rape (a type of spinach) mixed with pulped peanuts. The food was spread before the guests in such a way that they had only to stretch slightly in order to get to it. With appreciative gusto the guests delved into the fare and the conversation rose in pitch and volume.

Going through the motions of eating as he seemed to have suddenly lost his appetite, Zusa waited for another glimpse of the girl amongst those serving; to no avail as now they had retreated to allow the men to eat. His earlier hunger was forgotten as his heart continued to race at the thought of her deep brown eyes and on reflection; he was shocked at the almost cheeky sparkle they had emitted during their brief contact. *Who is she,* he thought to himself, and *why is she here?*

His reluctance to eat was noticed by Gemba who asked him if he was not hungry. Dragging himself back to the party he dipped his hand into a small bowl of water and reached into the pot of maize meal to take a palm full of the white mixture. He rolled the sadza into a small pointed ball, dabbed it into the bowl of gravy before attaching a small part of the vegetable and nut mix and taking a bite of the morsel.

He savoured the tastes and realised that the food had been well prepared. This brought his appetite back with a vengeance and he continued with the meal taking turns to address the other types of fine food on offer.
The meat had been cooked perfectly and its rich juices ran down his chin as he bit into it whilst the warm fat melted in his mouth like liquid gold along with the rich herbal gravy added to the full delight of the meal.

With well-orchestrated timing another procession of women appeared carrying pots of traditionally brewed beer and wound their way into the circle of men. Zusa saw that the girl was almost half way along the line but as she turned towards his direction a senior woman, possibly an aunt, redirected her to serve Makonde as he had already finished his first pot of the fermented brew. Zusa looked down and noticed that a pot had been placed at his feet and by the time he looked up he had lost sight of her yet again.

Shrugging his shoulders at the unfairness of the situation Zusa took the first cautious sips of beer, its husky texture running down his throat to add to a full stomach.
The feast continued into the night and the level of food and drinks was topped up by two or three constantly present

hostesses and there was no sign of the young women.

Freshly roasted goats meat was brought through, with additional clay pots of beer and the more that was consumed the louder the conversations became and more animated its delivery.

Large trunks of wood were thrown onto the central fire and it was poked back into life. The prodding caused bright orange sparks to rise into the sky along with the smoke and the hot embers soon caused the new logs to become well alight, offering a welcome core of heat to the rapidly cooling air around the assembly.

The bright yellow flames cast shadows across the seating arena, reflecting upon the kraal's buildings and the enclosing stone walls. Its intense light exaggerated the motion of the shadows of those around the fireplace like giants moving amongst the living. In dark contrast, areas where the fire light could not reach lent themselves to an overall macabre scene. It was an enormous tapestry of life being played out behind the performers without them being aware that they were part of it.

A while later, after the last of the food had been consumed, the serving women returned. Zusa caught sight of the girl and he could see that she was hovering around near the centre of the queue entering the fire-lit area.

She took a step forward, her eyes upon her aunt who was managing the proceedings, directing alternate servants left and right to begin the clearing of the empty pots and platters. With a darting movement, she slotted herself into a position, forcing one of the others in line to step back and as she reached the entrance to the gathering, she was directed left, towards where Zusa was seated. Without hesitation she knelt at his feet to offer him a fresh bowl of water so that he could clean his hands and whilst he was doing this she collected some of the empty dishes about her. Again, he saw her smile at his attention.
"What is your name?" he asked in a quiet voice.

She looked up at him and opened her mouth to speak but looking sideways she saw her aunt making a beeline towards where she was and dropping her head she rose quickly with both hands full of crockery. Unsure what was happening Zusa glanced about him and saw Makonde looking directly at him.

"So I see you have met my daughter, Shawana, young Zusa," he called across the fire in a strong voice.

With a start, Zusa's eyes opened wide at the comment. "Your daughter, sekuru? I did not know!"

"Ah, so you did not know this even after seeing her this morning near the water hole?"

"No sir. I really did not know!" Zusa was surprised that her father already aware of the encounter but then he remembered the large woman who had dragged her away. A few of the other men had picked up on the exchange between Makonde and Zusa and were having difficulty in suppressing their smiles as they saw this young man wriggle under the chief's interrogation. The conversation around the fire quietened down in expectation of some entertainment. Gemba leaned back to observe, realising that this must be the young woman who had flustered Zusa earlier on during the day.

Makonde went on, "So I welcome you into my house and I find you looking at my youngest daughter. What manner is this?" he demanded his voice stern in its delivery.

Thinking back to his conversation on the wall above the valley, Zusa remembered that the man had used the same tone when Makonde had first questioned him about his presence on the wall, only to discover he was not in trouble. Looking at the senior chief's face Zusa caught the same glint in his eyes and realised that he was being set up again but this time front of a lot more people. He paused to think before answering and the whole gathering held its collective breath to hear the response. "Well, great Chief," he paused and took a deep breath," all I was thinking was that due to the beauty of such an obviously well-presented young woman, I recognised that she must have been from a great and well-to-do family." He looked around to see who else was actually listening to the exchange and from his opening sentence he now had the attention of the whole party and the last of the conversations died. "From a really great family whose parental lineage must also be of equal prestige and grace so as to have been able to impart their own naturally-given refinement and esteem to their offspring."

As he finished he looked directly back at Makonde who for a moment stared back at him. Zusa heart raced as he thought, *have I said to much? Have I offended this chieftain in his own home?* Panic gripped his heart until he heard a few a few snickers from around the fireplace and, being unable to control himself any longer, Makonde let out a belly-shaking laugh and slapped his hand on to the top of his legs.

Everyone burst out in delights of laughter at the way Zusa had turned the conversation around and for a while the merriment continued whilst more beer was consumed. His words being repeated over and over, with some of the men mimicking his voice. A higher-pitched shriek from the kitchen area meant that the women gathered there had also heard the exchange and were sharing in the enjoyment.

"Well done, lad." Gemba leaned over to say. "Show no fear!"

The gathering stretched into the night. However Zusa did not get another glimpse of Shawana that evening. He smiled to himself. At least he knew her name, Shawana, meaning "Grace", and that was what she was to him: Grace.

Chapter Fourteen
A message at midnight

Zusa was ripped from his deep sleep by the mix of an urgently beaten drum and a large number of voices raised in panic and alarm. He lay still for while thinking that he might have dreamt the sounds but when the noises did not go away he decided to stir himself to investigate. As he moved Gemba also awoke and sat upright and voiced the same question all ask when awoken from a deep sleep, "What is happening?"

Zusa shrugged his shoulders in response. "I don't know, Uncle, it woke me too." Without another word the two got to their feet pausing to stretch before stepping out of their sleeping hut. The first thing they saw was that there were a lot of people moving about but what was really noticeable was that the city was alight with camp fires being brought back into fiery life and all of the huge security lanterns and beacons were burning brightly. The drum continued in its summoning tone and Zusa could see numerous torches being carried by people moving about the lower city. Turning to look at the top of the hill, he saw that the palace was also lit up.

"Hey soldier do you have any idea about what is going on?" Gemba called to a passing armed guard.

"There has been some trouble inland. A messenger has arrived from Belingwe to say that it has been attacked but we don't have any more details at this time," was the response.

Why would someone attack Belingwe?" Zusa asked his mentor.

Gemba took his time to answer, "Well Belingwe is one of the main stone-built stockades, a two days' walk west of Nyazimba. The site was primarily set to protect the iron-rich producing area and for central stocking of commodities for the area. I am sure it is not heavily guarded and the only military I know to be at this position was a company of warriors as it was midway between the fully manned Fort at Chimnungwa and the capital and was therefore under the protection of the two larger forces."

The older man thought of his conversation the previous afternoon about the unusual activities which had been going on around the southern border. "Zulus," he said under his breath. "They have raided before the border river had subsided so as to catch us unaware!"

Zusa looked back at him in shock.

"Zulus!" Gemba repeated. "Yes, it looks like they may just have raided us earlier this year. Come on, we had better see if we can find someone with authority." They moved into the stream of people filling the main corridor and turned left to go uphill towards the palace. The crowd thinned as they approached the summit and, as they got close to the King's residence, they saw Makonde entering the inner defence wall ahead of them. As they tried to push their way past the guards' station, the warriors blocked their path with their spears.

"No unauthorised entry," they said, their eyes searching for the first sign of defiance to their authority.

"Makonde!" shouted Gemba at the retreating back of the induna, "Chief, I have some information for you!"

In response to his shouted name, Makonde turned and saw the guards restraining Gemba and Zusa.

"Let them in, soldier," he called, waving his hand in command. Pushing by the guards Gemba walked quickly up to the chief and, as they got closer, Makonde was the first to speak. He said, "I see you have heard the news already. It would appear that someone has attacked our settlement at Belingwe."

"Not just someone," Gemba said, "I strongly believe that it is the Zulus attacking from the south!"

The statement made all within hearing range pause.

"It's too early in the season for them to cross the Limpopo. The river is still flooded and flowing too hard for anyone to cross," said one of Makonde's aides.

"No I don't think so," Gemba stated. "From what I have heard this has the hallmark of the Zulus' cunning nature and it would only have been a short time before the water level had subsided enough to allow a crossing."

"It can't be the Zulu! It has to be a large band of bandits or a group of San," the same aide interrupted, cutting off Gemba in mid sentence.

Turning on the speaker Makonde said, "Hold on, do not interrupt, let Gemba explain himself."

Gemba gave his explanation to his reasoning, referring to the conversation with one of the city's visitors the previous afternoon. He also recalled the occasion when the eastern borders had been attacked a few years ago. Something similar had occurred, just as he had explained earlier to Zusa.

Makonde stopped to think for a while. Making up his mind, he looked at Gemba and said, "Follow me; we are going to see the King." To his aide he added, "Send for this fellow who spoke of these strange activities and bring him to us in the palace." The aide walked away to attend to the direct instruction, giving Gemba an insolent scowl as he passed.

Turning on his heels Makonde continued his fast walk towards the palace with Gemba and Zusa falling in step behind his entourage. Passing through the corridors and the auditorium from the previous day Zusa saw that the palace guard was on high alert, with all of the entrances being guarded by at least two warriors. Priests and other officials were rushing about on unspecified missions and as the party moved beyond the staged area, one of the King's personal assistants rushed forward to greet the chief.

"Makonde, the King is awaiting you in the antechamber."

"Good. Show me the way."

"We should leave your understudies here," the King's aide said indicating Makonde's lieutenants, Gemba and Zusa. He was obviously nervous about so many people being in the immediate company of the monarch. "At least until after you have spoken to him yourself," he added in an attempt to lessen any impact his words had on those he had spoken of. "The Commander of the army, Kadenge, is already with him."

Taking the time to think about this request Makonde said, "Agreed, I will go and speak with the King and Kadenge first." He turned to one of his own party and instructed, "Ensure the training regiments are assembled and standing by."

To Gemba and Zusa he said, "Wait here. I will send for you." He followed the King's assistant through another entrance and was gone from sight.

Gemba looked around and noticed a wooden bench against one of the walls. "I think we should take a seat as this could take some time." They both sat down, deep in their thoughts leaning back against the wall. A number of other officials and messengers bustled in and out of the antechamber and surprisingly it was not long before both Gemba and Zusa were summoned to the inner meeting.

Raised voices could be discerned as they followed the messenger with the conversation getting louder at each step. After passing down a short corridor they entered a room which was in fact a natural cave with a high-reaching steep roof stained black by the smoke of countless fires and lanterns. The lower sections of the walls were covered with murals and some parts of it and the floor were covered with animal hides. Ceremonial shields and spears were mounted on the walls along with war axes and clubs, their handles wrapped with wire-wound multi-coloured glass beads all set in an intricate manner to impress visitors to the room.

The colours and complicated patterns of the beads indicated the value of such instruments. The chevron design, taken from the city walls, was apparent in vivid black and white globules of glass whilst brighter colours, orange, red, green and blue, set the intricate patterns in place. It was obvious that this was the city's main planning room especially in times of crisis; it was a warrior's room, the centre of which was dominated by a large table constructed from a single piece of flat rock balanced on four thick stone-carved legs. Gathered around this table were the King, Kadenge, the army commander, Zabesi, the head of the palace guard, Makonde and another seven high ranking members of the city and army. As the duo entered Makonde looked up and called them over to where he stood, the large group opened up to let the new arrivals up to the table.

"Your Majesty," Makonde addressed the King, "these are the men I mentioned to you who may have some information which I think could be relevant to the current situation." The King looked up and even in the tense atmosphere of the war room smiled at the approaching guests. "You met Zusa just two days' ago and this is his mentor Gemba who travelled to the city with him," Makonde said.

"Sire," interrupted Kadenge, "we really do not need advice from anyone at this stage especially just someone passing by who thinks they have a theory on what is going on!"

The King looked briefly at his army commander, his eyes ending Kadenge's comments before he turned to the newcomers. The King's face lit up at the sight of Gemba, "Ah, sekuru Gemba, of course I know you. It has been a long time, old friend." Even Zusa's heart missed a step at the greeting. Gemba had never indicated that he had met the King, let alone been a known acquaintance; Kadenge scowled at the exchange and moved away as he realised he had been on the verge of condemning someone who was obviously well known to the King.

"My liege, it has been a long time." Reaching forward they exchanged a warm handshake.

"Yes, it has been too long! Makonde tells me that you have something to contribute towards the situation."

Nodding his head, Gemba began to relate what he had already said to Makonde but in more detail. During his narrative, Yasini, Makonde and Kadenge interrupted him to ask a number of questions to glean details about a certain part of the recital. The man who had raised the initial concerns at the unusual events arrived during this briefing and he was brought straight into the room where he was also questioned in detail. The man was obviously overawed at the illustrious company. He stumbled occasionally in his recounting of the events and it was with obvious relief that he finally left the room, after it had been agreed that he had imparted all he knew.

Yasini turned to Kadenge and asked, "Have any of your scouts returned yet?"

"No, my King, but I am expecting them any time. I have instructed them to travel as far as Sampambi to see if they could find anyone else with more information."

"So what is the situation as we know it right now?" Kadenge stepped up to the table which had a three dimensional topographical relief map of the kingdom modelled upon it. In the centre was the fortress city of Nyazimba and expanding outwards were hills, mountains, forests, plains, rivers and lakes with villages and roadways shown in considerable detail.

"The person who raised the alarm arrived in the early hours of this morning, after he had run all of the way from Belingwe. He has told us of an attack on the garrison stationed at the settlement which had happened yesterday morning."

"Who was the man?" the King asked. Kadenge looked around as if to draw the information from the air, but Zabesi stepped forward to respond on his behalf.

"Well, he is more a boy than a man, sire. His name is Njeri and he was herding goats on a hill east of the town when he noticed a large number of armed warriors approaching from the south-west. He had risen early that day and was up on a hill looking for a stray goat after losing it from his father's herd the evening before. He said that this group of armed men, a force of a couple of hundred at least, attacked the town giving no quarter, killing even women and children."

"What happened to the military detachment based there?"

"The boy says that by the time the alarm had been raised and the town guard formed up they had been surrounded and were killed to the last man within a few minutes! The boy decided to go and warn his own family whose kraal was not too far away but by the time he got to his father's kraal, it had already been attacked. His parents were dead and their huts burnt to the ground. However, as he had not been able to find his younger brothers and sisters he decided to come here to raise the alarm!"

"Where is this young man now?" the King asked.

"He collapsed sire, once he had given his account of the events," Zabesi responded. "He is being looked after by our healers as he is exhausted beyond understanding."

"Another brave young man," the King said his voice etched with sorrow. The room fell silent at the last remark with all eyes on the King.

Chapter Fifteen
First reactions

Everyone in the war room was offering their opinion of the situation and the discussion extended well into the new morning but gradually, and in the absence of any additional information, the group drifted apart and re-gathered in twos and threes spread out across the room to discuss possible options open to them and everything else was left to the waiting game.

The war room had a balcony overlooking the city below and Kadenge who had been looking outwards was the first to notice a commotion at the main gate. The guards were hurrying around and even from that distance he could see that the wooden gate had been raised to allow someone through. Within a few seconds a lone figure emerged and a number of the guards took up station by the figure to escort the new arrival further into the city. Turning back to the gathering he announced, "One of my scouts is back; he is being brought to us as I speak!"

The room stirred in anticipation and Gemba spoke, the first time since his initial conversation. "If the King is finished with us we will now take our leave."

"No, sekuru, I would appreciate your contributions and wise counsel. Please can you wait and see what this messenger has to say?"

Gemba nodded his acceptance and retreated a few steps pulling Zusa back with him by the elbow to assume a subservient role of a listener at the back of the room. He had noticed how the army commander, Kadenge, had bristled at his introduction and the fact that the King had afforded him such a measure of respect.

There was a nervous atmosphere in the room while they awaited the arrival of the scout and each person handled its effect in his own way.

The King attempted to remain above the situation by continuing in mundane conversation with his subordinates. Zabesi remained loyal by shadowing his King standing at station at his ruler's left shoulder. Kadenge fidgeted to mask his anxiety, moving from one part of the room to another and pretending interest in the decorations upon the walls. Only Makonde appeared unaffected and continued to stand over the central map table, discussing some issues with his own men, occasionally despatching a messenger on some errand or another.

Eventually, a weary-looking warrior was escorted into the war room, abject exhaustion engraved onto his face and in his eyes. The dust from the road stained his legs and most of his body; his feet although hardened by years of walking barefoot were cut in a number of places. Bypassing the requirement for normal protocol in the presence of such an illustrious group of men the scout gave his report. He explained how he and his appointed second had run all night in the company of six other warriors, three pairs, with each team peeling off to its own destination as they progressed. His team had continued towards Belingwe at the instruction of his chieftain. He went on to describe how he had been guided in the dark by the light of large fires on the horizon from the direction of the iron-producing area. The duo had reached the Munaka hill range from where the source of the flames became more apparent by the advantage of the higher ground. At this position, they began to encounter the first of the refugees from in and around the area. From amongst these people he was able to gather enough information to warrant him returning to Nyazimba to make the first report. His colleague had continued towards the stockade, at least another three hours' hard run beyond. Another young man they had come across, who knew the area well having grown up there, had accompanied the other scout onward.

Because of the story from the refugees the scout had encountered, the initial reports carried by the young boy were confirmed. It would appear that, as Gemba had suspected, a large group of Zulus had attacked the town in the early morning, slaughtering the inhabitants as they awoke to the panicked commotion and then killing the warriors in the village to the last man. Within the hour smaller bands of Zulus had begun to attack other kraals throughout the district. The result of this was the killing of the men folk, imprisonment of the women and children and the plundering of the homesteads before the dwellings were set on fire. After further questioning, it was surmised that the force that had attacked the area must number at least two or three impi, possibly three thousand warriors. Additional reports would have to be assessed to gain the true disposition of the enemy, as an enterprise of this nature would be expected to require a larger body of soldiers.

The King looked up from the map table upon which he had set his eyes during the report. "Zulus," he said in a dark tone. Lifting his eyes he continued, "It is just how you thought, Gemba. They must have managed an early crossing of the great river to be here at this time of the season."

At this statement a silence loomed over the room with each person present lost in his own thoughts. The messenger was dismissed. Turning to Kadenge, the King asked, "Where else have you sent your scouts?"

"We have sent three large groups, each consisting of three sections of two-man teams." Walking up to the map table he indicated, "Each duo will splinter away along their instructed trail to certain areas to determine the extent of the invasion. The first group was sent south-west towards the traditional crossing points of the great river." He placed markers as he spoke. "The second group, from which this messenger came, was sent due west and the last north-west with instruction to travel as far as the town of Naletale. They will travel as far as Fort Chimnungwa to alert the forces there and to summon them to our assistance." As he stepped back the terrain model was covered with a fanned array of indicators showing the extent of the scouting parties' destinations.

Zusa shuddered at the information. *If we are*

sending search parties as far as Naletale, then what about my father's homestead at Mafuri, he thought to himself.

Gemba cleared his throat and the King looked at him expectantly. "If it pleases you, sire? If this large body of Zulu have already travelled from the crossing places on the Limpopo River and managed to get as far as Belingwe without the standing regiment at Chimnungwa reacting or sending us a warning, then we have to assume that the garrison may have already fallen to the enemy!"

All of those around the table felt the impact of his comment. If this was true then it meant the Zulu had already taken control of a very large portion of the nation.

"Never! That is impossible!" exclaimed Kadenge in a loud voice. "There is no way the border regiment could have been defeated so easily and without me being made aware of it." He paused and thought a little to himself, his hand held to his head. "No, never!" he repeated as if to convince himself further.

"What is the status of the city's garrison?" the King asked in a steady tone.

Kadenge quickly brushed over his last comments, barrelled out his chest and replied, "I am pleased to tell you that at present we have eight regiments totalling just fewer than three thousand five hundred warriors in the city. We have another regiment in the south-east garrisoning the two towns of Majiri and Runyanhi guarding the trading route to the coast. Your brother, Zimu, has his own regiment with over one thousand warriors based at his kraal in the north."

Nodding his head in acceptance the King turned to look at Makonde, "What is the status of the training regiments?"

"I have almost two thousand in training; the newest conscripts, about one hundred of them, have only been here two weeks. We could concentrate defensive training during the next couple of days so that they could relieve the city guard if and when they may have to move out."

"The palace guard?" was the next obvious question.

Zabesi replied, "We are at full strength sir, one

hundred and thirty in the barracks. I have already sent out the recall to any of the men who are away from the city on leave. I expect all to be accounted for by this evening, so these numbers can be expected to increase."

There was another pause in conversation whilst Yasini thought to himself. "When do we expect the remainder of the scouts to report back?"

"We should get more solid information by tomorrow noon, from those sent to the closer sites, but it could be as much as six or seven days before all of the groups are back and we have a full picture of the situation."

"Right," the King said, reaching a decision, "we cannot be seen to be waiting for another week before we react." The group unanimously agreed. He pointed down at the relief map model, its three-dimensional representation of the kingdom showing the mountains, forests and rivers in detail. "I propose we consider despatching the standing army consisting of the eight regiments to Sampambi, just south of the inland road. Its position guards both passes of the Munaka range that can be used to approach the city from the west. From this position, we will be able to react to the movement of the Zulus once we have accurately established the position of their main army. Our forces will be enough to hold either or both of the passes if need be!"

"Yes, sire, it is an excellent plan," said Kadenge. "We will meet them on a ground of our choosing and destroy them to a man for daring to think about attacking your Majesty's domain. I was only thinking the same thing to myself."

"Should we be recalling the outpost regiments?" interrupted the King.

"No, no your Majesty, we have enough men available to deal with this intrusion. My men are well trained and can easily defeat these Zulu dogs."

Makonde and Zabesi exchanged uneasy looks, not wanting to express their concern at Kadenge's easy dismissal of the real threat as it would appear that these Zulu dogs had very sharp teeth.

"It may be wise, sire," Gemba spoke aloud ensuring the tone of his voice was one of respect and not

Map of area around Nyazimba

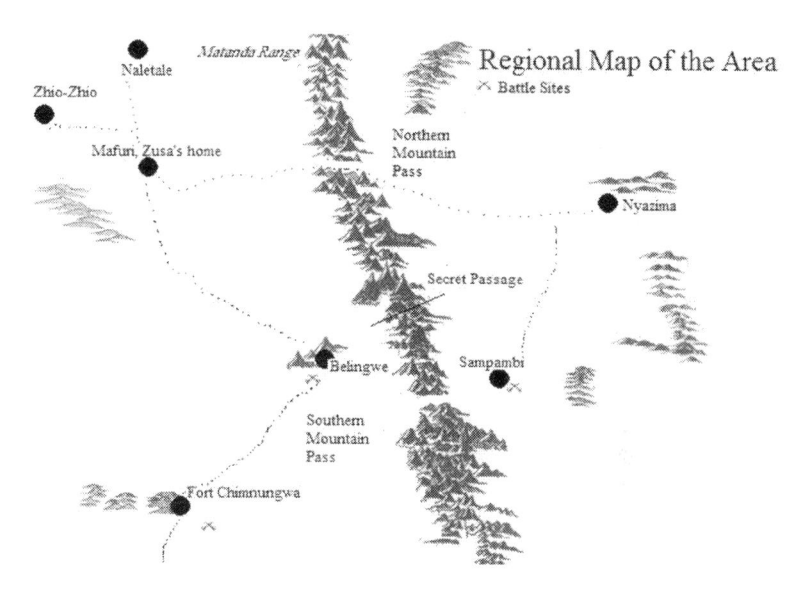

challenging to Kadenge, "to at least bring these extra forces into the city by way of a precaution. We still don't know what the full extent of the Zulu battle formation is at this time."

Kadenge rounded upon Zusa's mentor, a look of anger flashing across his face. "I believe that I am in a better position to be able to assess the ability of my own army and what our measured response should be, old man. Not you!"

"Enough," the King shouted, annoyed that Kadenge had let his emotions stifle constructive comments. "I suggest we despatch the army as agreed and await the remaining scouts before we finally agree how to commit our forces to a battle. Send for the eastern border regiments so that they are in the city as soon as possible and have my brother and his men meet our forces at Sampambi."

The King looked his army commander straight in the eye and said, "Ensure your chieftains fully understand the seriousness of the situation. They must take every precaution in the field and above all they are to remain vigilant. They are to establish the standard defensive formation for a field camp and then they are to await our further command. We will meet again this evening at sunset to discuss any updates. In the meantime we need to give our scouts the time to collect the intelligence we require!"

With this he turned and walked away from the group and disappeared down a corridor leading to the inner palace, his assistant running to keep up with him.

The room remained silent for a short time before Makonde spoke. "I propose we all," he emphasised the "all" whilst giving Kadenge a piercing look, "take the time to check the status of our own responsibilities so that we are able to speak with more informed confidence this evening in the King's presence."

The group broke up with each of the members leaving to attend to the numerous tasks the events of the day had forced on them, knowing time was not on their side.

Chapter Sixteen
A battle brews

The remainder of the night passed slowly but gradually, further information on the situation was made available by the return of more of the scouting parties. In addition, the steadily increasing number of refugees, displaced by the marauding Zulu, allowed for a considerable gain in intelligence. The capital's populace could not go back to sleep with the unknown threat still hanging over their heads and they watched the preparations of their nation getting ready to go to war.

By mid-morning, the eight standing regiments normally stationed in the city were assembled and they moved as quickly as their sections could to get out of the confines of the city. Thereafter the regiments moved purposefully eastwards with only two days' field rations and supplies carried on their backs. The logistics' support to sustain an army in the field would follow shortly but meanwhile the men would have to survive off the land by requisitioning additional food from kraals along the way. The men of the army moved with confidence but there was still the underlying fear of the unknown and many women and children accompanied their husbands or fathers to the outer boundaries of the city to where the fields had been newly planted with their crops. The army had fought and been victorious in a number of similar skirmishes over the last couple of years as the surrounding tribes and nations flexed their muscles in an attempt to expand their own domains. So it was with confidence that they left their families and headed towards the promise of a new battle.

The regiments walked in formation, four men abreast, the maximum the inland walkway could handle.

The dust from the passing of so many feet rose into

the still air marking their progress towards the far horizon. From outside the city it was easier to get an appreciation of the landscape around the city. High-rising hills and mountains surrounded the basin in which Nyazimba sat while the flatter valley floor suited their horticultural industry.

From the Zulus' reported position east of the Mtanda range and their city, the army commander knew that there were only two places where the enemy could freely pass as a cohesive formation. These were at Sese to the south and Kwana in the north, the passes only being a few hours' walk from each other.

This being the case, the Bantu army could be in a position by that evening to block either route the Zulus decided to use.

The army moved with determination knowing it was at least a full day's hard march to their staging position at Sampambi. From there they expected to hear from their high command on the updated position and battle order of the enemy and what would be expected of them. Numerous scouts were flung ahead of the march to ensure that the route of least resistance was used by the larger party of men behind them and to prevent any sudden surprise attack by Zulu skirmishers. High peaks and other hillocks were secured in advance in an attempt to prevent the expected corresponding Zulu scouts from using these sites to assess the response, size, strength and route of the Bantu army.

Once the army had moved away from the city their kin stood in silent groups watching until the last of the warriors was lost from sight and the dust disturbed by their passing was dissipated on the wind. Instead of returning to their normal daily rituals many just sat staring towards the horizon as if imagining the destination and the battle the army was rushing to.

The city became subdued and even the normally bustling water hole at the base of the hill was sparsely attended. For the rest of the day much of the common activity of the capital slowed down.

Building work on the valley complex had been halted

and the fields were left unattended with only the herds being led out to pastures close to the confines of Nyazimba.

At the end of the day the council of war gathered in the palace at the King's earlier instruction. However, Zusa did not accompany Gemba as he had decided to spend the time on his own, his concern for his family growing with each passing hour. He found himself drawn back to the place overlooking the city, atop the same inner wall on which Makonde had found him only two days earlier. He sat down looking eastwards in the direction where the army had long disappeared. *Two days*, he thought to himself and then said aloud, "So much has changed in two days." In fact his mind wandered back even further to the last couple of weeks, dwelling upon the leopard attack, his subsequent recovery, his summons to the city, receiving the King's honour and being able to see so much more than he thought possible. His thoughts again dashed back to think of his family at his father's kraal and wondered if the danger would spread as far north as that.

A soft footfall close by caused him to start and he looked around for its source. He sprang to his feet as Makonde's daughter, Shawana, walked towards him; he greeted her by name.

"Hello, Shawana," he stammered, and the first thing he could think of to say was, "what are you doing here?" as if it were she who was trespassing.

Smiling at the use of her name and the questioning of her presence in her own city, she replied, "I saw you from my father's kraal and I knew sekuru Gemba was with my father so I decided to come up here and sit with you!"

He realised that this was in fact the first time he had actually heard her speak a full sentence and he found her voice softly-toned with an underlying confidence. "Thank you, that is very kind of you," he said.

Shawana asked, "So what are you doing up here?"

Zusa paused for a few seconds measuring his reply. "I was just thinking about the events of the last couple of weeks. It has been such a hectic time for me. I have experienced and seen so much. Now we have this threat of the Zulus upon us." He paused. "I was just wondering about how quickly our fortunes change." He sat back down upon the wall, gazing eastwards again.

Shawana sat down next to him, sensing his feelings; she remained silent as if to share his thoughts.

The sun continued to settle upon the western horizon and the air cooled with its demise. For a while the fiery body balanced upon the ridge of the mountains, causing shadows to stretch out until they filled the lower valleys. Then with a final effort, almost with an audible sigh, it slipped below their formation leaving the world in a twilight, confused state as to whether it was day or night. The land darkened in the dusk, where colours lost their individual identity and became intermingled with one other. All this beauty was set against the blueness of the sky, lit up by the retreating sun. Within a few heartbeats the last of the bright sun faded and the horizon flared in golden shafts brushed with scarlet red, possibly an ominous sign of the blood that was about to be spilt.

Chapter Seventeen
In the war room

The war room was full and those in attendance were eagerly awaiting the King to return to take control of the gathering. Kadenge's scouts had continued to trickle in throughout the day and well into the evening, many being debriefed even before they had had a chance to quench their thirst. The majority of the reports were not favourable.

Without any pre-announcement the King and his immediate entourage swept into the chamber and dispensing with any prelude asked for an update of the situation. Kadenge reported on the new information he had received. Using the markers once again he indicated the confirmed positions of the Zulu forces along with the numbers which were thought to make up these formations. The largest concentration of attackers, at least three thousand Zulu, was still at Belingwe. Another large impi had left some time the day before and was last seen heading to the north. It was thought that this group was moving towards the key trading towns of Dhio-Dhio and Naletale. These indications were a further sign that the warring party was being meticulous in pillaging the towns and kraals further away from the kingdom's city. It was surmised that this was so that any response by the Bantu would be delayed due to the time it took for the news of the attacks to travel to the authorities.

The question was discussed by the group. "But if this was the case, then why has such a large portion of the army remained at Belingwe instead of accompanying the northern raiding party and adding their combined strength to it?"

This line of thought was argued over for a while. A

number of scenarios were discussed until the only reason that made sense was that the whole attack was more than just the annual raid expected from the south. The northern force had to be a diversion, a feint to lure the Bantu army away from the city leaving it unguarded! With this sudden revelation, the group took a collective gasp. If this was the case then their army, which had been despatched earlier on in the day, was heading into what could possibly become a pincer movement. The Zulus could now use both passes to cross the mountain range, to bring the Bantu army to battle. Even if the Bantu were able to take up a defended position within one of the two passes they could now expect to be attacked simultaneously from their front and rear.

Kadenge realised, with dread, that he had been totally out thought and that he had been fooled into wasting precious time waiting for additional information to reach the city before reacting. The news that had reached them was probably what the Zulu wanted them to know and if it were not for the young man's initial report it might have been many more days before they would have been made aware of the pending troubles. The army commander realised that the fate of the nation rested squarely on his shoulders and with that understanding he met the eyes of each of the other senior men present, their unspoken comments ringing loudly in his mind.

With a sense of sorrow Kadenge requested that he be excused from the meeting in an endeavour to get to where his army was before the Zulu managed to spring the expected trap and with the King's acknowledgement he left the room. The meeting continued and logistics and follow-up support were discussed in detail. Messengers were despatched to check on the progress of the eastern border guard regiments and to ensure that the King's brother had despatched his personal regiment stationed in the north and that it was on its way to support the impending battle.

All those present knew that time was going to be of the essence now for the assembly of these additional support troops. With a sense of dread, it was realised that the half-day's delay in making these requests had further compounded the seriousness of the situation. Eventually the meeting broke up. They planned to meet the following morning at sunrise for any further updates on the state of affairs. Gemba moved swiftly from the room in search of Zusa, knowing that he was going to have to be the bearer of bad tidings for the young man. The northern Zulu army was raiding villages, towns and kraals and Mafuri, his father's kraal, was right in its path.

He moved with purpose through the palace corridors, down the stage and across the auditorium towards where he had left his charge. As he approached the entrance to Makonde's kraal, he saw Zusa walking towards him accompanied by Shawana. Zusa saw him at the same time. Gemba's eyes and mouth were set in a grim expression and, without being told, Zusa knew the news was not good.

"What is it, sekuru? Is it the Zulu attack? Are my parents in danger?"

Nodding confirmation, Gemba explained the situation and that from the latest reports, Mafuri, his home, was in the direct path of the raiding Zulu.

"What can we do, Gemba?" Zusa asked his voice thick with emotion.

"The army has been despatched and there is no one else to send to the area as support. We will have to trust in Mware and that your father received some type of advance warning so that he could move the family away in time."

"I don't know, Uncle. I cannot just wait here to see what might happen. I am going home to see how my family are and, if need be, stand by them in this time of strife."

Gemba looked into the youngster's eyes and realised that nothing he could say was going to dissuade Zusa from going. It was the same determined look he had seen many times before when this young man set his mind to do something. "When do you expect to leave?"

"I will leave tonight as soon as it is possible. I intend to travel fast and light."

"But it is dark and it is not safe to travel."

"I cannot afford to waste even half a day. I will walk for a few hours before taking a rest so that I will be able to set off again refreshed at first light." He turned to go back to his sleeping hut to collect his meagre provisions when Shawana, who until now had remained silent, put a restraining hand on his forearm and said, "Zusa, I know I cannot make you change your mind as you must do what you believe in your heart is right, but please just take care of yourself."

Even through the tenseness of the situation Zusa smiled in thanks at her expressed concern, met her look, eye to eye, before he turned away, his stride full of purpose. As they paced their way back to their allotted hut, Gemba continued updating Zusa on what information he had and offered him advice for the return trip. He warned him to keep up his guard for the journey; he must continuously look for fresh spoor of passing bands of men while keeping an eye on the horizon or watching out for likely places of ambush.

"If in doubt, don't!" he stated. "I also suggest you do not use the Mushindi shelter that we used on our way here. It may already be in the hands of the Zulu. Give it a wide berth!" Agreeing with the advice, Zusa quickly gathered his possessions. Leaving his sleeping mat on the floor, he took his leopard skin trophy gifted by the King, walked up to his mentor and said, "Please can you keep this safe for me until I return!"

Realising the significance of the gesture Gemba looked hard into his eyes. In response he handed Zusa his walking stick which converted into a bow. "All right, but only if you take this with you in return. May it serve you well?" Taking this final gift in hand, Zusa turned away and made his way towards the water gate. Just as he was about to go through the gateway he heard someone calling his name. He turned to see Shawana rushing towards him; he thought he had seen the last of her up on the hill. Handing Zusa a small parcel, she said between gulps of breath, "I have packed some food for you so that you have something to eat while you are on the road. You may need it if you are going to travel quickly." Zusa realised that in his rush to get going he had forgotten the practicalities and preparations for travelling such as provisions. "Thank you,

Shawana!" he replied. "I had not even considered this." She smiled in response and blushed at his gratitude.

"Take care, Zusa, the countryside has become extremely dangerous since your arrival at the city," and with this, she stepped back so as not to hinder his journey. Zusa felt tears prick at the corners of his eyes because of the concern shown and turned to go through the city gate. Once through, he looked back and saw Shawana's slight figure, back-lit by the light of the city, standing forlorn on top of the wall watching him until the dark of the night hid him from her view. He knew she could no longer see him but the fact that she remained in position for a while later caused him to sense the seriousness of the situation and what he intended to do. He caught himself with this thought and said aloud into the night, "I have to get home. My family will need me."

It took quite a while before his eyes became fully accustomed to the surrounding darkness following the bright security fire towers of the city. Even after he had passed over the first rise on the main road Nyazimba remained a bright beacon behind him staining the gently gathering mist caused by the cloudless sky above him. The starlight of an African night was in full splendour. Even without a moon, the heavenly bodies cast enough light to show the wide inland path of pale sand through the gloom of night. Zusa's bravado was enough to keep him heading homeward and he settled into a measured pace. The recent sounds of the city were soon exchanged for the sounds of the wild with the gentle breeze rattling the numerous leaves and swishing the grass with its passing.

The incessant chirping of the night-time insects was all-encompassing. The insect noise ceased at times as he passed too close to one of their hiding places, marking his progress along the road, only to resume once he had safely moved on by. Zusa knew that the threat of meeting one of the big cats, lion or leopard, was remote since he was still close to the mass of humanity in the city. However hyenas, the environment's scavengers, were attracted to that which repelled the former and could be a concern. Snakes were his greatest threat as he chanced disturbing them while they were resting on the warm sand, absorbing the last of the day's heat from the soil. Most snakes, by nature, would move away as they heard someone approaching, but a sleeping reptile would not know you were there until you stepped on it. This is what makes the difference between a life and death situation. With his eyes roving ahead left and right, he continued into the night in his urgent quest to get home.

Zusa gauged that he had been on the road for half the night and he felt weary from the fast pace he kept up and the constant strain of trying to remain vigilant. He eventually came across a natural refuge where he felt he could rest in safety. It was a large elevated rock, slightly off the path, with another overhanging stone which afforded shelter from the elements whilst offering concealment from animals and humans.

Marking the position of the potential hide, he continued walking on the path for a while longer but as he moved forward, he began to purposely step onto the firmer patches of the road and the larger stones to reduce signs of his spoor. Once he thought he had left as little sign of his passing as possible he jumped off to the side of the path and made his way through the bush, back towards the rocky outcrop he had discovered.

He approached what was to be his hiding place for the remainder of the night with care, stopping and listening for any sounds which should not really be there. Checking the space carefully, he prodded the gaps with his walking staff for any unwanted bedfellows.

Not finding anything untoward, he squeezed himself into the space. After taking a deep drink of water from his flask, he covered himself with his cape, made a cushion for his head with his hands and, in no time, was fast asleep.

Chapter Eighteen
A foolish thing

The Bantu army awoke early although having arrived at the place known as Sampambi late the previous evening. The position they found themselves in was blanketed in mist, the result of cool air and the residual moisture still in the ground from the recent rains. The all-encompassing wall of grey limited the men's visibility to less than twenty paces and, at the edges of the camp, the trees and bushes all faded into the mist, lending a ghostly image to the scene. It's covering of moisture deadened sounds masking their source and direction. The air was still, which was why the white vapour had stayed in place for so long, however the sun managed to shine above the eastern horizon, like a silver disc in the enfolded landscape. The higher the sun climbed the more intense its light, reflecting its rays in the vapour and causing a white-out effect.

    The Bantu army's campsite, selected during the dark, was a short march from the base of the Mtanda range near the southern mountain pass whose rock formation had been visible even then in the near distance. The two sides of the breach through the natural obstacle, reaching into the night sky like jagged fangs, had been clear to see when they had arrived but now the persistent haze had obscured even these.

    Men spoke in low tones as the regiments readied themselves for the day ahead. They had camped on the eastern side of the pass surrounded by a light forest which had offered some overhead cover and whose openness at base level offered enough space for the sprawling encampment.

    The army had crossed a small river to get to this position and the flowing watercourse was now to their rear.

It had offered the men the chance to refill water flasks emptied during the hard march. Following normal practice and as soon as the camp was set up, skirmishers and watchmen were set up at about one hundred paces from their outer perimeter. These guards would be changed throughout the night at regular intervals to prevent the risk of the tired men falling asleep at their posts. The remainder of the army, comfortable and confident in their position on their home soil, lit camp fires to ward off the chilly evening and so that food could be prepared. These fires, left to die down during the remainder of the night, were revived with dry grass and twigs, the smoke causing a number of those around the fireplaces to cough as it swirled back into their faces as they blew the flames into revival.

A sudden commotion from the direction of the road they had travelled made those more inquisitive to enquire as to its source. From the grey curtain, Kadenge and his personal guard emerged and rushed into the camp making straight for the regimental chief who had already convened his command for their morning briefing. Kadenge's body was stained from travel, proving that he had been moving for most of the night. Despite the tiredness showing in his eyes he demanded an immediate update on the status of the army.

Briefly he was told of the uneventful day and early evening trek to this position and how it had been decided to camp away from the passes where the ground offered better defence.

"What about the regiments you sent to guard the passes? Have you heard from them this morning?" Kadenge enquired.

A look of nervousness crossed the senior induna's face. "You did not instruct us to precede as far as that, sir. Your instructions were for us to encamp at this point between the passes so as to be in a position to react if either of the passes were breached by the Zulu. We arrived and set up our normal defensive structure for the night."

Kadenge exclaimed in a loud voice, "So you have left the passes open and unguarded all night?"

"Yes sir, but we have had the standard perimeter

guards around the camp."

Kadenge threw his arms into the air and shouted a command. "Assemble the regiments immediately and have one of your lieutenants inspect the perimeter guard. I want us to be able to move away from this position as soon as we can." He turned back to the unfortunate chief. "Your camp fires have been like bright beacons, burning all night. Even we were able to see where you had camped from the road." He paused, as if by slowing down, the chief would understand what it was he was trying to say. "I am sure the Zulu are converging on us as we speak."

The senior man he was addressing opened his eyes in surprise, "But you told us that their forces were still some distance away and we would have time today to prepare," he said.

Kadenge lifted a hand to stall the protest. "Yes, I know what we told you but it may be that we were wrong. The Zulu have planned their attack well and although we are not completely aware of their activities, we feel that everything they had done up until now has led to where we are today and that they are going to attempt to entrap us here."

Messengers and lieutenants began running around the camp to attend to the newly-issued commands and as soon as the last of his orders was put into action, Kadenge took the time to rinse his mouth with water from a proffered cup. Looking around at the hectic activity, he noticed that some of the army's regiments were still partly hidden in the settled mist although he could just make out their hurried preparations. He ordered another chief to assemble the scouting parties so that he could direct them in their search for the Zulu position.

As he looked towards the western boundary of the camp Kadenge could just make out the ghostly shadows of what had to be his perimeter guard pulling back.

Sensing that something was out of place he looked again, soon realising that the lieutenant he had sent to recall the guards was actually preceding "his men". Other senior men notice Kadenge's shift in attention and also turned to see what had grabbed his attention. From within the mist, the man was running hard, his arms flailing in an attempt to gain as much pace as possible and he was shouting an indiscernible cry, which caused a number of the command group to lean forward in an attempt to make out what it was he was saying. Glancing beyond the sprinting man, Kadenge realised that "his men" were also rushing forward but unusually in an even and well formed line. They were hunched over, elongated shields pointing the way. Their attitude was of determined stealth. The lieutenant kept on running towards the chiefs position and finally, as he got within shouting range he called again in a voice full of panic, "Chenjeru, *beware* Zulu!" He dragged out the syllables of the last word. Kadenge's mind clicked, the shields were wrong; his men did not carry shields of an elongated design. "Zulus!" he shouted to relay the warning, "Zulus! We are being attacked! Men, form up into your battle lines." His warning cry was taken up by others and the alarm was raised. The warriors closest to the senior men were the first to reach and they too picked up the battle cry, shouting the warning and for their fellow men-in-arms to rally.

With a final rush the shadowy figures behind the running lieutenant burst from the mist bank, their ostrich-feather plumes and sheep-skin-covered lower legs defining their nationality and it did not take the sight of the short-shafted assegais and large shields to further announce the arrival of the Zulu. In a straight line over three hundred enemy soldiers burst from the clouded concealment conveniently offered by nature and they were immediately into the front lines of the newly-stirred Bantu. Many of the Nyazimbian warriors had not been able to retrieve their weapons or those who had were struggling to form into their regiments and they milled about, confused at the panicked shouts and commands.

The first of the Bantu to die were those closest to the mountain range and to the direction from which the surprise attack originated. Although many of these men were unarmed, they reacted to their martial training and in moments of sheer bravery, they fought with their bare hands, grabbing razor-sharp blades as they were swung about and stabbed. The sharp iron headed assegai cut fingers from hands and pierced bodies and limbs and the pre-determined outcome of the one-sided attack was not altered in any way by their selfless sacrifice. With their cries of pain and agony loud in the still air, all their bravery managed to do was to slightly slow down the attacking wave giving just enough time to allow those Bantus further into the camp to arm themselves properly. These men were able to gather into some semblance of a formation in order to be better prepared to meet the continuing assault. Kadenge's elite personal guard had reacted quicker than the other troops and, although they were tired from their full night's hard march, they immediately formed a solid cordon around their army chief.

  Shouted commands from the other regimental commanders caused the Bantu army to form their lines and as soon as an assembled formation was established, they were directed towards the developing melee. Stepping forward in a well ordered line, almost five hundred Bantu soldiers approached the contour of conflict. However, by the time they had advanced so as to relieve their comrades the Zulu had managed to wipe out the first line of Bantu warriors.

  The continuing Zulu attack, although it had lost some of its initial impetus, advanced towards this new force in a less regular line. The two sides met and their shields and weapons clattered loudly in the morning air, with shouts of defiance and cries of pain echoing across the plain. Without the advantage of surprise the smaller Zulu force's momentum became spent and sensing the increased resistance they began to fall back in good order, in a well-rehearsed fighting withdrawal. As they retreated they drew the Bantu soldiers back along with them into the further hidden reaches of the mist. With the withdrawal they left the bodies of over two hundred Nyazimbian soldiers lying on the ground. A few of the bodies moved in the agony of their grievous wounds whilst others twitched in the final throes of death. These gestures were unnerving in the jilted motions of their limbs. Their torsos had been ripped open and the salty, iron smell of fresh blood hung in the air mixing with the more repugnant odours of stomach cavities pierced by the broad blades of the assegais.

The initial opposition to the sudden Zulu attack had been pure reaction to the circumstances and no solid Bantu command structure was yet in place to control the first Bantu counter response. As if sensing this, the Zulu fighting force continued to retreat in good order. The Bantu formation in direct contact with the Zulu now became the attacking force; closely following their enemy which was disappearing into the haze and it was soon lost from sight and out of communication range with their commanders.

Only the harsh sounds of the confrontation indicated their steady progress away from the main Bantu force. Recovering from the suddenness of the attack Kadenge took immediate command and despatched runners to instruct the engaged Nyazimbian force to extricate itself from the attack and pull back to the camp. "This cursed mist," Kadenge said to himself. "It concealed their attack until the last minute. We didn't have a chance to see them approaching."

The sounds of battle rattled deep in the vapour-filled air. Shouts and screams could be heard as man fought man in its deep unfathomable recess. The clash of spears against shields echoed across the plain, steel on steel, wood on wood and then, for just a moment, the noise died. It was just for a split second and then the uproar continued but this time noticeably higher in intensity and as it reached a climax, the harsh sounds caused a flock of birds to arise in flight from their overnight roosting tree and take to the air, their squawk of alarm added to the din. The shouts of aggression peaked and then changed to the sounds of severe panic. Those still in the Bantu camp looked at one other in confusion at the change in tone of the battle, which continued for a few more minutes. Its source and direction was confused as the wind swirled and eddied about the plain and the echoes from the mountain range. For the first time that morning the breeze blew from the rear of the Bantu position reducing the volume of the confusing sounds of conflict, forcing the horrifying sounds towards their source. Then, as if a switch had been thrown by a giant's hand, the battle clamour stopped. There was not a sound to be head, yet the silence was deafening.

During the opening period of the battle sequence the remainder of the Bantu army had wisely used the time available to them and the commanders and chieftains had managed to form them into a resemblance of a standard battle order. It was hastily centred on Kadenge's position and that of his personal guard, the most experienced and battle hardened warriors in the army.

Many of the men gathered in the remaining regiments exchanged startled expressions as the silence from the battlefield dragged out and the senior men positioned in the ranks suppressed the few uneasy murmurs of discontent which arose. A few gusts of wind had managed to clear the mist away from the immediate vicinity of the Bantu camp and Kadenge was able to assess both his position and the disposition of the remainder of his army. With this knowledge, he realised that his force had been reduced by over seven hundred men, with the deaths from the initial surprise assault and the fact that their first attempted sortie had been suddenly cut off as if in mid-sentence. He knew that this was not a good omen; he had been on to many other battlefields to think it any different.

His remaining army was now made up from less than three thousand men. It was more than likely closer to two thousand eight hundred and so he had in effect lost one and half regiments, with not much to show in return other than a few Zulus whose bodies lay strewn amongst his own dead before him.

The Bantu army had arrayed itself into a formation with four of their regiments in the front rank and the remaining two and a half behind them as a reserve force. Both lines were orientated in the direction in which the Zulu raiding force and that of their counter-attack force had disappeared, their eventual destination still shrouded in a blanket of white about whose reflecting wall stood approximately fifty paces to the front of the Bantu lines.

As Kadenge looked more intensely the haze swirled in the strengthening breeze and, as if the Bantu army had exhaled its collective breath, the mist moved away from them for a few pace lengths and then, reversing its direction, it steadily advanced onto their position, its action almost mystical. The commands of "steady" and "Tighten up formation" steeled the ranks as the ghostly effect of the phenomenon rippled through the waiting army.

Two Nyazimbian warriors emerged from the white curtain of fog. They were weaponless and blood poured from numerous stab and slash wounds all over their bodies. They staggered on their feet, hands held outwards in supplication to their waiting comrades as if appealing for help. The murkiness slowed in its advance and then stopped for a few heart beat as if nature was holding it back. The breeze returned in a sudden exhalation and the white misty curtain was blown away to reveal the full Zulu army standing shield to shield on a higher position to that of the Bantu. Their formation had a large and deeply layered centre body with two horns curving to their front, left and right, known as the head of the bull.

The enemy were calmly set out before the Bantu and numbered in excess of four thousand men. Kadenge realised that his depleted forces were greatly outnumbered. His mind raced as he thought to himself, *the two Zulu forces which had been discussed at the palace yesterday, must have rejoined sometime during the night and moved through the unguarded passes early that morning.* A hiss of contempt escaped from his mouth and one of his men voiced his concern, "Now we weren't expecting that!" A few of his comrades chuckled at the over statement. His friend added, "Well if we were to move around a little we might have them surrounded." The responded laugh had Kadenge snap a command, "Silence!"

A low moan had arisen from the other Bantu ranks brought on by the proximity and suddenness of the appearance of the enemy. With their mode of concealment whipped away, the Zulu had no need to hold back any longer and they advanced at a sprint in a well-ordered, tight formation. They were solid in their arrangement as a result of their excellent training and co-ordination, which was moulded together by their strong discipline. This was further strengthened in the silent manner they advanced without the need of their commanders to call or redress its structure, only the sound of their pounding feet and the occasional rattle of assegai against shield revealed the true intent of the human wave. The attacker covered the short distance between the two groups very quickly, killing the two surviving Bantu soldiers as they were overtaken.

The Bantu front ranks wavered and their nervous commanders shouted encouragement to stand steady and confirming final instructions. Taken aback by the unexpected change in time-honoured tactics, even the Nyazimbian army commanders were startled at the surprise, advancing manoeuvre.

Traditionally the warring parties should have spent some time exchanging insults across the gap separating the two forces. A few brave souls would pluck up enough courage to hurl a couple of spears at the opposing side. Eventually the remainder of the two armies would become stirred into a final frenzy before throwing themselves at each other. However, in this case, like the waves of a large body of water tumbling loose stones on the shoreline, the Zulu broke upon the static line of the Nyazimbian army with a mighty roar.

The centre of the attacking force had a depth to it, six or eight men, and these reinforcements quickly and eagerly replaced any Zulu warrior who was killed or injured. The Bantu were not as fortunate. Their line was less dense and within a very short time, holes had been ripped open in their static defence.

Kadenge's personal guard of seasoned troops in the centre was the mainstay of the force and the pivot upon which the structure of the army held, as their strength and manpower was gradually whittled away.

The swiftness of the attack had meant that the Bantus' traditional opening volley of spears had not been delivered in a co-ordinated fashion. Individual warriors who had the experience to realise what was happening managed to throw a number of spears at the last moment. Some found their mark but with their foe now shield to shield, the advantage of the balanced throwing spear was lost and its long design and construction now hampered their users as the weapon could not be wielded easily in the tight throng of humanity in hand-to-hand combat. On the other side, the Zulus' shorter assegai was perfect for this type of battle and although it could still be thrown at short distances it was used with a more devastating effect if the warrior combined its action with the use of their elongated shields. Hooking the Bantus' shorter protection out of the way, it exposed their foe's underarm and chest, into which they plunged their large iron blades, deep into the living flesh. The razor edge easily pierced the bodies, inflicting the same terrible wounds seen earlier during the opening skirmish. On withdrawal, the suction of the blade made a slurping sound and the cry of, "Ngadhla, *I have eaten*," poured from the mouths of the victors whilst the agonising screams of the victims filled the air.

All along the Bantu front line, sections of the second rank and those reserves which had not had to step into the breach caused by the death of their fellow warriors, managed to release two additional volleys of spears, inflicting a few more casualties within the main body of the Zulu attackers. This did not affect the leading edge of the force which just continued in its close chest to-chest slaughter of the Bantu.

Kadenge's personal guard had also taken some casualties but it remained a coherent fighting force to be reckoned with. Their solid presence in the centre of the line managed to hold the Bantu army together.

As the Nyazimbian army fought to hold the defensive line the true purpose of the Zulus' unusual formation
became apparent. Their extended horns overlapped the Bantus' left and right flanks, enveloping the warriors with its extreme edges which curved around to catch the defenders to the rear. With this manoeuvre, the Bantus' brave but uncoordinated attempt to hold a protective line became all-out carnage.

The cohesion of Kadenge's force also disintegrated and the line-to-line battle broke into numerous melees with islands of unfortunate Bantus becoming surrounded by the Zulu. They were eventually killed where they stood – no quarter was asked for and no quarter was given.

The final act of the ill-fated battle was around the Bantu army commander's central position with his men forming a last protective circle around their charge. The locale around those still standing was littered with the dead and dying, the majority were Bantu but a good number of Zulu had fallen to Kadenge's sentinels.

As the battleground noise subsided, the surrounding forces around the last point of resistance paused in their quest and briefly pulled back in respite. For a moment, Kadenge thought his men had managed to push the enemy away but, during the lull; he was able to look beyond the immediate horizon of what had become his own little and insignificant world for the duration of the battle. Now he realised the extent of the situation. The Zulu army, although damaged to some extent, was largely intact and had simply gathered around this last position.

With a final thought of his family, wives, and children, their limited future and the shock at what this aggressive foe was capable of, he pushed himself between two of his men and took a position in the front row. He knew he had failed his King and his nation by underestimating the true threat of the invasion. Calling upon Mware, he gathered his men with a few shouted commands, for one final act of defiance. Once those around him were in place, taking a deep breath he filled his lungs and led with a song. It was not a song of sorrow.

It was a song of gladness, its words expressing the expectations of their nation in defending their realm and that the sacrifice that they were about to make was for the benefit of their homeland and city. Neither of which any of them would see again. The Zulu continued to close around the band as if listening to the chanted words:

> *"We are the rocks who stand through time,*
> *We are the foundations for all our kind.*
> *When you face us, we will not give in,*
> *We will fight you until the end. "*

With a final shout, the last of the Bantu warriors exploded in a sudden and unexpected charge towards the encompassing ring of Zulu, scattering themselves like an exploding seedpod of a Mopani tree and exposing themselves like this, they died individually, a warriors death, in a final and brave defiant attack.

With the last of the Bantu dead Modena walked amongst the fallen inspecting the battlefield which was littered with the slaughtered. His men were moving amongst the bodies despatching any Bantu who showed any sign of life, splitting the bellies of the corpses with their broad blades in honour of the brave men to release their spirits and not to leave them trapped in the bodies.

He could read the story of the battle, depicted by the lines and avenues formed by the dead and he could see where the fighting had been the fiercest. Continuing to the position where Kadenge had stood at his last post, Modena saw that even in their last charge the Bantu had killed and wounded another thirty-six of his own men.

However, the Zulu chief had good reason to be pleased with his men's performance. They had force-marched most of the previous night in reaction to the arrival of the Nyazimbian army at Sampambi, whose progress had been observed by their own scouts. The Zulu scouts had remained out of sight by retreating just in front of the Bantus' advancing skirmishers.

The last leg of the approach to the battle ground had been much simpler for the numerous Bantu camps' fires had guided them over the last few miles.

Despite this, tired as his men were, not long arrived from their long night's travel, they had performed admirably. The Zulu induna's gathered around him as he looked across the battleground. "They fought a little better than I expected; I must admit they died bravely" he said. The group agreed in unison. "What are our casualties?"

"We have four hundred and twenty-seven dead and one hundred and twelve seriously wounded. There are another three hundred and seventy-two walking wounded," a lieutenant reported.

"Do we have word on Digane's northern raiding

party?" he asked next. For once Modena had been informed of the approaching Bantu army, he had had no other option but to withhold the support troops which had been destined to follow Digane's forces and to lead them here. At the time the decision was based on the fact that the main Bantu army had committed itself to the field. Modena thought at the time that the impi chief would just have to manage with what men he had available to him.

The same lieutenant responded, "Only that they have progressed as planned and that they have managed to capture many women and children. There has not been co-ordinated Bantu resistance. Plunder and livestock from the area are already arriving"

Modena assimilated the information. His mind struggling with the decision to immediately marching upon the stone city of Nyazimba or sticking to the plan in raiding the surrounded villages before any more of the Bantu population escaped his net. He knew the city was vulnerable and defenceless with their main army dead at his feet. However, the city walls were still formidable in their defence and if he attacked now he would still lose a large number of his men, even to untrained defenders. He smiled to himself; even baboons can throws rocks from their outcrops he thought. It truly was a tempting prize. This scenario had been discussed prior to the invasion and it had been agreed, actually his King had ordered it, that he used this time to catch as many slaves and to capture as much plunder as possible.

Already, vast herds of cattle were being driven back towards the great river so that as soon as the furious waters subsided they could be taken across at the fords, which would be revealed by the lowering waters. The captured women and children were still being held inland. Unlike dumb animals, these people still needed a substantial force to guard them so that they would not be able to escape on the homeward march.

"So my chief," one of the elders spoke, "do we attack the city? It is only a hard day's march away." Many eyes searched their leader's face for the first sign of anger at the direct question.

Modena paused before responding. "No," he said, "we stick to the original plan. The fact that we have been able to deal with the main fighting force so early on in our campaign means that we will be able to roam the area at will. Let the last of the Bantu baboons stay behind their high walls. At least we know where to find them." He laughed at his own humour and he was joined by those around him. "We will pull back to Belingwe to regroup the men but we will leave large guard parties at both of the passes where they should be able to prevent anyone getting any more information back to Nyazimba. We will use the army to continue to raid the district and then wait for the full reunification of all of our forces before moving on to the last stage. Once we have fully assembled, we will march on the city and finish what we have begun."

As they left the killing fields the men of the victorious Zulu army did not look back. Their dead had been collected for the correct burial rites but the Bantu were left where they had fallen and in the brilliant blue sky above the fields of carnage the hungry vultures were already gathering.

Chapter Nineteen
The way home

The fingers of the morning sun gently brushed across Zusa's face and the changing light made him stir from his sleep as the golden glow stretched across his closed eyes. As he opened them the bright glare made him wince and for a while he was confused as to where he was. Then he remembered, the reported events of the previous day and his decision to travel home that night, and he became instantly awake taking in his surroundings. He had slept deeply and his legs were aching from lying in the same position all night. Edging out from under the overhanging rock shelter, he reached for the parcel of food Shawana had given him as he had left the city. He ate quickly, washing down the dried meat with a mouthful of water before stretching his muscles in anticipation of the day's travel ahead of him. From his elevated position, he noticed that he was closer to the Mtanda range's northern pass than he had realised which meant he had made good progress during the night. He strung the bow given to him by Gemba, as he knew he was entering what had possibly become enemy territory and there was no guarantee that the next person he met was going to be one of his kin.

With a final look to gather his bearings, Zusa made his way back to the inland road. Once on the well trodden path he noticed that the track was well imprinted with the passing of many bare feet. They were going in the same direction as he was and he correctly surmised that the tracks were from Kadenge and his entourage who had left the city just before he had on their way to join the main army formation. Zusa also knew that the tracks could be expected to branch off to the left and travel south for a few hours towards the southern pass at Sampambi.

With the rising sun behind him he began his arduous trip home with a slow walk gradually building up his pace until he was able to maintain a fast mile-consuming trot. He remembered Gemba's advice and continued to scan his immediate vicinity in addition to looking further afield for any other sign of danger.

He soon approached the mountain pass and all looked clear to him until abruptly two humanoid forms stepped into the path ahead of him, Zusa realised that he had already allowed his mind to wander for he had not seen or even heard the figures approaching. Reacting to the imminent danger he threw himself into the foliage to the left of the road in an attempt to conceal himself in the low bushes. He landed heavily on one side, his arms underneath him, winding himself in the fall. He paused to listen for any sounds of alarm or pursuit: There was nothing! The only sound he heard was the swish of the gentle breeze through the grass and the call of the wild birds. *You fool,* he thought to himself.

Taking the weapon Gemba had gifted him he swung the bow into a forward position and fitted an arrow so that it was ready for immediate use. It was difficult to move quietly with the weapon in his hands but as no one had shouted a challenge he edged his way back towards the pathway. Taking care, he crawled back towards the path so that he would be able to peer through the curtain of vegetation to see if he could identify who had stepped out in front of him onto the trail. He edged forward and using one hand he parted the last strands of grass between him and his target. There in front of him were the two figures. He laughed aloud, with relief. For in the middle of the path "guarding it" were two very large baboons, standing on their hind legs, looking around and appearing very humanoid. They were reaching up to pick fruit from a tree which overhung the road but at the sound of his anxious merriment the animals jumped into the cover of the bush with a loud bark, like that of a wild dog, and they quickly disappeared from sight.

Getting back to his feet, Zusa brushed the dust from his lower body and legs and carefully moved towards the place where he had last seen the baboons. They had not gone far, having followed their natural instinct in a moment of danger, to climb a tree where most of their natural predators, other than the leopard, would not be able to follow. As the animals saw Zusa pass by they ducked their heads pushing their lower jaws forward whilst opening their eyes wide and emitted a challenging stuttered bark. Zusa heeded the warning signs knowing well what a fully-grown baboon, standing eye to eye, could do to a person. Not only was the strength of their arms formidable but their savage fangs could easily tear flesh from bone.

Zusa's pace increased with the downward inclination of the road once he was through the mountain pass. Taking advantage of this as, in the distance, he could see the higher ground to which he needed to ascend where his father's kraal and his other kin's homesteads were situated. However, he still had a full day's hard walk ahead of him and he knew it would take a little longer than normal as he took his mentor's advice to take a route well clear of Mushindi, the stone-enclosed half-way house which was just on the other side of the mountain pass he had traversed. Once he cleared the last of the natural obstacles he cut a route north through the dense bush so that he would be able to rejoin the main road further inland.

****

From their position on the other side of the river and slightly higher above the battlefield, two men from Kadenge's ill-fated Bantu army had witnessed the final slaughter of their comrades, seeing their commander cut to the ground after the last desperate charge. Shame and guilt churned their stomachs as they had been unable to rejoin their regiment as the watercourse had been between their allotted guard post and where the main army had encamped. Realising that their forces had been resoundingly defeated they knew that they were the only eyewitnesses to the massacre and that it was their duty to get back to the city to inform the King of the disaster.

The older of the two spoke for the first time since the completion of the horrendous massacre.

"Chemwapuwa, my friend. This is truly tragic for our people. Our friends lay dead before us; it looks like we are the only survivors." His colleague nodded his head in agreement, his eyes watering at the humiliation. "You are right, Goredema! We had better let the King know what has happened here." Gathering what few possessions they had with them they slipped away, cutting the through the thick bush to find the main highway to the north.

****

Zusa spent the rest of the day concentrating on getting back to his father's homestead. As he travelled he noticed with concern the increasing number of pillars of smoke rising into the air from numerous positions in the direction he was travelling. Even as he looked another dark plume began to rise ominously into the clear sky, the smoke leaving a smudge across the landscape.

The hours quickly passed and for mile after mile he alternated between walking and trotting, his heart consumed with concern for his family's well-being. Just as the sun began to sink towards the horizon his apprehension spiraled as he came across the first of their neighbours' homesteads, destroyed by fire and laid to waste. He did not have to investigate any further as the stench of burnt flesh assailed his nostrils and finally, unable to contain his emotions any further, he broke into a run towards the place which he had known as home for all of his life.

His breath caught in his chest as he pumped his arms and legs, his gasps loud in his ears. Over the last rise in the ground he raced forward only to skid to a halt within a short distance.

The sight before him was what he had feared following the scenes he had witnessed along the road. His eyes saw but his mind did not want to accept what was before him. His father's kraal, his home, lay before him.

The six huts which had made up the farmstead were now just dark rings marked on the sandy terrain. They had been razed to the ground by fire, the mud and dagga walls cracked by the intense heat that had engulfed the structures. The wooden rafters were blackened and leaning like accusing fingers pointing to the sky. A light grey ash from the grass thatch lay deep in the destroyed buildings from which wisps of smoke were still escaping caused by the hot embers glowing in its depth, occasionally being fanned back in to life by the eddying winds. He could see that the wooden corral and fencing which had marked the immediate part of the living area had been broken in two sections where an entry had been forced.

After his fast march throughout the day he now walked slowly towards the smouldering ruins, his mind full of dread at what else he might discover. As he got closer to the main hut he could see two bodies within the ruins. The limbs of the burnt bodies were frozen in grotesque positions, their hands now claws grasping empty air. Even at this distance Zusa knew one of the corpses to be that of his father, identified by the intricate copper bands of rank and seniority upon his shriveled left upper arm and the other, from his size, had to be his brother, Chenzira.
Guilt racked his body and he sank to his knees in the dust knowing in his mind that he should have been here to stand by his family in defence of their home, instead of being in another place delighting in the glory of recognition. Shouting into the wild he screamed, "Why, Mware, why has this happened?" His only answer being the crackle from the burnt house. He lifted his eyes; hands raised beseechingly to the sky and shouted, "Father! I am sorry. I am so sorry that I was not here to stand with you and Chenzira. I have failed you when you needed me most." He slapped his hands into the ground in front of him, the pain it brought unnoticed in his sense of loss and failure.

Tears unashamedly stained his face at his sense of remorse and guilt. Pouring the soil of what had been his father's land over his head in mourning, he knelt in this position until the sun sank below the horizon plunging the landscape into dark shadows, and the land cooled.

It was the same darkness and chill that filled all of the corners of his heart.

****

The two survivors from the Zulu massacre arrived at the city well after dark that evening. The city's watch fires were a beacon for the last hour of their quest to return home. They emerged from the hostile and unlit landscape and stood below the main gate wavering on their tired legs as they hailed the guards on top of the wall. Those on duty summoned the lieutenant in charge of the post and once he arrived he demanded the identity of the strangers in the dark. "It is Chemwapuwa and Goredema of Kadenge's regiment. We have grave news which needs to be relayed to the King." Satisfied as to their identity, albeit curious as to what they had to say, the lieutenant assembled the gate guard before allowing the fort's entrance to be unlocked. The exhausted men walked through the corridor and collapsed into the arms of their comrades their tale of horror already spilling from their mouths.

Realising the importance and ramifications of the report the lieutenant instructed the two men to be silent until they were in a more secure location to impart their tidings. However even these few words of the defeat caused a ripple effect throughout the city and before the men were escorted to the palace, word of the ill-fated battle spread across the city like a wild-bush fire, burning out of control.

****

Zusa laid on the hard ground near the ruined homestead well into the night, the smoke from the burnt-out ruins playing over him adding its bitter sting to his already reddened eyes. The hut which contained the bodies of his father and brother emitted some warmth to the side of his body facing the building while the cool evening air chilled the opposite part of him. With his eyes closed he let the difference in temperature symbolise his inner turmoil. The heat was like the love his parents and family had offered him all of his life, while the chilling cold represented the sense of isolation he now felt and he was somewhere in between the two. A young man whose life had been shattered by the violent actions of others and he was all alone in the night. He did not want to do anything other than draw near to where his father had died, trying to draw a last message from the departed.

His exhaustion and the effect of the strong emotions caused him to fall into a light slumber. He drifted in and out of confusing dreams where the death of his father at the hands of the Zulu played repeatedly in his mind. He could see the figure of his father but no matter how fast he ran or how far he reached out his arms he was not able to get to him in time to change the outcome.

Eventually the dream changed and just at the point where his father was murdered, he turned as if to face where Zusa was observing the scene. He smiled and said, *"Zusa my son. You being here would have made no difference. Mware has greater things for you."* The picture in his mind faded and the last thing he heard from his father was, *"I love you, my son. Look after your mother."*

A repetitive scratching noise brought him out of his dream filled sleep and he lifted his head to locate the source of the sound. His voice croaked in the dark, "Father," he said, "is that you?" as he peered into the night. The deep red glow of the embers below its layer of ash affected his night vision and the burnt-out homestead became a lone island within an impenetrable sea of darkness.

The memory of what had happened flooded back to him but before his mind was seized by the dread, the strange sounds were repeated and he stared harder into the gloom in an attempt to identify the cause.

He sensed rather than saw a movement in the night and a pair of red eyes reflected the dying firelight, accompanied by a horrific low chuckle which caused the hairs on the back of Zusa's neck to rise in revolution.

Hyenas, *Bere*, the wild bush's undertakers, had gathered at the smell of death and corruption that had been spread on the wind. Although their presence appalled Zusa, he knew that he was in no immediate danger. The timid nature of the animal meant that he was safe from the beast until they had gathered enough courage caused by the inactivity of their prey or until abject hunger drove them forward. He picked up a rock and hurled it at the scavenger hitting the ground at its feet, and the beacon of its eyes disappeared as it loped off into the night.

Sitting up, Zusa knew he had to pull himself out of his misery and decide what he had to do. Although he had found the bodies of his father and brother, he realised that there was no sign of the rest of the family, his mother, sister and youngest brother. His mind replayed the dream and the last words from his father, *"I love you, my son. Look after your mother."* He straightened his back and thought to himself, *Look after your mother,* Father had said. He had not seen any more bodies. Maybe they had managed to escape and were hiding in the surrounding bush too afraid to come home. Maybe they were waiting until they knew the Zulu had gone for good. Rising to his feet, he cupped his hands and called out their names as loudly as he could, "Amai, mother, it is Zusa. I have come home. Where are you?" turning a little after each shout until he had completed a full circle. The only responses were those of the wild, underlaid by the snicker of the hyenas, which reminded him of their proximity. Other than that, his desperate calls into the night remained unanswered.

He knew he had to see the night through the best way he could and trust that the morning light would find him in a better place both physically and mentally. He walked to the damaged corral fence and pulled a number of broken stakes from the ground. He needed light and heat to ward off the scavengers and the crack of the breaking wood caused the marauding hyena to retreat a little more into the dark.

Zusa could not bring himself to heap the dry wood onto where his father and brother lay so instead he used one of the other huts whose walls had also crumbled. He threw the wood onto the hot ashes, added a few handfuls of dry grass and fanned the flames back into life and within a short time the wooden poles were well alight. The effect of the rekindled fire reflected onto the trees and bushes surrounding the kraal. He sat with his back against the wall of the hut where he had found his kin, to guard them from the prowling animals, watching the effect of the flames as dancing shadows. Finally, exhaustion overcame him and he fell into a restless sleep.

It was the increase in rancid stench that brought him out of his slumber. As he opened his eyes, he came face to face with one of the hyenas which had finally plucked up enough courage to step into the ring of firelight.

Unfortunately while he was asleep, the bonfire had diminished in its intensity, the closing darkness giving additional boldness to the animal. The beast's heavy head hung low between its shoulders and its large eyes looked straight into those of Zusa. Its ears, upright and rounded at their ends, swivelled at the confusion of sounds. Zusa shrugged forward, the sudden move causing the beast to lope backwards a few steps before it overcame its fright and stopped to look at Zusa over one shoulder. Its hind legs, now towards Zusa, curved downwards as if weakened, giving the appearance of a cowering creature but its large jaw and teeth were evidence of the real danger it represented.

Grabbing one of the glowing wooden poles from the fire Zusa jumped to his feet and waved the flaming branch above his head whilst shouting at the top of his voice, "Yah, yah, get away from here you carriers of witches. Get away from my family."

The animal once more skidded away out of the fire lit area only to turn back to face him again. Its eyes remained two spots of red in the dark, unblinking. Taking his bow Zusa quickly notched an arrow and sighted on the fiend. Holding his breath for a few seconds Zusa let loose with the projectile. He was rewarded with the thud of a strike and a painful howl. The animal retreated further into the darkness. Twice more during the night Zusa drifted into sleep and on both occasions a sixth sense caused him to awaken in time to tend the fire or to make enough noise to hold back the encroaching of the wild.

Eventually the false dawn announced itself on the

horizon and with it Zusa knew he had a number of unpleasant tasks ahead of him day.

Firstly, he had to bury his father and brother and even with the limited resources available he knew had to do this with as much honour and respect as possible as he did not know when or if he would return to perform the correct burial rituals. He also knew he had to inspect the ruins of his father's kraal so that he could piece together what had actually happened at the homestead and finally, he knew he had to find what had happened to the rest of his family!

Zusa began his search of the compound. Amongst the broken-down buildings, he discovered lengths of rope and two cured ox hides which had been overlooked by the raiding party. He decided to wrapped both of the burnt bodies in the skins and bind them with the leather thongs. The task was the most unpleasant thing he had ever done, made worse by the knowledge that they had once been his kin. The smell was the worst although the smearing of the skins even at the gentlest of touches made the bile rise in his throat.

Just as he finally secured his sibling's body, he tugged on one of the ties and cracked one of his brother's arms like a dry twig whose moisture had been removed by the hot sun. At the sights, sounds and smells Zusa stepped away a number of times to vomit the contents of his stomach, the vitriol tearing at his throat as it ripped its way out his mouth. He took the time to take a few deep breaths to regain control of his feelings and, after wiping his mouth with the back of his hand, he continued the grisly task.

Eventually, both his father and brother were secured within their ox-hide cocoons and they were ready for burial. Their bodies did not weigh as much as the living person had as the fire had consumed much of their flesh, and what was left had been burnt to charcoal. He carried them one at a time to a place around the back of the homestead where a rock outcrop with large boulders overlapping each other formed a cave. Once the bodies were placed as far back as he could manoeuver them into the recess, he sealed the entrance to the burial chamber with loose boulders and stones, placing them carefully so that wild animals would not be able to disturb their final resting place. Once he had completed his duty he took the time to invoke the memory of his father and brother. He spoke aloud, "Baba, *Father,* I ask that you find rest and peace in this place overlooking our home." His eyes shimmered with tears at the mention of his birthplace. Cuffing them aside he went on, "Thank you for your strength, love and guidance. I heard you last night. I promise you that I will find Amai, Mende and Rudo and I will bring them home." He gazed around the burial area nodding to himself at its position. "I do not understand why this had to happen but I do know is that I will avenge your deaths." His heart filled with the injustice of what had happened to his family.

With this, his mind turned from the thoughts of the dead to those of the living, to his mother and surviving siblings, and he knew that it was what his father expected of him.

He went back to the burnt-out homestead and cast around the immediate vicinity of the kraal looking for signs and clues. From the multiple spoors he was able to decipher what must have occurred as early on as yesterday afternoon, as the imprints had retained precise sharp edges, not smoothed off by the wind. Again his heart ached at the timing of it all: if only he had left Nyazimba a day earlier. It was clear that at least ten men had run onto the kraal, their footprints defined where the balls of their feet touched the ground with plumes of dust kicked backwards indicating the speed of their approach. The burning of other homesteads must have forewarned his father, for it appeared that they had managed to bar the wooden gate from the inside. This perimeter defence had been built to keep out four-legged beasts not humans and the attackers had quickly defeated the barrier. There were pools of bloodstained dust where Zusa imagined his father and brother had managed to kill or wound a couple of the attackers before they were overwhelmed by sheer numbers and succumbed to the attackers' blades. The places where they had fallen were stained with their blood, the drag marks of their heels led from these spots to what had become their funeral pyre upon which their bodies had been unceremoniously dumped. Zusa smoothed over these marks and covered the pools of blood with a thin layer of sand as if to erase what had happened to his family at this place. He caught the tears that welled at the corners of his eyes, whipping them away in annoyance. "Enough, Zusa," he shouted to himself, "you have a lot to do before you can afford yourself any more sorrow!"

A mass of footprints showed how the remainder of his family had been herded into the centre of the kraal before being led away to the south in a single file. They must have been tied together, pieces of frayed *tambo, rope,* had been thrown aside. *They were captives,* he thought to himself, *a small mercy but at least they were alive.* A surge of hope swept through him. "Mother", he said to himself, touching the ground where their footprints were with his fingertips," I am coming for you, Mother."

Exhausted by his forced march the day before and his restless night, Zusa knew he needed to get some sleep before backtracking to see where the Zulu had taken his family. He knew he would be of no value to his family if he was not able to keep up with the captives' group. He chose another small kopje not far from his home. It was a place insignificant enough not to warrant anyone having to explore or control its summit but he also knew it well and where all its hiding places were for as a child he had spent many days playing in and around the area.

Taking what few possessions he had, he made his way up the small hill to a rock cave, decorated by the wild San with multiple brown-coloured animals and stick men armed with bows and spears. Ignoring what had appealed to him as a youngster he managed to crawl into a narrow crevice and within moments of putting his head down he fell into a dreamless sleep.

Chapter 20
Panic

The King hurried into the war chamber as soon as he had been informed of the horrific news borne by the two warriors. Walking into the room he discovered that the city leaders had already assembled in expectation of the meeting. In front of the group of leaders, the two soldiers recited the events leading up to the rout and the ensuing defeat in battle. They managed to do this in the near perfect recollection of a society which had not yet developed the art of writing. Goredema gave the blow-by-blow account, from the sudden appearance of the opening attack, to the mystical manifestation of the Zulu main army from out of the mist. Although horrified at the ease of the defeat, the use of the new fighting tactics was of particular interest to Makonde and Gemba. When Goredema tired from the monologue Chemwapuwa took over the tale by describing Kadenge's last stand. The group of senior men began to understand the true horror of what could possibly lie before them. The Zulu were taking no prisoners; it was to be a fight to the end.

    The two men were eventually dismissed but it was decided to keep them within the boundaries of the palace so that they could be questioned for further details of the events if need be, but it was primarily an attempt to prevent the city from panicking at the news. This measure proved to be pointless, for soon after the two men had left, a royal court messenger arrived to inform the King that the populace of the city was gathering and that they were expecting him to make an appearance to calm their fears or at least quash the rumours of a great defeat. For a brief moment even this natural leader of people was lost for words. No other occurrence in his nation's history came close to what was unfolding before them. Yes, skirmishes had been fought and there had been defeats in the past but never had there been a complete slaughter of a regular standing army and so there was no precedence for such. All that he did know was that he had to act fast so that the situation did not get any further out of control. Already the noise from the streets and housing areas below was louder than normal.

The rumour of the conquered forces meant that almost every household would have been affected by at least one death, possibly more, and the mourning had already begun. Drums were sounding for the dead accompanied by the wailing and singing which formed part of the funeral ceremonies. With death existing so close to life, African nations had learnt to expel all their emotions at the funerals of their loved ones. With the harshness of life, the living had to be free of the burden of loss and guilt so that they could continue for the sake of those left behind. This was because much of their time was spent eking out an existence that there was not a lot of time left for luxuries, prolonged grieving being amongst them. Turning to the messenger the King responded, "Tell the people to gather at the place of meeting, Pamusangano, in two hours, and I will address them then!" The man left to ensure the instruction was carried out. "So what is the current situation and what are the suggestions for what we must do now?" the King asked those in the room, his voice echoing off the walls.

The group remained silent, with nothing to say, each man remained deep in reflection. It was not an occasion for short thinkers and quick speakers, but a time for consideration when there might well be no more chances after what was discussed today to get it right. It was clear that their first hurried action, the sending of the army, had greatly contributed to its defeat and the resulting fact was that their city now lay wide open and undefended to the enemy. As the next senior military man in line, most in the group looked at Makonde for some reaction. He was studying the relief map, his eyes moving quickly over the three-dimensional display.

He spoke in a low voice. "We know where the Zulus were yesterday morning and from the two survivors we know they headed west back through the southern mountain pass. What we need to do is to confirm this before we can finally agree on a second confrontation."

"Another confrontation, Makonde!" one of the others exclaimed. "We have lost our army! Who or what are we going to confront the Zulu with?"

Makonde pulled himself to his full height and stared down at the doubter. "After the last meeting with Kadenge just before he left for the ill-fated battle, Gemba and I performed a census of the city and surrounding towns so that we could assess what warriors we had left available to us." He looked into the eyes of each of those present receiving nods of encouragement to go on. "At present we have two regiments of experienced warriors, that is eight hundred men. These forces are primarily men from the city's perimeter guards and a good number of recently retired soldiers who can still be considered fit for action. In addition to this I have over one thousand two hundred trainees many of whom have just about completed their training in my camp. We have also received over four hundred and fifty volunteers, mainly older ex-soldiers either injured or retired. This brings the total figure of our forces to about two thousand six hundred men."

"You can add my palace guard to that, that's another one hundred and sixty seasoned troops," Zabesi added.

"Actually make that one hundred and sixty one including me," the King said.

"You, your Majesty!" his aide exclaimed. "You cannot expose yourself in battle. The risks are far too high!"

The King spun around to look at the last speaker and shouted. "Too high you say! What risk is too high? The risk the men in Kadenge's army put themselves in and died for!" He paused and took a deep breath, "Alternatively, is it the risk I ask other men to expose themselves to, simply because I say so? Do you really expect me to let them go in my place?" The aide cringed at the harshly delivered words. The King went on, "What good is it being a King of a nation if the nation no longer exists?"

He paused. "No, a nation is measured by its people. I will stand with my warriors even if means it is for the last time." The look on his face dared anyone else to challenge his decision. Realising the passion he had spoken with, he changed the tone of his voice and went on. "With that now clear, how do you suggest we now meet the Zulu?" The King directed his words at Makonde.

"Sire, there are two trains of thought. Ideally, if we decide to do nothing and wait here it would eventually draw the Zulu to the city where we can use the strength of the walls to our favour. We have even discussed a plan to let their regiments gain easy access to the lower part of the town. Once they are in the zones we have prepared for them, we will use the narrow corridors and high walls to split their forces and deal with them piecemeal instead of taking the Zulu on as a whole unit!"

"It carries its risks letting them in," the King said.

"Yes, but as I mentioned, if we were to manage their entry into the city it could work very well in our favour. We all know that a determined enemy, given time, could breach our walls. These walls have always been there as a means to slow an enemy down, not to stop them altogether. Rather we know when and where they are going to make the breach so that we remain in control."

"What is the alternative?"

"We take the battle to them," Gemba said, a serious look upon his face. Those around him returned a look of amazement at the suggestion. He continued, "Again at a place and time of our choosing now that we know of their new battlefield strategy." His comments were met with continued silence.

The King thought to himself for a while and then said, "Explain your idea."

The old man went on, "There is still no guarantee that the Zulu army will attack Nyazimba. If the city was their main objective they would have marched on it as soon as they had defeated Kadenge but they have not done this. I feel that their main purpose is to raid the districts far enough away from the capital so that any reaction by us would mean sending more scouts to find them and then having to manoeuver our forces to meet them. Kadenge's army must have seemed a gift laid out for them at Sampambi. Once in the open the Zulu tactics simply out-performed our own well known and advertised battle formations."

It was as if a light went on inside the King's head as Gemba's reasoning became clear to him. He finished the line of thought on Gemba's behalf. "Ah, this was so they can steal our cattle, women and children in safety, instead of blunting their fighting force against our high walls."

"Yes, sir. They know that after such a campaign, we would still remain wide open in the city to further attacks any time throughout the season, and at a time of their choosing they could return to pick up the pieces!"

****

Zusa had woken up a few hours earlier and had already taken up the spoor of the caravan of captives. Fortunately the group he was tracking could only travel as fast as its slowest walker and there were young children in the group. The Zulu captors were confident in their occupation of the high veldt as their raiding parties freely wander at will. He had to hide on two occasions as roaming war parties came close to his position, their presence fortunately being well announced by undisciplined chatter and singing.

At other times Zusa saw lone figures or small groups of two or three people moving as cautiously as he was and he assumed that they were other refugees from the sacked villages and kraals. Each time these people had been beyond verbal communication distance and he was too intent on following the tracks made by what was left of his captive family to attempt to take on any other responsibilities.

As the hours went by Zusa observed from the sign of converging tracks that three other groups of enslaved women and children had joined up with the group he was following. The spoors became congested and he was soon unable to distinguish one group from the other; the only common theme was the southerly procession it made. The individual spoor of his family members was long lost in the increasing throng of humanity.

Inevitably more Zulu warriors joined the main group, evident by the signs of the amassing footprints, possibly as additional guards, although Zusa doubted this. Instead it was possible that this was just for the convenience of the returning raiding parties to enjoy each other's company and for them to travel as a group. Zusa's earlier vision of bursting into a small group of Zulu warriors and rescuing his family slowly faded as the reality of the situation dawned upon him. Already he was outnumbered beyond imagination but maybe he could discover their final destination and lead a rescue party back to the place.

As far as he could tell the main Bantu army was only two or three hours away on the other side of the Mtanda range, whose high crest he could see in the near distance. The Zulu captors seemed to be following this ridge of high ground as a natural point of navigation.

By mid-afternoon, Zusa seemed to have gained on the enlarged group of captives. Eventually he almost stumbled on to the perimeter guards who had been set while the prisoners were being rested. Zusa decided to find a position which overlooked the incarcerated Bantu so instead of getting too close and risking discovery he used the mountain range to gain a height advantage so that he could look down on the gathering. Although the high ground was extremely rocky, it still had a lot of good cover with medium- sized trees and numerous bushes holding precariously on to the hillside. It was between these that he expected to be able to hide. To cross the mountain range anywhere other than the two passes seemed impossible for the summit of the mountain range had a ridge with a peak of sheer-faced cliffs, their tops flattened by a curious quirk of nature which made them unassailable. He carefully climbed onto a ledge on the mountainside. It was the one he had selected from below to give him the best view over the captives. He could see that the prisoners' position had been chosen and prepared with some care and it was ideal for the processing of so many detainees. He could see that food had been stored to feed the expected multitudes whilst a river offered plentiful water. The prisoners were already in the throes of despair, realising that their fate had been sealed. The majority of the captives sat dejected with their legs outstretched in front of them, with children resting their heads on their mothers' laps. Not many of them had the energy to move around but he soon picked out the familiar form of his mother and his heart soared at the discovery. She was sitting to one side with his sister's head on her lap and his brother Mende standing as if on guard at her right side. He smiled to himself at the sight; they were alive and looked reasonably well. The Zulu were keeping their captives in good condition and had not pushed them hard. Thinking to himself, he wondered why they were in no hurry or even concerned for the inevitable Bantu response from Kadenge's massed forces?

****

    Back in Nyazimba the place of meeting, known as Pamusangano, was actually part of a natural phenomenon, consisting of a naturally formed cave with incredible acoustic properties, which managed to amplify a speaker's voice considerably. It focused its sounds at a position in the valley below. The cave was accessible via the audience chamber and faced south towards the valley complex. The entire populace of the region, the hilltop fortress, the inhabitants from the newer valley town and those from surrounding kraals and villages, gathered at a point below in the valley where the audible effect was at its greatest.
    Although everyone had heard the rumours and with the city already in mourning, the crowd awaited their liege's address with an air of expectation and hope. Maybe what had been heard was not true, maybe the Zulu were not even in the Masvingo district and they had assorted conversations until the appointed hour.
    The long sounding of the Kudu horn trumpet announced the imminent arrival of the King and the throng of people rose to their feet with faces lifted to the cave

platform above them. They waited in silence. Instead of the pomp and ceremony normally reserved for a King's address, no aide pre-announced the arrival of Yasini and the first person the gathering saw was, in fact, his majesty. This break in protocol rippled throughout the people and the air of expectation and anxiety increased.

Lifting his hands he greeted the assembled people who called back their respectful response. "My people," the King went on, "today I stand before you with a heavy heart." With the opening statement the crowd's anticipation sank like a stone to the bottom of a well. "I am the harbinger of dire news." He lowered his arms and allowed his chin to settle upon his chest for a moment. Taking a deep breath, he looked forward again. "I know that you have already heard rumours that there has been a great battle between the Zulu and our own forces under the command of Kadenge. It is true and I can confirm that the outcome has not been favourable to us." A low moan escaped from the mass of people below, loud enough to be heard by the speaker on the platform and Yasini's stomach tightened at the audible sense of their feelings. "Our regiments were set upon by a large Zulu army yesterday morning on this side of the Mtanda range near the southern mountain pass at Sampambi. They were soundly defeated and so far we have only had two survivors return to the city."

The crowd's response was louder and wails of anguish, at the loss of family, rose above the din and clatter of conversation. The haunting funeral sounds, made by the women by rolling their tongues and making a high-pitched, drawn-out, "woo woo", and the painful cries of fatherless children, filled the air.

The King had to raise his voice over the din of the crowd. "I know this is a shock to all of us here and that our immediate future is unclear but we," he indicated a number of city officials who had filed onto the platform behind him, "are working on another strategy. I appeal for all of you to remain calm and for you to await further instruction on what we it is we want you to do over the next couple of hours and days." He stopped in his narrative as the crowd settled down to hear the next words. "I do not want panic or hysteria to reign across the city. We believe we have a number of workable options open to us even at this stage. In fact as I speak we are already gathering another military force to defend the city and we are making arrangements to move women and young children to the secret hiding places in the hills." He paused again but this time for effect and the sounds of the crowd faded. "Again, I ask you for your continued devotion to the kingdom and our society. We will not allow ourselves to simply disappear into the night as a mythical civilisation whose stone monuments are all that will mark our passing."

Gaining momentum he raised his arms to stress the point. "We have not survived for so long for such an end to our culture and for it to vanish without a trace. We have fought in the past, for the right to set down our roots in what has become our homeland and we have progressed well beyond that point which our ancestors established so long ago. We will offer righteous defence to what is ours to defend and I am calling upon all the people of the kingdom to stand as one in the face of this adversity."

During his speech the wailing and cries of pain gradually lessened as the impact of his words were felt throughout the gathering. They were listening and believing in their King's word and true to his calling Yasini had managed to evoke enough of his people's pride in order to unite them against a common enemy, the Zulu.

****

Back on the mountain range, Zusa had been able to observe enough from his vantage point and he now knew it was time to try to make contact with Gemba who could be expected to help arrange a rescue attempt for the Bantu captives below. Based on the slow progress of the incarcerated they would not have moved too far over the next couple of days so they should be easy to locate again. They were at least another fifteen or sixteen days' travel from the large boundary river in the south. This should give the Bantu army enough time to arrange to cut them off further down the path and well before they got to the southern border crossing places.

The hours he had spent on the side of the hill observing had left him thirsty and his water gourd only contained a couple of mouthfuls. From his position high on the mountain he could see the pass where he had encountered the baboons the previous day. He stepped around the rocks and boulders, taking care not to dislodge any stones, which could cascade down the slope to alert anyone to his presence. With his slow progress he was able to make out the peaks either side of the mountain pass, which rose to the left and right of him. He decided that it was now safe to climb down the slope to make use of the road which led through the gap.

Once he was down on the road, he realised that the immediate approach from the direction he was travelling was hidden from the view of anyone guarding the entrance especially with the increase in the number of Zulu who seemed free to roam across Bantu land. With caution, Zusa slowed down and left the road so that he could observe what might lie ahead from a position of concealment. The going was difficult, but as he broached the rise he was rewarded for his patience with the view of two fully armed Zulu warriors standing in the middle of the road.

Although attentive to their task they were relaxed in their stance. Fortunately they were looking away from his position and in the direction of where Zusa wanted to go. With a heavy heart he pulled back out of sight; his route home was blocked.

****

The mood within city was simmering like a boiling pot of water with only its lid keeping its contents in place. Feelings and dispositions were barely in check, whilst messengers and officials hurried about on endless errands on the instructions of the elders. They were organising the assembly of a second army while also arranging for the shoring-up of the city's defences and the evacuation of non-key inhabitants. If a siege was mounted against the city, and if the commanders of the new army decided to remain within the walls during this action, then they did not need the unnecessary burden of additional mouths to feed. The fighting men would also be in a better state of mind to fight knowing that their families were hidden safely, deep in the secret places in the mountains.

In the training ground outside Makonde's home a mix of older boys and men were going through their training regimes with a number of instructors shouting corrective commands to keep the warriors moving. Another group of senior men were observing certain individuals to rate their military prowess so that they could be graded into the hastily raised regiments. It was important that a number of full regiments were assembled purely from the more experienced warriors so that these could act as the cornerstone of the planned military manoeuvre with the balance of the warriors arrayed about this nucleus formation.

Prior to the women and children evacuating the city they had been directed to collect provisions from the surrounding countryside, along with any food which was ready for harvesting such as pumpkins and nuts which were brought into the city's storehouses. Livestock, other than those corralled for the garrison's consumption, had been driven away, well out of reach of the Zulu whilst water was collected and stored in the large city cisterns. Men collected rocks and small boulders from the hillsides, which were strewn with them, and these were stacked at strategic locations about the city walls to be used as missiles if the walls were stormed. Wood and dry grass was also piled up for use as illumination during a night attack.

****

Back behind cover, Zusa was thinking to himself. *"The Zulu commander must have set up a guard outpost at Mushindi",* the place where he and Gemba had spent the night on their travels to the city. This was evident from the smoke emitting from cooking fires within the confines of the wall. Zusa decided that he was not going to be able to afford the time in trying to get to Nyazimba through the other pass to the south and even then he would more than likely find it guarded as well. *"Maybe I could wait for nightfall,"* he thought to himself*," but that would mean wasting the rest of the day. No, time is not on my side."* He knew he had to get by these guards as soon as possible and then, with a final hard run, he should be at the city sometime in the early evening.

Realising that he was going to have to fight his way through, Zusa prepared the bow and arrows he had with him. He checked the tension of his weapon by pulling gently on the string before slowly letting it go back to its curved rest position, not allowing it to twang in case the noise attracted attention from the nearby guards. He only had eight arrows left in the quiver and he took the time to inspect them. Selecting what he thought to be the four truest examples, Zusa advanced to get as close to the guards as possible.

As he peered through the foliage he could see that the two guards he had observed earlier were still chatting easily to each other. The young man decided that the warrior facing him would be his first target as the other with his back to his position would lose precious time after his comrade had been hit to react to the situation. Zusa thought this should give him enough time to reload. He eased his back against a large rock. He had managed to close to within twenty paces of their position without discovery but the last gap was in the open and there was nothing else left to hide behind.

He quickly poked his head around the large boulder he had taken final refuge behind, his bow ready with an arrow notched. *"Good, the men were still in the same position,"* and he pulled back into cover. Taking a deep breath he began to draw on the bowstring, when he heard a third voice calling. Chancing another look at the guard's position showed that a third warrior had now joined the group. Now he was well outnumbered. *"There's nothing left for it"*, the young man thought. He edged around the rock and took aim at the newcomer, whose eyes widened as he saw Zusa emerge from hiding. The warrior opened his mouth to sound the alarm. With a snap Zusa let fly the first arrow which sang through the air catching the first target cleanly in the throat, silencing his attempted warning. Blood spurted from his open mouth, his eyes wide as he sank to his knees with both of his hands gripping the arrow shaft. The other guards were spellbound by the sudden closeness of death and they lost vital seconds looking around for its cause. By the time the men had recovered from the shock Zusa had managed to reload and loosen another arrow which found its mark in the upper torso of a second warrior. The dying Zulu managed to raise a strangled sob as the iron arrowhead found his heart. It ripped the muscle apart and he died on his feet, his body falling in a tangled mess half over that of the first casualty. A look of triumph etched itself onto Zusa's face at the death of the warriors from the nation responsible for the murder of his father and brother.

  The last guard turned towards the threat, his shield at the ready, which he used to deflect Zusa's third hurriedly dispatched projectile. Without any hesitation the assegai-armed man charged the young bowman's position only twenty paces away, a distance he covered in a just a few seconds. Zusa knew he could not afford to fight at close quarters; his bow against an assegai would be no match and so he stepped back out of sight of the charging warrior, behind the rock, dropping his bow as he went.

  Glancing at the discarded weapon the Zulu sensed an easy victory, as he thought the young man had panicked and run away. Rushing forward, he spun around the corner of the boulder only to find Zusa kneeling down; his knobkerrie held above his shoulder, his arm tensely loaded like a spring. As the Zulu reached his position, Zusa swung the club with all his strength at the exposed knee of the guard. It made solid contact which crushed the kneecap with a pop and in an instant rendered the fast moving warrior crippled. Even as the guard fell to the ground he tried to stab Zusa with his spear but missed. He landed heavily on his shield with a sharp clatter and shouting a panicked cry of alarm.

Quickly rising to his feet Zusa sidestepped the out thrust assegai, knocking it out of the way with one motion whilst with a fluid counter-action bringing his fighting stick back with a vicious swing to connect with the downed warrior's head. The man's skull split with the impact and his eyes immediately dimmed, as if a switch had been thrown, his body crumpling in an untidy heap.

Zusa stood above the dead man, panting hard, his chest heaving from the efforts of the last few minutes. His body was shining with sweat at the exertion and the stirred-up dust stuck to this moisture turning it in to a thin layer of mud, like dark patches of beige war paint. He held his position for a few seconds and listened carefully to see if the group had any other comrade's close by and if the scuffle and muted shouts had raised any suspicion. He was relieved to find that his attack on the outpost had gone unnoticed.

The big question for him right now was for how long and how much of a head start could he expect to gain before the dead soldiers were found and others were sent after him? If he hid the bodies he might be able to extend this period of discovery even if was only for a few precious minutes. Quickly making the decision he dragged the three corpses off the pathway and into the bush so that the thick vegetation would hide them.

It was hard work as the men were large. Once this was done Zusa went back over the ground and covered the dark puddles of blood with dirt and swept away the drag marks with a leafy branch broom. Not wanting to waste any more time he cast a final look over his handy work, satisfied that he done the best he could he collected his few possessions and stepped back onto the track home and began a fast trot toward Nyazimba.

Chapter Twenty-One
A new beginning

It was a new day, the third since the destruction of the Bantu army and Zabesi, the commander of the palace guard, had been put in charge of the newly assembled army. He was a tall and muscular man and his stature commanded respect. Before this promotion, he had controlled the King's personal guard after proving himself in a number of skirmishes with the tribes on their eastern border. The remaining Bantu troops accepted his appointment as a matter of course.

After the rigorous training the men had been receiving over the last two days, they were now allotted to specific regiments and as predicted, there were just over two thousand five hundred warriors who could be fielded. Their battle formation was now designed around an arrangement of three strong defensive lines instead of the traditional individual regiments. This had meant that they could use what little time they had left available to them working as a large core group. Training regiments and their individual manoeuvring was not something that could be accomplished over such a short period. The city guards retained their unique regimental status along with the palace guard who would be used as shock or support troops if the need arose.

Zabesi had wisely thought to gather as much information on the Zulus' latest disposition so a more informed position would enable him to choose under what circumstances and at what location they would next meet the enemy. With this in mind he dispatched twenty scouting parties to cover a wider swath of territory. This formation was in the shape of a crescent which stretched from below the southern and to beyond the northern mountain passes so that the outer tips would encompass the known Zulu positions. Reports already back indicated that although the main Zulu army was still on the far side of the mountain range, the enemy had full control of the routes through the natural stone barrier. Constant updates were being fed back to the city by runners at set stations which meant that any new situation report only took a few hours to get back to the city leaders.

Refugees from other inland villages and kraals continued reporting the events occurring throughout the the high veldt including the details of the Zulu raiding parties on Naletale, Dhio-Dhio and Khami, three of the kingdom's largest trading towns. Their own local chieftains, loyal to King Yasini, ran each of these towns. Unfortunately for the Bantu, these important sites had only token defences with few permanently based warriors and were, therefore, wide open to a surprise assault. The majority of these sprawling complexes were unfortified with wide-open decorative walls. These sites, deep within the kingdom, and far from many of the Bantu adversaries had in the past relied on this sheer distance as their first line of defence. The towns did have central refuges to which the Bantu populace could retreat, if given advance warning. These internal defensive structures were well-sited and anyone who had managed to make their way into the safe-keep could expect to survive as they could be defended quite well even against the most determined of attackers. The Zulu army would have been aware of this and their assault would have had to be swift to catch as many captives as they could before they managed to secure themselves in the fortifications.

Nyazimba continued to swarm with activity stimulated by the underlying apprehension of the unknown threat caused by the Zulu occupation of such a large portion of the Bantu Kingdom. However, for the first time in the last couple of days, the city council was seen to be acting proactively instead of being forced into a position of reacting to what the enemy seemed to be dictating.

The remainder of the city's population had been allotted duties and they had taken to their responsibilities with rugged fervour. As the key tasks were completed, such as the stocking of food and water, or wood and grass and weapons, they were then dispersed to their hiding places within the hills to join those who had gone ahead, leaving only the essential inhabitants and warriors in the city.

Just after sunrise, the war council was meeting for another of its now regular conferences when a messenger stepped into the room to inform Gemba that Zusa had just entered the city and was asking for him. With relief, Gemba asked the King if he could be excused for a short time, and he followed the aide to an antechamber where Zusa was waiting. As he stepped into the room, Gemba's greeting smile froze in place as he saw the expression on the face of his charge. He knew straight away that something was terribly wrong and quickly walked up to the youngster, gripping his shoulders, "What has happened, are you injured?" he asked

Zusa let his chin fall to his chest, tears welling in the corners of his eyes. In a low voice he recounted the events since his departure from the city three days ago. He choked through the description of the scene at his father's kraal and when he explained his discovery of his father's body along with that of his brother he had to take a number of deep breaths to get the whole story out. His tears freely ran down his cheeks at the recital, as the sights, sounds and smells came rushing back to him. Knowing that Zusa should be left to finish without any interruption Gemba began wondering at the fate of the rest of the family, Zusa's mother, sister and young brother. His concerns were soon answered when Zusa explained how he had managed to reconstruct the attack from the spoor left on the ground. He went on to say how he had managed to track the raiding party which had captured them back to the holding centre west of the mountain range. In conclusion, he quite casually explained the killing of the three Zulu guards with his bow and thereafter his uneventful return trip to the city. Looking up as he finished Zusa said, "We need to get the army to intercept the slave train as soon as possible, before it gets out of range! They are not too far away if we set off immediately." He paused for few seconds, thinking back to three days previously when Kadenge had left just before him to command the Bantu army in the field. This time it was the expression on Gemba's face which indicated that something else had happened while Zusa had been away. "What is it, uncle? Has something happened to Kadenge?"

Gemba took his turn in relating the events surrounding the defeat of Kadenge's army, and it was with a heavy heart that Zusa realised that the rescue column he had assumed would rush to the aid of his family no longer existed and his family was now truly on its own and at the mercy of the Zulu captors. The old man went on to inform Zusa of the King's address to the people and the decisions which had been made. A lot of what his uncle said made sense to Zusa explaining the activity of the community he had noticed as he had made his way through the city earlier. The settlement had been a lot quieter than normal which he had thought was possibly due to the reported attacks but instead he now saw it was due to the partial evacuation of the city.

"I know you have travelled far over these last few days and are still in pain with the loss of your family," Gemba said to him in a gentle voice, "but I am sure the King would be interested in your accounts of the Zulus' behaviour on the high lands."

Still stunned from the shocking news, as well as being extremely tired from his travels, Zusa followed the older man, in a daze. The war room had more people in it than the last time he had been there, but the King was at the head of the central relief map of the kingdom, upon which were a few new markers indicating the last reported positions of both Bantu and Zulu forces. The conversation was more controlled and exchanges were even debates with the King managing the discussions and the overall impression was one of consolidation, far from the panic and strain of only a few days ago.

Without any preamble, the King straightened up and greeted Zusa as he entered the room. "Ah, my young warrior returns."

Gemba spoke and related his conversation with Zusa and the situational map was updated with the information the young man had brought back. When the old man recounted the murder of Zusa's father and brother and the subsequent imprisonment of the remainder of his family, the King expressed his condolences and regret but added, putting his hand on Zusa shoulder in sympathy, "We will do our best to get our people back, including your kin, once we have dealt with the more immediate danger, their main army."

Noting the Kings words, Zusa asked, "So we have a plan to confront the Zulu again?" as he regained a little hope in what had appeared to be a desperate situation.

"Yes, we have a number of options but what we have finally chosen to do is based on what the Zulu do next!" He walked over to the map pulling Zusa with him, those around the table opening up a gap for them to get closer. "We have managed to assemble a second army and although it is not as well trained and equipped as Kadenge's forces were, we trust we will have enough men available to perform the task in hand, provided they are used wisely and to attack a portion of their army at a time. We could wait within the walls for the inevitable attack and this, we feel, is what the Zulu command expect us to do. However, this would be of their timing and on their terms and would allow them to amass all the military they have available for such an endeavour. We know they have split their forces and sent large bodies of men to attack a number of our towns and cities but their main force of less than two thousand six hundred warriors is still based at Belingwe. They have almost a thousand men in the field and out of direct communication right now, so if we time it right, we will be able to engage their main force as it is, under strength. We are just waiting on the latest reports before we make a final decision."

Zusa grasped the situation but now it was his turn to answer a few questions put to him by those in the meeting!

The gathering was overawed at the description of Zusa's use of the bow and arrow to defeat the Zulu guards who had been in his way at the pass through the mountains. The bow and arrow had never been used for an offensive weapon, even in a defensive action. Its uses were for hunting, as traditions of war had been maintained until now, and the hand-to-hand fighting with spear and shield had always been the custom.

The Zulus had opened their enemies' eyes to the realisation that times were changing and so the old tactics would also have to change. The fact that a young man had killed three warriors with considerable ease using his bow meant that its effective use should not be overlooked and its inclusion as a weapon should be seriously considered for future battles. The traditionalists amongst the group still advocated the pure use of the spear and shield and what the strength of a solid wall of trained warriors could be expected to achieve.

"Yes, this is true and undeniable," Gemba replied, "but the Zulus have moved their battle sequences beyond this. They simply wait until we have spent our throwing spears before closing on an effectively unarmed opposition. Their shorter spears are more suited to close combat."

One of the newly-appointed lieutenants responded, "A warrior can close the distance of a bow shot very quickly and once an arrow has been fired, the bowman is also defenceless. Even if the bowman manages to reload he may get off another shot before he is forced to defend his position or to run away."

Yasini and Zabesi listened to the exchange, both observing the different factions and their arguments, letting the discussion govern itself as a way to enable the expanded thinking of the group.

"What about accuracy?" another said. "Zusa seems to have a natural skill but it takes a long time, possibly months of practice to be able to hit whatever you are aiming at. We do not have the luxury of time to train more bowmen." There was a moment of silence as this point was considered. What was the point of discussing an option that was not immediately available to them?

Zusa interrupted and spoke in a clear voice. "Yes, it would take time to train true bowmen to hunt single beasts or men but even if a group of children fired their arrows collectively at an elephant enough would hit it to cause it some damage."

"Yes, but I wouldn't want to be staying around to receive its attention afterwards," someone said. Easy laughter echoed in response throughout the hall.

Zusa also smiled, his eyes alight. "Yes that is true, but we are not trying to hit just one animal or one man are we? The true effectiveness of our arrows would be if they are fired in large volleys in the direction of the enemy. It would mean that the enemy would have to slow down to defend themselves, possibly holding their shields high, leaving their front undefended to a line of spear men."

The men around could see he was thinking this through as he was speaking. For a moment he stuttered his opening sentence. Then something new appealed to him and he went on in a stronger voice.

"I suggest we look at fielding our normal regiments but use bowmen to add their weight to the defence by firing from behind or to the side of our own regular troops." This time the stillness was one of stunned silence as everyone in the room grasped the importance and significance of the statement. All at once they spoke aloud, each one now perceiving himself a professional in the newly-proposed tactics which had just been suggested. Ideas on other applications abounded until the King called the meeting to order.

Raising his hand above his head, he turned to Zusa and Gemba. "If we are to consider this option, how many bows are there available for us to use? How long would it take to train warriors in their basic use?"

Gemba responded, "Sire, there would be a hunter's bow in most households but additional instruments could be made reasonably quickly from resources around the city. If you were to direct the weaponsmiths to fashion iron-head arrows we could easily arm enough warriors to become an effective force within a few days."

At the mention of the word "warriors", the stillness in the room returned as the realisation hit them. They were already undermanned and there were not enough men to redirect into this force; it would leave their front lines severely weakened.

Zabesi voiced the unspoken thoughts, "We cannot relieve the main force of any of the spear men to train them as bowmen. We are as far stretched as we can be already. It's simply not possible to divert any of the men, no matter the promising potential of such a tactic. Don't forget it is still, as of now, an unproven gambit."

Zusa spoke again, his voice gaining in confidence, "You are right, we cannot afford to reallocate men, but we can use boys. You do not have to be a grown man to use a bow and we have many boys too young to stand in the battle lines but still old enough and eager to use the new weapon. Don't forget all of these boys will have used a small bow at some stage during their years of growing up, even if it was just in a game." At that point, he remembered seeing a boy bring down a wood pigeon on the day he had first arrived at the city.

The room again erupted at Zusa's words; Gemba reached over and tousled Zusa's head in congratulation. Zabesi called everyone back to order and began issuing instructions to messengers and his lieutenants. Firstly, all boys aged fourteen and above were to gather in the King's auditorium at midday. Secondly, he sent for the master weaponsmiths to measure their ability to meet the expected demand for projectiles and additional bows.

Lastly, he turned to Gemba. "With these new options open to us and the prospect that we may now have the difference required to meet the Zulu in the field on an almost even footing, I would like you to take over the defensive preparations of the city including the planning of a final evacuation as the last resort."

The King added, "Yes my friend, I will leave the royal family in your care, safe in the fortress, but if the worst happens, I expect you to get them away to safety so that the family may continue to govern once the Zulu have moved on." He paused in thought, "If we are defeated, their survival will be enough to resurrect the nation but it is all we can do or expect at this time." He turned to the gathering and asked, "Has my brother sent word as to when he and his regiment expects to arrive?" Everyone shook their heads from side to side. Exasperated he looked away from the group, worried his face would reveal his feelings, *"Where was he?"* the king thought to himself. *"I know we have had our differences but to hold his resources back in a time like this is paramount to treachery."* Unable to express his concerns he turned back to the meeting.

Zabesi turned to Zusa. "You, young man, have proven yourself to be of outstanding bravery. In the face of multiple dangers you have shown that you are able to continue to think at a strategic level." He paused in his delivery. "I appoint you as chief of the proposed bowmen regiments. You will be responsible for the selection, training and arming of the new formation and in your honour they will be known as the Mbada, *the leopard* regiment." He took his copper band of rank from his arm and fitted it to Zusa who remained shocked and silent at the turn of events. The rest of the group acknowledged the official recognition, clapped their hands together and shouted, "Mbada, Mbada."

The King stepped up to the table. "I am pleased with what we have achieved today. You all have your new assignments and duties and I want you to get on with it immediately, the lack of time is going to be our biggest enemy. I will address the gathering of the boys this afternoon with Zusa and use the meeting to inform them of our intensions and his appointment as their leader."

The meeting broke up with the senior men leaving to attend to their allocated tasks.

Zusa spent the next few hours making additional plans and arrangements whilst wrestling with his inner turmoil. He soon realised the enormous extent of his new responsibilities. They were the direct result of the few words he had uttered earlier, and he understood that stating your opinions was definitely a lot easier than putting them into action. It was to be his final decision which of the young boys would venture forth into battle, bringing with it the possibility of their deaths. It was his responsibility to teach and train these boys, in the short time given, in the use of the weapon and the tactics they were to employ in the field. And finally, it was his responsibility to lead the regiment, his regiment the Mbada, the leopards, into battle.

His mind was brought back to the present with the announcement of the arrival of the weapon smiths. Each of the masters was adorned with his trappings of rank, prestige and honour. They carried themselves with a dignity which expressed their age and knowledge; none were without the signs of time-honoured silver-streaked hair, a sure sign of their wisdom. One or two of the men were so well blessed with silver grey hair that their heads almost glowed.

They shuffled into the room, knowing that their summons was linked to the current events. They had as a community, elected to remain at their stations within the city, producing replacement weapons as fast as they were able with the combined efforts of their younger apprentices. The fire of their forges glowed all through the night, staining the dark sky, while throughout the day the smoke from the processing announced the ongoing increased activities. They had taken over the gold furnaces to increase the production of iron, as its dull properties had become more precious than the yellow metal. The gold-metalworkers became willing semi-skilled assistants in the iron workings, recognising that their contribution and skill from working with molten metal was immeasurable at this time. The art of combining simbi, in the correct proportions of ingredients, was critical to the result. The accurate temperature of the furnaces was also a significant part of this art, along with the number of times the glowing metal was heated, folded and reheated to ensure the resulting tool was correctly formed whether it be spear blade, knife or axe head.

The visiting group consisted of seven men and once they had assembled they were led further, accompanied by Gemba and Zusa, into one of the palace's inner chambers. In recognition of their seniority, carved wooden stools with high backrests were placed in a semi-circle in front of the King's throne. Not much had been said until this stage but as the King stepped into the room with Zabesi at his side, the madala's, *old men*, gave their greeting of respect to their monarch, bowing their heads in reverence.

Acknowledging their status within the community the King asked for the group to be seated, an honour in the presence of the nation's leader. The weapon smiths' appointed representative voiced their combined appreciation at the mutual respect shown and even though the seriousness of situation was pressing, pleasantries were exchanged. Polite coughs were made whilst the gentle clapping of cupped hands, giving a pleasant popping sound, expressed their loyalty and commitment.

Once these ceremonies were exhausted, the King began the meeting by recounting in a measured tone the events of the last few days, many of the details already well known to the gathering. Yasini took the time to explain how serious the situation was, including the city's increased preparations and counter-actions for dealing with the enemy. This last part included Gemba's appointment as protector of the city in the King's absence, and this was well received by the elders gathered. The King concluded with the proposal and suggestions of Zusa and the plans they now had to assemble and equip a regiment of bowman. At the mention of this, Zusa moved forward from the back of the room where he had earlier taken an unobtrusive position, his head bowed in respect to the company, to sit on his haunches to the left side of the King's throne, clapping his hands in greeting.

The senior weapon smith said, "Arise, master Zusa, and take a seat," while he indicated a spare stool, "for amongst men we must speak as equals and your favour with the King stands you in high regard with ourselves. Explain what it is you wish of us."

For the next few minutes, Zusa explained the concept and what he had envisioned for the design of the weapon. He explained how existing bows were being sought throughout the city as they spoke and any found were being sent to the main armoury to be inspected for their suitability. The main issue with this would be their pulling strength, which would have to be matched to the bowman, or in this case the "bow-boys"; they smiled at his comment. Sinew bowstrings would be the only consumable required and extra strings would need to be issued to the regiment before they entered the field of combat. "It is the design of the arrows which will require your expert attention," he said. The group looked on patiently, waiting for him to continue. "In the past we have used large arrowheads which were sufficient in bringing down most game. What I am looking for is a modification to the hunting arrow. We will require this new arrowhead to be just as heavy but with a longer, narrow point." He scraped the design onto the ground in front of the men and they all looked over to see what was required. "I want to be able to puncture the Zulus' shields, deep enough to damage their arm! Barbs should also serrate the edges so that they cannot be pulled out too easily. Enough of these stuck into a shield would make it very difficult for the holder to use and they may be forced to discard it."

Three initial design options were discussed in depth before the group agreed on the final specifications along with the suggested manufacturing procedure. The final solution was based primarily on the concepts which made it possible to build such devices in large enough quantities, meeting the time constraints for the short-term demand.

Satisfied, the meeting broke up with the weapon smiths' commitment to begin the manufacturing of the prototype samples straight away so that the mass production of the final design could commence once it had been finally tested and approved. They did mention that this would mean diverting scarce raw materials originally destined for spear manufacturing to this new venture.
This was debated and finally accepted as part of the course to war.

Zusa and Gemba left the room at the same time to attend the next meeting with a collection of men and women who had been conscripted for the construction of the arrows. These tasks included the collection of reed shafts from the riverbanks, attachment of the manufactured iron head and the fletching of the shaft with goose feathers, which affected the flight and accuracy of the projectile. The group was made up of forty people and would remain under the supervision of one of the weaponsmiths. Although it was intended to fire the projectiles en masse, the importance of regular construction was stressed, as this would affect its performance and the user's ability to control his action including the drawing and releasing of the arrow. The only outstanding issue was to agree on the final length of the arrow shaft, which could only be determined once the prototype arrowheads had been manufactured, sometime later on in the day; in the meantime, the collection of the raw materials would go ahead.

Taking a short break at the end of this meeting, Gemba and Zusa took the time to discuss the situation to see if they had forgotten anything. It was agreed that they had covered most eventualities and all that was left to do was to find the bearers of the arms and that responsibility rested with Zusa, for Gemba had a lot to do in his own role as city protector and it was time he attended to his own errands. "I will see you later on in the day," Gemba said.

"That's alright uncle, see you later on." As Zusa walked away, he saw Shawana moving with haste towards him. The last time he had seen her was three nights ago just before he left to find his family and she looked as beautiful as he remembered. Maybe it was because he had spoken to her a couple of times that he found he was not as self-conscious in her presence.

"Zusa," she called, "I am so pleased that you are back. My father sent word of your arrival and I wanted to speak to you before I left."

"You are leaving? Where are you going? Why?"

Then he remembered Gemba's task for evacuating the city of non-core personnel and dependents and he knew that Makonde would also be sending his family to safety. Before she answered, he cut in, "Sorry, what a stupid question, I do know where and why. I have just left a meeting where it was being discussed!"

She looked into his eyes. "I just wanted to say how sorry I was to hear of your father and brother!" Her eyes glistened as she blinked away the forming tears. Zusa's mind had been preoccupied until that stage and his emotions flooded back as he watched her control her feelings and to save her from embarrassment he looked away. A hard lump rose in his throat.

She went on in a gentler voice, "Our family has packed all of our essential belongings, as we are only being allowed to take what we can carry. Valuable possessions which cannot be ported are being sealed in the secret caverns and caves of the dead below the city."

Nyazimba practised a method of caring for their dead and the majority of the deceased were respectfully placed in an ancient cavern whose unique drying properties were such that it preserved the forms of those who had died. Even those, entombed generations before, were still intact and recognisable, although fragile to the touch. The entrance to this cavern was a secret closely guarded by the royal priests but it was rumoured to be accessible from within the fort, somewhere within the palace walls.

"When are you leaving?" he asked her.

"Right away," she replied. "I am told our destination is almost two days away. Are you coming with us?"

Zusa flushed at the direct request but also at the fact that due to his age, and in normal circumstances, he should have been evacuated along with those preparing to leave. "No, I am not going with you." He took a deep breath. "I have been appointed by the King to establish a new fighting force, the Mbada. I am to form a regiment of bowmen to travel with the main army!"

This concept was difficult for Shawana to understand, "But we have never used bowmen before," she said.

Zusa smiled. "Yes, we know. Your father has given me considerable support with the council. After what happened to my family, I cannot just sit by and await the outcome of the conflict as a spectator. I am now part of it no matter what happens." He went on to explain how he had managed to track his mother, brother and sister in the captivity of the Zulu slave camp. "My father is dead and so it is left to me to do what I must to rescue them. If that means I have to go with the army for me to perform my duty then that is what I choose to do."

Shawana reached into a side pouch and took something from within. Opening her hand, she showed Zusa a carved ivory pendant of a leopard's head, its mouth wide open in a snarl. It was attached to a thin leather thong. She reached up and placed the ornament around Zusa's neck, tying it in place with her nimble fingers. As she stood on her toes to do this her face got very close to Zusa's and they flushed at the near contact. Once she had tied the ornament, they stood there face to face, looking deep into each other's eyes.

"Take this please," she said, "Take it with my heart." And without another word, she twirled on her feet and walked quickly away so that he could not see the tears returning to moisten the edges of her eyes. Zusa touched the carving, which was warm from the contact of her body but as she disappeared from view, the heat in the ornament also dissipated and faded until he had neither of them. All he had in his mind was the look on her face as she said goodbye. Leaving him feeling lonely, but he knew that the thought of her parting words would be enough to bring him back.

Chapter Twenty-Two
Dhio-Dhio

Digane was disappointed; he had originally expected to have been returning by now to have joined up with the main Zulu army in jubilation, with his brethren at Belingwe shouting his praise and honour. Instead, he was walking at a pace equal to that of the captives, raked from the countryside by his depleted raiding party. He lamented Modena's decision to keep behind, as his supporting forces, the other half of Digane's impi. Instead of sending them as planned, to strengthen the last part of his campaign, attacking the Bantu trading cities of Dhio-Dhio and Naletale. He had begun his march northwards with three hundred men and now, with the casualties, that number was down to less than two hundred warriors.

The aggressive move by the Bantu army out of their city so early in the campaign had almost caught the Zulu unprepared and too spread out across the district. However, a sharp-eyed scout had detected the movement of the force as it left the city along the northern road and it had been enough for the main army to reform and respond. His raids had also cost him far more men than they had expected. A typical example had been one of the attacks he had personally led where a man and his young son, in a remote kraal, had managed to kill two of his men before succumbing to the blade themselves. He remembered forcing his way into the homestead by breaking the wooden stockade. *Well the family had paid for that as the survivors had been taken into captivity,* he thought to himself.

Another mistake they had made was the burning of the abandoned homesteads as they advanced. The plumes of smoke had alerted the larger communities that something was amiss and by the time he had closed on the towns, the element of surprise was gone with the population taking to their central refuges along with much of the expected plunder. If he had had the additional men he could have risked mounting an assault on these decorative fortresses. These central retreats had not been designed to keep out a determined attack but even so, from the safety of these stone walls, the Bantu had managed to keep up a barrage of stones, large rocks and spears whenever his men had attempted to assault the hill the fort had been built on. He also did not have the resources or time to mount a prolonged siege and so it was decided to pull back with what men he had left, using the few captured Bantu to carry away what limited spoils could be found. He did not know what the penalty would be for his failure to achieve all that had been set for him to do but at least he knew he would have Modena in his corner due to his decision which affected the outcome of the raid. The success of the previous day's battle should pacify their King but one could never tell until the time they actually confronted him face to face, knowing his dedicated and experienced executioners were never far away.

Digane had also hoped to have travelled ahead of the returning column but again the limitation in the number of men he had available meant that everyone was needed to escort the slaves and the bounty they were transporting.

On the return trip word had reached him about the success of the battle at Sampambi and he wanted to ensure that he was also associated with such a resounding defeat of their enemy. Even as he held these deliberations in his mind, the column of women and children stumbled once again to a halt as yet another prisoner fell to the ground in what Digane knew to be a deliberate attempt to slow him down and to frustrate his desire for a hurried return.

This time he lost patience with the feeble attempts of the other prisoners to get the middle-aged woman back onto her feet. The anguished cries of those around her increased in intensity and Digane stormed across to where the commotion was taking place, pushing the crowd aside, stood over the women on the ground and without a moment's hesitation plunged his assegai deep into her chest as she lay on the ground. She did not even give out a cry, her eyes just opened in surprise at the sharp pain before they glazed over in death. Those prisoners close enough to witness this act of violence screamed as Digane withdrew the blade of his weapon, with a hollow sucking sound. Turning on them he pointed his bloodstained assegai at the dead woman and shouted, "That is what is going to happen to the next person who stops or falls down and to everyone else after that. There will be no more discussions. No more attempts to persuade you to keep getting back on your feet. There will be no more words to convince you to keep on moving. You will simply die and your body will be left where it falls for the jackals to fight over." His eyes glared at the individuals around him, his anger unchecked. Having wiped the blade on his victim's body, he stormed back to the head of the column, shouting commands to keep on moving. He also clipped a young boy who was too slow in getting out of his way across the head. The child's mother managed to grab and pull her son to the safety of her bosom so that her offspring's pain induced cry did not anger the Zulu chief any further.

As Digane regained his position at the head of the column, one of his senior men asked if it had been a wise thing to do, killing the exhausted woman. Digane's anger flared once again and he subconsciously took a firmer grip on his spear shaft. Undaunted and obviously used to his chief's outward rage, the other Zulu stood his ground looking deep into the induna's eyes. "You cannot kill every one, Digane," he said, his voice firm in its delivery. "We must let the women and children rest, they have been walking all day. Otherwise you will have to kill and keep on killing, just to maintain your authority!"

Digane let his shoulders slump at the remark, his anger quickly fading with understanding. "You are right, my friend, I have been pushing the group too hard. We will walk as far as that river over there," he indicated with a pointed finger, "and we will take a rest."

The area he referred to had a number of trees near

which would offer good shade from the blazing sun. Satisfied, Digane's comrade nodded his acceptance and he moved back down the column encouraging the captives with the knowledge that that they only had a short distance to go before they could sit down and have some water and food. With a final, tired effort the caravan of captives shuddered forward, most of them having to pass by the place where the woman had been murdered, averting their eyes at the sight of death.

The Zulu chieftain moved well ahead of the slave train and even as the captives were being allowed to take water from the river, he isolated himself by sitting on an ant hill overlooking the surrounding terrain.

"It's a long way to Chimnungwa," he said to himself, "but that's where we need to get the captives to." Looking at the desolate group, he took a deep breath and finally resigned himself to the task.

Chapter Twenty-Three
Mbada, the leopard

The King's outdoor auditorium was bursting with the excited chatter and shrill calls of a younger generation. Their mysterious summons to this special site, without any explanation, fuelled their active imaginations. The majority of them thought that it was still unfair that they were about to be sent away to positions of safety even if the reason had been thinly disguised as the role of protectors to the women and livestock in the mountains. Even these juveniles could not miss the movement of so many dignitaries around the palace and their excitement increased as each new person was identified going in or out of the King's chambers.

Speculation had reached fever pitch when a pounding drum called the gathering to order, the abrupt silence a stark contrast to the babbling that had filled the stone-lined arena just a few moments before. All eyes were drawn to the higher stage where palace guards stepped into view followed by the King and, in his wake, Zabesi and Zusa. The sight of the young hero was enough for the excitement to return but their conversation was quickly stilled by a shouted command for silence from Zabesi. The King put his hand to his mouth to conceal the quick smile that sprang to his face and once he had managed to control himself he was able to project an expression of seriousness, enough to quell even the liveliest of the youths.

Once he had their full attention, the King spoke with a loud and clear voice. "Umfana, *young men*, I can imagine that you are wondering why you have been called to this meeting so promptly." A few nodding heads in the crowd confirmed this statement. "Well that is the reason why

I am here to speak to you this afternoon." He paused again and the crowd held its breath in anticipation. "I do not have to spell out the exact situation our nation finds itself in today. Many of you have already been affected by the dramatic turn of events which have occurred over the last couple of days. Many of your own clan, friends and family, lie dead on a battlefield not far away from here." He let that statement sink in for a while. "A battlefield which was one not truly of our choosing and I have to say that your personal sorrow is shared by the whole nation."

The King simply announced the fact that Zusa had been commissioned to recruit, train and equip a regiment of bowmen and as he explained what it was they were proposing, using the young men of the city, their shoulders and backs straightened as they collectively understood the impact of what was being suggested. They were not going to be used as a rear guard, as so many of them thought they would be; no, they were going to take an active part in the salvation of their kingdom.

The King concluded, "I am not guaranteeing you all a place in the Mbada regiment, as that honour will be based on your own efforts and at Zusa's final discretion. Nor am I promising you glory or even survival. Never before has the nation found itself to be in such a weakened position to have to call upon a generation of young men such as yourselves to assist in its protection. It is not easy for a nation's leader to have to send the future of his kingdom into battle, but unless I do this there may be no kingdom for you to live in, in the future." The auditorium was completely silent now. "It is not fair for you young men to be exposed to the horrors of war at such a tender age; a war whose very experience will steal the innocence of your youth from you. But these are not normal times. Although it was a difficult decision to make, it was agreed that better we risk this than risk losing the prospect of your future and that of our state."

It was a long speech, especially for the young to concentrate on, but the message was clear. The Bantu nation's back was against the wall and they were being given the opportunity to be part of the solution. The King nodded for Zusa to carry on and he walked off the raised platform followed by his personal guard.

Zusa knew the time was now upon him to make his final choices; it was no longer just about him and his family. His responsibilities were beyond that and it was the decisions he made now which could well affect his future and that of those whom he had been selected to command. A slight murmur had returned with the exit of the King and Zusa knew he had to regain control of the assembly immediately. He stood tall and in a commanding voice spoke, "You were not given leave to talk. You will get the opportunity to do that on your own time but right now you are on the King's time." He looked across the gathering, of about five hundred boys, their faces attentive and eyes full of anticipation. "It is my duty to assemble a regiment of bowmen. The idea is new and unproven but we will perform our tasks with the determination needed so that we can serve our people." He lowered his voice a bit and went on, "I too as a young man have been a herder for my father's livestock. I know of the imaginary games we played with our friends and the battle practice we had with our fighting sticks. I am sure most of you have either made your own bows or at least managed to handle your father's hunting bow in the past. Now it is going to be for real. It is the time for us to stand up and be counted. It is time for us to stand with the new army and for us to lend our efforts, and possibly our lives, to the cause." The gathering listened attentively. Raising his voice to its original level he instructed the group to re-form into lines. Leaving the platform he walked amongst the group indicating for the older and larger boys to fall out of line and to go to the front of the area.

Once he had selected ten boys he asked their names and explained that he wanted to use them to assist in the initial command structure of the training regimen. He was careful to explain that this was a temporary appointment. The posts might be confirmed later when their own efforts justified their senior positions.

The remaining boys were divided into ten groups of approximately forty to fifty individuals. Each of the new company leaders was to question their allocated group as to their experience with the bow. From this exercise, it was established that the majority of those present had some knowledge of firing a bow and arrow, even if it had only been at small animals and birds.

During this selection period, another messenger arrived to inform Zusa that one hundred and twenty eight bows and a large quantity of light arrows had been located and delivered to the visitors' enclosure where Gemba and Zusa were accommodated. It had been decided to keep the youths' training camp and exercises within the city to restrict the possibility of their enemy becoming aware of the unusual preparations.

One by one the newly formed companies followed their assigned leader in single file to the area set aside for their training. Once there Zusa found that Gemba had arranged for the visitors sleeping huts to be cleared so that the trainees could be barracked. He had also established a firing range, complete with straw-stuffed, life-sized targets fitted with shields and spears. The new recruits again exchanged excited chatter but this time their appointed guardians controlled it with a few disciplined words. As the ten companies marched in to sit in the allotted area, Zusa had time to speak to Gemba. "Well, Uncle, I have my boys now," he said,

"Yes, but are they your warriors?" Gemba responded, patting Zusa on his back as he walked away.

Is that all Gemba is going to give me? Zusa thought to himself but pulled his thoughts back with a measure of guilt when he remembered the full extent of his mentor's responsibilities over those of his own.

Zusa instructed the companies to stand in line and he had each of the boy's fire six arrows, so that they could have their personal skills assessed and graded. As could be expected, some of the projectiles flew over the targets set at a distance of fifty paces; however a good percentage of them found their marks. Some of the arrows did not even reach as far as the targets, with the arrows either burying themselves in the sand of the firing-range or skittering along the ground leaving a trail as if their bowman did not have enough strength to consistently draw the bowstring to send the arrow straight and true.

By now, the significance and seriousness of the situation had begun to sink in with the boys. Instead of the expected ribbing of those who missed or did not have the strength to keep up the firing pace, words of encouragement were called which the senior boys wisely left unchallenged, as the open gathering quickly became a consolidated force. In between these sessions the group that had last fired was occupied in collecting the spent arrows so that the group awaiting their turn could re-use them. Some of the arrows were broken from repeated firing and others were lost over the city boundaries but enough remained to complete the task in hand.

By late afternoon, the boys had completed the initial grading exercise and they were served with refreshments of water and fruit, which they consumed with the gusto of youth. During this time, another one hundred and seventeen bows had been collected from homes throughout the city and they had been delivered to the training ground. There was a promise of at least another one hundred by the end of the day.

Families had sent some of the bows for specific individuals and Zusa was careful to ensure they were correctly handed over to the right individual although these new owners were expected to share them until the time when enough weapons would be available for the whole regiment.

Zusa used the break time to discuss the individual performances with the selected seniors, all of whom had shown themselves to be of enough maturity to remain in their position. He explained that the remainder of the day would be spent in free practice and firing at the targets. Zusa and some of the more experienced bowmen moved up and down the line correcting the boys' stance or simply telling them how to hold their weapons and aim, offering one-on-one advice. This attention paid off and many of the new bowmen bloomed before Zusa's eyes. Eventually he had to demand that the companies of trainees stop target practice as the sun had begun to set and the straw Zulu targets were becoming difficult to see in the waning light.

The band of trainee bowmen were led off to their allotted huts, ten boys to a hut, and five huts to a company. Food had been prepared earlier and its aroma quickly attracted the boys' attention.

Zusa found he was exhausted from his previous all-night travel and full day in training, but he knew he still had to attend the evening meeting in the war room before he could think about retiring for the night. He was one of the last to arrive but still in time to hear the latest report on the main army-training programme. Zabesi was pleased with the progress which had been made, and the new army had responded well to the accelerated exercises. The King turned to Zusa to enquire as to the status of the bowman training. Zusa explained what headway had been made and that they had just established the skill level of the recruits.

The master weapon smith also arrived to reveal the fruit of their day's labour and the heavy arrowhead sample was presented to the gathering. Zusa was the first to pick it up, turning it around in his hands whilst assessing its design. A number of other heads had been fitted to reed shafts of varying lengths and combinations of feathered flights. Zusa also tested them for stability and balance to find which version could be the optimum design. He balanced the selected arrows one by one on his finger, moving the position until at the exact halfway point along the length of the shaft, the arrow tilted forward indicating its action if it was in free flight. Smiling, he looked up, and realised that the rest of the group had been observing his assessment of the projectiles. "Excellent," he said to the master smith. "The results are exactly what I had in mind. I will begin testing first thing tomorrow morning so that we can agree upon a final design," he grinned, "but this one," he held up the arrow he had already selected, "this one feels just right!"

Gemba took the offered arrow and assessed it for himself; with a brief nod he handed it around the table where each member in turn took the time to look at the new design. The arrowhead was as requested, a miniature but elongated spearhead, razor-edged with an equally sharp point. The rear of the iron arrowhead had a number of serrations angling backwards to stop it being withdrawn from flesh or shield. The arrowhead was set into a reed shaft, a warrior's pace long, with the base of the iron tool inserted into the hollow tube and bound with copper wire to hold it firmly in place. A tree resin had been used to further assist in gluing the assembly together. The other end of the arrow was equally as important as the killing end, as its construction would determine the stability and characteristics of the projectile in flight. Three large goose wing feathers had been stripped of one side of their plume whilst the quill, with the remaining part, was inserted into a split in the reed.

Once all three guides had been secured with more of the tree resin glue, the split end of the shaft was bound tight with a thin length of copper wire. A groove for the bowstring was then carved at such a position that when loaded and fired, the feather flights would not interfere too much with the bow shaft and limit any chance of deflection. Humbly pleased with the praise given, the weaponsmith left the meeting and the discussion turned back to the tactical situation.

It had been confirmed that, the main body of Zulu was, in fact, at its lowest number since the Bantus had managed to keep the garrison under observation. It would also appear that some of the other towns had fought harder than had been expected by the enemy and additional warriors had been required to deal with the pockets of resistance, The Bantu scouts reported that another batch of Zulu was preparing to leave on yet another sortie or raid in the next day or two as supplies were being assembled and packaged. The news pleased the King knowing that his people had not simply crumbled and given up at the first onslaught. This would give hope and purpose to the reorganised army. The time was now for Yasini to decide either to attack this weakened group or wait behind the stone walls for a co-ordinated and mass campaign attack by the Zulu.

All options were discussed at length but Zusa had trouble concentrating on the conversation and Gemba noticed his exhaustion and took him by the arm to lead him away from the meeting, which could be expected to go on well into the night. Zusa protested but Gemba said, "Sleep, Zusa, you will be no good to the King or your regiment if you are too tired to think straight. You have done your part today, and any final decision tonight will not be affected by your well-earned absence." A member of the palace staff appeared at Gemba's summons. "Show him to a guest room in the palace."

"No, sekuru," slurred Zusa, "I will sleep in the same accommodation as my troops!" Clutching the manufactured arrows in one hand, he stumbled for the exit and, guided with a caring hand by the servant, he left the palace.

Chapter Twenty-Four
The awakening of the leopard

The next morning Zusa awoke at first light. He got up and hastened to the target range where the well-peppered targets were placed, looking the worse for wear after their attention from the trainee bowmen the day before. Modifying the targets, he made sure one of the hide shields was facing directly forward, while another target's shield was positioned above shoulder height as if to protect its head. He paced backwards and stopped at the demarcated line. He set the new arrow designs point downwards in the ground for easy retrieval. Looking at this instinctive action he thought about what he had just done and realised that this procedure could be used for the process of quick firing but immediately concluded that its disadvantage would be if his men needed to remain mobile. A way to hold the spare arrows would have to be arranged as quickly as possible. He made a mental note to speak to the weaponsmiths about it!

Taking the first arrow, he fitted it to his bow and carefully aimed at the centre of the shield facing him. Holding the bow in his left hand he stretched the arm forward, slightly skywards. As he lowered it to nearly horizontal he inhaled and held his breath, drawing back on the string with his right hand, which also secured the notched arrow in place. As his aim centred on the target he paused before loosing the projectile.

With a twang, the arrow leapt from the bow and, in a blur, crossed the space between the two points in the blink of an eye to bury itself at the extreme bottom of the shield.

Off the mark, he thought to himself. The arrow was made front heavy by the shaft being too long, which caused it to drop too much during its flight. A second and third trial with the other examples of this design confirmed his findings each time with similar results.

Next, he selected the extreme opposite of the first, these arrows being shorter in length by over three hand spans. This time, on release, the arrows tended to tumble end over end to arrive at the mark almost sideways and not presenting their pointed heads to penetrate the targets, obviously nowhere near the standard he was looking for. In fact, just to be sure, he retrieved the first six arrows shot, pleased to find that some were difficult to pull out of the shield. He walked back to where he had left his bow and fired them again, satisfied that the outcome was very similar to the first round in both cases and in his mind, he rejected these designs.

By now, the sun had risen a little higher into the morning sky and many of the bowmen recruits had left their huts and were watching Zusa's experiments from a respectful distance.

Further up the hill the King had also been watching the young man test the new arrow designs, sensing his dedication and patience. Not rushing to conclusions but testing and testing again to arrive at a firm result. He was joined on the palace balcony by Zabesi. "He is a true man," the commander said.

"Yes, you are right! I have said it before but may my future kingdom belong to such men as he?" During the previous afternoon both men had taken the time to observe the bowmen's preparation and training from the same vantage point and although the opening rounds had been ragged and erratic, they noticed the marked improvement toward dusk as Zusa and his appointed assistants tutored the regiment.

Back in the bowmen's enclosure, Zusa finally reached for the last design. It was his choice arrow - the one that he had assessed and announced to be the best sample the night before in front of the war council. Pausing for a drink of water he saw that he had gained an audience and smiled at their patience.

Turning back to the task and almost with relish, he fitted the last arrow design to his bow. The spectators collectively took an involuntary deep breath as he did, each going through the bowmen's action in their own mind as Zusa took up the tension on the weapon and released. The projectile seemed to have taken on a life of its own as it sped towards its target and with an almost pleasing swish the arrow buried itself the full length of its head into the shield, enough to penetrate flesh if held too close to the body behind its protection.

A spontaneous cheer resounded from the crowd and even the King and Zabesi smiled as the sound floated up to where they stood. The regimental lieutenants walked over to be nearer to Zusa as he shot the last two arrows. Each performed in the same manner, penetrating the shield to end in a neatly grouped cluster. The senior boys walked to the target with Zusa to discuss his final verdict. The mock Zulu shield bristled with the arrow shafts, their heads buried deep. In fact, they were so well embedded that they could not be pulled from the target and the shield had to be broken to be able to retrieve them. "I guess this is the one," Zusa said in a calm voice. The rest of the crowd broke into laughter at his statement of the obvious.

Walking back, he spoke to the group with him. "I need to attend another meeting with the town elders shortly. Get your companies to rotate between free-fire practices after they have eaten their breakfast. Once this has been done I would like them to continue for another hour before you take them on a run beyond the new valley construction sites and return to the range. As each company arrives back, I want them to fire three arrows in quick succession and I want to you to assess the best results. This exercise will possibly be closest to the way we can expect to be used in battle, quick movement, followed by the need for accurate shooting. Is this clear?" A number of affirmations were given. "Good, carry on."

Making his way towards the palace he knew he was a little early and so he decided to visit the weaponsmiths who were using the furnaces of the gold refinery so as to increase the production of the metal arrow and spear heads needed to re-arm the regiments. Passing through the royal audience chamber he walked straight across the area as opposed to his normal route left of the palace entrance. The walls of the audience chamber were bedecked with the seven stone carvings of the city totem, the Rukodzi, *the hawk*. The largest example was set at the doorway to the refinery; its golden eyes reflecting as if it contained an inner life. As he went to go through the doorway he looked more closely at the carving, as under normal circumstances, the average citizen did not have the ability to get as close to the statues. He stopped and a shudder ran through his body. What he saw was that, instead of the normal fish-bone chevrons, like those on the other bird statues around the chamber, the base of this figurine had in fact been engraved with miniature bows and arrows. The biggest surprise was that the animal depicted on the column upon which the bird was set, was a leopard, its front claws extending in detail and dug into the stone, its mouth open wide in a fierce silent snarl and its eye set with a bright red stone.

    A voice behind him made him jump, and he looked around to see Gemba standing close by. "I was wondering how long it would take you to see the significance of the royal appointment." He stepped up to the effigy. "This was the last and greatest carving handed down by our ancestors, and it carried with it a tale offering the key to a great peril which would befall the nation at some stage."

    Zusa's mind spun at what the older man had said, at the impact and clarity of such a prophecy. "It's beautiful, so well carved." They stood side by side for a while and Zusa asked, "How are your preparations going?"

    Gemba replied that everything was going as planned but just that it was taking longer than he initially expected.

    "Well I guess we need to get on with what needs to be done, I have to speak to the weaponsmiths about the chosen arrow design." He went on to explain to Gemba the results of his tests who agreed with his reasoning. As they spoke they moved through the stone entrance into the stone walled manufacturing area, which they saw had been reorganised to maximise the capacity of the industry.

    The smoke from the hot furnaces was being directed skywards through the long clay-formed chimneys; their length calculated to generate the correct airflow to get the furnace to the critical temperature to smelt the iron, working in conjunction with the leather bellows, which were operated by relays of younger artisans and apprentices.

The lumps of smelted iron were pulled from the coals using long iron tongs. The blacksmith then folded the glowing metal and pounded it into shape on the large anvils set in the ground for this purpose. The noise, heat and smoke created a horrific environment but the measured rush of people from one point to the other showed it to be an organised chaos. As soon as a finished arrow head was thrust into water to cool, the hiss and steam adding to the smog, it was passed on to others who were sitting before large pumice stones used to sharpen the metal edges and sharp iron chisels to add the serrations. At this point this part of the process ended; the result was numerous evenly-produced and well-sharpened iron arrowheads set in neat rows. However, on the other side of the industrial area, fletchers were completing their own contributions by working on bundles of reed shafts which had not been cut to an agreed length. The goose-feather flights were attached by a time consuming procedure. The flight feathers taken from the locally hunted common goose were stripped of their barbs on one side, leaving the shaft and half a feather attached. To be able to attach three of these to the arrow shaft, a special bulbous root had been dug up and mashed before being boiled in a pot, until only a white sticky paste was left. This mixture was poisonous and those handling it had to take special care. The gluey substance was mixed with charcoal that caused the paste to harden and was used to hold the flights in place.

At the same time, other labourers were pounding the dried leg tendons of a large deer until it broke into very thin yet strong individual fibres. The deer sinew was tightly wound around the feather assembly and once left to set it became as secure as could be expected. Thin copper wire was used to complete the process.

The master in charge of the production area walked over to where they were standing and greeting them both by name. After responding, Zusa showed the old man the arrow he had decided to have mass-produced. The man nodded his acceptance and without another word moved over to where the two parts of his product facilities were awaiting to be married together.

"How many will you be able to produce, master?" Zusa called after him.

"The slowest part of the process is the iron work, but we are producing the heads at two other sites outside the city and we expect to finish about two thousand heads a day. We have found a quicker way to make them by using flattening iron bars. The final assembly of the arrow is not a problem as we can use less skilled workers to do that."

"Excellent, what about the bows? How many of those do we now have?"

"I have four men making the instruments and they are producing about sixty-four bows a day between them. In fact since yesterday there are eighty ready for immediate allocation." As they spoke they had walked over to the area set aside for the iron head attachment. The weaponsmith pointed to numerous clay pots. "We have gathered tree resin from the forest which is different from the glue used to hold the feathers in place, and we have burnt softwood to make a very fine charcoal. We will cut into the top of the shaft to allow us to slide in an arrowhead. We then mix the tree resin with the charcoal, which makes the natural glue harden, and then we use more of the deer sinew to tighten the setting to complete the arrow"

Zusa was nodding his head at the detailed explanation and from the knowledge being imparted by the master weaponsmith he knew he had nothing to add to the refined procedures.

"Good. I can't believe what actually goes into the preparation, it is truly amazing." He paused whilst taking a last look around. "I will send some of my men for the completed bows as soon as I get back to my camp," Zusa said. Further, congratulating the master for his effort and that of the people he had working with him, Gemba and Zusa left the area for the scheduled meeting at the palace.

As on the previous occasions, they found most of the

other delegates already there and all it required was for the King, Zabesi and Makonde to arrive, As soon as they appeared, Zusa could tell by their attitude that things had changed from the last time he was there. The King opened the conversation with his regular request for a status update on preparations. Zabesi was the first to speak. "I now have eight hundred and seventy-three experienced warriors under my direct command and they are fully equipped and ready for battle."

The King followed on, "With my personal guard now numbering two hundred and seven, after a number of those on leave made their way back to the city, all are fully equipped and my men are eager to get into the field. I have also sent another message and instruction for my brother Zimu to make his way to a position near the southern pass and that he is to wait to meet the rest of our army."

At the mention of Zimu being instructed on where to meet the King's forces, Zusa realised that some decisions must have been made about possible deployment in his absence.

Makonde's turn was next. "My trainee regiments are as ready as we can expect them to be. They have completed the normal tests and trials and are of an excellent quality. There is nothing like placing fire in their bellies or revenge in the hearts of men to get them motivated." His smile was one of pride in his own men. "There are one thousand two hundred and eighty-nine soldiers who can be sent to the field but we are waiting for about three hundred shields and over four hundred spears to fully arm them."

At the mention of the deficiency in arms, the group looked at Zusa, knowing the impact his arrow production had had on the capacity of the city in meeting the increased demand for spears.

Stepping forward he began his report. "I have four hundred and fifty bowmen in training, over half are fairly competent and armed with bows and the remainder should be armed by the end of today. They will require more time and instruction to hone their skills. Fortunately, most of the boys have hunted with bow and arrows in the past so many of them have been able to start with the basic knowledge. I am working on them to respond to commands and tactics at this time."

"Time is something we may no longer have," the King interrupted; the room went silent, waiting for him to continue. "This morning our scouts have reported that the Zulu regiment we thought was preparing to move, actually left during the night. We are trailing their movement to ensure it is not just a lure or an attempt to entrap us again. Once we confirm that this force is going to be out of touch of the main Zulu army we will march on their main position." He moved to the map table and pointed at an area just outside the captured town of Belingwe and on the far side of the mountain range. The three dimensional map model indicated a gentle horseshoe-shaped valley. "This is the position we have selected to confront the Zulu. The key to this is for us being able to get close enough to the Zulu army without them being aware of our presence so that when we present ourselves for battle, it will be too late for them to contact and recall their far-flung regiments for assistance." He placed a marker on the west side of the mountain range which appeared incomprehensible as it was beyond the well guarded north and south passes, and in fact other indicators proved that there were still Zulu warriors at these posts.

Zusa looked up. "But that is beyond the mountain! How are we going to arrange a surprise attack without the sentinels at the passes becoming aware of our presence and announcing our approach?"

The King smiled at the question. "Not all is as it may seem, young man. We have a plan to get our men into position," he finished, winking at Gemba.

"Okay that is all right then. Assuming we are able to burrow under or flyover the mountain, then what is stopping the Zulu from simply falling back to another position to wait until they are reinforced and their numbers are more favourable for a counter-attack?"

"A very good question, Zusa. The answer is simple - their plunder. They have spent the last few days ransacking homesteads and capturing our people. They are not simply going to leave their spoils of war behind and run away. Besides that, they are over confident in their ability to defeat us in open battle as proven by the actions only a few days ago at Sampambi."

Zabesi took over from the King and said, "We know that we have had to choose the lesser of two evils here. Ideally, if we could be certain that after raiding the countryside, the Zulu would leave, then we might decide to mount a few spoiling raids on their prisoner columns, without risking the remainder of our army to an all-out battle. But we don't believe they are going to simply go away." He looked at Zusa knowing that his mother, brother and sister were captives and it was their very lives that were being discussed, along with the future of hundreds of others. "The city offers far too much temptation for their greed and we must assume that once they have re-gathered their strength, they will attack us here."

Makonde took up the conversation. "As poorly prepared as we may feel we are, this opportunity is the best option for us at this time. It allows us to choose the time and place of the confrontation. "

As he finished he looked back to the King, who completed the narrative. "It is our plan to bring the Zulu to battle the day after tomorrow." The room went quiet at the voicing of the plan. "This evening we will send large skirmish parties to clear the vantage viewpoint overlooking the city so that we are certain that we are not being observed when the army leaves the city early in the morning. They will travel in three groups so that their passage is not written in the skies by the dust which the combined army would generate." He pointed again to the table map. "As there are no large groups of Zulu reported this side of the mountain range, we will use three different routes already mentioned and meet up at this position here, by late afternoon." He pointed to a place slightly north of the southernmost mountain pass. "We will rest the men there and during the evening we will make use of a secret passage to cross through the mountain range. This tunnel means we will arrive near the stockade where the

Zulu are encamped about two hours before dawn. This will give us an opportunity to rest for a while before the day's expected battle."

A hidden tunnel. Zusa now understood how they were going to be able to arrive unannounced in the Zulus' rear position, without having to fight their way through the natural passages.

The next hour was taken up with the finer details for the planned march, preparations and attack but halfway through, Zusa asked to be allowed to return to his regiment to check on their status. The King agreed but as Zusa turned to leave he said, "Zusa, I know time is not on the side of your bowmen and their need to practise but I urge you to get what you can done today and have your men ready to leave with the rest of the army tomorrow."

"Yes, your Majesty, I understand. The Mbada will be ready and you can count on us." Leaving the chamber Zusa took time for his sight to adjust from the internal gloom to the brightness of the daylight. The palace was still shrouded in smoke from the weapons manufacturing site not far away; the smoke stung his eyes and he had to wipe away the tears caused by the acrid fumes. He knew he had so little time in which achieve so much. At a brisk walk, he headed back to the bowmen's training ground. As he arrived, he saw the last of the companies just returning from their forced run into the valley. Without a break, they were instructed to form into a line and fire three arrows in quick succession. Tired from the run, some panicked at the command and fired wildly, missing their targets by a considerable distance, but Zusa was pleased to see that the majority kept their cool, remembered their recent instruction, and made use of their skill. Soon the Zulu dummies were bristling with arrows.

He walked into the centre of the area and summoned his lieutenants. "Dismiss your men and meet me back here, I need to discuss something with you all." The trainees gratefully took the time to take a drink of water during which Zusa went on to explain, in confidence, the ever-changing national situation. He told them that the bowmen regiment only had the remainder of the day to cover a number of tactics that they could be expected to employ in the field, as they would be leaving for battle that night. "We will use this time to perfect two main actions. The first is the massed volley-fire which we have been practising since yesterday. As you know this demands accuracy and coordination. How do you feel your individual men have done at this exercise?"

Each lieutenant had his say and the consensus was not too bad although sixteen of the younger boys had been identified as having no aptitude at all for using a bow and their continued presence could distract and endanger the rest of the regiment.

"All right," Zusa said, "have these individuals report to me after the meeting and I will speak to them." His heart felt heavy at the thought of having to send some of the boys away but he knew that with his responsibility there were going to be both highs and lows of command. This would be the first of the lows.

"We are still short of over eighty bows, Zusa," one of the other boys said.

"Send a detachment to the weaponsmith at the palace, he will give you enough to fully equip those still without." Turning to the others he went on, "The second action I want rehearsed today, is multiple-impact shooting." He went on to explain that he wanted the regiment to work on firing a first round of arrows into the air to arc down onto the target and then to quickly reload and fire a second volley, horizontally, so that it arrived at the same time, in effect doubling the impact. Understanding the principle, the trainers started back to their companies, whilst the other young man, tasked to collect the completed bows, took those boys still unarmed to collect their new weapons.

Zusa strode to one side of the ground as the sixteen boys earlier identified as not being able to bear arms walked towards him, their faces full of apprehension. He instructed them to sit on the ground and he followed suit. *Here I am*, he thought to himself, on the other side of the authoritative line, having to pass judgment on boys who are only just a little younger than myself. *What am I to do with them? All they have done wrong is not being able to fire an arrow correctly but their hearts and minds are in the cause otherwise they would not have even been here!*

A notion came to mind and he spoke. "Warriors of the Mbada," they all smiled at the greeting, "I am sure you are wondering why you have been sent to see me." He could see the question in their eyes. "Well I have selected you from amongst the whole regiment for a special task." He looked towards the range where commands were being shouted in correction. "No commander can be expected to face an enemy unless he has good, strong and reliable communications. You have been chosen because of the fact that you are swift on your feet. I want you all to be my personal messengers and I will be expecting you to carry my instructions during battle to the rest of the Mbada without any delay."

The faces beamed back at him with their new responsibilities explained. "Are you up to the task?"

"Yes, sir," they chorused back. "Well fall in then, one to each of the lieutenants, the rest to stay here with me and await your commands." With a scramble, they jumped to their feet at Zusa's very first order to them, the leopard's messengers.

Chapter Twenty-Five
The route to war

The next morning, as so many times in their previously ordinary lives, the young warriors of the Mbada awoke at their first summons. However, instead of going out to herd the family livestock this day, they were going to war.

The army was stirring and, as explained the evening before, it had to move as quickly as possible and so their field provisions were going to have to be carried by the troops. They were expected to be in the field for two or three days and so the first two days' supplies were going with them in their backpacks. If they missed this chance and the campaign lasted any longer than that, then they ran the chance of being greatly outnumbered and at the risk of another defeat by the Zulu's larger, combined force or otherwise they would be manoeuvering until another opportunity to meet in battle presented itself and they would then have to resort to foraging.

The sun would not rise for a while but the different sections of the army formed up in their companies with the regular army regiments in their barrack areas. Without the need to broadcast their intentions, the senior regiment led by Zabesi moved out first. The route they would take, cut south-west from the city, crossing the Nuanetsi and Lundi rivers at the known river fords, before heading towards the assembly point at the village of Kezi, situated in the shadow of the Mtanda Range.

Once this formation had cleared the city gates, Makonde's mass of trainees struck out. This second force travelled in an almost straight line westwards from the city. The group started well and a brisk walk was achieved in no time.

The King took the last assembly consisting of his royal guard and the Mbada, accompanied by last minute volunteers which was made up from another four hundred and twenty-three men and boys who had found their way to the city in the last few days and who had expressed their desire to join with the new force. Chemwapuwa and Goredema, the survivors from the first battle, had attached themselves to this group so that they had a chance to regain some honour. Amongst these additional recruits Zusa had noticed his arch- rival, Pimi. The last time they had met was over two months ago when Zusa received his wounds from the wild cat. Subconsciously, Zusa reached across to rub the scar tissue which had healed, leaving the scratch marks still bright and ridged on his shoulder and arm.

For some reason Pimi would not look directly back at him. Seeing Zusa in this environment Pimi had decided to keep away from the leader of the Mbada. He knew his boyhood foe had been recognised by the King and appointed to a senior position and based on his own principles of life, he thought he was now wide open to receive his just rewards. He shrank back when ever Zusa looked at him, trying to disappear into the background, shivering at the thought of when an excruciating revenge could be expected to occur.

The Mbada remained under control and any boyish excitement was contained as the senior boys held the regiment in tight formation as they snaked their way out of the city and towards the assembly point on the main inland road. This, the easiest of the routes, had been selected for this group due to their lack of field experience. The road, although longer in distance, would still be quicker and easier to traverse. The King was column commander and he knew his personal guard would offer support in case the young bowmen encountered the Zulu along the way.

Further away, Zabesi's warriors had kept up a good pace with the route being well known by a number of warriors in the group and the areas of difficulty, even in the dark, were navigated with ease.

It was only the water crossings that were felt to pose

some danger. The column commander decided to approach the fords with care. Even a token hostile force could cover these natural defensive choke points. The narrow crossings acted as funnels for game and man, filtering from the vast, surrounding open plains. As the regiments approached these obstacles scouts had to reconnoitre the area and only once they were satisfied that there was no major opposition in waiting did they give the all clear for a larger shadow force to cross. The aim of this secondary force was to form a bridgehead to cover the main column's passage through the fords. The army commanders knew that nothing could be worse than their forces being caught during a water crossing, the army divided by the natural obstacle. Fortunately, neither river caused too many problems and when daylight arrived, Zabesi knew he would get to the assembly place very close to the time agreed.

Makonde's group was beginning to struggle with a combination of problems. Although not as young as the Mbada, this assembly did not have much field experience, especially that which was required to move as a large coherent force at night. Some of his companies became split whilst avoiding natural obstacles such as rocks and thick forests and, throughout the night, time was wasted searching and re-forming the units. The only river they had to cross was running a little faster than they had expected as the banks were at their narrowest at this point. One soldier had lost his step and as he fell into the flow he dragged another of his colleagues into the water with him and they were quickly swept away and, although search parties were sent to both sides of the river, it was feared that they had both perished.

Another unsettling occasion occurred was when one of the scouts disturbed an adder which had wound its self in a coil on the warm sand for the night. His foot trod on the reptile and he was bitten on his shin. The man died quickly after the agony had strained his nervous system until it simply collapsed.

These events had caused the remainder of the column to become nervous and their pickets and scouts began to jump at the slightest thing. False alarms were raised and, in one case, a scout mistook another one of his men for a Zulu, which almost resulted in the killing of the man.

Eventually, towards daybreak, Makonde was compelled to call an early rest so that the column could re-form as they had once again become stretched out across the grass plain. At this stage he decided to break the army group into four smaller sections. These, he thought, would allow the individual commanders to keep track of their men's movements. This proved a successful remedy and good progress was made for the rest of the morning.

The swiftest progress was achieved by the King's force. To begin with the path ahead of the column glowed pale in the light of the half moon which was enough to indicate the direction. This part of the main army was also the smallest of the three sent out that night and there had been no mishaps. The King's presence held the group together and by dawn they had covered the distance they had expected to and the pace was increased as it got lighter. Two short breaks were taken leading up to midday to rest the group. The first on the road and the second at the junction where they had to break off from the main road to head south to the scheduled meeting place.

The heat of the day gradually increased but fortunately their route was tending towards the higher ground and the stiff breeze channelled by the mountains offered some relief. By mid-afternoon, the King realised that he had pushed the youngsters quite far and he made the decision for an early rest.

Some of the lads simply fell asleep where they settled and Yasini decided to call an impromptu meeting. Indicating the sleeping forms he said to the senior men, "We have travelled well but I can see that it has taken a lot out of the younger men. We will give them a bit more time to rest. Once the group is refreshed, we will have to make a final push towards Kezi. Just before sunset we will stop to have our last rest before we join up with Makonde and Zabesi." Those in the group agreed with their leader's statement.

The King's experienced guards became the ears and

eyes for the younger group although the hard travel was also taking a toll on their mature fitness and strength. However, their pride would not let it hinder their duty and so they stayed on watch. A while later at an indication from the King, these men moved amongst the sleeping forms to rouse them from their slumber. A few moans escaped from their lips before they remembered in whose company they were and they struggled to their feet. Shoulders and backs were sore from carrying their packs, bows and arrows over the long distance but they had just reached the mid-point and they still had many hours' travel ahead of them.

Eventually the day drew to an end and the three columns were all converging on the assembly point. The first to arrive was, as expected, Zabesi's group and they made immediate use of the fast flowing river to quench their thirst and to wash the dust of the road from their bodies.

Surprisingly, the King's party with Zusa's Mbadas, arrived a short while after with Makonde's force limping in over two hours later than expected. It was not a time for recrimination and the senior men from all groups gathered around their King for a briefing. He took a parchment from his backpack and spread it out on the ground in front of them all. "Sekuru Gemba has reminded me where, as two younger men many years ago, we managed to find a hidden passage through the mountain range. I do remember the day although not the exact route, but with Gemba's detailed directions I know we will manage to find it again." The diagram consisted of a number of jagged lines and indicated some type of path.

Their most skilled scouts were summoned and the map was shown to them. One of these men had heard the rumour of the passage but he had never seen it with his own eyes.

The animal skin parchment marked the line of the mountain range with the northern and southern passes shown clearly. A number of settlements were also indicated with the travel routes and other natural barriers, such as rivers in between, drawn in some detail. The secret passage was represented by a dotted line, snaking across the high ground with some additional features of the surrounding terrain and other signs, which should show the way through. The daylight would be gone in about two hours and so the scouts were sent ahead to confirm whether the route was still open and available to the Bantu army.

Prepared food was eaten cold while their thirsts were quenched. Most of the men sat, talking in low voices although there were quite a few who sat on their own in silence. Weapons were checked again, shield straps tightened and Zusa had his men string their bows.

A while later one of the scouts returned to report that they had in fact found the path drawn on the parchment. He explained that after an initial steep climb, the path folded back on itself a number of times where it eventually appeared to end against a sheer wall of rock, a dead end. However, a small ledge off the precipice actually took one around this barrier, then once over a number of step-like boulders, there was a crevice in the mountain side. The tunnel was wide enough for one man to pass through at a time and it sloped downwards quite considerably. The scouts had managed to penetrate the passageway for over five hundred paces before a rock fall stopped their progress. From the blockade they could make out what must be the opening on the other side of the mountain, as they could see distant light. The rock fall would take a couple of hours to clear, as they did not want to make too much noise in case it attracted the enemy's attention.

The rocks would have to be carried out of the corridor so that they would not hinder the passage of the troops expecting to pass through it.

King Yasini thought to himself that the clearing of the passage would delay their planned arrival on the far side of the mountain. To move almost three thousand men quietly through this narrow passage was going to take the remainder of the night. Reaching a decision he said to Zabesi. "Get your strongest men working on clearing the blockage, have them form a line so that the rocks can be passed from one to another. We will continue to rest the troops this side but we cannot afford to light any fires so they must remain their companies and await the call for them to begin to traverse the mountain passage.'"

The chiefs and their lieutenants patrolled the resting army to ensure that the instruction to keep quiet and for there to be no fires was enforced. There was no real need to do this as exhaustion had driven many to find a convenient place to rest and they had already fallen asleep.

It was completely dark by the time Zusa stirred and, for a moment, he was disorientated and could not work out where he was. He had done so much and travelled so far recently that his mind reeled. Rising to his feet, he quietly moved through the dozing forms around him, so as not to disturb the regiment. He managed to locate the command post set up to handle the tunnel excavation work and thereafter the logistics of getting the men safely through the rock channel. As he arrived, he heard the final report from the men tasked to clear the rock fall that the way was now open and he sat down in the circle of senior men. The only problem remaining was how to direct this mass of men through the difficult terrain in the dark to the other side?

Zusa spoke. "I may have a solution for you! Something Gemba gave to me before we left the city!" He reached for a grass woven basket, which he had carried all day. As he lifted the lid a dark green glow almost filled the basket and its illumination was enough to reflect in the eyes of those who were in the gathering. Someone said in a voice full of awe, "Glow beetles!"

"Yes," said Zusa, "Gemba spent the last night we were in the city collecting as many of the larvae as possible and he was fortunate enough to stumble across a rich patch of them." The glow-worm or beetle larva has been known to shine continuously for hours at a time without any apparent provocation other than a good shake of the insect, which results in a satisfying light. Those best for this predictable reaction are often fully-grown larvae which will soon be pupating, a part of their preparation for adulthood, and at a time when the larva's body is undergoing all manner of internal changes. Zusa took a specimen from the basket and secured it to a small stone with tree resin.

Even at this movement the worm glowed enough to offer an indicator which could be used to mark a safe path, although its illumination would not be enough to alert anyone looking from further afield. After a number of congratulatory words, the insects were glued to small rocks. The scouts were directed to set the finished glow lamps along the dark mountain pass.

Once the conversation settled, Zabesi turned to the King and said, "Sire, we have had no word from your bother Zimu and there is no sign of his regiment so far."

The King remained silent at the questioning statement. His own doubts were reflected in his eyes as he slowly answered. "I am sure Zimu is well aware of the seriousness of the situation and has probably been delayed by enemy action! He may have been forced to take a longer route to join us here. I am sure he will catch up with us by tomorrow morning." The ensuing silence hung in the air as each of the group took in what had actually been said.

Eventually it was time to begin moving the men, and Zabesi was directed to take his experienced warriors through the tunnel first, to form a protective wall on the far side. They would then be followed by the Mbada regiment so that their ranging weapons could be used effectively from the hillside if need be, followed by Makonde's large group with the palace guard bringing up the rear.

For the next five hours the men made their way along the glow-path and though the secret passage, all in relative silence. The only moment of concern was when two men fell from the cave exit, after losing their footing on the rock-strewn path and falling to their deaths down the steep cliff face. The noise of the rebounding rocks echoed throughout the area and the complete Bantu army froze in place, waiting to see if the noise had raised the alarm. Although the men fell to their death they had kept quiet and had not shouted during their fall and the only other sound was the wet, meaty thump as their bodies broke across the boulders below.

It was now only two hours to sunrise and the Bantu army was sectioned into the predetermined groups across the forest floor so they could get as much rest as possible whilst maintaining a state of readiness. The light of the Zulu campfires from within Belingwe on the far hill burned brightly in the night, the silhouettes of the buildings stark against the back-lit stage. The Zulus were obviously lax following their success over the last few days.

Now was the time for the army of Nyazimba to put aside all doubts and to concentrate on what needed to be accomplished, knowing that once the sun rose, they would have to face their foe and, with their backs literally against the wall, they knew that it was to be a moment to do or to die.

****

The thought of being safe was relative to those in the protective cave formations. Shawana was keeping a number of younger children quietly entertained whilst others bustled around them with clay pots and sacks of provisions being carried to the far end of the underground complex. The noise of so many people moving around echoed throughout the chambers and even whispered conversations resonated so that they were heard by everyone in the high roofed cave. The only light was from the daylight streaming through the main entrance which looked like an open mouth, and a few rocks added the eerie impression of sharpened teeth.

The refuge had been used for generations for the protection of the population; although not for quite a while as the newly constructed city walls had kept most enemies at bay. Those in the caves knew that times were now different and only strict discipline kept noise and the smoke from their camp fires under control.

The herds of cattle and goats were further away from the city in steep walled valleys. A number of younger boys were watching over the wealth of the nation which also provided fresh meat and milk to the isolated community.

Shawana was simply going through the motions with the children as her mind was at a place a lot further away.

Her father had led the second section of the army from the city whilst Zusa was with the King at the head of the Mbada regiment. *Where were they right now*, she thought to herself? *Were they safe? Had they found the Zulu?* Her mind was in turmoil as she struggled with everything which was going through her mind. She had only met Zusa a few days ago but her heart raced whenever she thought of him. She closed her eyes and asked Mware to keep him safe! One of the children noticed her and asked if she was unwell. "Is your tummy sore?"

"No," Shawana replied and turned away as her eyes glistened, "no, I am all right, I have just got a bit of dust in my eyes." Nodding her understanding the child lost interest and went back to the game and she whispered under her breath, "Keep him safe, Mware, keep him safe!"

Chapter Twenty-Six
The last battle

On the other side of the mountain range, the Bantu regiments stirred and awoke to find themselves shrouded in a fine haze which blanketed the veldt upon which they had settled in the early hour of the morning. The air held a slight chill from the cool night but it would not be long before the sun burnt off the mist and the temperature rose. It was deathly quiet with even the incessant noise of the insects absent.

A few coughs from men clearing their throats broke the silence and gradually the sounds increased becoming more discernible, the rustle of leaves and grass and the sounds of many men stirring. Shrugging off the stiffness and cramps from their cool night on the ground, the army began to come alive.

A breakfast of cold millet porridge and dried meat, washed down with the last of the goat's milk, was hastily taken while the final preparations for expected conflict were completed. Leather thongs were tightened on shields, spear handle grips rewound and their blades honed with rubbing stones. The drawn out rasps as the stone crossed the metal was enough to set even the bravest nerves on edge in anticipation of the battle. The priests who had travelled with the army moved around the wide spread warriors, offering words of encouragement for the day ahead. Men murmured to each other in muted conversation but the occasional chuckle indicated that their spirits remained high.

Further away, in a group, the King, Zabesi, Makonde and Zusa met for one last time before the battle was expected to commence.

The first question Yasini asked was, "Any sign or

news of my brother and his forces?"

"No, sire," Zabesi replied, "We have not heard or seen anything of the Zimutu regiment." The King nodded his head at the statement; his eyes betraying his hidden thoughts.

Makonde joined in, "The lack of support from your brother's forces is going to be felt! Maybe we should consider holding back until we find out where he is?"

"That is going to be impossible," the King responded. "Look around you. We are exposed here and cut off from the city by the mountain range we crossed last night!" He turned away to hide the anger he had at his brother's failure to arrive. "No," he said in a calmer voice. "Today, we make a stand. We still have surprise on our side and we will go ahead with our original plan." He looked at each man in the group in turn. "Tell your men this. Today we stand, today we fight and today we will win. Let's move the men out."

The regimental leaders made their way back to their formations that had been patiently awaited their return. The army broke camp on instruction and formed into the pre-planned battle-lines. Their preparations were complete before the sun orb rose fully above the horizon. Movement orders were given in quiet voices and as soon as it was light enough to be able to see the man in front, the final command was given to move forward to the appointed battlefield, scouted the previous evening.

There was no idle conversation, just the occasional order to dress lines or to raise shields. The front regiments passed by the night picket guard positions given away by the flattened foliage caused by their regular patrols. The forest through which they passed had trees with trunks as thick as a man's leg, grey in colour, speckled with white lichen and stained with a green furry moss. It was known that this particular growth flourishes on the east side of a tree, which is exposed to the light and warmth of the sunrise, and it can be used to navigate by touch, in the dark.

The tree branches and leaves of this forest were high enough so as not to interrupt the immediate line of vision and the forest floor was covered with long grass, which swayed with the breeze, limiting an open view beyond the woodland's boundary.

All night the enemy's campfires had burned deep within their protective fort and their smoke had stained the low mist brought on by the clear skies. This eerie, glowing vapour had continued to swirl in the morning breeze. The bark of a baboon echoed across the land and with an explosion, which caught even the battle hardened with surprise, the first of the large flocks of resident weaver birds took to the air from their overnight tree roosts. The thought that raced through the leaders' minds was, were they disturbed by something or was it just time for the birds to take to the air?

Under orders to remain quiet, the senior men suppressed any attempt at conversation; however, the movement of so many warriors could more be sensed than heard. The occasional cracking of dried twigs and leaves, the kicking of loose stones or the accidental rattle of spear against shield completed the sensory spectrum.

Breaking through the perimeter of the woodland in which the army had encamped, the frontal regiments pulled up in shock. Before them, they found that their enemy had already arrayed itself in a battle formation only two hundred paces in front of their position although in the soft light of the morning the enemy's disposition was difficult to make out.

The Bantu army had thought that their final approach had gone undetected but, obviously, something had given away their element of surprise, for their enemy had had time to prepare before the planned assault. Yasini's first thought was, *is this connected to the absence of my brother and his troop? No, he would never dare! Have we done enough? Are we ready?*

Sensing the surprise of the lead Bantu warriors, their commanders called loudly, halting the second and third waves of soldiers before they broke cover to reveal their battle formation and strength, to the waiting Zulu.

After much debate in the city, the army of Nyazimba had been restructured, based on lines of seniority and experience. Following the first fateful battle against the Zulu, ten days ago, the front line was now made up from the remainder of the experienced warriors in two regiments, just over eight hundred men strong.

The second line consisted primarily of the new recruits who had been in training at the time of the invasion but who had not been sent with the ill-fated main army. More numerous than the former, over one thousand two hundred, its lines were strengthened with retired warriors, some of whom had been instructors at sometime. Many of these senior men were really looking forward to the battle, especially as they had thought their days on the battlefield had passed them by.

The third and last line of warriors consisting of all manner of men and was where Zusa had been placed with his regiment of four hundred and fifty Mbadas, armed with their newly revived weaponry. They were with another group of three hundred and sixteen boys, younger than those in the bowman regiment, along with some older men, well past their prime. These would be the Bantus' last resort. No one else would stand between the invading Zulu army and the city of Nyazimba if the battle got as far as this. It was part of the plan that this last body of men was there to project a perception of depth in the defences of the Bantu force, which in reality did not exist. Not everything is as it seems in battle and deception was considered a major part of the strategy.

Zusa looked about his position and realised how much he missed having his mentor close by him especially at this time. Gemba had been instructed to stay in the city and had had to be almost physically restrained from trying to join the army. Furthermore, it was not until the King had personally instructed him that he agreed to remain within the defensive walls of the city.

The King had placed himself to the left of the front line formation, where he was surrounded by two hundred and seven of the palace guard.

Other senior chieftains stood by this position so that they would be able to pass on the King's instructions as messengers. From here, Yasini was able to see the whole valley and surrounding area which was soon to become a part of their history either in a resounding defeat or in spectacular victory.

Both warring armies were arrayed at a similar height but on parallel wooded hillsides, separated by a gap of almost two hundred paces. Between these positions was a grass-covered area dipping into the valley before flattening out across a distance of about fifty paces, the killing ground. The grass was short, possibly recently grazed by a domestic herd as the area offered some natural shelter, with the end of the valley curving around and shaped like the hoof of a buffalo. Both the Bantu King and the Zulu chiefs had made use of one of the numerous gigantic anthills on which they had climbed to gain a commanding view of the battleground.

For a while the two factions stood in silence looking at each other in a drawn-out game of nerves with only the breeze causing the sound of rustling leaves, grass and trees. Occasionally a nervous cough was heard from within the ranks.

Eventually, the Zulus stirred after a high, prolonged command from their chief. As one they responded with a deep rumbling war cry of "Gee", which carried a note, low enough to vibrate in the bellies of their foes. In a single motion they presented their shields forward, which until then had been held edge on to the battlefront, minimising their frame. All of a sudden, what had first appeared as a broken formation of men spread out, becoming a virtually solid wall of armed warriors. The manoeuvre was accompanied by a clatter of assegai against shield. The techniques had an immediate impact on the front line of the Bantu formation who almost as one, let out a breath of surprise, It appeared to the waiting Bantu that they had already been overlapped and outflanked by their enemy, which from an initial estimate must have numbered well over two thousand men.

King Yasini immediately sensed the effect this aggressive stance had had on his men and he called out further encouragements, his voice carrying clearly over his own forces, who in turn managed to steel themselves at the reassuring sound of their King's words. "Steady men. Hold fast, they are just trying to intimidate you."

A voice behind him was heard to say, "Well it worked didn't it?" A few chuckles from the men around him defused the comment and even the King smiled at the words. Turning to Zabesi, he commented, "Look at that. The Zulu have extended their lines in an attempt to outflank our forces. As we know how many men they have available to field, it must mean other than at their centre," he pointed with his spear, "the two flanking forces, the ox horns, are only a single man deep."

Zabesi nodded his head in agreement. "Yes, your Majesty, I agree with what you say, but look beyond that position," he indicated with an outstretched arm, "I can make out what must be some form of reserve force standing behind their commanders!" A mass of Zulus could just been seen milling around within the cover of the tree line.

"Yes I can see them now." Yasini paused to think and then went on. "It is time for us to put our new ideas to the test. Have Zusa march the Mbada regiment to the extreme right-hand flank of the Zulu position. Tell him that he is to keep the regiment well out of sight of the enemy so that they cannot see the movement. Once he is in position, he is to remain hidden until the battle lines have joined.
Tell him that at some stage I will signal for the retreat of our troops with three trumpets calls. The Zulu can be expected to be drawn backwards with us and I will use another four long trumpet calls to signal to Zusa to advance to the hill line and fire into their flank and rear."

"Yes, my Lord," Zabesi responded and strode away to hand on the instructions. Chemwapuwa and Goredema had been close enough to hear this conversation and they looked at each other for a while before Goregema's mouth broke into a wide smile.

"We are going to avenge our friends, for today will be a great battle." His colleague nodded his head in agreement. "Yes! Today is a good day to kill or be killed." By now, the traditional chants and exaggerated gestures of the two armies had begun. The braver warriors stepped out of line and shouted a challenge normally accompanied with a twirl in the air, showing their backs to their foe before strutting back to their position with their arms waving in a stiff legged walk. The hooting and jeering of the other troops added to the raucous behaviour with many of the men becoming extremely animated in their gesticulations and the lines wavered with the increasing aggression.

The regimental commanders on both sides were having difficulty in restraining their men and the urge to charge increased as the blood-lust grew. Behind the Zulus' antagonistic stance was the need to overpower a weaker foe; to the Bantu it was a matter of revenge and ultimately their survival.

The King had insisted earlier that every effort was to be made to bring to the battle site the large bass war drums normally used to call an alert at the city, as their sounding drowned most other noises and the note carried over a great distance. There were twelve of these gigantic instruments and they had been taken apart to get them through the mountain tunnel. Now they were reassembled and were being rolled into position behind the Bantu line and within the cover of the trees. At a signal from the King, the percussionists began their measured beat, calling all to arms.

Behind the lines, Zabesi found Zusa in his position deeper into the trees out of sight of the enemy and he passed on the King's instructions. Zusa felt a rush of adrenaline and excitement at being given a directive so early in the confrontation. This was especially so as he had not known if the King was going to give his men a chance to prove their weapons and new tactics as they had had so little time to refine their use.

Grasping immediately the King's intention, Zusa turned to the Mbada and summoned his section leaders. Wide-eyed they listened carefully to what was now expected of them. The instruction was given to string the bows. Some of the smaller boys needed help from their heavier colleagues to bend the bodies of the bows and in attaching the sinew string. The bows were carried on the march unstrung for two reasons, the first being that the tension of the wood and string would weaken from prolonged strain and secondly, moving through thick brush and low trees would catch the weapon and slow down the warrior.

Leather pouches of arrows with about thirty projectiles in each were thrown over their shoulders for ease of access and portability. Now properly prepared, the Leopard regiment moved off, section by section, to circle around the forming battle lines and all the while, the sound of the war drums followed them to remind them of the urgency of the manoeuvre. Zusa took one final look around to ensure all his men had moved off and turned to follow the group. As he started, Pimi stepped into his path, backed up by at least another eighty of his own boy-warriors armed with shield and spear.

Zusa pulled back in alarm, looking for support in what would appear to be an opportune moment for his childhood foe to enact a final revenge. Sensing Zusa's reaction Pimi called out, "No, Zusa, we are not here to harm you, we," he indicated those behind him, he paused, "well actually," he said, "I want to help you." He emphasised the word "I".

Zusa was shocked by the gesture and asked in an incredulous voice, "How Pimi? What is it you are suggesting to do?"

Pimi responded, "By being able to guard the flanks of your regiment. I heard what the King has instructed you to do and it is no good you attacking whilst your men are at risk of a counter or flank attack." Zabesi had stayed to ensure that the Mbada left as instructed and he had heard the exchange; Zusa looked at him and questioningly said,
"We hadn't thought of any protection. Will the King let Pimi and his men go with me?" The chieftain thought to himself. "Yes I agree. I will tell the King what we done. Now go," he said, "and may our ancestors go with you."

At that, Zusa stretched out his hand in an offer of friendship. Pimi responded to the gesture and shook it with delight. "Let's go, brother," he said and with a final sweep of his arm, Zusa led the spearmen into battle. With a spring in their step the group followed Pimi and Zusa who were running shoulder to shoulder at a hard pace to catch up with the bowmen who were already fifty paces ahead of them. The sounds of the opposing armies faded behind them whilst they jumped and side-stepped over and around rocks and shrubs. They eventually caught up with the Mbada and the two groups joined just at the point from where they were able to loop around and move up the right hand side of the battlefield. The climb was hard and the need to remain silent made it even more difficult.

Once near the summit, Zusa called for a halt and indicated that the enlarged group should go to ground. Crouching over, he summoned the section leaders of both bow and spear regiments, to him. He pointed to Seki and said, "Get the most reliable marksmen from your group to reconnoitre. It will be no good if we run into the Zulu flank guards and they raise the alarm. If you locate any, deal with them." He looked into his eyes, the meaning all too clear. Seki acknowledged the command and moved away to his section.

Quietly, twenty bowmen broke away from the group and merged into the green wall of the forest and disappeared from sight. Zusa continued, "Pimi, have your men form in line to guard our flank over there." He indicated an area about fifty paces away and at ninety degrees to the bowmen's position. "The Mbada will assemble in two lines here but we will await the King's signal before we break cover and attack the Zulu. I intend to keep a small force within the forest as a mobile reserve." In a louder voice he said, "Everyone must keep out of sight until I tell you to move forward. Is this clear?" He looked around the group receiving nods of acceptance. "Alright move out and await my next order."

The Mbada mingled for a while until the formation was in directed into place; Pimi led his men away to the instructed position where they created a line just within sight of the bowmen. Zusa's self-appointed bodyguard, made up from the reserves, moved forward with him in search of the break in cover so that he could ascertain their position in relation to the main battlefield below. He knew he was close to its edge because the sounds of the challenging calls and chants were becoming clearer as he crept forward.

He broke cover just in time to catch the first real aggressive movement of the opposing armies. The Zulu moved first. They had grown weary of the waiting game the Bantu had seemed to be happy to play all day and, as one, their lines rushed towards the Nyazimbian army.

Once the first stirring had been made the front line of the Bantu army also reacted, started off by a missed beat of the giant war drums. Taking firmer hold of their long spears they stepped forward at a fast pace. As the gap between the armies narrowed the warriors shrugged off their last vestiges of civilisation leaving only the discipline of their training to hold their lines against the rising desire to race to the kill. It was important that the integrity of the Bantu front line met the Zulu whilst they were still in an even formation otherwise their enemies could easily decimate them.

As planned, once the warriors of the Zulu first line begun advancing and had committed themselves to battle, the second wave of Nyazimba's warriors also hurried forward, following their front line. Two sections broke left and right to act as a stop gap and to prevent their front line from being outflanked by the Zulu ox-horn formation, whilst the majority of the formation ran on towards what was going to become the battlefront's centre.

The Bantu front line continued to move forwards at an even, measured pace until the piercing note of a trumpet sounded, and then they slowed to a walk and finally halted. They dug the butts of their long spears into the ground and securing them in place with their feet, the warriors angled their weapons so that they left the iron-tipped head at the chest height of the approaching Zulus. Bringing their shields around to offer a form of defence they called in union, "Tapedza, *finished*. We are here!"

The drums reverberated even louder and the direction from where they sounded became confused by the repetition of the bass notes, echoing in and around the valley walls.

The Zulus howled at the unexpected change in the

formation of their foe, as they had thought that they would be able to close on the Bantu in their now traditional ox-horn battle order, to sweep aside the Bantu spears and shields before plunging their assegais into the torsos of their prey. Although slightly daunted, the Zulu continued to rush at the spiked defensive line, shouting and screaming their anger.

In a well-choreographed movement, the Bantus' second wave continued to stride towards the imminent point of impact. From a gentle trot they accelerated and reaching a sideways, crab-like sprint, they heaved their spears, in unison, into the air, with a grunting cough that merged into a roar of defiance.

The air became darkened with almost eight hundred heavy spears being thrown and within the seconds it took for the flight of the weapons, the Zulu attacking line was ripped apart with many of the projectiles finding targets. Behind the spear throwers were other men carrying spare spears so that the throwing line could re-arm in as little time as possible and continue to rain down death from afar. This second wave of spears was thrown. However by now, the enemy was wiser and they held their shields above their heads in order to deflect the attack from above, a number of spears still broke through to embed themselves in the flesh, whilst some shields became over burdened and unwieldy with the weight of multiple javelins sticking into them and they had to be cast aside. Just as the Zulus had learnt a lesson, so in addition, had the senior Bantu warriors, for as soon as the Zulu shields were lifted into the air to deflect the spears, the front line Bantu combatants retrieved their grounded spears and stabbed at the exposed bodies of the Zulu arrayed before them.

By the time the Zulu line reached the stationary spiked defensive line the impact and momentum of their charge had been lost. Many a Zulu, not expecting this change in tactics, became impaled on the barrier whilst those who had managed to slow down in time were trying to pound aside the hedge of spears in an attempt to close with the warriors beyond.

With Zulu after Zulu falling to javelin or spear thrust

the attacking line faltered and began to give way. The Bantu defensive line now became the battle's advancing offensive line and the only way forward was to step on or over the fallen bodies, which were stabbed where they lay to ensure that they did not rise up again to attack after they had been passed over by the warriors.

With this violent move forward a number of the front line Bantu warriors were killed or injured and fell out of their positions. These gaps were immediately filled by the less experienced troops behind them. However, these replacements in turn, seemed to become casualties even quicker than the former and the Bantus' ready reinforcements were beginning to dwindle. But still the drums kept on their constant beat encouraging them forward.

The Nyazimba induna's hurried about, directing reserves into place whilst a third and fourth hail of javelins were thrown over the heads of the front line embedding themselves into yet more Zulu warriors. The effect of the last two spear volleys was weakened as they had been thrown from a stationary position and as the targets were now more spread out.

The Zulu flanking troops had by now managed to swing around the Bantus' central force's position and with a clash of shields, they made contact. They were immediately slowed by the depth and strength of the Nyazimba second line wing. However, the Zulu were able to slam into the shield wall formation and their tactics of getting in close to their targets now paid off. Assegai blades were plunged into the bodies of the men facing them, their metal surfaces flashing in the early sunlight whilst blood spattered and the screams of men in pain and dying rose on the air almost drowning out the constantly present war drums. More Nyazimbian warriors fell and were quickly replaced and when there were no reserves available the lines closed up to prevent gaps being left open in the line. Gaps which would be taken advantage of by the more aggressive Zulu.

Backwards and forwards the lines surged, like waves breaking on the shores of a lake but gradually the Zulu battle line began to buckle under the Bantu answering deep-layered offensive. Sensing the loss in momentum, the Zulu commanders, on the hill behind their lines, sent in a portion of their reserves, about eight hundred men. In a wedge formation and in support of their brethren, the group sprinted down the hill towards the centre of the front line where there was a fierce melee taking place between the two forces of front line troops, assegai against spears.

The Bantu static defence had successfully prevented the Zulus from getting too close and with the accompanying launching of spears from behind, had taken down almost four hundred of their enemy.

Even with this disadvantage, the Zulus' superior training had allowed them to edge past the spiked defence. Killing even more of the experienced Bantu soldiers, they had opened up wide gaps towards which the Zulu reinforcements were now heading and in the blink of an eye, the Bantu line broke and enemy troops poured through the breach, killing and maiming as they vented their fury on the insolent Bantu.

A shout of, "The line has broken!" caused King Yasini to turn his head quickly in an attempt to grasp the situation. Realising that the Zulus had indeed broken through his men sooner than he had expected, he shouted to the bearer of the kudu horn trumpet, "Sound the recall immediately!"

The resulting sound dragged out the three tone call, fast, fast, slow, which caused a number of the battling soldiers to turn their heads at the unexpected signal, with many of them paying for the momentary lost in concentration with their lives.

With the hesitation that a change in battle plan or formation modification brings, the Bantu were now on the back foot and the breach in their line widened as the wedge-shaped attacking force pushed through. The Nyazimbian warriors attempted to disengage with the enemy and withdraw to the apparent safety of the rear defensive row at the tree line. Confusion had taken reign.

The retreating front ranks stumbled into their own reinforcements, some of whom were still pushing forward in the heat of the battle either not aware of the new command, or too full of battle lust to hear. The once orderly ranks of the Bantu became fouled with the attempted withdrawal and the King knew that unless control was re-established soon, it would lead to serious bewilderment amongst the ranks, which in turn could result in a full and uncontrollable retreat. Realising the full extent of what had happened; he called to his royal guard to follow him, and without hesitation, leaped into the centre of the muddled formation in an attempt to regain control of his army. It was a dangerous move to attempt in the midst of a full-blown battle. Knocking aside some of his retreating warriors, Yasini knew he needed to use his personal force and presence to stiffen the line so that the planned tactical withdraw could take place. He raced through the ranks, jumping over prone corpses while calling out orders to keep his royal guard around him as a coherent fighting force. At best, he had just seconds to prevent the situation becoming an uncontrollable rout.

Chapter Twenty-Seven
From the lookout

In the City of Stone the sun had just begun to rise: its golden and red colours staining the eastern horizon. Gemba was on the highest part of the mountain fortress looking west; in the direction the three columns of the new Bantu army had travelled two days before. He could picture their last trek towards the unknown. The only thing they did know though was that the Zulu had swept the first Bantu army of over three thousands warriors aside in what had been a change in traditional tactics or protocols of war.

Gemba could imagine in his mind the exact route taken by the second, hastily prepared army, sent out, not fully trained and with little experience. Zusa's newly formed regiment of bowmen was the main cause of his anxiety, and only because of the King's personal instructions was he convinced to remain in the city instead of accompanying Zusa to the battlefield.

The enemy had been reported as still being camped in and around the fort at Belingwe, which they had captured well before the King had even been made aware of their presence in his kingdom.

Gemba was further agitated that the King's brother, Zimu, and his regiment of over one thousand warriors had not materialised from Zimutu where their garrison was based in the north of the Bantu nation and Gemba knew they had been summoned with enough notice so that they could have joined the King on his way to the confrontation.

Maybe they had been delayed and decided to meet the King further along the planned route of the march, Gemba thought to himself. Messengers had been backwards and forwards all night with the last getting through in the early hours of this morning, making his report only four hours old, showing that the King's brother had still not arrived! "Where could he possibly be? The King needed these men; otherwise the outcome was far from being determined in their favour!" he said aloud.

This messenger had also said that the King's army had camped for the remainder of the evening with the Zulu campfires in sight of their hidden position. Their route through the secret mountain passage had gone as planned and the morrow would bring about some form of conclusive battle. Gemba smiled to himself at the memory of the boyhood mischief which had revealed the existence of this way through the mountain range. *It has served us well this day*, he thought to himself.

The sun had cleared the horizon by this time and although the countryside to the east was bathed in light from the clear blue sky, the west was still shrouded in a grey shadow and would remain so until the sun rose higher into the sky. The morning breeze carried the clean scent of the night and the promise of a new day across the plains below.

For safety the city had been closed up tight. The remaining skeleton fortress guard was on a high alert with three watches taking turns to man the lookout points and walls. Those off duty were available at short notice either eating or catching up on lost sleep within the barracks. The main city gates from both the east and west approaches had been kept closed and all the interlocking passages had been blocked with warriors controlling movement between these areas. All unnecessary travel. had been curtailed with some areas higher up on the fortress hill made out of bounds for many of the remaining citizens.

The security of the city was firmly in Gemba's hands and he had formulated the present structure of the defences. Two mobile reserve forces of fifty men were held in strategic positions in each of the welcoming chambers east and west of the city near the two main gateways. It would be through these areas that any attacker would have to pass to penetrate the city. From these vantage points the reinforcements could be rushed to any vulnerable area being assaulted or weakened by an attacking force. Both sides of the fortress were well protected by the gigantic stone walls and the only way through would be via the guarded gateways. Even if these were broken into and the entrance tunnels penetrated, their narrow, restrictive design would mean that only one enemy soldier would be able to get through them at a time and thus could be easily dealt with.

Gemba had personally inspected the north face of the hill upon which the city was built and he realised that, although an approach from this direction would be extremely difficult, it could assailed by a determined foe. He had the villagers stack rocks and large stones above the bottlenecks and natural pathways in the terrain so that they could be rained down upon an approaching army. The city walls were at their highest point here so an attack from this direction would be improbable but all contingencies had to be planned for.

Gemba had even arranged for an early warning system to be set up and manned day and night. He had sent trusted men and in one case some older boys to key hilltop locations, which were in the line of sight with Nyazimba's highest observation point, so that signals by fire at night or smoke by day could warn the city of an approaching danger. The effectiveness of this scheme had been put to the test the day before. The sounding of the kudu horn trumpets had raised the alarm, after the signal towers to the south-east of the city had sent a column of smoke into the air. The trumpets' reverberation had caused a mild panic as the Zulu were thought to be at least three or four days away and to the west. Gemba had made his way as fast as he could to the watch tower while the main guard turned out with half the force being dispatched to reinforce the guards on the southern entrance gate and walls.

For the next hour Gemba had strained his eyes for the first sight of the cause for the distant alarm, when suddenly, a young boy standing near him shouted, "There look on the hill crest. Warriors are approaching!"

After a little more searching and the boy pointing with his finger, Gemba eventually saw the approaching men, like ants moving in single file. At a fast trot they disappeared from sight as they descended into a valley only to reappear a short while later, but a little closer. From this distance, their formation was eventually deciphered and with relief, Gemba realised that it was the two border guard regiments from Majiri and Runyanhi, returning to the city in answer to their summons. Gemba had sent another message to these groups for them to make all haste once he had realised that the King's brother just might not make it to the planned assembly position in time.

    Majiri and Runyanhi were two small fortresses which were used to guard the trade road to the coast, whilst providing fixed points of secure accommodation for travellers along the way. The stone fortress of Majiri was the first stop on the trade route; it consisted of a number of concentric circles with sixteen demarcated areas containing huts and holding areas.

    Runyanhi was a little smaller but, like its neighbour, it was also a well-equipped, natural stronghold.

    As the reinforcements made their way up the southern entrance's stone stairway, the newly-arrived men were received by cheering crowds, almost as if they were returning victors. Their numbers would swell the depleted garrison troops which had been stripped to bolster the King's force. Even before they had the opportunity to recover from their travels, the warriors were put to work helping to shore up the city's defences.

    Before the ordered the lockdown of Nyazimba the usual two-way traffic of the living city was distorted by the one-way inwards transfer of people carrying water and foodstuff consisting of millet grain, root plants and fruits. Some of the nation's animals, cattle and goats, along with their fodder, had been corralled within designated areas on the outskirts of the town, within the walls. The remainder of the national herd had been sent into the secret valley locations spread throughout the surrounding mountains and hills where they had been left to their own fate.

It was expected that a number of these would be lost to predators but this was a far better option than having the whole herd driven off by the Zulu. The newly grown grass in these meadows would keep the animals well sustained until they were retrieved.

Gemba caught himself with this thought: *Once or if they were ever recovered* he contemplated. As soon as this thought had passed through his mind he chastised himself at his defeatist attitude. "Not if at all, but definitely once the Zulu have been driven off," he said aloud as if in final confirmation.

The previous night he had had the perimeter guards set on full alert with all of the watch towers manned and light towers well fuelled. Preparation for this action alone had occupied a large portion of the available work force, cutting and ferrying enough timber to keep the hungry fires burning all night. The forests from where this fuel was cut were almost half a day away to the north, as the city had consumed the surrounding lumber over time, and so this increased distance had affected the rate at which it could be ported into the city.

The thick, sticky black sand, known as tara, from the southern lower valleys, four days' journey away, was also stockpiled, with a well-timed trading caravan arriving just two days previously. The traders were pleasantly surprised at the eagerness with which their entire consignment had been purchased and paid for with gold by the city fathers.

This newly discovered material had been found to have a number of useful properties. On a small scale and in a lightly heated state it was used to treat open wounds or better still, to help complete amputations by sealing the wound in an airtight manner whilst its temperature cauterised all the blood vessels in an instant. Although this remedy appeared to be a kill or cure solution a surprisingly large number of patients had recovered fully which far outperformed previously used procedures and known cures for these conditions.

The second, more advantageous asset of this product was the ease and intensity, both in heat and light, at which it burnt. A small flame was enough for the material to catch alight and even a heavy downpour of rain could not snuff its fiery activity, and strong winds just boosted it so that it would burn until it consumed itself completely. If added, in smaller quantities, this tara contributed to the watch tires and fire torches used by the city. It was also the key to the early warning arrangements from the furthest perimeter guards.

Gemba made a note to himself to investigate these marvellous properties further once time was less pressing. There could be additional applications for such a wonderful substance but he knew they had to learn to control its strength first, like knowing how to stop it from burning once it was no longer needed.

On top of these preparations, the miners from the surrounding gold and iron mines had been summoned to bring in the last of the metal-bearing ore. The iron was still being processed into new weapons as fast as the smiths could produce them and after the mass-produced arrowheads had been completed the gold smelting had been restarted so that any other essential materials could be purchased with its currency if the products were traded before the Zulus made it to the city walls.

Gemba reminded himself to ensure that these artisans were also sent to safety once their tasks were complete in order to preserve their knowledge for future generations in case the city fell to the invaders. Their experience and understanding would take generations to replace. These craftsmen were primarily in their old age; however their apprentices were the future and would have to go with them although he knew that the younger men would not want to leave their city undermanned.

Reminding himself of the King's own words to him, "No matter how much we feel we should be doing something in order to satisfy our own desires and needs to be fighting the Zulu, we must not lose sight of the greater picture, that being our nation's ultimate survival, and so I ask that we ensure that all craftsmen, farmers, women and children are preserved so that the nation has the chance of a rebirth in case we are defeated in battle." Gemba knew he too might have to give a similar speech when the time came for these people to leave.

The royal family, all the King's wives and children

together with most of the city's women and children, had been sent to the holy caves of Chamavara and Dengeni, north-east of Nyazimba. At these places, the resident priests and priestesses would look after them until the conflict had been decided. The paths to these cave complexes were known only to a few and large quantities of cattle had been driven behind the masses to cover the traces of their footprints. These caves were two days' walk away from the city and had always been used in times of strife.

Another key reason for the evacuation of the city had been necessitated by the newly-imposed food rationing which had been put into place so that the limited resources could be used to their best effect, feeding fighting men and key city personnel. Water had been collected and stored in giant clay urns within the city and these would be kept topped up, right until the time they lost control of the water gate guarding the dam below.

From his observation point, Gemba took a last look across the landscape before he began the long walk back into the city to complete yet another check on the perimeter and other ongoing preparations. Many of the remaining people in the city, seeing him walk by, raised their hands in greetings to the Madala. Others stopped him in the street in conversation even if it was just in an attempt to allay their own doubts and fears about the coming days and to draw on his confidence.

One by one, Gemba took the time to address each question and at other times he gave an instruction or correction to someone working on the defences as he passed by.

His presence had a calming effect on those he interacted with and so he continued this regular activity for the remainder of the morning stopping neither for food or refreshment, for he knew that time was their first enemy and there were still many things to be checked and checked again.

It was during his morning round that the city alarm was raised once again, catching many who were going about their business unaware. Was this just another patrol coming in, a messenger from the King or was it the real thing, the Zulu? Gemba was in the western reception area at ground level. Looking up to the sentry tower he called, "Which signal station has given the warning?"

"None, my sire, it is not a warning signal I see many warriors, maybe one thousand in number and they have crossed the fields below the west gate; our guards have managed to close it and they have taken up their defensive station on the ramparts."

"What!" Gemba thought in horror, "How did such an army get by our outposts and so close to us without alerting our guards?" At a run he headed for the main gate to be in a position to assess the situation first hand. The reserve guard had also turned out and there was a rush for them to man their allotted posts. Gemba wisely left these men to go ahead of him.

Feet stamped on the bare paths and the scuff on the stone steps was mixed with the cries of alarm and orders. Shields and spears rattled in haste but by the time Gemba had managed to make it through the narrow passages to his intended destination; all the posts were calling in reports of their state of readiness.

Just before the main gate was another closed, controlled entrance and as Gemba walked up to it he indicated for the guard above it to raise the portal so that he could go through.

With a rasp of wood against stone the door panel was raised, the man above grunting with the effort. As it was halfway up, Gemba bent over to duck beneath it and as soon as he was through, he called for it to be lowered and locked back into place. He continued to the right of the east gate and arrived at it just in time to see the unidentified warriors stop before the outer perimeter gate on the far side of the river in an open and even formation.

With a start, he realised that his men were standing on their defensive wall and talking to someone on the other side, not an action expected in a time of a frontal assault by an enemy. The induna in charge of the first line defensive wall was animated in his conversation with whoever was on the other side but after a few minutes of discussion the guard turned towards one of his men, shouted an instruction at which the messenger left his post to run towards Gemba's position. *Well I guess my questions are about to be answered*, he thought to himself. The breathless messenger arrived at the base of the inner protective wall and once he caught sight of Gemba he shouted, "Sekuru, it is the King's brother, Zimu, he has arrived with his regiment and he is demanding we give him access to the city!"

Gemba was confused at the revelation of who had led these soldiers to the city. He thought for a few seconds to himself. *What is Zimu doing here? He should be with the King! Why is his regiment here instead of being in the field with the rest of the army?* Making a decision he said, "Tell Zimu that someone will be down to speak to him shortly." The messenger spun on his feet and raced back with the instruction.

Gemba used the time taken to get off the inner wall to think about the new situation. By this stage, a number of other senior men had joined him and were discussing the unexpected turn of events. He looked at one of these men, Mudede, whose eyes indicated the unanswered questions. He asked, "What will you have us do, Sekuru?"

"Send twenty warriors to accompany me to the outer wall so that I can hear with my own ears why Zimu is here and not with the King! Once I have gone down you must close the inner city again and keep all the men at their posts. If there is treachery afoot, then it will be for you to defend the inner city to the last."

With measured steps, Gemba retraced his way back towards the main passageway with his escort following closely behind. The inner city gate took a while to open as it had two thick-wooded gates which had to be raised, but once through the tunnel Gemba stepped into the bright sunshine and began the walk to the causeway, river and beyond to the outer perimeter wall. It had taken some time to get down to this position and Gemba had used it to think about the predicament.

As he got closer he could hear voices raised in anger although their exact words were muffled by the dividing stone wall and difficult to make out. By this stage the guards on top of the walls were becoming nervous at the presence of the King's brother on the far side and the insults being directed at them.

Gemba caught the last words by the induna in charge of the perimeter defence: "Ehe baba, I know what you are saying but I am obeying direct orders."

An angry deep voice responded, "Who dare issue instructions which you choose to obey over mine?"

"The King of Nyazimba dares," Gemba answered on behalf of the induna, as he stepped onto the parapet. "He is obeying King Yasini's, your brother's, instructions." He moved forward to the edge of the stone wall so that he was looking down onto the massed Zimutu warriors. Behind him his escort appeared which caused Zimu's men to react, a murmur arising at the sight of the reinforcements.

"Ha ha, Gemba, I should have known my brother would have left the city in the hands of someone like you, instead of entrusting it to his own blood," Zimu exclaimed.
He was an almost identical image of the King although less regal in stature and younger by twelve years, tall, dark and forbidding with his tokens of office, a decorative ceremonial axe in one hand and his pure white ox-hide shield in the other.

"Well I am sure the King also sent clear and detailed instructions to you," Gemba responded. "Didn't he ask for you to join him with your men at the place where he expects to meet the Zulu. Why are you here instead?"

Zimu bridled at the challenging question. "Who are you to challenge my decisions and my whereabouts? I have decided to come to the rescue of the city!" he shouted.

Unaffected by Zimu's anger, Gemba had another query, "How did you get by our watch towers? We were not..." Gemba paused; he was going to say warned but said instead, "advised of the King's brother's approach."

Sensing the hidden meaning of the response, Zimu answered, "Well, some of my brother's people recognise my authority and position within the nation and they did as they were instructed. I thought to surprise the people of the city in order to give them a sense of hope."

Alarmed, Gemba cut in, "And what about the men at the watch post?"

"Ah, your concern for your King's subjects which are not really your responsibility is touching Gemba, but don't worry. Other than one lad, who is nursing a sore head from a lesson well learnt, they are all well. In fact, some of my men are standing watch with them at this time. Now open the gates so that I can offer my protection to the King's wives, his children and the heir apparent, the King's eldest son, Shira."

Gemba was becoming increasingly concerned because it was clear that Zimu had deliberately avoided joining the King before the expected battle and had instead moved on the city with his force intact. A city which he knew full well was weakly defended and without its ruling monarch present. It left Gemba in a political dilemma, as protocol stated that the King's brother, or any other senior member of the royal family, should be welcomed into the city with open arms. But never before had this occurred with the King actually not being in attendance to receive them.

"Have your guards stand down and open the gates in greeting to me, Gemba," demanded Zimu. "Immediately, before you risk offending your King's blood by refusing me and my regiment hospitality."

Gemba knew he was trapped between his responsibility to the city and the common courtesy to be afforded to his liege's younger sibling.

"Of course, sire, at once. I will announce you to the city but you should know that the royal family has already been sent away and are in hiding for their own protection. They will not be able to benefit from your sacrifice of travel and offer of assistance."

Darkness flickered across Zimu's eyes and was noticed by Gemba, who was watching for some reaction to the news. "Well, allow me refuge anyway. We have travelled far in order to come to your aid. My regiment will offer you a welcome addition in manpower to the defences."

Gemba saw an opening and responded, "According to our custom, Zimu, you are most welcome into the city, but you know that no more than your immediate entourage and personal guard are allowed into the inner limits. Your men will have to make camp outside the walls."

Zimu baulked at the suggestion. "What, and leave my men outside the city, open to a sneak attack and risk of being trapped between the Zulu and the city walls? I tell you again, Gemba, let us in," he shouted, waving his arms in anger.

Knowing the dangers of allowing over one thousand soldiers loyal to Zimu into the city, Gemba also saw the other side of the situation. If the Zulu did manage to get past the King's forces and make it as far as the city then they would need every Bantu man they could to get onto the ramparts in defence.

A plan formulated itself in his mind. *He would let Zimu's troops into the city but only as far as the inner defences and this meant that Zimu's regiments would have to take on the responsibility of guarding the perimeter and water gates. It also meant that he could pull back his men currently doing performing this duty, giving him additional men of his own to redistribute elsewhere. The only glaring problem was that he would be trapped within a ring of Zimu forces. No, he could not allow that. He would maintain the southern gateway with the relieved forces, leaving Zimu only the responsibility of the western defences.*

Looking down at where Zimu stood he said, "Sire, you are so right, we need to put aside etiquette for the sake of the nation," and he went on to explain where Zimu's regiments were to encamp. "We will provide some food but I suggest you send foraging parties out to supplement the meager rations available."

Sensing a form of victory, Zimu exclaimed, "Thank you, Gemba, you know you have done the right thing. Now let us in, as I am tired of speaking up to you like this. It hurts my neck!"

"You will have a wait a little while longer whilst we undo the barricades. I will go and supervise it so that you will not be delayed any longer than you need to be," and Gemba left the platform before Zimu could respond and make any further demands.

Calling one of his guard party Gemba began to give quick instructions. "Have Mudede notify the royal household servants that we will soon have a visitor and that he is to keep the men allocated to the palace on full guard. I also want the eastern gate reinforcements, the Majiri regiment, to move on to the inner-wall, above the west-gate and for them to stand out in the open in full view." After allowing the messenger enough time to get up the hill and pass on the message to Mudede, Gemba moved towards the barred gateway and called for the thick wooden gate to be opened. Once it was fully raised he cautiously moved through the entrance until he came face to face with Zimu. "Greetings, sire," Gemba said. "Welcome to King Yasini's city."

Zimu smiled in response although the expression did not quite reach his eyes. "Thank you, Gemba, I will remember your timely judgment and actions to my brother on his return," the threat apparent in the delivery of his words.

With that, Gemba stood aside to allow free passage to Nyazimba for Zimu and his regiments.

Chapter Twenty-Eight
The battle continues

As the King's small regimental reinforcements arrived at the fighting edge of the battle Zabesi found himself on the right hand of his liege. Arriving just in time, he managed to counter an assegai thrust directed toward Yasini's chest. He swung with his shield deflecting the attacker's weapon. Stepping forward with a loud shout, he plunged his spear into the stomach of the Zulu warrior, who responded with an anguished scream of pain. To the King's left, more of the royal guard took positions forming the core of a fighting retreat.

By this stage the battle had moved backwards and forwards and back again across the small valley's basin and Zusa, high on the hill top, was still waiting for the pre-arranged signal to attack. With horror, Zusa saw that their lead regiments were being whittled away, whilst being outflanked. He had heard the trumpeted call for the planned pull back and expected his own signal any time. He was tempted to react to the situation unfolding below and have his regiment begin the attack but he had been given strict orders not to attack until commanded. "Come on my King, give us the signal!" he said to himself.

His regiment of bowmen had remained hidden, although some had poked their heads out of the cover of the forest to see what was happening, only to be severely reprimanded and forced back into shelter. It was one of these incursions by the young bowmen which attracted the attention of the Zulu chief.

He had been on the verge of committing the remainder of his reserve forces, which could have countered the number of Yasini's royal guard's interventions, shoring up the Bantus' weakened centre. Their weight and experience increased the resistance to the last Zulu sortie.

Realising that there were some Bantu above and to their far flank, the Zulu commander redirected a detachment towards the point where the curious head had revealed itself. At this stage, he was not fully aware of the strength of the group hiding in the tree line and so the regiment he dispatched was instructed to take a circuitous route to arrive at the rear of this gathering, whose presence on the hill could be potentially lethal depending upon its exact structure and intent.

To ensure his instructions were carried out to the letter the Zulu chief sent his blood brother to command this force. He further added that once they had dealt with whoever was in the thicket he was then to bring his men back down the hill to join the battle below. Calling to the Mbera Impi, the induna led the men off at a run and in a moment they had disappeared from sight.

With this, the Zulu chieftain decided to hold back the last of his reserves, almost four hundred warriors, just in case the Bantu had another trick planned. These men were becoming impatient; evident from their constant aggressive stance and moves, but a simple command brought them back to order. Shouting his orders to the fidgeting soldiers, he realised that it was those incessant Bantu drums which were causing him to lose focus and concentration. He wished he had the manpower to send around to deal with that nuisance as well but he had not been able to assemble any more men, as a portion of his regiments was still in the field.

Whilst the Zulu were responding to their planned strategy, Zusa realised that the call he had been expecting might never come, especially once he saw the King lead his royal troops into the centre of the clash below. The armies quivered at the force of the impact and counter charge, its entity created by the myriads of men from both sides, the combined force taking on a life of its own.

Taking a last look around, Zusa made his decision and called to his regiment behind his position. "Mbada, get ready. Stand to," and in response, his bowmen rose from their concealment to a place where they could look into the low stretching valley at the spectacle, which until now had only been an indefinable noise.

The full impact of the story being enacted before them was immediately apparent to the young troops. Zusa took a deep breath and in a steady voice, he called out, "First rank, forward," and half of the regiment stepped two paces out of the cover of the thicket. After a few heartbeats, "First rank, stand by!" In unison, this line reached into their leather holders for a projectile and notched their first arrow to their bows. "Second rank, forward and stand by," on this instruction they took up a place behind the first row, notching their own arrows at the same time. "I want the special detachment to stay in cover," Zusa said and a look of disappointment crossed the faces of the twenty men kept aside as they realised that they were not to be included in the opening attack.

Slightly below their position and about eighty paces away, Zusa could see that the tide of the battle seemed to be turning in favour of the Zulu and his King's army was gradually being pushed back towards their starting point. Although this had been part of the original plan, Zusa could see that it was not going the way the Bantu command had predicted. The Zulu had not fully disengaged and had instead kept the pressure on the Bantu as they pulled back and there was no discernible gap between the two forces.

If they fired now, the Mbada had the added pressure of possibly hitting their own men.

At this stage, the Bantu main army's right flank was facing the bowmen's position, and the backs of the Zulu were presented to them and unprotected. Zusa decided to show his hand. "Aim at the Zulu in the front of you. I want every one of the first arrows to count, so take care in your aim. Don't forget that you are shooting down hill so that you should aim low, otherwise your arrows will go over the Zulu," he instructed the first rank.

Over one hundred arrows were pointed at the line of men; "Ready," he said, pausing as the tension was taken up on the bowstrings and they were drawn back, their arms straining from the effort, "Release!"

With a unified twang, the arrows sped across the short distance, some overflying their targets to stick into the Bantu shields beyond, with one of the arrows taking a Nyazimbian warrior in the throat, his scream lost in the overall chaos and din of battle. Fortunately, the remainder of the volley found their intended targets, burying their heads and shafts deep into the exposed backs and sides of the Zulu warriors' line. The immediate result was that over sixty of the enemy fell to the ground, many of them killed outright by the iron-tipped arrows.

"Second rank, forward," the first rank pulling back from the edge, "take aim," another delay while the boys took up the strain. He repeated his earlier caution to aim low then he shouted, "Fire."

Pausing to assess the combined effect of the two volleys Zusa was able to see that the enemy below was in a state of confusion from the unexpected assault and as soon as the second volley hit home there was absolute panic.

Many Zulu turned around to face the new danger and the Bantu warriors against whom they were fighting immediately took these men, stabbing with their longer spears, killing them in an instant.

In reaction to the attack thirty-two Zulu warriors broke away from their regiment, turned towards the threat and rushed the bowmen's position. Bare-footed and quick on their feet they ran up the small hill. Presenting their shields they formed an unbroken advancing line. Their fellow warriors quickly filled the gaps these men had left in their front line. However, their sudden departure meant that their offensive line was no longer able to push forward and it only just managed to hold its defensive position in the face of the Bantus' renewed counter-drive.

The first rank of Mbada had already set their second arrow onto their bows and without instruction, fired a more staggered round of projectiles towards the advancing menace, many of which pierced the hide-covered shields, slowing down the sudden counter-attack. Some of the Zulu fell out of line, maimed or injured. The second row of archers fired as soon as they had also reloaded. However, there were still twelve of the assaulting Zulus on their feet and they were only ten paces away when Zusa realised the danger. "Everyone back, fall back," he shouted and the bowmen quickly stepped back to be swallowed up by the thick bushes and trees.

The Zulu warriors charging the hill became confused, for one moment, the ridge of the hills was teaming with Bantu archers, but in a single breath, they had disappeared from sight. They kept on advancing, knowing that they could not leave this danger to their rear.

Zusa had kept his reserve force to one side of the current position of the retreating bowmen and as soon as the assaulting Zulu entered the tree line, these bowmen fired a co-ordinated volley, at point blank range. The Zulu had thought the Bantu to be in the process of running away but it was too late for them and in a short space of time all of the attackers in this band of warriors were knocked off their feet, either seriously injured or dead.

Recovering from the ever-changing situation, Zusa called out again, "Mbadas to the front line, quickly now, back into position." In response his men rushed forward, some pausing to offer the coup-de-grace to the injured Zulu as they passed to ensure that none arose behind them.

By the time the regiment had regained its initial position, the battle had moved past them and once again a large section of the main Zulu force had its unprotected backs to the bowmen. The line of targets was angling diagonally away, with those closest to the Mbadas position being the most exposed. The bowmen automatically prepared for the next shot.

Meanwhile, in the centre of the battlefield, King Yasini had kept the main force together and with his enforced yet measured retreat, he had regained control of all of his forces and the battle. The surprise arrow attack a few minutes before had had an effect on this outcome as it had reduced the pressure on his right flank but as suddenly as it had started, it had stopped. Looking up, the King could see the bowmen melting into the tree line with a party of Zulu warriors chasing the retreating figures. With a grimace he knew that the young men up on the hill were on their own as he was in no position to dispatch assistance and even if he could he knew that by the time his forces reached their position, the outcome would have already been decided.

In the time taken to contemplate this, the Zulu army had once again surged forward in a renewed wave, their screams, shouts and cries echoing amongst the clatter of shields, spears and assegais. Standing in the front row with his thin line of warriors spread about him Yasini let all thought of what might be happening on the hill go, and he was quick to use his shield to deflect a blade which had been jabbed towards his throat. The defensive move left the assailant open to a counter-thrust and the King buried his spear into the gaping mouth of the warrior, and the sharp point pierced to emerge from the back of his head. A wave of red spurted from between the lips of the man which had, uncannily, closed around the spearhead. The weapon's point severed the spinal column and the head flopped to one side. As the body fell, Yasini lost his grip on his spear, his hand slippery after it had been drenched by the surge of blood.

Now weaponless, the King had no choice but to deflect a second attack with his shield, before turning the protective cover horizontally to use its edge to slash at his attacker. As Yasini cut across at eye-height, the man flinched backwards at the move.

The Zulu blinked realising that the attack was a feint and moved back to offer the killing blow to the unarmed Bantu King. With a grimace, he lunged forward in triumph, his assegai held high ready to descend into the upper body of his foe. As he committed to this action, he realised that his opponent was not acting as one who was staring death in the face and in a split second he saw a look in the King's eyes as he reacted. The Zulu warrior was too slow to prevent the King's shield from being swung back to crush his larynx and the impact jarred his head with a force which knocked him off his feet. Lying prone, the warrior suffocated and died, unable to draw a breath past the ruin of his crushed throat.

An outstretched assegai killed the Bantu warrior to the immediate left of Yasini and as he fell, he knocked his chieftain to his knees. Another Zulu shield lashed into view to catch Yasini on the side of his head stunning him and he sprawled to the ground. Glee ran though the Zulu line as the warriors almost fought each other to order to gain the honour of dispatching their enemy's head of state. An inhuman scream and shout of rage raced across the fallen King's position and with a fierce movement, Zabesi forced his way forward and managed to stand over the prone form of his liege, with his men standing side by side with him in a protective pack, their surge forward forming a blister in the Bantu front line. Other warriors pulled their stunned King to his feet, dragging him out of immediate harm. Within a few paces, Yasini had recovered his senses and regained his balance, shaking off the helping hands. Stooping to pick up a fallen spear he spun on his feet, a little dizzy but he steeled himself and called for those closest to him to rally to the position where Zabesi was now holding his own defensive battle in an attempt to give his King the opportunity to be pulled to safety.

As Yasini arrived back in support of Zabesi, he felt the front line slacken once again. Looking up he saw that the Mbada had returned and were aligned in careful formation at the tree line above him. Zusa's arrows were again scoring direct hits on the Zulu line and the enemy was falling to the projectiles.

Unfortunately some of the Bantu warriors facing the Zulu were also hit, causing sudden and unexpected openings in their line. The enemy immediately exploited these gaps. The attacking Zulu fighters stepped into the breaches to stab left and right, opening the break in the defences even wider and filling it with their own comrades. It was only the stinging arrow attack which was preventing the Zulu taking full advantage of the tense and finely balanced situation.

Realising the knife-edge the battle was poised upon, Zusa kept up his constant command to reload, aim and fire, trying to coordinate mass volleys for maximum effect.

Every so often Zusa picked out a particular individual below, who showed a talent for rallying or commanding the Zulu in the field and he personally fired his weapon in order to deny the enemy the benefit of reliable and effective command.

The sounds of war from below his position filled his head almost to distraction but he was still able to sense a change in his immediate environment and he looked around curiously for the cause of his unease. As he looked across the two lines of bowmen he saw the fluid movements of his men firing into the mass below. Nothing wrong there, he thought to himself. Turning around he sought out the group of reserve troops, some of whom had also sensed something was amiss, and were glancing over their shoulders towards the north of their position but from where he stood he could not make out what they were looking at.

Suddenly, Pimi's regiment skirted back into sight. Although only seen fleetingly through the brush and trees, Zusa could see some of the appointed guard regiment moving to new positions of concealment before turning back to face the direction from which they had just come.
Zusa caught his breath as he made out beyond them a large group of Zulu advancing through the forest in their now classic bullhorn formation. *Now what was he meant to do?* He knew that the ranging, advantageous effect of his bowmen would be lost attempting to shoot through the forest into this new threat. He realised that the fate of the Mbada regiment was now in Pimi's hands and his regiment of spearmen

Pimi could be seen exhorting and organising his troops into defensive positions while his scouts probed the advancing Zulu line, maintaining contact but not being drawn into a frontal battle. The numbers were about even but the Zulu were seasoned warriors, up against boys who had only just finished their basic training. This could be expected to be a one-sided battle. *Maybe Pimi could hold them until the King sends reinforcements!* Zusa thought.
He caught himself, speaking aloud, "Reinforcements! Ha, what was I thinking?" He realised that they were too far

detached from the main battle and the King was probably not even aware of the situation the Mbada were in. "Well I guess it means that it is all up to us now to sort out this situation."

With a smash of shields, the two sides of spearmen joined in combat and the Zulus' experience showed immediately as a score of young Bantu went down to practised assegai strokes. Realising the seriousness of the situation Zusa had no choice but to stop the Mbada from supporting the main battle below once again and to look to defending themselves.

In a loud voice he called for the Mbada to about face and group up as closely as possible. He split this group again, his commands flowing easily, so that the formation became rectangular in shape, four ranks deep. "Now listen to me carefully. I need to you to do something we have not trained for," he shouted above the increased level of noise from the melee less than thirty paces away from them.

A few of the young boys kept glancing nervously at the fight on their perimeter. Zusa called them to order. "Look at me and listen to what I am saying." The turned heads snapped back at the command. "I want the first row to fire on my command and then kneel while notching their next arrow, then the second, third and fourth are to follow suit on my command. Do you understand?" he added, looking across at Pimi's men who had slowed the Zulu advance a little but they were still being driven back bit by bit, blow by blow.

"Ehe, *Yes*," the Mbada responded in unison.

Zusa filled his lungs and shouted into the forest, "Pimi, pull back, pull your men back." He waved his arms to emphasise his instructions. The spearmen's resistance had drawn the Zulu to one side of the Bantu arrangement and already the attackers on the flank closest to the bowmen, almost thirty in number, were edging their way towards the new formation.

"Front rank ready, take aim," Zusa commanded as the Zulu advanced on the bowmen in a rush. "Fire!" Forty-five arrows flew across the short distance, the front row of bowmen immediately taking to their knees.

"Second rank, fire," following suit they also knelt. The arrows were volleyed and this segment of the Zulu attack stopped as if they had run into a solid wall.

"Third rank, fire."

****

On the front line of the battlefield, the King knew that he had to stay where he was to keep the force together. Shouting encouragements and with Zabesi now at his side, he caused a renewed surge in the thinned-out row of men.

Unfortunately, this containment was again negated by the sudden loss in support from his bowmen on the high ground. Looking up he could not see what had caused it this time and all he could make out was that the young bowmen had re-orientated their formation and, from their stance, they were obviously facing another foe that must be attacking from their rear. He knew that they would have to look after themselves as he still had no one to send in their support.

The Zulu heaved forward and again the Bantu line gave. This was happening each time the Zulu induna's called for a push and he did not know how much longer his men could absorb the pressure.

He shouted above the noise of combat to Zabesi to order in the final reserves. It was to be a now or never decision, either fully commit or be left wanting in defeat. Covered in his enemies' blood, Zabesi turned out of the battle line and raised his spear in signal to the last of the Nyazimba reserves.

Bodies littered the small valley. Injured and maimed warriors crawled for safety or lay still and stupefied where they had fallen, their blood seeping into the soil, whilst entrails and severed limbs lay spoiled about.

The third and final wave of Bantu, who had kept themselves hidden from the battle until now, burst from the cover of the tree line. Although ragged, the impact of having yet another fresh group of three hundred armed Bantu join the fray had the desired effect upon the Zulu who had been fought to a standstill, shifting the delicate balance of the battle once again in favour of the nation of Nyazimba. Screaming in challenge, this group mixed with the heaving mass of humanity although the scene did not depict it so clearly. It was nature's inbuilt instinct to survive which brought out the animal in man to the surface and kill or be killed ruled the moment.

Although it was not a tight, interlaced, fighting force, the impact of Nyazimba's last reserves stopped the Zulus' forward motion and for the next few minutes the Bantu regained some of the territory just lost, although measured in mere paces.

The King and his senior chieftains continued to rally their weary soldiers but by this stage in the battle both sides had lost a good third of their initial fighting force which had assembled only a short hour before, but now it looked as if the Bantu were in the favour of the god of war.

As he looked around, the King's heart jumped to his throat as, with a roar, an unexpected Zulu reserve force broke cover and, in a solid formation, they hurled themselves at the right hand side of the battle line and even before they had arrived, King Yasini knew all was lost. Four hundred fresh Zulu warriors were going to hit his flank where he was the weakest and most exposed.

****

Back on the hillock, Pimi's men had managed to disengage themselves from the Zulu raiding party and he had led them at an angle away from Zusa's position. This allowed the bowmen to continue firing into this separated Zulu force's line. Over half of Pimi's spearmen had fallen to the assegai but their sacrifice had given the bowmen the precious time needed to face the new danger.

Although the bushes and low branches had deflected a high proportion of their arrows, the Zulu warriors still fell to the defensive bow and arrow attack.

With a rush, a final detachment of Zulu, who had turned back toward the bowmen, burst through the shrubbery at the extreme end of their box formation. In an instant, fourteen bowmen had fallen to the bloodstained assegais. The once steady lines dissolved as the Mbada had no other defences such as a shield or spear to hold back the Zulu attackers. The detachment of bowmen scattered in all directions. More of the young men were chased down and stabbed in their backs by the battle crazed Zulu.

Zusa knew that he was fast losing control of the situation and that he was no longer in communication with over half of his force.

The remainder of the bowmen regiment near him, tried to re-orientate themselves to confront the last Zulu attack which had scattered their brothers-in-arms. The fighting became hand to hand, a fight surely in favour of the assegai wielding enemy.

Zusa's reserve force was trying to get into in a firing position so as to be able to offer some form of counter-strike against the Zulus who were slaughtering the boys from their regiment.

Suddenly the last of Pimi's spearmen, twenty-eight in number, raced back into the fight, slashing and cutting into the rear of the surviving Zulu. As their enemy turned to meet this more menacing spear-wielding foe, the surviving bowmen fired at point blank range into their unprotected bodies and within minutes, the battle for the hillcrest was over. All of the Zulu were dead or dying along with almost one hundred of the combined Bantu force, with at least half the survivors spread across the forest and largely out of sight. It had been another very close encounter with death.

Wasting no more time Zusa turned his attention back to the main battle below them. Breaking through the tree line once again he was just in time to see the last of the Zulu reserve running down the hill from their position, cutting across at an angle with intention of hitting the main Bantu army on the furthest side of the battle. Even before the threatened onslaught arrived he could imagine the effect this rush of Zulu warriors would have on the Bantu army. From his position of height he could also see what must have been the remainder of the royal guard gathering around the King. They were attempting to forestall what seemed to be the inevitable.

Without hesitation Zusa went to shout a command but found his throat was parched dry from his exertions and the adrenaline rush of the last quarter of an hour. Swallowing hard was not enough so he reached for his water gourde at his hip, unstopped the bottle and took a quick sip to quench his thirst.

He shouted at the top of his voice, "Mbada, Mbada, rally to me." Those closest to him formed up straight away. Time was critical. As they gathered round him he shouted for them to pick up any stray arrows as they might well be needed, and then he led his remaining force towards the new attack phase developing below.

Moving from the concealment of the tree line the Mbada left the forest in a ragged line. They covered half the distance downhill before Zusa called an instruction for the bowmen to load their bows. In a few heartbeats and, without having to detail the target, he called for the release of a volley of arrows and just over one hundred of the projectiles flew across the short distance tearing into the sprinting Zulu reinforcements, many of whom were hit.
As they fell, they brought down others running behind them. Confusion again reigned on the Zulu side as a second, more ragged volley of arrows, hit the group but with equal effect.

The Zulus' coordinated attacked became splintered and, instead of a solid line of trained warriors hitting the weakened and exhausted Nyazimbian army, it made contact piecemeal and its desired impact was dampened and did not affect the tenuous balance of power at all; it was just more meat into the grinder.

The Zulu soldiers on the front line, seeing the way their support had been ripped apart, began to slacken in their forward drive. In response the Bantu fought harder with the added encouragement of the slaying of the reserve force. The bowmen were easily distinguishable on their hilltop position and they could be seen redressing their formation above and behind the Zulu line. Their numbers were continuously increasing with those bowmen earlier scattered now finding their way back to their regimental line. The length of the bowman's battle line began to grow and at the sight, the heart went out of the Zulu army and their formation simply broke.

It began with those to the rear of the Zulu line. They simply stopped pushing and then they gradually began to fade away. Soon afterwards they were followed by the two flank guards who peeled away in retreat. One by one, the tired enemy soldiers began to switch to the defensive, carefully stepping backwards over the ground which had been so expensively won. Their commanders attempted to keep the men together and to structure them facing the Bantu, but once the first men had begun to turn their backs and head towards their own lines, the effect on the main fighting force was total and absolute.

The bowmen continued with their covering fire but already some of the men had no more arrows left to fire and they stood still, watching the effect the remainder of the regiment was having on the battle below. From their position above, it could be seen that the complete throng of humanity was moving in the direction of the retreating army.

The leading edge thinned out, pulling away from the Nyazimbian army. Totally exhausted, the Bantu army had no reserves left to follow up the retreating Zulu and they soon halted in their slow advance and eventually stood still, watching their enemy leave the field. After the last of the surviving Zulu had disappeared from sight over the valley summit their commanders, who had become mere spectators to the tragedy which had unfolded below them, took one last look before following their defeated army.

The victorious Bantu owned the battlefield, their ragged formations standing in the place from where the Zulu had broken, staring at each other, astounded after the long drawn-out encounter.

Then the drums stopped.

In dreadful silence, the battlefield lay before the survivors, Stunned into this state by the sheer ferocity of the events and further still by the horror of death which was stretched out before them, they could only stand and contemplate the scene before them.

The dead lay two or three deep, in discernible lines indicating where the fighting had been the fiercest, Limbs of those still clinging onto the threads of life, moved feebly with their cries of pain and anguish rising on the breeze. The smell of spilt guts and the flood of blood filled the nostrils to make the stomach heave at the stench.

The King also stood with his men, motionless, staggered by the enormity of the situation and like everyone else; he too just stared at the scene.

Zabesi moved to his side and, at his approach, the King looked at him. His newly-appointed commander had been injured a number of times with several slash wounds to his head, arms and legs, which ran freely with his blood whilst his body was splattered by that of others. Dust had stained these damp patches so that they became mud which clung to his limbs and torso. "Well, sire, we definitely showed them how to fight!"

Yasini chuckled at the simple statement before the true success dawned upon him and in response, with his natural ability to lead, he became galvanised into action.

Messengers were sent scurrying on errands with two of them being dispatched to Nyazimba to carry the glorious news of the victory and to call for a relief column to help with the wounded. Healers who had travelled with the army were summoned so they could begin attending to the injured. Others ran from regiment to regiment to call the surviving chiefs and section leaders, who soon gathered around their King.

Yasini had reclaimed his position on the large anthill used during the opening stages of the battle. Once all those who could be expected to be at the meeting had arrived the King indicated for them to sit, a request contravening custom but in full recognition of their efforts as the majority of them were wounded to some degree. Zusa had managed to join the group after making his way directly down the hill from the position he had established, elated at what had been achieved.

From this location they could see that the battlefield before them was littered with the bodies of men from both sides. The story of the past hour retold in the lines of the fallen, where comrades had stood their ground side by side, and died, side by side. The smell of death had already begun to permeate and fill the valley with the iron sharpness of massed blood mixed with the putrid scents of spilt entrails and gouged limbs.

Gradually, the remainder of the Bantu army re-gathered and, as tired as they were, the regiments re-formed so that the losses could be accurately accounted for and the reports begin to flow in to the gathered chiefs.

Eventually the final tally was known. It was found that the first wave had taken the main brunt of the battle and of the eight hundred, who had started the day, only five hundred and twelve were still fit or considered walking wounded, the rest were dead in their lines. The census also indicated that the second and third waves had lost another four hundred and seventeen warriors between them. This was due primarily to their lack of war skills and for the most part caused by the almost catastrophic collapse and break through by their determined enemy. They had been saved by their King's valiant efforts and physical presence during the critical stages of the battle.

Following the hand-to-hand fighting on the ridge with the Zulu the Mbada had been reduced to less than two hundred and fifty bowmen still fit to fight with another twenty-three wounded but in a state where they could be expected to recover fully. Pimi's regiment had lost half its number and due to the ferocious close combat, all those lost were dead. Only forty of the boys who had run with him only a short time before were still alive, amongst these was Pimi, although he had suffered a serious wound on his left arm.

After listening to the full report the King stood; his people around him looked up at his face expectantly. "My children," he began, "today we have saved our nation from the very jaws of oblivion by taking on the greatest of our warlike neighbours. Over these last days we have lost family and comrades, friends and brothers, but we have survived and we still remain a force to be reckoned with." He paused to let his words sink in. "We have met on the battlefield the people of the short spear, and we have shown ourselves not to be wanting in our ability to defend our people." His voice rose in the strength of the delivery.

Looking further around he continued to meet the gaze of those in the group but when he got to where Zusa was seated, he saw the mix of pride and despair in the young man's eyes. He continued in a softer voice, "Today we had no other choice than to force the horrors of our ultimate survival upon the future generations of our people. Today, young men have lost the innocence of their youth and they have been rushed into the harsh reality of becoming men. Today, our young men stood to be numbered among the heroes of past generations when they used their new weapons to offset the attacks of the Zulu."

He stood for a few moments gathering his thoughts. "In honour of what has happened in this valley today, let this place forever be known as Ngomahuru. This will be the place of the big drum."

He went on to say, "Zusa!" Zusa looked up slowly at the sound of his name. The gathering turned their eyes towards where he sat. The King continued, "You led your men into battle where their contribution was instrumental in bringing about the ultimate victory, and although your regiment suffered many casualties, you must know that they followed you because they trusted you. Their hearts were dedicated to the cause for which they gave their lives. Do not dishonour their sacrifice by mourning their passing but you should count their deaths as a victory for our civilisation!"

Raising his voice again to include the whole group, the King went on, "I know we are all exhausted and I wish I could order you to take a well-earned rest but we need to follow up the Zulu retreat. My first reason for this is that they will lead us to where they have taken our people as hostages. Secondly, we must not let any remnant of their invading army return to their homeland. I want their defeat to remain a mystery and as a warning to others who may think about attacking my kingdom in the future."

Zabesi stood. "I will go, my King. Give me the honour of bringing our people home!"

Following this statement, the rest of the surviving members of the senior regiment stepped forward in support of the chieftain. The King nodded his acceptance of this gesture of loyalty.

"And I too will take my regiment of bowmen in support," Zusa said with a clear and determined voice and the remainder of the Mbada stepped forward to back their leader.

Smiling, the King said, "Go, my young chiefs! I send you in my name. Go and bring our people home."

Chapter Twenty-Nine
In pursuit

As soon as Zabesi and Zusa had taken their reduced regiments in pursuit of the broken Zulu army, King Yasini dispatched twenty warriors to Belingwe, which was only a short run away, in order to liberate the town. The Zulu had been seen to simply bypass the refuge in their haste to get away from the battleground. When the detachment arrived they found that the town had been looted but worst of all, the cattle pens were empty. The warrior in charge said, "Our people have already been moved, no wonder the Zulus had been happy to desert the town." The men around him nodded their heads in agreement. "Well search the buildings to make sure none of the Zulu have stayed behind! While you are at it make sure any food or drink is taken to the battlefield, they are going to need it."

The king received the report and the fact that the captives had been moved strengthened his decision to go after the remnants of the Zulu force. With nothing left to do here except leave a token force in the town he decided to get his entourage, the remainder of his palace guard and about nine hundred other warriors, including the injured, back to the Nyazimba as quickly as he could. It would probably mean another night in the open before the large train of people would eventually wind its way back to the city but he did not want to travel ahead and leave his warriors who had overcome so much.

It had also been agreed for a burial party to remain at Ngomahuru to take care of the dead from both sides and to collect spent weapons and provisions.

It was difficult to get the depleted army moving again but it was not advisable to stay near the battle site as the spread of disease would be rampant once the sun touched the bodies. The city was also defenseless and the King needed to get back as soon as he could.

Gradually the surviving warriors moved away but as predicted the evening found the group too far away from the city to make it home safely that night and a halt was called so that the weary troops could be rested. Those on litters, too injured to walk, were set to one side and the medicine men were administering what they could to either treat the injuries or at lease ease their pain and suffering. The walking wounded were not faring too well either, with many falling behind during the day's march. These men continued to trickle into the camp for the next couple of hours, normally accompanied by a close friend or relative who had taken it on themselves to ensure the safe passage of their kin.

As the camp was being prepared another messenger was sent ahead to the city to make sure that the garrison was made aware of the Bantu army's status, the Zulus' retreat and that Zabesi's men were close on their heels.

In the firelight, the King took his time to visit the injured men and twice during the early evening he was with two individuals as they died. Eventually his aide insisted he rested, stating, "You will be no good to govern and lead everyone else if you do not get enough rest, sire." Reluctantly the King agreed to take a rest and, as soon as his head touched the rolled blanket pillow, he fell asleep.

It was in the early hours of the following morning when the perimeter guard heard someone approaching. It was not somebody trying to hide their approach and, although it was assumed to be a messenger from Nyazimba, the camp guard was called to arms just in case it was a roving Zulu raiding party. Some had been reported to still be roaming the kingdom, out of touch and unaware of the defeat that had befallen their army.

A shield wall of thirty warriors stood to as the messenger arrived and was escorted to the watch chief. "I have a message for the King," he said.

"The King is asleep and cannot be disturbed."

"Sekuru Gemba has sent me with an urgent communication for the King." Pausing, the messenger gauged the man before him weighing up how much of the message he could reveal without breaking his oath to deliver it for the King's ears only. Realising that the chief was simply safeguarding his liege from being awoken for a trivial matter, he made a quick decision and said. "The King's brother, Zimu arrived at the city on the morning of the battle. As we stand, he and his full regiment are camped within the outer walls of the town!"

Shock registered on the face of the senior induna and, without any further hesitation, he went to wake the King.

At the gentle touch on his shoulder, Yasini awoke and sat up, confused at his environment and dizzy from the lack of sleep. The man informed him of the arrival of the messenger from the city and the basic information the envoy had been forced to impart, in order to get to see the King.

Yasini listened in silence, thinking through the full ramifications of the information. "Send the messenger to see me," he said. Within minutes the courier arrived and crawled on his knees to where the King was seated.

The man took his time in relating the full details which Gemba had entrusted to him to convey to the King. Adding to what he had already told the senior induna, he elaborated about how and when the King's brother had managed to gain access to the city. The King chuckled at the words of Gemba standing on the wall asking his younger brother why he was here and not at the battlefield where he was expected, as he imagined his old friend standing up to his unruly brother. He was also encouraged to hear that the old man had managed to keep the majority of Zimu's men cordoned off in the army barracks. Gemba had also brought the city's remaining garrison troops into an inner circle to hold the high ground and deny access to the palace.

The best news was that, along with this section of the palace, Gemba and his men were still in control of the southern gate whose point of entry was up the steep cliff face and so the city could be reinforced from this direction if need be. "Call my palace guard and have all of my chieftain's get ready! I need to meet with them as soon as possible!"

The camp came to life as the senior men were summoned to the place where the King was sheltered. Campfires were re-stoked until the flames emitted more heat and light. The men gathered around the largest of the campfires and a short time later Yasini walked into the centre of the meeting. "Men, just as we have finished with one danger we may very well have to face another!"

The group looked directly back at their monarch, straight faced and serious, not trying to second guess his words. Yasini went on to recite all that had been told to him by the courier and at the end of the explanation no one spoke. The significance of the situation was clear. Although the King's brother did not have full control of the city, he had over one thousand fresh soldiers inside the main city walls. The only positive fact was that there were over four hundred loyal Bantu warriors on the inner wall ramparts. Included in this were the warriors from Majiri and Runyanhi, the King was pleased to hear, who had arrived just after the main force had left the city.

"Well I guess the good news is, once we get to the city walls and approach the water gate, we will have Zimu's forces surrounded," someone offered. The resulting laughter eased the situation.

"What do you want us to do, sire?" one of the senior lieutenants asked.

"How many men do we have?" Yasini asked Makonde. "We only have about five hundred fit and able to fight, sir, with at least another four hundred who could still hold a spear. Unfortunately nowhere near enough for a frontal assault!"

The King responded, "Well we will hope it does not come to that." He paused in thought. The group waited until their leader spoke again. "This is what I want you to do. I want three hundred of our fittest men to leave as soon as possible and for them to find a route back to the city out of sight of Zimu's troops. Once they are there they need to use the southern gate which is still controlled by the loyalists and enter the city." A few heads nodded at the instruction. "Later on, during the day, the remainder of our force will approach the city and I will confront my brother as to the reason why he is there? It will be interesting to hear what he has to say!" A few more chuckles. "The day could go either way but with our men reinforcing the existing garrison troops, I trust we will be able to persuade Zimu to come around to our point of view!" No one responded to this, as all understood the impact of the statement.

Another messenger was dispatched to inform Gemba of the arrangements and to give him notice so that he could be prepared to receive the extra warriors. This stage of the plan needed to be completed by first light and it was going to be a hard run for those being sent. The messenger was also to inform Zimu that the King's force was expecting to arrive at the city after midday the next day and that he would appreciate his brother meeting him with an honour guard of his troops at that time.

As soon as the chosen men were assembled, the three hundred troops disappeared into the darkness to make their way home.

Those who had been left behind for what was expected to be a clash of wills at the very least the next day, spent the remainder of the night in final preparations.

By early morning, the camp had been fed with the last of the provisions available. The stone city was only three hours' walk away from their present position and scouts were sent ahead to see if they could perform the same trick Zimu had used by having their people in the city's watch-tower not report their early approach.

Yasini wanted to catch his brother off guard as much as possible, as he did not want to give him any extra time to prepare for the expected standoff.

Those who were unable to walk without assistance were left in the care of a number of healers, with the King promising to send further assistance as soon as possible. With the last of the preparations complete, anyone who could carry a spear was led towards the city.

As they travelled, the King pondered on the possible reasons as to why his brother had gone to the city instead of joining him on the battlefield. The instructions he had sent to him a few days had been extremely detailed and specific so he would like to hear the logic behind this potentially treasonable event.

The temperature was still mild and so the march home was kept at a brisk walk. The formation passed below the watchtowers that, to the King's pleasure, remained silent. Their occupants were convinced by the message sent ahead and out of loyalty to their monarch, the signal fires remained unlit. It had been a risk as Zimu could have easily manned the stations with his own men and so Yasini would have been forced to show his hand sooner that he had wished.

They continued along the main inland road and through the supporting cultivated fields of the city complex. As they approached the last turn in the road from where they could expect to be observed from the high points within the city walls, they stopped to redress the lines. The more able-bodied warriors were moved to the front line with those less so, stationed behind so as not to advertise their true weakened state. The kingdom road was only wide enough to allow men to march four abreast and so the formation was modified around this restriction with the intention of marching to a position parallel with the city wall but just out of spear range. Once there, the army would stop and turn to the left to offer a wide, extended wall of armed warriors.

The column rounded the last bend and set before them was the city, the fortress standing proud on the hillock overlooking the lower defences and, at its highest point, the anticipated signal flag which indicated that Gemba was still in control of the palace and inner fort. Many a warrior's eyes brimmed with the sentiment of seeing their home again, a luxury compared to what life had had to offer them only two days before.

The Bantu warriors kept in step, placing their feet heavily upon the ground, stirring the dust to create a cloud which belied the actual size of the force. The drums sounded the step and the column of men moved onto the flat plain in front of the city walls. As the formation reached its full length a double drumbeat brought the men to a disciplined halt. For a few seconds there was a silence and then, with another double bass note, the formation turned to its left and with a crash of spears against shield the warriors announced their presence.

Movement above the first gate indicated a flurry of activity and twenty or thirty men appeared on the wall above the closed gateway.

The King had his royal shield lifted into plain sight of all those in the city so that no one would be able to say that they did not know who it was in front of them.

More people could be seen hurrying about across the hillside inside the city and the King knew that many of them were his loyal subjects looking down on to the place where his brother and his regiment were inside the fortress. These people would also be able to see what his brother's regiment was up to within the safety of the outer wall defence.

Yasini stepped forward, heading towards the gateway with a number of his guard close by, with shields on hand just in case an ill-advised spear was thrown. He continued to walk to within shouting range and called aloud, "Open the gates for I, King Yasini, have returned to my city!"

Silence rewarded his effort and so he called out again, "Open the gates for I, King Yasini, leader of the nation of Nyazimba and chief of all Bantu have returned to my city and I demand immediate entrance."

A few seconds later the unmistakable figure of his brother, Zimu, stepped onto the platform, his men clearing a space for him. "Is that really you, Yasini?" he asked, peering as if shortsighted and unsure of who was before him.

"You know it is me, Zimu! Why are you in my city and not in the field with the rest of my army?" Emphasising "my" both times, his voice echoed off the granite walls, deep with emotion and frustration.

His brother held his arms open wide. "It is you, good brother. Blessed is Mware, for he has seen it fit that you have survived the horrendous battle."

Yasini returned the statement with silence.

Zimu hesitated before going on, "I was late in assembling my troops and thought I had missed the battle so I decided to come here directly to safeguard the city!" *The fact that he had arrived a full day before the battle was left out of the explanation,* Yasini thought to himself, *but that will be a discussion for another day.*

"Well as you can see I am back now and I want access to my city. Have the gates opened. We have wounded that need attending too." There was no immediate reaction to his command and he spoke again.

"Zimu, I thank you for performing your duty in defence of our capital but now I ask that you have your men leave so as to make to room for my weary soldiers."

The confusion was clear on Zimu's face as if he was trying to assess the threat of the troops arrayed before him outside the wall. He knew there had been a great many more men in the army when it had left the city, and that they had not all been killed in battle. In his mind he was trying to work out where the balance of power was.

He attempted another gambit. "I can see that there are so few of your warriors left, we should be able to share the barracks until the time we confirm the danger has passed and our nation is safe," he said, his head moving from side to side as if searching to see if the King had more forces hidden out of sight.

"If you had been on the battlefield with us you would know that the Zulu have been resoundingly defeated and that they are no longer a threat to us," Yasini shouted back, his anger just under the surface but clear in the words carefully chosen. He paused, watching his brother have difficulty understanding and adapting to the situation. "And in reply to our requirement for space, my whole army is here, brother! Look behind you!" His drummers sounded a fast tattoo on their instruments, the notes bouncing off the granite structures and hills.

With this signal Zabesi's troops, who had secreted themselves within the city that morning through the far gateway controlled by Gemba, ran onto the highest defences above and behind Zimu. In an about-turn of tactics, they used the Zulus' manoeuvre of simultaneously turning their shields to the front on command and, as the Zimutu regiment turned and looked upwards, they were presented with a solid formation of warriors, fully armed, and with the advantage of the high ground.

Zimu had also turned to look behind him as the clamour of so many men getting into position reached his ears and his face fell at the sight. He almost stumbled at the shock of seeing so many Nyazimbian warriors to the rear of his position. Immediately he knew he did not have time to re-orientate his own soldiers who were waiting just below the main wall upon which he stood, facing his brother. Even now as he watched, the King's men were extending themselves over the city, taking control of walls and the carefully constructed choke points, which they were familiar with. Gates were slammed shut and locked into position, isolating the major part of the city from the Zimutu supporters.

Stuttering with disbelief at the sudden change in circumstances, Zimu quickly turned back to the King, a broad smile on his face, hands outstretched. "My brother, you have misunderstood my intensions." His voice had changed from one of confidence to that of subservience, his words almost whining in their delivery. "I have only been performing what any loyal subject would do and that was safeguarding his King's palace until the time he returned."
He glanced down to someone behind him, saying something to an individual out of sight. Yasini's guard attentively shuffled a little closer to their charge, their shields at the ready.

Zimu disappeared from his position above the wall and Yasini tensed himself for the first signs of betrayal. Another burst of activity and the city gate was raised with the sound of wood sliding against stone and Zimu came hurriedly through it toward Yasini his arms open wide in welcome. "Welcome home, my King, my brother. Look, I have brought my men to serve you as you requested!" He knelt as he arrived at the position where Yasini had waited. The royal guard inspected his form from afar, in case he had a concealed weapon, but from his minimal battledress, there were no signs of anything which could cause harm to the King.

Behind his brother the Zimutu regiment began to thread their way out of the city taking care to appear submissive with their spears strapped to their shield and then both held in an arm stretched over their shoulder position so that they could not be easily drawn upon and used.

Looking down on his brother, the King thought about the attempted treason and considered how best to deal with it. Now was not the time, his nation had too much to recover from. Following the widespread Zulu attacks, he would need a unified nation and not a senseless civil war, to rebuild the damage caused. He was not even sure if Zabesi and Zusa had managed to release the enslaved Bantu yet, let alone if they had reclaimed much of the wealth lost to the enemy, and it would be a couple of days before he knew definitely. He had to make a decision based on what he knew right now. The tension was high as Zimu, still on his knees, kept his head bowed.

Zimu knew that all it would take was a single gesture from the King and one of his men would not hesitate to kill him with a simple stab of his spear. It would be a quick death, reserved for nobility, and he would be fortunate not to have to share the long, drawn-out death of a common traitor.

The King decided on his course of action and reached out slowly so that the movement was not misinterpreted as aggression and pulled his brother to his feet. "Thank you, brother," he said in an even voice. "Your King recognises your actions and the true eminence of your heart," the real meaning clear to both men, "and one day, once our nation has been rebuilt you may well receive your just reward!"

Brushing past Zimu, who felt physically weak, wobbling on his knees, Yasini strode towards the open city gate with his guard falling in closely behind him. From the parapets above, his warriors and townspeople cheered his entry as he led his army in a triumphant return from war.

Chapter Thirty
Mapedza, it is finished

Zabesi and Zusa conferred whilst on the march as to what their next action should be. They were leading their regiments toward what was thought to be the last stronghold of the Zulu. A messenger from the King had caught up with them to notify them that the captives were not at Belingwe and that the Fort at Chimnungwa was where they were expected to be, based on information from a captured Zulu. The alternative could not even be considered at this time.

Their combined force consisted of over five hundred fifty, newly seasoned troops. Amongst them were the palace guard as it was felt that their discipline was going to be needed for the final eradication of the enemy, two hundred warriors, Pimi's forty surviving spearmen and, finally, just over two hundred bowmen from Zusa's Mbada regiment. Not a great force, but it was still the largest coherent force in the region following the defeat of the Zulu at Ngomahuru.

With skirmish troops and scouts flung ahead of the force keeping pressure on the retreating Zulu, no quarter was given to those found on the road, who were either too tired from exhaustion or too weak from their wounds to put up a fight, and they were dispatched with as little ceremony as possible. Their cries for mercy were loud in the ears of their fellow comrades, driving the retreating mob forever southwards, to the perceived safety of the fort at Chimnungwa.

From their tracks, it was thought that fewer than four hundred Zulu had escaped. The only co-ordinated withdrawal was that of their chief, Modena, his lieutenants and personal guard of thirty two men.

Once this group had left the field their numbers began to increase as lone warriors rallied to their leaders call. This re-forming cluster of men was the first concern of Zabesi, for it was clear that this command group had a calming effect on the terrified and demoralised warriors in full flight. *If it continued to reassemble like this then the Zulu might just be in a better position to offer a more structured resistance once we catch up with them.* Zabesi thought to himself.

The commanders pushed their men onwards, encouraging them as the day progressed however many Bantu warriors, tired from the battle, fell out of formation along the trail.

Just before darkness the Bantu core group found that it was down to less than four hundred weary men. Zabesi knew that to continue running like this carried the risk of his depleted force blundering into a trap. He did not want to risk this and besides, the stragglers must be given the opportunity to rejoin the group during the night.

A halt was called at an easily defendable position, although they knew that the chance of having the Zulu double back and attempt a surprise assault was low. Those bowmen still with the leaders' group made further use of their weapons by hunting a buffalo and two large deer. The meat was roasted on open fires which gave warmth to the men around them. Throughout the early evening, the troops who had been unable to keep up the punishing pace staggered into the camp, their final miles being directed by the campfires and the smell of cooked meat.

The whole army was exhausted; however a rota for guard duty was issued, as lessons from the past week had shown the catastrophic result of not maintaining a state of readiness in the field. The remainder of the men fell into a deep sleep soon after consuming their share of the food and although the smell of blood attracted scavengers, the scent of humans and their constant movement around the camp and firelight kept them away.

At what had become the accustomed time to set forth each day, the army was roused well before sun-up and the refreshed group of men was fit for what was promising to be a good day for killing Zulus.

Zabesi wisely led his men at a more sedate pace so that when they eventually caught up with the retreating Zulu, they would still have the stamina to be able to fight a full battle. He knew that by now the escaped Zulu would have reached and joined up with the garrison troops at the fort. More wounded and dead Zulus were found along the trail to Fort Chimnungwa, marking the route taken by the retreating soldiers. Zabesi had instructed that those men found alive were to be spared. The Bantu blood lust had faded overnight and those captured would be interrogated. According to one wounded warrior there were now less than five hundred Zulu warriors left to face. *The retreat must have cost them a lot more than previously imagined.* Zabesi thought.

The Bantu army ran all that morning and as they closed on the captured fort, they began to witness the earlier devastation of the Zulus' indiscriminate sacking of the surrounded kraals and mines. Bodies had been left where they had fallen and many were at an advanced stage of decomposition with body parts scattered by the attentions of the scavengers. As the Bantu warriors approached, vultures flew lazily up into the air before settling in the branches of nearby trees. There they patiently waited until the army had passed and it was safe for them to return. Revolting as it was, Zabesi knew he could not be distracted by diverting his available manpower to attend to the correct burial of his people. This task would have to wait for another time, for those still alive had a more urgent duty set before them, other than worrying about the dead. His seasoned troops silently filed pass the grisly scenes, their anger at the desolation laid before them strengthening their resolve to bring the Zulu to a final justice.

A few hours later the scouts reported to Zabesi that the fort was just over the next hill and that they had managed to catch some of the Zulu watch-keepers at their posts. However, a few Zulu had managed to escape the surprise assault and a warning had been raised, alerting those who waited in the town fort beyond.

Zabesi and Zusa broached the hillcrest on the road which led straight down towards the town's main gateway. The sandy road in front of them dipped for a hundred paces before climbing again so that the top of the fort's stone walls was only slightly higher than the position where they stood. Armed men could be seen filing into the stronghold and, even as they watched, the strong wooden gates were swung closed.

A ridge of ground rose on one side of their position, to a tree covered hillock. With a gesture Zabesi indicated for Zusa to accompany him and they made their way to the top. From this position they were able to scrutinise what was going on inside the fort's defensive walls and they were able to make out the activity within the stockade. As expected, the Zulu had drawn all of their remaining men into its relative safety, protected from a direct attack. The inside of the fort's main wall was stepped with a low-level stone parapet from which a guard could easily defend against a anyone attempting to scale the wall and, even as the commanders watched, they could see numerous warriors using the ledges to look back at the Bantu force. They knew that any determined rush of the walls would require the majority of the troops they had at his disposal. In reply it would be extremely easy for the Zulu commander to concentrate his own men at this point of attack to counter the assault.

In this type of action, a smaller defending force could hold off an attacking army many times larger until it was whittled down enough to engage on an even footing. It was noted that the Zulu garrison had even had the opportunity during their short period of occupation, to erect additional grass-roofed structures as accommodation for the increase in men being lodged inside the stronghold.

It was not the sight of the remaining Zulus in the fort or even their defensive preparations which received Zusa's immediate attention. It was the view of the town's cattle stockades which were teeming with the women and children of his nation who had been captured over the last week by the Zulu raiding parties. He looked at Zabesi and asked, "Why have they been left unguarded?" he indicated the position with an outstretched arm.

"I am not sure Zusa, possibly the Zulu are expecting us to be content with the recovery of our people and herds thinking that once we had them back we may decide to leave them alone. Maybe they think that we are too weak to try and attack them in the safety of the fort."

As in confirmation and support of this train of thought another Bantu scout reported that vast herds of cattle and goats had been found in two adjacent valleys unguarded other than by a few young Bantu herd boys.

"Bring them to me," Zabesi said, "let's see if they have anything to tell us." Twenty young men we brought to where Zabesi and Zusa were waiting and when questioned all of the boys relayed the same message given to them directly by the Zulu chieftain. *Take your people and livestock and leave us alone!*

Zabesi turned to Zusa and asked, "What do you think?" he eyes fixed on the young man's face.

"They seem to be well protected inside the fort and if they have provisions, they could last quite a while." He paused to think, "We could contain them here and end for reinforcements!"

"Yes we could" Zabesi replied but the King has his hands full dealing with his brother and besides that, there is nothing stopping the enemy sneaking away under the cover of darkness in the time it will take to amass a force!" To maintain an effective siege around the fort the Bantu would require at least four or five times the number of troops they had at their disposal.

"The King did say we were to eliminate this force and leave no trace of its existence." Zabesi and Zusa turned back to look down onto the fort. They could make out a party of Zulu looking back at them on the hill. "I am sure they are trying to work out what it is we intend to do as well," Zusa said. Both sides stared at each other across the void.

Zabesi decided to take the immediate option open to him and he directed a band of his men to go down to the stockades in the town, taking care to approach from the opposite end from where the fort was situated. It took some time for the men to get into position and as they arrived at the wooden stockades they found the entrances barred but unguarded and, within a few seconds, the gates had been flung open and their people began streaming away from their temporary prison, some supporting or carrying those for whom the incarceration had been too much to bear. The commander sent other troops to direct the mass of humanity away from the town. It had been agreed to set up a temporary camp at a site a few hundred paces back along the road from which they just had travelled. Zusa tasked one of his lieutenants to see if his family had made it this far; their fate had long since been placed in the hands of Mwari!

"Okay," Zabesi said to those around him. "The Zulu have handed over two of the reasons for our relentless pursuit of them. I think they will be content just escaping with their lives at this stage, although the measure of the length of their lives will then be determined by their ruler for their failure." The man's fierce reputation and his inability to accept defeat was well known in the region. "They are already condemned to death!"

A muted cry behind the group drew their attention and Zusa turned to see his mother, brother and sister being led towards where he stood. Moving away from Zabesi, Zusa ran to his family, their cries of delight rising above the general babble of the multitude of people milling below their position, as they were directed towards the proposed camp. Zusa's mother began to cry aloud, "I thought you were dead, my son." She reached for him just to convince herself that he was really there. His brother and sister clung to his legs as if to draw strength from his presence. Zusa's tears streamed from his eyes as his pent-up emotions from the last few days tore through his heart. Zabesi led his group away from the scene to afford them some privacy and to allow Zusa to regain his composure before his peers.

Between the many questions and demands Zusa assured his mother that he was quite well. He explained how he had followed them from their homestead to their first prison camp. "I saw you, little sister, with your head on amai's lap." She shied away at the recollection. Turning to his brother he went on, "And you, umfana, *young boy*, I saw you standing guard over the both of them." He ruffled his brother's hair, and who beamed a smile in return.

From this initial description, Zusa's mother realised that he must have found his father and older brother's bodies at the kraal. Sensing the unspoken question Zusa looked back at her and nodded his head. "I found them, Amai!" He bit his lip when recalling the scene. His mother sniffed a tear away at the memory. "I managed to retrieve their bodies so that we can pay our respects correctly later on and giving them the right form of burial." His resolve cracked as the family unit burst into tears at the thought of the loved ones who had given their lives in the protection of their home.

Zabesi cleared his throat, which brought Zusa back to the current situation, and he gently extracted himself from the embrace of his mother. "Amai, I have things to do right now, so you must to go down to the camp which is being set up and wait for me there."

A look of confusion crossed her face. "But you came here for me, didn't you? What else could be required of you, my young son?"

"He is no longer a young boy, Amai," Zabesi said in a deep voice from behind them. He walked over to the family group. In a few words he explained how Zusa had been appointed by the King to raise a regiment of young bowmen and how he had led them into battle the day before. He explained that now was the time for them to deal with the Zulu below them in the town and Zusa was part of that solution. Zusa's mothers face expressed a mixture of emotions, knowledge that her boy was far too young to bear such a responsibility yet pride in her son who had become a man in the short time since he had last been at home.

"I have to go, mother," Zusa said, removing himself from the firm hold she had on his arm. "Don't worry, I will find you later on and we can all catch up with what has happened and be together again!"

"Take care, my son, we will be waiting for you," she

said before turning away to follow the person who had waited patiently to guide her to safety. Zusa's heart felt heavy at the sight of his mother being led away, with his brother and sister trailing behind, the eyes of both reflecting the confusion and misunderstanding of the events. He raised his hand, more to give himself some encouragement than for his family. His mother just kept on walking away, her head cast downwards, but just as he was about to lower his arm, his young brother turned and acknowledged the gesture, a smile flashing across his face in acceptance.

Now knowing that the remainder of his family was safe, Zusa walked back to where Zabesi was standing, studying the Zulu in the fortress below. Zusa waited for the senior chieftain to acknowledge his presence and, after a while, Zabesi glanced at Zusa then back at the enemy.

"We can't simply let them go away unpunished," he stated in a loud voice.

"Yes, you are right," agreed Zusa and a period of silence followed. "But how will we smoke them out from behind those walls? We all know what it takes for a determined enemy to break into one of our fortresses!"

Zabesi turned his head to stare at him in astonishment. "We do just as you say, young man. We smoke them out! Look," he pointed, "they have built grass shelters in case we decided to lay a long siege on the fort." The grass of the huts was bright yellow in the sunlight.

Zusa saw the solution at the same time. "We smoke them out. Yes that is what we will do!"

A plan was quickly formulated and four hundred of Zabesi's spearmen began to work their way down via the hidden route which had been used by those who had freed the prisoners, keeping out of sight of the Zulu in the fort.

The remainder of the Bantu force was kept on the hill, in the bottleneck caused by the rising ground on both sides of the pathway. This group had been tasked to prepare a defensive barrier, by cutting tree branches and thorn bushes then weaving them into each other to form a chest-high fence. It was stretched across the road to form a barricade and act as a line of protection for those behind it. A small detachment would be able to hold this line against a counter attack. The rescued population position was a few hundred paces behind the defence.

Zusa led the Mbada to a position behind the large group of spearmen who once were in the town, continued to advance on the fortress. Amongst the looted provisions stored in the town's warehouses they had found clay jars of black tara, along with imported cotton cloth. Before the Mbada had left the battlefield at Ngomahuru they had scavenged spent arrows, sometimes having to perform the gruesome task of cutting them from the flesh of dead Zulu or breaking apart shields so that the arrowheads were retrieved undamaged. Even after this action, the archers still only had twenty arrows each. Zusa reminded himself that this could well be the weakness of his regiment especially in a long field campaign. He would have to find a solution to the problem of replenishing projectiles for the future.

The newly-discovered cotton cloth was tom into strips and wrapped around one hundred arrows. These were then dipped into the pungent-smelling sticky liquid until they were saturated.

With the final preparations completed the bowmen were formed into lines out of sight of the fortress while in front of them the spearmen offered protection with their shield wall. With a signal from Zabesi who was guiding the forces from his on the hill, the men moved forward, shield to shield, their spears poking through and extending to their front. As they cleared the line of houses closest to the fort they grounded their spears and over-locked their shields into an even, impregnable barrier.

The gap between the Bantu force and the fortress' walls was about fifty paces. Behind this defence the first line of about a hundred bowmen stepped forward with the specially prepared arrows set in their bows.

At a command from Zusa another warrior walked down the front line of the Mbada with a burning firebrand. As he passed each of the bowmen he lit the arrow set in their weapon, which caught fire with an even-burning flame. Droplets of tara leaked from the mass at the end of the reed body and fell to the ground like stars falling from the night sky, their passage marked by a miniature tearing sound, to form small pools of flames at the feet of the archers.

As every group of ten arrows was lit, the command was to fire was given and the bowmen shot the flaming projectiles in a high trajectory, up and over the stone walls to land on the internal buildings. Immediately puffs of smoke could be seen emitting from the grass-thatched roofs, the arrows delivering fire deep into their layered construction. A hive of commotion was seen as the men inside the fort attempted to extinguish the flames, using leafy branches beating to snuff the burning grass whilst precious water was consumed to wet down the other roof expanses. Once the complete salvo of fire-arrows had been shot, the second row of bowmen stepped forward and fired a volley of normal arrows to hinder the attempts to put out the fires. Many of these arrows, although fired blindly into the billowing smoke, found their mark and the warriors inside the fort were forced to give up fighting the flames to protect themselves. Eventually, with the wind adding its force to the flames, the whole of the fortress looked as if it was on fire and the smoke was so thick that Zabesi could no longer distinguish individual men inside the ring of stone.

For a while, all that could be heard was the steady crackling of the flames interspersed with the explosion of dry wood cracking under the heat. The Bantu warriors continued to await the first reaction of their enemy.

When time began to drag, Zusa thought that the Zulu were going allow themselves to be burned to death within the inferno. He was tempted to twist the tail of his enemy by firing another round of arrows into the ring of fire but then, with a sudden clatter, the wooden gates were flung open and the Zulu warriors poured out of the citadel, screaming their fury. The smoke billowed from over the top of the walls and partly concealed their rush towards the line behind which Zusa and his men stood. He shouted a command; his bowmen prepared their weapons and had enough time to fire a full volley at a high angle in the direction of the charging enemy, the passage of the flight of arrows was hidden by the bright glare of the sun. But onwards the Zulu formation ran like a wedge pointed at the centre of the Bantus' position.

The front-line spearmen dropped to their knees, shields, and weapons presented forward, leaving the bowmen behind them with a direct line of fire. This time, the entire regiment let loose a combined volley straight at the attacking foe. The Zulu were rushing forward with their shields set in front to deflect and block as many of the expected arrows as possible, which they knew were going to be fired at them. As this coordinated volley slammed into the Zulu, the previously-fired, high trajectory projectiles had completed their upwards flight and now rained down death on the uncovered enemy. The iron-tipped arrows pierced heads and entered bodies through chests and backs. Men were ripped from their feet to stain the earth with their life force. As these men fell in untidy heaps on the ground they left wide gaps in the Zulus' shield wall and through this, more arrows were released from closer range. Those Zulu still pouring from the fort stumbled over the dead and dying, which broke their attempt to affect a final chance of victory. Once again, it had been snatched away from them by the presence of the bowmen.

As the remaining enemy could not close on the Bantu position, it was decided to take the final fight to them. A shouted order caused the wall of Bantu spearmen to move forward in unison.

As the last of the arrows were spent, the bowmen put their weapons across their neck and shoulders and exchanging them for their knobkerries which had all along carried the fighting stick as a secondary weapon they followed the spearmen into the melee for the kill.

The advancing Bantu line cut the distance to the fort by half and as they moved forward they managed to curve their formation into a semi-circle, imitating the Zulu ox-horn, so that their enemy would not be able to out flank their force.

The smoke from the fortress continued to thicken as

the provisions inside the burning buildings added to the conflagration. Screams and shouts marked the killing on the front line and the shield walls continued to beat away at each other, the Bantu out numbering the depleted Zulu who still managed to tear holes in the lines, however these breaks were filled with a mass of bowmen wielding their fighting sticks, smashing and breaking bones at their impact.

The number of escaping Zulus running from the fort dwindled to a trickle; the Bantu line relaxed, as it appeared that it was finally over. The stunned men looked around at each other, their throats parched from the sudden excursions whilst the smoke caused their eyes to smart.

Unexpectedly, from out of the smoke, twenty large Zulu warriors raced at a sprint, led by none other than their chieftain, Modena, his badge of rank clearly on display. With shouted battle cries and screams of defiance they burst upon the front row of the Bantu spearmen, stabbing and hacking in their well-proven style of fighting, sweeping aside the Bantu shields before piercing their broad blades into the unprotected trunks of their opponents.

Zusa shouted commands in an attempt to regroup the forces, but the bloodstained Zulus managed to keep up the pressure on their targets by keeping close and pushing up against the Bantu brittle shield-wall, not giving them a chance to step back so as to be able to use their longer weapons more effectively.

The clatter of assegai and spears against shields together with shouted insults and cries of pain reverberated across the battlefield. From the hillock Zabesi saw the small Zulu detachment pierce his defensive line below and he ordered the reserve troops guarding the road to rush in support of their men. Their cries of joy at being released to attack added to the confusion below as they rushed towards the confrontation.

The small Zulu force continued to fight and in a short time they managed to kill and maim eighteen Bantu warriors for the loss of only two of their own. Their assegais continued to flash in the sunlight, flicking bright red blood as they hacked and plunged their blades into the warriors they were facing. Modena continued to rally his men, fighting with them, calling encouragements, urging his men onwards. The dead, who lay two or three deep in places, hindered their way forward and they had to clamber over the bodies in their attempt to advance.

This gruesome obstacle gave enough time for the Bantu reinforcements dispatched by Zabesi to reach the place where the fighting raged and, with the momentum from their downhill rush, they slammed from the rear, into the surviving group of Zulu. Another four Zulu quickly fell to the attack. This released the pressure they had kept on the force being led by Zusa. Eventually the numbers of Bantu warriors on the field was stacked against the Zulu and the surviving Bantu spearmen managed to overlap the attackers, outflanking and surrounding them just as the Zulu had done to Kadenge's army at Sampambi a few days before.

The Zulu warriors continued to fall to repeated counterstrikes until only Modena, their chieftain, was left standing. He was bleeding from numerous wounds across his body and the blood of those he had slain covered his face and arms. Without respite he continued to fight, slashing and stabbing, spinning to catch those all around him, daring anyone to get too close.

The Bantu formed a circle about him and he was left standing in the centre. He jabbed at those around him daring them to take him on. Eventually he reached too far in one of his aggressive actions towards the ring of men and a spear managed to break through his defence, plunging deep into his chest. The pain caused him to stiffen and drop his guard, his shield falling away, an arrow flashed across the distance into the centre of his body, burying itself fully into his torso.

Those around the Zulu chieftain looked up to see Zusa in their front row with his bow outstretched and held steady towards Modena.

Blood leapt from the Zulus mouth as his lungs were pierced and his heart torn in two. He died on his feet, his hands clasping the shaft of the arrows for a few seconds before his grip relaxed and he sank to his knees. The life faded from his body and it fell inanimate to the ground.

The din of the battlefield faded until only the cries of the wounded and dying could be heard above the crackling of the blazing fortress whose smoke irritated the eyes of those standing near. The flying embers from the burning grass stung where they landed on uncovered skin and when it was wiped away it left a smeared, black, sooty stain.

The battle was over. It was finished, *Mapedza*. The invaders had been punished fully and the last of them now lay dead at the feet of those upon whom they had attempted to impose their own ill-conceived values.

The Bantu warriors began to cheer; their sounds of delight rang true. From his position on the hill, Zabesi waved his arms in congratulations and from behind him the recently freed Bantu women and children streamed across the rise to join in the victorious celebrations below.

Made in the USA
Charleston, SC
01 October 2013